Chap

Fathers, do not exasperate your children; instead, bring
them up in the training and instruction of the Lord.

Ephesians 6:4 (NIV)

Crossland, Texas
Saturday, June 4

Chance Brayden-Dearling lifted his eyes toward home, that mocking
cross above his parents' front door. As it gleamed in sunset, a tremor
of anger shot through Chance. He quenched it, though, and walked
on, opening the door. His younger brother met him in the foyer, and
Chance grew tense. Before he had left town, they'd had an argument,
and Chance had said some harsh words. Now, he wasn't sure of his
reception. "Hello, Victor."

"¡*Hermano*! You're back!" Victor slapped Chance on the shoulder.
"Welcome home."

Chance relaxed. "Are Mom and Dad home?"

"In the living room."

Chance met his grass-green eyes. "How's Mom?"

"Sad, grieving." He fingered the silver cross on his necklace, and Chance
frowned. Victor only rubbed that cross when he was afraid or worried.

"What's wrong?"

"Since I got in from Austin, Mom and Dad have been acting strange.
They keep walking off, huddling together, and whispering like they've got
something to hide."

"Like what?"

"That's the million-dollar question." Victor led Chance to the living room, where they found their parents snuggled on the couch, their heads close together.

At Chance and Victor's entrance, the couple stood, their eyes bright and shining with tears.

Their mother rushed toward Chance, her arms open. "You're home!"

Chance hugged her, savoring the warm comfort of her arms, then he stepped back, looking at his parents. "Hello, Mom, Dad."

"Welcome back, son!" His father said. "You're a mighty good blessing for these eyes of mine." His father beamed happiness, with nothing but love in his hazel, gold-framed eyes.

Even after all these years, Chance was amazed by how much his parents loved him, how much they expressed it in word *and* deed, even when he failed and disappointed them. More than anything, he wanted to make them proud and show them how much he truly loved them.

Before the Dearlings adopted him, he had almost given up on life, hope, love, happiness, and family. But they had taught him to love and trust again, and they had given him a brighter future, a happy home, and new hope, and he was grateful, truly indebted to them. "I've missed you both. More than you know." Chance kissed his mother's light-brown cheek before hugging his father, then firmly shaking his dark-brown hand.

"We've missed you, too." Tears welled within his mother's light-brown eyes as she glanced from Chance to Victor. "We've missed both of our sons."

"Don't worry, Mom," Victor said. "I know I'm your favorite."

"I don't have favorites."

"Of course you do." He grinned. "Me."

She swatted his arm. "That's not even true."

"Actually, it is," Chance said. "He's always been the dark-haired prince."

She pinned Chance with her eyes. "You're both princes, and I love you equally."

"No worries, Mom. I'm not jealous. Really, I'm not."

Victor smirked. "That's because you're Dad's favorite."

Their father looked at Victor, his eyes serious behind his glasses.

"Neither your mother nor I have ever made any difference between you boys. We love you both, and we've raised you as best we could."

"Easy, Dad!" Victor smiled. "I'm not complaining. Chance and I know you love us, that you've sacrificed for both of us over the years. We love you, and we're not going to fight over you. Promise."

There he goes again, Chance thought, *ever the light heart, ever the mediator, ever the perfect son.*

Before Chance had left for Dallas to investigate the Jessica Morano kidnapping, he and Victor had argued about Chance being antisocial and becoming even more a lone ranger in his personal and professional life. Victor had called him an iceberg, a fortress of solitude, and that had rubbed Chance wrong. It was like his brother didn't really know or even understand him, nor could he fathom how a traumatic childhood could turn a man cold, weary, and aloof.

Even though he and Victor shared the same house, it felt like they lived worlds apart. Everything seemed to come easier for him than for Chance. "You don't have to fight; you usually get everything you want," he said.

Victor's smile faded. "Not everything, *hermano*."

Nearly everything, then. Everyone loved Victor: mothers doted on him, women chased after him, men befriended him, and teenagers flocked to him in droves. Compared to Chance's life, his was relatively calm, practically perfect. "What battles have you fought? When have you ever struggled or faced adversity?"

His brother sighed. "You got me, Chance." He raked fingers through thick, curly black hair. "Living for me now isn't about fighting battles. It's about sacrificing all I have and giving selflessly for a greater good, a better purpose."

"That's my point: Your world is pleasant, comfortable, and secure. In it, there's no need for jealousy, disappointment, or conflict. There's only room for love, goodness, and laughter—butterflies, hearts, and roses."

"There's nothing wrong with love, beauty, or peace."

"You always have a safety net."

"I lost my whole family, too."

"But you weren't beaten like a dog, discarded like trash."

"I guess not. I was just an orphan, poor and homeless."

"You had a grandmother who loved you, which is more than I had after I lost my mom."

Victor crossed his arms. "I'm not competing with you. We both lost people we loved, and we both suffered a lot."

"The only real difference between you and me is that I haven't let my adversities or losses cast a dark shadow over my life, defining who I am. Every day I choose not to wallow in misery, and I choose not to fight everybody who crosses my path. I'd rather be a peacekeeper than a fighter, and I'd rather live in love, not war."

Live in love, not war? How naïve could Victor be? He still saw the world through the eyes of a child. He still believed that good always triumphed over evil, that love could cure anything, that God could fix any problem.

His brother had never known war; he had only known peace. Neither had he seen the face of rage and hatred or the ugliness inside of people, but Chance had, and he still did. "The peacekeepers rarely act, and they aren't truly on the front lines. The warriors and soldiers are; they're the ones suffering pain and abuse, sacrificing their lives for the greater good. They're the defenders of the weak—the ones fighting other people's battles."

"So, you think I'm the weak one, and you're the family warrior, its fearless soldier?"

Chance didn't flinch but met his brother's stare. "I'm on the frontline, ready to protect this family against all threats. You, Mom, and Dad are the ones who are too dependent and too complacent. You've put your trust in some invisible God, praying that He'll intervene and work things out. But I'm a realist, and my faith isn't in some Spirit but in flesh and blood and weapons I can actually see and use."

"You're going too far, son," his father said. "God is real, and He *is* relevant."

"To you, Dad. Not to me."

"That's because you think He's hurt you."

"Hasn't He?"

His mother touched his arm. "God loves you. Why won't you accept that?"

"I don't need Him or His love. He's not my crutch."

"Everybody needs God, son."

"I don't, Dad. I'm not that weak nor helpless."

Victor unfolded his arms. "So we're all weak because we believe in God and we trust Him?"

"You're naïve," Chance said. "About God and life. You, more than anybody, trust too easily and let people take advantage of you. That's why you, more than anybody, need protection, supervision."

His brother glared at him. "I'm a man, just like you."

"I don't believe in fairy tales or have the faith of a child."

"There's nothing wrong with child-like faith. If you read a Bible, you'd know that." Victor wagged his olive-tan finger at Chance. "And I'm twenty-nine years old, not eleven. I don't need you as my defender or warrior anymore. I've got all the armor I need in Jesus."

"Then, you've got nothing, and you're defenseless, with no armor at all."

"Chance!" His mother gripped his arm tighter. "God is good, just, and holy. Don't disrespect Him, especially in this house."

"Your mother's right, son."

Chance saw sadness in his parents' eyes. "I'm sorry. Forgive me?"

His father nodded. "Always."

Chance's mother released his arm. "Why won't you stop rejecting Him?"

"I'm only doing to Him what He's done to me."

"Honey, God loves you and—"

"I'd rather not talk about Him."

His mother stole a glance at his father, then bobbed her head. "All right. I'll let it rest."

"I'm sorry I wasn't here when Granddad died."

"You're here now. That's all that matters."

"Still, I should have been here for you." Instead, he had been gone for two months, and he had barely phoned or kept in touch. Guilt gnawed at him.

His mother caressed his face. "You had a case. I understand." She lowered her hand. "Now, come and have a seat, *relax*, so we can talk some more." She led him to the couch, then sat down between him and his father.

Chance held her hand. "You look tired, exhausted."

"I haven't been sleeping. I've been having headaches."

"Have you seen Dr. Allen?"

"I'm waiting for the test results."

"Why didn't you call us?" Victor asked.

"I didn't want you to worry."

"You're our mother," Chance said. "And we don't keep secrets. That's a family rule."

"I made a mistake. I'm sorry."

"When will you know the results?"

"Soon."

Victor propped his arms on his legs and pressed his hands together. "You'll give us an update, won't you?"

"Of course I will."

"We can't lose you, Mom."

"I'm not planning on dying anytime soon."

"Whatever the cost to keep you here, I'll pay it. That's how much I love you." Fire lit Victor's eyes, and for once, he seemed ready to battle—fight.

Chance felt the same.

Their father was the backbone of the family, but their mother was the ever-beating heart. More than anyone, she was Chance's anchor, his calm during every storm, and he couldn't bear the thought of losing her to sickness or death. "Promise you won't leave us, Mom."

She looked at him, tears in her eyes. "I can't make that promise, honey. One day, I'll have no choice but to leave."

"Not today."

"You still need to be prepared, at least for the possibility."

"Promise you'll fight for us. Promise you'll do everything in your power to get well."

"I will."

"You won't keep any more secrets, shutting us out?" Victor asked.

"I'll be honest."

Their father draped his arm around her. "Are you ready, love?"

She nodded. "It's time."

"For what?" Chance asked.

"Sharing the truth—a family secret." His mother inhaled, then exhaled deeply, loudly. "I haven't been honest with you boys, especially about my past. Now, there's no hiding the truth."

"Tell us."

"When I was sixteen, I gave birth to twins, a baby boy and girl."

Chance fell back on the sofa like he'd been punched in the gut. "What?"

"As a teenager, I got pregnant."

Victor scratched his head. "You had twins?"

"Nathan left for college. Later, I found out I was pregnant. Daddy made me call Nathan and break up with him, and he wouldn't let me see him again or even tell him about the babies. Nathan didn't learn the truth until years later after I had lost the twins."

Chance had always heard an infection had left his mother barren, that she couldn't conceive. He leaned forward. "What happened?"

"I only know what I was told. It was a difficult delivery. I was bleeding internally, on the brink of death. I slipped into a coma. When I woke up, Daddy told me the babies were gone, dead. I never saw them nor cradled them in my arms. Later, doctors told me I couldn't have any more babies. I was hysterical, devastated." Pain sliced across her light-brown face, and sorrow clouded her light-brown eyes.

Her babies died. How fair was that? Chance raised his mother's hand and pressed it to his heart. "Why didn't you tell us?"

"I didn't want to reopen that wound, relive that loss—that ache." Tears slid down her face. "I blamed myself. I thought I had done something wrong, that God was punishing me, and that got me depressed. After Nathan and I reunited and got married and we began a family with you and Victor, the twins were still a painful part of my past. I never mentioned them, but they were never far from my thoughts or my heart."

His mother pulled her hand from Chance's so she could wipe tears from her eyes. "For thirty-six years, I've grieved those babies, and February the twenty-first has always been a hard day for me. I used to lock myself in the bathroom, reliving that awful day, crying until I was empty. Finally, your father convinced me to remember the twins in joy, not in sorrow, so I began celebrating their short lives, always placing a couple of white roses in a purple vase in the kitchen window on the birthday."

White roses. Chance sank back in his seat, recalling the countless times he had seen those white roses in the kitchen window. He had always assumed they were romantic gifts from his father to his mother. "Why white roses?"

"They symbolize purity—innocence—hope for a new beginning."

Chance traded glances with his parents, suddenly curious. "You and Dad have kept these babies secret for decades. Why tell the truth now, especially if it dredges up unpleasant memories, painful emotions?"

"On his deathbed, Daddy confessed that he had lied, that the twins hadn't died but that he and his friend and family lawyer Richard Williams had planned everything, and they had made arrangements to put the babies up for adoption."

"They're alive?" Chance asked.

His mother nodded.

"How is that possible?"

"Leah was sixteen, still a minor, when she gave birth. There wasn't even a guarantee she would survive the birth or regain consciousness. So while she was battling for her life, her father, Laban, was calling in favors from his friends and plotting to get rid of her babies—his own grandchildren."

"Why?" Victor asked.

"Laban was a proud, strict, unforgiving man. His wife had died when Leah was ten years old, and he was a well-known man, a deacon in the church—considered upright and good-natured in the community—and he was ashamed of his pregnant, unwed daughter.

"Although he respected my family, especially my father, a minister, Laban never condoned my relationship with Leah. So, after I left for college and she found out she was pregnant, he took advantage of the situation and pressured her to sever all contact with me. After she did, he packed her bags and sent her away to the Bethany House for Girls because he thought her sins were disgraceful, unforgivable, and they reflected badly on *him*."

Chance's mother sniffled. "After I gave birth and slipped into the coma, Daddy put his plan into action, and he got custody of my babies; then, he and Richard separated the twins and sent them home with two adoptive families."

"That sounds criminal—illegal!" Victor said. "Even if you and Dad were teenagers, you should have been included in deciding your kids' future."

"Neither Laban nor Richard believed us ready or mature enough to raise the babies or provide them with a stable family, a good home," their father said. "I was in college, clueless about what was really happening at home, and Leah was still in high school, completely under Laban's control."

Chance rubbed his chin, trying to wrap his mind around what his parents were telling him, what his grandfather had done. "At least with you, the twins would have been together. They would have been well-loved. I can't believe Granddad dropped a bomb on you, then died, leaving you to face the fallout." Although Chance had always thought his grandfather a bit of a dinosaur—extinct and rigid—he would have never thought him cruel and heartless. The man had taken his daughter's babies—his own grandkids—and tossed them out like unwanted newspaper; then, he had lied, claiming they were dead.

"Would he have confessed if he wasn't dying?" Victor asked.

"Of course not," their mother said.

"Can you forgive him?"

"I already have. I just can't forget what I've lost because of him: those first years, first words and steps of my children, first kisses and graduations, likely weddings and grandchildren."

Chance's father hugged her. "All isn't lost, love. We might be down, even delayed, but we're not done nor defeated." He kissed her forehead. "We've got their names, so we'll find them."

"You know the twins' names?" Victor asked.

"We confronted Richard with a lawyer, and he told us. The boy's name is Daniel, and his adopted family, the Winwards, were originally from Sutton, Georgia. The girl's name is Leisha, and her adopted family, the Laurences, at that time lived a few hours from here in Corinth." He glanced from Chance to Victor. "That's all we have, but still, it's good news."

Chance didn't know how to respond to this apparent *good* news. He knew he should be happy that his parents' biological children were alive, and he *was* glad that they had found out the truth. He just didn't know how these new siblings would change the dynamics of the Dearling family, and that made him unsettled.

He searched his parents' faces and saw the expectation, joy, and hope. "You want to meet them, invite them into our lives, this house, don't you?"

"Your mother and I want to meet them, know them, and build a relationship with them if that's possible. But neither of us can travel now and make this reunion with the twins a reality. Leah's under doctor's orders to rest and refrain from stress and travel, and I'm the senior pastor at the church, so I'm compelled to stay as well."

They need me, Chance thought. *I've got to help them. It's the least I can do.* Forcing all his reservations aside, Chance decided to give his parents what they wanted—a reunion with their biological children. "Since I'm the private investigator, I'm the logical choice for finding the twins. Would you and Mom like me to find them?"

A fire lit in his father's eyes. "You'd do that for us?"

"I love you."

"It wouldn't be an imposition?"

"We're family, Dad. I'm willing to give everything to help you and Mom, even without you asking."

His father smiled through tears. "Thank you, son."

"Count me in, too," Victor said.

"Don't you have to work?" their father asked.

"I'm on summer vacation."

"What about your volunteer work at Hope Recovery?"

"I'll take some personal time."

"Are you sure?"

"I've logged in enough time to take a well-deserved break."

Their mother dabbed tears from her eyes. "Thank you, Victor. You, too, Chance."

"We're glad to help," Chance said.

"For *that*, I'm truly grateful." Her smile was like sunlight breaking through dark clouds, and beneath it, Chance felt love and warmth.

"How do we proceed?" she asked.

"Victor and I can divide the task, each of us seeking out one twin. That way, we're not wasting valuable time and resources."

"That sounds reasonable."

"I'll fly to Georgia since I'll likely have better success with the son." Chance glanced at his brother. "Since Victor is Prince Charming and has a way with women, the daughter might be more comfortable with him."

"When do we leave?" Victor asked.

"After your birthday."

"Sounds good to me."

"What do you think?" Chance asked his parents.

"We have the most amazing sons." His father looked at him, his eyes searching. "But are you comfortable doing this?"

"It's not a problem. Really."

"Well, thank you again. I'm mighty proud of you both."

"Don't get too excited about a happy reunion, Dad. There's no guarantee the twins will accept you. After all, you and Mom are strangers, and they're just as likely to toss Victor and me out as to welcome us into their families."

"Your father and I will write letters of introduction, explaining who we are and the events surrounding their birth," his mother said. "We'll also get documents from Richard to verify the truth."

"Documents will help, but they may not secure the twins' cooperation."

"Your mother and I walk by faith, Chance. We expect good even though we may not always see it."

"Faith can't solve every problem, Dad. It can't make strangers love you." Chance's own experiences with Ray Brayden had taught him that lesson. No child-like faith, birthday wish, nor bedtime prayer had changed his birth father from a violent monster to a loving parent.

"It's true that love can't be forced, but faith is still the key that unlocks every closed door. Without it, it's impossible to move mountains or to please God."

"I respect you, Dad, and I accept your beliefs, but I'm not interested in pleasing God. For me, He's no better than Ray Brayden. When I needed God most, He was absent, invisible; He abandoned me."

"God loves you, son. He's never forgotten you, forsaken you, nor has He left you alone."

"Really?" Chance laughed drily. "Mama believed in Him, and she prayed every day, yet, despite her faith, He remained silent, distant. He left both of us in pain and misery, and He did nothing to save us, especially from Ray."

"He protected you, provided for you. He kept you safe until Ray left and the abuse ended."

"After three years!" Tears stung Chance's eyes. "Even then, God took Mama, the only parent I loved. He left me alone, with nothing and no one."

"Never alone, son. God has walked with you through every fire and every storm. He directed your steps and led you to us. All because He cares, and He loves you."

"I can't imagine what He'd do to me if He actually hated me." Chance had put God behind him, and he was fine relying on himself. He certainly didn't need God's love or His interference now that he was an adult and could fight, defending himself. "Enough about me and the Almighty. Okay?"

"All right, son. I won't force the issue."

"So tell me: How are we supposed to convince these twins to come home with us—to meet you and Mom?"

"Just find them, give them the letters and invite them to Crossland. If it's God's will, they'll come."

Chance lacked his father's faith. He hoped for the best for his parents' sake, but a life full of hard knocks had taught him happy endings were more in fairy tales than real life; they were extremely rare. "So be it, Dad. We'll start this journey in seven days, after Victor's birthday."

Chapter Two

And we know that in all things, God works for the good of those
who love him, who have been called according to his purpose.

Romans 8:28 (NIV)

Parkland Place
Friday, June 10

As he spent his thirtieth birthday at home on the basketball court
with Chance, Victor was thankful. His life today was a far cry from
what it had been twenty-two years ago. Then, he had been eight, dirty,
dispirited, dehydrated, homeless, and living with his *abuela*, Milagros
Ortega, in a shelter on Lyons Street.

That was where Pastor Nathan Dearling had found him, and that
was when he had befriended Victor's grandmother and had become her
and Victor's guardian angel. After Victor's grandmother died, Nathan
and Leah, honoring the elderly woman's last request and following God's
guidance, had adopted Victor.

That first night in the Dearlings' home Victor had lain in bed, scared
and crying. Even though he loved his new parents, he had missed his *abuela*.

Hearing his cries, Chance, thirteen at that time, had strolled into
Victor's bedroom, climbed onto the bed, then hugged him, offering
assurances and comfort. He had recounted his first night with the
Dearlings; then, he'd said, "We're brothers now, you and I. Nobody's
gonna hurt you, at least not while I'm here.

"Plus, Mom and Dad are good people. They love you." He had
tousled Victor's hair, then promised to take care of him like a good
big brother. Forever. From that night on, the two truly had become
brothers—united, inseparable.

"Are you going to daydream all day or toss me some water?" Chance quirked his dark-brown eyebrow as he sat down on the grass, a white towel on the ground beside him.

"Sorry." Victor leaned down, grabbed two bottles of water and a sports drink from the blue cooler, then handed the water to Chance and sat beside him.

Chance twisted the lid off one bottle, sat the second beside the towel; then, he doused his head in clear liquid and raked sun-tanned fingers through his layered, dark brown hair. "You played a good game, especially for an old man." He lifted the towel, drying himself.

Victor tilted his head. "The score was one hundred to eighty-five. Either your head wasn't in the game or you let me win."

"You won, so enjoy it."

"Thanks then. I will." Victor removed the lid from his sports drink, then gulped the orange drink down, his mind drifting to his past again.

His parents' quest to find their birth children had sparked thoughts of his own birth parents, Roberto and Rosaria Ortega. He had been three when they had died in a car accident in Puerto Rico, so his memories of them were somewhat faded.

If his grandmother hadn't saved that one family photo of them cuddling him when he was born when she had returned to Crossland, Texas, with Victor, he wouldn't have even remembered their faces.

He lowered his drink, searched his brother's face. "Do you remember your birth mother?"

"Every day."

"Why don't you talk about her?" As an adolescent, Victor had grown accustomed to sharing stories of his life with his *abuela*, yet Chance had always kept his experiences with his mother private. Even though Victor was always curious, he had stopped prying into Chance's past, assuming his brother would share when he was ready. But Chance had never let down his guard, nor had he really given Victor a good glimpse into his thoughts or his heart.

"Sometimes, it hurts to remember how Mama lived, how she died." Chance massaged his temple as though trying to scrub the bad memories away.

"Maybe it wouldn't be so painful if you talked about it. Maybe then you'll find what you're looking for—peace." Victor had been leaning on Chance since he was eleven years old; now, he wanted Chance to lean on him. "Tell me about your mother."

Chance remained silent, staring ahead, and Victor knew he was shutting him out again. *He still won't trust me with his past or his pain,* Victor thought, and his heart sank in his chest.

After five minutes, Chance laid back, his head cushioned on his arms, and he glanced overhead toward the clear blue sky. "Her name was Eileen, and she was a registered nurse."

"Do you look like her?"

"She had short hair that framed her face like light-brown feathers, and her eyes were like large, clear-water pools of light that seemingly saw straight to my heart. She looked fragile, but she wasn't." He closed his eyes. "Safety and love for me then was being cradled in Mama's arms, with her chin resting on my head." He smiled, seemingly lost in his memories. "I always told Mama I loved her beyond the clouds, and she always said, *I love you beyond measure.*" Chance opened his eyes, and they were shimmering like two sea-blue oceans. "That was Mama, full of love."

Victor remained silent, afraid to spoil the moment.

"Mama was too faithful, too forgiving, too loving. Ray took advantage of her all the time, and she was his favorite punching bag, and she couldn't protect herself or me."

"Why didn't she leave him or have him arrested?"

"He threatened to track us down and kill us if we tried to leave. Mama was scared he'd actually do it."

"What happened to him?"

"He left."

"Did you ever hear from him again?"

"No."

"And your mother died?"

"From a brain aneurysm." His dark blue eyes gleamed with tears in the sunlight. "After that, I was put in foster care, and I was shuffled from one miserable foster home after another, and I fought every day just to survive."

"When did your life change?"

"On July the fourth, my eighth birthday. Kingdom Family sponsored a picnic for foster kids, and that was when I first met Mom and Dad. Even though I was silent, distrustful, and unresponsive, they kept trying to befriend me, and they didn't leave me alone for the duration of the picnic. I still don't know how they did it, but before that day was over, they won a smile from me and a little piece of my heart."

"If Mama's death was the worst day of my life, the best day was when the Dearlings adopted me. They saved me, and they've done nothing but love me since. For all they've done, I'll never be able to repay them."

"They don't expect payment."

"Still, I wish I could be an ideal son—one who makes them proud."

"You've done that, and they love you already. You don't have to earn what they freely give. Mom and Dad just want you to be happy, fulfilled. They want you to live a life of purpose, giving love and receiving love, and possibly even having a family of your own."

Chance shook his head. "That's one dream that won't come true. I'm not getting married, nor am I bringing any child into this messed-up world."

"Why not?"

"I'm not turning into Ray nor passing on any of his genes."

"You're nothing like your birth father."

Chance laughed drily. "I look just like him."

"The physical resemblance doesn't matter, Chance. Your heart, spirit, and soul do. You're a good guy—a protector, not an abuser."

"According to Mama, Ray wasn't always angry and violent either. When they met, he was a prince—quite the gentleman—and when they were first married, he was the model man—a good doctor, a loving and attentive husband. Within three years, though, he quit working at the hospital, began drinking heavily and using drugs; then, he completely changed, became more monster than man, inflicting pain, inspiring fear."

"You're not Ray, and you can't let fear paralyze you and keep you stuck in the past. Like everyone else, you deserve a great future—a family —a wife, some kids."

Chance sat up and faced Victor. "I have all the family I need—you, Mom, and Dad."

"What about the twins—Daniel and Leisha?"

"They're strangers, not family. And even though I'm glad Mom and Dad know about them, I don't see a reunion happening, not anytime soon."

"All we can do is pray for the best."

"I stopped praying after Mama died."

"It's never too late to start again or give God a chance."

"He already had one with me, and He lost it." Chance slapped his hand against his right thigh, then stood. "If we don't want to be late for your surprise birthday party, we'd better shower, change clothes, and drive over to Mom and Dad's."

Victor sighed. "I really don't need a party. I told Mom to skip it this year."

"She loves you, and she wants to celebrate, so let her."

"She needs rest."

"She'll rest tomorrow." Chance clapped a hand on Victor's shoulder. "Let's just enjoy the day. As a family. Because tomorrow I'll be catching a flight to Sutton, Georgia, and you'll be driving to Corinth."

"How long do you think we'll be gone?"

"A few days. A week. There's no telling."

"How long before you give up?"

"Every assignment is different, and this one's personal. About Mom and Dad. So, I can't come home until I've done my best and exhausted all my resources. I owe Mom and Dad that much."

"Is that all this is for you, an assignment, another way to repay Mom and Dad?"

Chance lowered his hand. "What else can it be?"

"A privilege and a gift. We'll be the first to meet Mom and Dad's son and daughter, and we'll be the ones to return them home. It's not about fulfilling any obligation or repaying any debt. It's about blessing Mom and Dad, making them happy, and giving them the greatest gifts we can give them—their firstborn children, the first fruit of their love."

"For once, be realistic, Victor. There's a possibility of failure."

"I believe in God, Chance. I have hope, *faith*."

"I hope your faith doesn't fail you." Chance collected his empty bottles, then draped the towel over his shoulder. "I've got to shower. I told Dad I'd get you there on time, and you know I always keep my word." He walked toward the back door, opened the screen, then disappeared inside.

Victor tilted his head back and looked toward heaven. "Lord, show him how to forgive, how to love You. Let him know he can trust You, even with his anger, his past, his pain. Above all, draw him to You so You can speak to his heart and help him accept Your love and receive Your Son and Your grace."

Chapter Three

Lord, I know that people's lives are not their own;
it is not for them to direct their steps.

Jeremiah 10:23 (NIV)

Sutton, Georgia
Sunday, June 12

*A*t six o'clock in the morning, Chance sat in bed, in a white T-shirt and blue pajama pants, in a motel room, his laptop perched on his outstretched legs and his preliminary file on Daniel Winward at his left side. In the week since he had first learned of Daniel's existence, he had discovered the basics about the man.

He was an only child. His adoptive parents were Elec and Marissa, a high school principal and public librarian. His full name was Daniel Michael Winward, and he held degrees in Divinity and Counseling. He was an Associate Pastor at Increasing Faith Worship Center under the guidance of the charismatic Senior Pastor, Dr. Asa Eli Joseph.

On paper, the man seemed upstanding—someone Chance's parents would admire and love, a son after their own hearts. But Chance was skeptical. He didn't trust that Daniel Winward was as honorable and righteous as he seemed. And he wasn't sure there weren't any skeletons lurking in the man's closet, some hidden vice or indiscretion that could affect or haunt the Dearlings, should it become known that they were Daniel's birth parents.

For that reason, Chance was biding his time. He wouldn't tell Daniel the truth until he had assured himself that the man wasn't a threat or liability. That's why he was online, searching for more information on Increasing Faith Worship Center and its staff.

Chance found a recent photo of Daniel Winward, and he instantly noticed the man's resemblance to his father, Nathan Dearling, who was six-feet-four inches, with dark-brown skin, dark-brown hair, and hazel eyes. In contrast, Daniel had trimmed dark black hair and clear gray eyes. Otherwise, he resembled Nathan Dearling in stature and appearance.

He's their son, most definitely, Chance thought. He clicked on another screen, then scrolled down until he found the schedule for the weekly services.

Browsing through the itinerary, he found out Daniel would be teaching the Men of Valor Sunday school class and the Wednesday Night for Learning, NFL, Bible study.

Chance shut down the laptop, returned it to the case on a nearby table; then, he stepped from the bed and walked to the bathroom for a quick shower. He wanted to find the church in time to observe Daniel Winward in his Men of Valor class.

After his shower, Chance got dressed, putting on a royal blue shirt, leather jacket, and blue jeans. He fastened his silver watch, then grabbed a compact Bible from the motel's desk drawer. He figured he might as well carry it with him, even if he doubted he would open it or even read it.

Collecting the key to his rental car, his cell phone, and his wallet, Chance strode from the motel on his way to the one place he thought he'd never visit again—church.

Chance arrived at the church and parked the car with fifteen minutes to spare, and for five minutes, he just sat inside the car, peering through the windshield at the majestic gray and purple building that seemingly stretched toward the sky. Already families dotted the parking lot, streaming toward the glass doors. If he didn't join them soon, Chance knew he would be conspicuously late. So he unsnapped the seatbelt, tucked the cell phone in his right pocket, then grabbed the Bible and stepped from the car.

Inside, a female greeter with reddish-brown hair and green eyes approached him, with a plastered smile on her face. "Welcome to Increasing Faith." She handed him a folded church bulletin. "God bless you."

"Thanks." He walked past her to the Information Desk, where an Asian woman with long black hair and dark brown eyes stood and smiled.

"How may I help you, sir?"

"I'm looking for Pastor Winward's class."

"Take the corridor on the right, then find the third door on the left. Signs are posted beside each door, indicating each class."

"Thanks." Chance followed her directions, easily finding the room and the last vacant seat near the end of the third row among four arched rows of men of different races and clothing.

Apparently, the men knew one another. They were hugging, shaking hands, and chatting. A few waved and nodded their heads at Chance, offering smiles and words of welcome, but he didn't encourage any conversation or intimacy. Instead, he dismissed them, turning his head away.

Surveying the room, he felt like an outcast—a lone wolf among sheep. *Why am I here torturing myself?* he thought. *There must be some other way for me to discover the truth about Daniel Winward.* He was contemplating his exit when Daniel Winward entered the room and shut the door behind him.

Dressed in a yellow shirt, navy blue blazer, and dark denim jeans, the man walked in confidence, with a Bible tucked beneath his right arm. "Good morning, everyone. Welcome to Men of Valor. For those of you here for the first time, I'm Pastor Winward, but most of my friends here call me Pastor *Win* because that's what I'm called to do for the glory and honor of God—win souls."

"Good morning, Pastor Win," the men all chimed.

Daniel smiled, then sat on a stool, laying his Bible on the adjacent table. "Before we begin every lesson, we always pray, then spend at least fifteen minutes eating and fellowshipping. So, if you would, bow your heads, close your eyes, and give reverence to our heavenly Father." He bowed his head and closed his eyes.

I'm not doing this; I'm not praying, Chance thought, glancing around the room, watching heads go down like rows of dominos.

When his head was the only one still up, he felt a prick of uneasiness within his spirit, and he could hear his parents chiding him for being rebellious and irreverent. Finally, he lowered his head and listened courteously but with a hardened heart as Daniel prayed. When the man finally said, "Amen," Chance raised his head and watched as the men left their seats and formed a line at the refreshment table.

Daniel left the stool and chatted with a cluster of men for a few minutes before moving on—laughing and clapping others on the back. As others talked, he earnestly listened, as though he were invested in what they were saying, in them.

Warding off greeters, Chance lowered his head and wondered how he would endure a full day of church with the saints when someone lowered a plate of fruit in front of him. He raised his head and stared into searching gray eyes.

"You seemed lost and alone over here." Daniel smiled at him. "I thought you could use the food and the company."

His stomach empty, Chance graciously accepted the plate. "Thanks." He plopped a couple of grapes in his mouth, expecting Daniel to leave now that he had performed his Christian duty in feeding the hungry, but the man surprised him, sitting down beside him.

"Is this your first visit?"

Chance nodded. "I'm not a churchgoer."

"You have a name?"

"Chance Dearling."

"Nice to meet you." Daniel extended his right hand, and Chance accepted it, returning his firm shake. "Are you from Georgia?"

"Crossland, Texas."

"You're a long way from home, then."

"Yes, I am."

"Is this a permanent move?"

"I'm on assignment, working, actually."

"What's your profession?" Daniel's stare was as intense as a laser beam, and Chance almost felt like Daniel was peering beyond his eyes, deep into his soul.

"I'm a private investigator."

"Wow! That's impressive."

"It's a job, nothing more."

"Even a job can be a calling, ministry, or mission field—an opportunity for you to touch, impact, and transform lives, all for the glory and honor of God."

His job as a calling, a ministry, or a mission field, really? Surely, that was a joke. Chance laughed. "Believe me, I'm just an investigator. I'm nobody's minister, role model, missionary, or hero."

Daniel studied him. "A minister doesn't always stand behind a podium, nor does a hero always wear a costume, uniform, or mask. He can live a quiet, ordinary life but use his God-given gifts to do great, extraordinary things."

"That's not me, nor is that my life."

"Well, I imagine you still work some interesting cases and travel extensively."

"Generally." Chance raised another grape to his mouth, then chewed slowly, hoping Daniel would take the hint and go away.

He didn't.

"How did you learn about Increasing Faith?" he asked.

"The Internet."

"And what brought you to my class—Men of Valor?"

Lying wasn't in his nature. So Chance decided he'd be honest with Daniel...to an extent. "I was curious—about this class and you, the minister."

"Are you a believer?"

"I believe in my family, myself."

"Are you seeking God, then?"

"I'm not looking for Him, nor am I here begging for His love, acceptance, or forgiveness."

"Yet you're here—in this church, in this class, on this day." Daniel palmed his hands on his thighs. "You may not be pursuing God, but He's definitely pursuing you, Chance."

"I don't need Him, and I don't want anything to do with Him. Not anymore."

Daniel raised an eyebrow. "You're angry?"

"With good reason."

"Did you lose someone?"

"My birth mother."

"I'm sorry for your loss." He put his hand on Chance's shoulder. "Is she the reason you're mad at God?"

"Partly." Chance pulled away from Daniel's touch, but he felt compelled to share his past, his pain, his misery. "This loving God of yours let her die, and He left me broken. He took everything from me—my mother, my home, my innocence, my faith." Chance met Daniel's unwavering gaze. "He left me alone—orphaned."

"Where's your father?"

"If there's any justice, he's in jail or dead. He beat my mother for years, then finally walked out, leaving us alone."

"Did he abuse you, too?"

Chance saw the same compassion in his father's eyes reflected in Daniel's, and he was drawn into the warmth. Even despite his best effort to rein in his emotions, he couldn't stop talking or revealing the thorns in his heart, the skeletons in his closet. "Verbally and physically from the time I was three until I turned six."

"I'm sorry for that pain and suffering, and I understand how you feel."

"Was your father abusive? A drunk and an addict?"

"He's always been my hero."

Chance pulled away from him. "You don't know me, nor can you understand me. In comparison to my life, yours was probably picture perfect."

"You're making assumptions."

Chance tilted his head. "You have a story?"

"Every man in here does." Daniel motioned toward the others in the room. "God never promised that any of our lives would be easy, but He did warn that we would all have crosses to bear—that we would have to pick them up, carry them, and follow Him."

"Just what I'd expect to hear from one of God's cheerleaders."

"I'm no different from you, and I'm not oblivious to your pain. You've been hurt, you feel betrayed, you're angry, and you resent God."

Daniel placed his hand back on Chance's shoulder. "You're entitled to your feelings."

Chance snorted. "I don't need your permission to be angry with God."

"Of course, you don't. However, you should know those feelings—anger, hatred, bitterness, unforgiveness, and resentment—are like poison in your heart, Kryptonite for your spirit and soul; they make for certain death and separation from the eternal Source of life, as long as you hold on, clinging to them.

"They keep you bound in guilt, in pain, in suffering, in torment, in the past, in the desert, in the wasteland, too, and if not removed completely, they become everlasting barriers between you and God."

"You're the one who's bound to a jealous, indifferent God. I'm free from His tyranny."

"God isn't vindictive or capricious. He's permissive, but He's good, loving, merciful, faithful, and just—the same yesterday, today, and forever."

"That's your interpretation."

"It's an accurate depiction, just the same. The Book of Job, in chapter five, basically says, blessed is the one whom God chastises because God bruises but He binds up; He wounds but His hands make whole. What this really means is God allows us to go through storms and trials, to encounter obstacles and mountains, and He doesn't always remove them, but He journeys with us, empowering us through His Word, His Son, His Spirit, and His strength so that we persevere and overcome as victors, not victims, and we prevail against every opponent and adversary and come through any trial and storm as more than conquerors through Him who loved us.

"And in Joshua 1:9, God even instructs us, saying, 'Be strong and courageous. Do not be terrified; do not be discouraged, for the LORD your God will be with you wherever you go.'"

Chance shook his head. "That's all meaningless to me. I don't need someone else quoting Scripture. I get enough of that from my adopted father."

"He's a preacher?"

Chance nodded. "He's on a mission to save my soul."

Daniel squeezed Chance's shoulder. "You may not be ready to surrender your life to God or accept Jesus as your Lord and Savior today, but He's still here, patiently waiting for you to grab on to Him, cling to Him, and invite Him into your heart, your home, and your life."

"You might as well give up on me, Pastor Win. I'm not here for a sermon." He didn't need Daniel Winward hopping on that bandwagon to save his lost soul. He was self-sufficient, self-reliant—a survivor—and he didn't need God as his Lord, Savior, Protector, or crutch. He could take care of himself.

Daniel lowered his hand. "Regardless of your motives, I'm glad you're here, and I hope today's lesson blesses you."

"I'm not into sermons, and Bible lessons bore me."

"Chance, you're here for a reason. If you come with an open heart and a willing spirit, I think you'll benefit from today's message."

"I don't share your faith, Pastor, so why should I care about your message?"

"Because it deals with redemption, and it's meant for people just like you."

"I don't need anyone saving me."

"We all need salvation, even from ourselves." He glanced at his watch. "Are you staying for the morning service?"

If I had my wish, no, he thought. *But this isn't about me; it's about Mom and Dad. They're depending on me to reunite them with you, their firstborn son.* "That depends on who's preaching."

He smiled broadly. "I am."

"Then, I'll stay."

"Good." Daniel stood. "It's time for our class to begin." He returned to his stool, signaling everyone to finish their refreshments and return to their seats.

Chance's mind strayed as he finished eating the fruit. *What's wrong with me today? Why did I even agree to sit through an entire church service? What's worse is I've practically shared my life's story with this man— this stranger.* He didn't understand the man's appeal other than he bore a strong resemblance to the only father Chance had ever loved. Today, indeed, was a rare day for him.

Daniel cleared his throat, lifted his Bible, and commented on his lesson. "This morning, our journey and the precursor to today's sermon begin in Ephesians 4:1, which says, 'As a prisoner for the Lord, I urge you to live a life worthy of the calling you have received.'"

Chance lifted the Bible he'd brought from the motel from the floor, then flipped the pages, fumbling until he found the scripture. *This is pure torture. I hate sermons.* Stonily, he listened as Daniel recited the verses, then closed his Bible, his eyes scanning the crowd and sweeping over Chance.

"We were created in love for love and for giving, and as servants and prisoners for the Lord, we're to glorify God and worship Him in spirit and truth, to live lives that testify to His goodness, grace, and mercy." Daniel looked at Chance, his eyes riveted on him.

"If we're not living for God, then who exactly are we living for? And, if we're not serving our Lord and Savior, Jesus Christ, who are we serving—ourselves, other people, or that adversary many still don't believe is real—the devil?" Daniel's gray eyes seared Chance's. "Search your heart, my friend, and ask yourself these two questions: Who am *I* serving? Who am I living for?"

Chance closed the Bible, Daniel's words and his challenge ringing loudly in his ears, even in his mind: *Who am I serving? Who am I living for?*

Chapter Four

"Ask and it will be given to you; seek and you will find;
knock and the door will be opened to you.

Matthew 7:7 (NIV)

Corinth, Texas
Monday, June 13

After spending a few hours at a computer at the Corinth Public Library, Victor discovered that Leisha Laurence was a family lawyer practicing at the Offices of Wright, Laurence, and Arrollo.

Content with what he had learned, Victor had returned to his room at the local bed and breakfast, and he had phoned the law firm to make an appointment.

Now, as he waited in her office, Victor noted the décor—the cherry wood desk with three photos: one of an older dark-skinned couple, presumably Leisha's parents, flanking a tall, serious teenage girl whom Victor assumed was Leisha; one of two graduates hugging, Leisha and a laughing young woman with creamy white skin and long windblown red hair; and the last photo was of Leisha dressed in black, kissing a white puppy.

On the left wall, college degrees were framed, and beneath them were framed verses: Philippians 4:13: "I can do all this through him who gives me strength."; 2 Corinthians 5:7: "For we live by faith, not by sight."; and Philippians 3:14: "I press on toward the goal to win the prize for which God has called me heavenward in Christ Jesus."

She's a woman of faith, Victor thought, pleased by the discovery. *Maybe she'll be more receptive to meeting Mom and Dad, to giving them a place in her life, in her heart.* He was contemplating how best to broach the subject of her adoption and a reunion with the Dearlings when the office door opened.

Victor turned, and his heart jolted, battering his chest like pounding elephants, and he gasped, for the first time in his life, utterly speechless because in person, Leisha Laurence was magnificent, glorious, *hermosa*—quite beautiful. She had smooth, unblemished brown skin, a long curtain of dark brown curls that cascaded over her shoulders, alluring tiger eyes, which were the color of amber, and full heart-shaped lips.

Leisha Laurence crossed the threshold and stepped inside with authority, confidence, and poise. "Sorry to keep you waiting."

Even her voice struck a chord in Victor's heart, thoroughly enchanting him, and he leaned forward, drawn to her like a moth to flame.

"I'm Leisha Laurence." She advanced, extending her right hand, and Victor tilted his head back, giving reverence to her. Even as she paused, her lips slightly parted. In a blouse the color of sunset and a chocolate brown pantsuit, she stood graceful yet commanding. "Is anything wrong?"

"Excuse me." Victor composed himself.

"I'm Victor Dearling." He accepted her hand, wrapping his around hers, and for the first time in eight years, he felt a connection with a woman—a touch of lightning. Before he could savor it, she stepped back, her eyes wide and her forehead puckered—creased.

"Nice to meet you, Mr. Dearling. Are you here for a divorce?" She glided around the desk and sat comfortably behind the barrier.

"I'm not married."

She slid a legal pad in front of her, then lifted a black pen, nestling it between long, slender fingers. "Custody of a child?"

"No children either."

"How can I help you, Mr. Dearling?"

"Call me Victor, please." He removed the letter and envelope from his parents and Richard Williams from his jacket pocket, deciding against prolonging the inevitable. "I'm not here as a client, looking for your professional services."

She frowned. "Why are you here, then?"

He raised the letter and envelope and handed them to her. "These will explain." As he watched, she opened his parents' letter and perused it, her face an expressionless mask.

Finally, as she finished reading the letter, the façade cracked, and she clutched the letter to her chest and lifted skeptical eyes toward Victor. "My parents are Dr. Leander and Brianne Laurence, not some unwed teenager and her boyfriend."

"Your parents never told you that you were adopted?"

Fire shot from Leisha's eyes. "I'm not adopted!"

"If you don't believe what's in the envelope, call your parents and ask them."

She glared at him. "They died in a car accident four years ago."

"I'm sorry for your loss. My parents died in an accident in Puerto Rico when I was a boy, no more than three." He pointed to the envelope on the desk. "If you'll read the documents from Richard Williams, you'll find proof of the adoption—even a newborn baby photo. At your leisure, you can verify everything."

Leisha dropped the letter, then grabbed the envelope, ripping it open. As she removed the photo and documents and scanned them, she began to quake, her hands trembling and her eyes filling with tears.

Victor's first instinct was to go to her and comfort her, but he fought the urge and remained seated instead. "Are you convinced?"

"That's my baby photo, and the documents seem legitimate, easily verifiable." She let Richard's document and the photo slip from her fingers, then lowered her head and cupped it within her hands. "My parents lied to me." Tears streamed down her cheeks. "They didn't even mention this twin brother—Daniel."

The pain in her eyes and the tremor in her voice drew Victor closer. "From what I understand, they never knew about your brother. As far as the adoption, maybe they didn't want reminders of your past—your birth parents."

Leisha raised her head and dried her eyes. "You didn't know the Laurences, so don't make excuses for them. The truth is, they lied to me, all my life." She stiffened her spine, trying to compose herself despite her tear-swollen eyes. "Who are you exactly?"

"Victor Ortega-Dearling—a friend, if you'll let me be." He leaned forward, drawn more by that glimpse of vulnerability than by any physical beauty she possessed. "Your birth parents, Leah and Nathan Dearling, adopted me when I was eleven years old."

"You're an adoptee?"

"Yes."

Her eyebrows drew close together. "You're not Black."

"I'm Puerto Rican, my brother Chance is White, and the Dearlings are Black. None of that matters, though. We're a family." He palmed his hands on her desk. "I love Mom and Dad completely, and they're my parents in every way."

Leisha exhaled and brushed a wayward curl behind her ear. "I'm sorry if I offended you."

"You didn't."

"I still don't understand why you're here, dumping this family secret on me."

"My parents couldn't come, so I'm their emissary."

Her expression soured like spoiled milk. "What do they want?"

"A meeting with you in Crossland."

Leisha's curls flounced as she shook her head. "That's not happening."

Victor felt the needle prick of disappointment in his heart. "Why not?"

"Genetics don't make them my real parents. To me, they're no more than strangers, and I'm not obligated to meet them anywhere, anytime."

"Please, give them a chance—an opportunity to get to know you."

A face of stone confronted him. "They had their chance when I was born. They lost it when they let me go. Now, it's too late."

"They didn't voluntarily give you up. You were taken from them."

"I don't need surrogate parents."

"Mom and Dad don't want to replace your parents. They just want to spend quality time with you and build a relationship with you." Victor grabbed Leisha's hand and pulled her toward him, and her eyes got wide. "Aren't you curious—about them, your family history, your twin brother?"

"I've known about them for mere minutes, not a lifetime."

"Then don't make a rash decision. Pray about it, talk to your minister, or get advice from a friend, but don't ignore the truth, don't harden your heart, and don't shut the Dearlings out of your life because you're hurt, angry, afraid." Victor rubbed her hand, caressing it. "Will you keep an open mind, please?"

Leisha pursed her lips and glanced down at their hands before facing Victor again. "I won't promise to meet them, but I'll take what you've said into consideration."

"Thank you." Victor preferred a slow "yes" to a hasty "no." While Leisha was thinking, he'd be praying. "I'm sorry for blindsiding you."

Leisha pulled her hand from his and rolled her chair back. "It's not your fault my parents lied to me, then died, taking their secret to the grave."

"Still, I'm sorry I upset you and made you cry."

Leisha waved her hand. "I'm a strong woman, not made of glass, so I can handle the truth." She laughed drily. "And I'm a lawyer, required to be tough, have a thick skin."

"Thick skin usually covers a tender heart."

"*Mi corazón es fuerte, lleno de paz, Señor Dearling.*"

"*¿Qué?*" A smile tugged at Victor's mouth. "You speak Spanish?"

"Occasionally."

"I'm impressed."

Some of the tension left her face. "I'm not fluent, just average—good enough to carry on a conversation with some of our Hispanic clients."

"I'm a Spanish teacher, going on six years at a private Christian Academy, and you didn't sound average to me." He wondered what other pearls lay hidden within Leisha Laurence. "So, what led you into family law?"

"A dream of helping families in need, especially children."

"That's commendable, selfless."

"I'm no saint, nor am I seeking any praise, Mr. Dearling. I just follow my conscience and try to do what's right."

Victor appreciated her candor, her humility. She was a fascinating woman, one he was interested in learning more about. "Have you ever been married?"

Leisha crossed her arms. "Why does that matter?"

"You're a mystery—currently a blank page in this book called Life—and I'd like to know your story. At least as much as you're willing to share with me."

"There's not much to learn. I haven't been married, nor am I divorced."

"Engaged?"

Leisha raised her hand, pointing to a ring-less finger. "I don't have any children either if that's your next question."

He recalled that passion, that ray of light in her amber eyes as she spoke of her motives for pursuing family law. "You love kids, don't you?"

"They're like sunshine to me, full of light, love, life, and warmth."

"I feel the same." He was curious about what else he and Leisha had in common. "I work mostly with teenagers at Kingdom Family Academy and at Hope Recovery, a rehab and resource facility for recovering teen addicts, and I've noticed that most of them are hurting. Many are lost—broken, battered, bruised, and abandoned—and others are merely fighting to survive—seeking hope, love, salvation, deliverance, and peace anywhere they can find it." He raised his hand to his chest. "They all touch my heart, and I gladly sacrifice whatever I have so they'll have whatever they need to live, survive, and succeed."

"Then you're an advocate, too."

"I'm just an open vessel; God's my Source, my Stream."

"That's how I feel."

"Then we're more alike than not." Even though they had just met, Victor felt a kinship, an intimate connection, with her. He felt bound to her, and he didn't want to leave, but he knew she needed time alone—time to digest all that she had just learned. He glanced at his watch and realized they had been talking for an hour. "It's late, and you're probably tired, ready to go home, so I'll go now." He rose, and Leisha did as well.

"Where are you staying?"

"Blessings' Bed and Breakfast."

"For how long?"

"That depends on you."

"Then, you might be here indefinitely."

He grinned. "I'm persistent, so I won't mind camping out on your doorstep, making a nuisance of myself."

"So you're going to stalk me into compliance?"

"I'll give you some privacy, time to consider Mom and Dad's request. But I'm not leaving town, not in defeat. I'll do everything in my power to convince you to come home with me, and I usually get what I pray for, including what I want…if not sooner, then later."

"You're that confident you can sway me?"

"I walk by faith, not by sight." He bowed his head. "Good evening."

"Good evening, Mr. Dearling."

"Victor, please."

She sighed. "All right! Victor."

"Do you like roses?"

"Why does it matter?"

"I'm just curious."

"Yes, I like roses."

"What about candy?"

"Chocolate's my favorite."

"Mine too."

Leisha waved him away. "Goodbye, Victor."

"Until next time." He waved, then walked to the door, opened it, and crossed the threshold, happy and encouraged—his spirit lifted, his heart pumped up—full.

Chapter Five

You have searched me, LORD, and you know me.

Psalm 139:1 (NIV)

Sutton, Georgia
Sunday, June 19

For the past week that Chance had been shadowing Daniel Winward, he had been thrust into a veritable faith arena—a place where his convictions were challenged, where God was worshipped and glorified continuously, and where a wayward soul was constantly encouraged to increase his faith—to hope again, to return home.

"Be free!" Daniel had commanded last Sunday, vigorously shaking his Bible. "Be not bound to the sins of your father or mother. Be not bound to anger, lust, depression, loneliness, pride, shame, or fear. But be bound in righteousness to Christ." Daniel had lowered the Bible to his heart. "I challenge you all to choose this day who you will serve."

Daniel's words hadn't left Chance empty and indifferent, but they had dropped like pearls into the bowl of Chance's spirit, and they had left him bowing his head and palming his hands, with unexplainable tears stinging his own eyes. For the first time during a church service, Chance had actually cried, and he didn't know why.

On Wednesday, he sat through another Bible study with Daniel, this lesson titled "Arrested," coming from Psalm 139:23–24. After Daniel had prayed, then requested that everyone read the verses aloud, Chance reluctantly complied, blending his voice with the others, saying, "Search me, O God, and know my heart; test me and know my anxious thoughts. See if there is any offensive way in me and lead me in the way everlasting."

Daniel had sat on a stool with a Bible in his hand, and he had taught on being called, anointed, and arrested by God.

"If you've been arrested," he said, "you're God's completely, and He has authority over you and your life. He watches over you, catching you when you fall, lifting you when you sink beneath the burdens of the world, and reeling you in, romancing and capturing your heart and soul.

"He draws you to Himself, and you're at peace, for you know He is your strength, joy, hope, peace, and salvation. He gathers your fragments, restoring you—redeeming you—so you're not alone, wounded, rejected, or lost, and when you allow Him to arrest you, when you invite Him into your heart, you gain true freedom. You have authority, dominion, and power, all through Him, the Son of God, Jesus, the Anointed One—the Christ."

His lesson had left Chance wondering whether God was, indeed, knocking on the door of his heart, seeking entrance, or whether He could gather the broken shards of that shattered heart, piece them together, and restore peace and joy to Chance's heart, pouring in it pure—untainted—love.

Now, today instead of celebrating his parents' thirty-third wedding anniversary with them in Crossland, Chance was again at Increasing Faith Worship Center, sitting in the sanctuary and waiting for the service to begin. He had learned what he needed to about Daniel Michael Winward's character—about his integrity, his heart—and Chance felt more at ease sharing the truth about the Dearlings, inviting Daniel into their home and their lives.

After worship through the ministry of music, Dr. Asa Eli Joseph, a lumbering man with a salt-and-pepper afro that glistened beneath the lights, rose to the podium, immaculate in his three-piece navy suit and pink shirt, and he gave a rousing sermon titled "Wounded yet Worthy," which he said was inspired by Joseph, the Dreamer, and Jesus, the Savior.

Dr. Joseph stood composed but with spiritual fire, resting his hands on the clear, see-through podium. As he commenced his sermon, his voice rose and fell like water against sand over the congregants.

"You're worthy," he said. "Even broken, dirty, foul, and discarded, YOU matter, and you're worth all God's love, favor, and care. All you have to do is DREAM beyond your present circumstances, ACT in faith, making a change, and BELIEVE in God and in the value and worth of yourself."

He left the podium and walked across the stage, his eyes fixed on the congregation, seemingly on Chance. "So, if there's anyone in your family who has wounded, betrayed, or abandoned you, today's the day to turn that pain over to God and forgive him or her so you can be free and live worthy of your calling, your purpose, your assignment, your destiny.

"The Passion Translation says of God in Psalm 139:3–7, 'You are so intimately aware of me, Lord. You read my heart like an open book and you know all the words I'm about to speak before I even start a sentence! You know every step I will take before my journey even begins.

'You've gone into my future to prepare the way, and in kindness you follow behind me to spare me from the harm of my past. With your hand of love upon my life, you impart a blessing to me. This is just too wonderful, deep, and incomprehensible! Your understanding of me brings me wonder and strength. Where could I go from your Spirit? Where could I run and hide from your face?'

"So meditate on these words, hide them in your heart, and receive this truth: God loves you and He knows who you are, and where you are, spiritually *and* physically.

"And take this to heart: Even though you've been hurt, God can heal you; even though you've been bruised, He can bind you up; even though you've been broken, His hands can make you whole, and even though you've been wounded, scarred, and completely messed up, you're not disqualified, but you're worthy—of love, healing, redemption, salvation, deliverance, freedom, Jesus—*God*."

As an image of Ray flashed in Chance's mind, he lowered his head and pressed his right hand over his heart. For years he had been harboring hate for the man, and that hatred was doing nothing but destroying everything good in Chance's life.

Was it time for him to release that poison and move on into a place of healing, restoration, peace? Could he truly forgive Ray and leave the past behind?

Countless times his father had urged him to forgive Ray, soften his heart, repent, and return to God, but he had been a brick wall—unforgiving and intractable. His heart had been hard, his mind rigidly set. *How do I forgive a father who hated and rejected me, who stole my innocence and took pleasure in pounding every ounce of love, hope, and happiness from me?*

"Recall Joseph and Jesus," the minister said. "Joseph was betrayed by his own brothers and sold into slavery, yet years later, he forgave and embraced those same brothers, telling them in Genesis 50:20, 'As for you, you meant evil against me, but God meant it for good in order to bring about this present result, to preserve many people alive.'

"Also, Jesus was betrayed by Judas, one of His chosen disciples; He was denied by His friend Peter; and during His trial—His persecution—He was deserted by those He had taught, served, and loved. He was wounded and battered for us—for our sins—for 2 Corinthians 5:21 says, 'For He [God] made Him who knew no sin to be sin for us, that we might become the righteousness of God in Him.'

"So you see, Jesus—equally the Son of God and the Son of Man—was pierced for *our* transgressions, crushed for our iniquities, and the punishment that brought us peace was upon Him. He bore our sins in His body on a tree so we might die to sin and live for righteousness, and by His wounds then you and I now, who surrender our lives to Him and receive this gift of love, this gift of grace, have been healed, forgiven, saved, delivered, redeemed, and reconciled to God, and we live in the presence and spirit of God, trusting as Romans 8:28 says, that all things work together for good to those who love God and are the called according to His purpose.

"That means this day—today—is *your* day—your chance to be like Joseph and forgive those who've hurt you. It's your chance to accept Jesus' sacrifice, His gift, and come, putting aside your fears, reservations, and resentment, so you can be delivered, cleansed, healed, and set free."

Dr. Joseph closed his Bible and extended his hands toward the congregation, inviting those in need forward, to the altar. "You're loved. You're valuable. You're worthy. So lose those shackles, break those chains, draw near God, keep your eyes on Him, and come."

Even as droves of people stood, making a surging wave toward the altar, Chance felt a burgeoning flame in his heart, a consuming fire in his chest, and he felt compelled to rise, walk forward, and draw near the altar—*God*—but he quenched it, remaining in his seat, his head down, the motel's Bible clutched in his right hand.

He hadn't come here to find God or surrender his heart; he had come only for Daniel. For his parents.

You may not be pursuing God, but He's definitely pursuing you, Daniel had told him. Now, his words replayed in Chance's head like an unforgettable song on the radio. *You've been hurt, you feel betrayed, and you're angry. You resent God. You're entitled to your feelings. However, those emotions are like poison. They keep you bound in the past, in the desert, in the wasteland. Be free! Be not bound to the sins of your father or mother. Be strong and courageous.*

Chance raised his head and dried his damp cheeks, and he stood, slowly wading through years of brokenness and pain, grief and anger, toward the altar—that spot of light and hope where Daniel stood before a weeping woman, his forehead pressed against hers, his hand resting on her shoulder, and his lips quivering in fervent prayer.

Chance's heart thumped like a thousand needles against his chest, and fresh tears stung his eyes. *I can't do this,* he thought, and every negative, disparaging word he had ever uttered against God and every misdeed he had ever committed in his quest to live life on his own terms flooded his mind.

I'm not ready or worthy of a place at this altar. Why would God forgive me when all I've done is reject Him, blaming Him for Ray's violence, for Mama's death? Why would He acknowledge me when I've denied Him, even Jesus? Is it even possible for someone like me to change, to forgive, to trust, to love... someone perfect, holy, righteous... like God? How can God even love me like a son? My own birth father couldn't.

Chance's resolve wavered, and he stepped away from the altar and sat down on the nearest pew. Instantly, he felt depleted—completely empty—and a wave of disappointment washed over him, like a blanket over his heart, shutting off the light in his spirit.

He waited until everyone had gone from the altar and Daniel stood alone before rising again and approaching Daniel. "Excuse me."

"Chance! I'm glad you came." Daniel clapped his left hand on Chance's shoulder and offered his right hand. "Did you enjoy the sermon?"

"It was...compelling."

Daniel studied his face, seemingly searching for something. "Did the Word speak to you? Did you get a revelation, any new insight?"

Chance lowered his eyes. "What do you mean?"

"Did you feel God's presence, hear a still small voice urging you to come forward, feel something tugging on your heart, drawing you closer to God, to the altar?"

"The only voice I heard was the preacher's, and all I felt was strange, not like myself at all. For no reason, I got emotional, started crying, and I hardly ever cry, at least not in public."

"That's God, knocking on your door, trying to get your attention. But you're still a doubter, an unbeliever. You won't step forward and take that leap of faith so He can heal you, redeem you, and deliver you."

Chance met Daniel's eyes. "Maybe my heart's too hard. Maybe I'm so broken, I can't be fixed, so lost I can't be found, and my soul can't be won, even by you, the great Pastor Win. Maybe I'm beyond salvation, beyond hope."

Daniel squeezed his shoulder. "Sometimes, courage comes when you allow yourself to be completely vulnerable, when you surrender control and let God take the wheel in your life, while you sit in the passenger seat, going wherever He takes you."

Chance sighed. "I don't have your faith. So I don't know if I can entrust my life, even my soul, to a Spirit I can't see, hear, or feel. If God is real and He cares about me, He wouldn't hide or remain silent. He'd reveal Himself clearly or at least show me that I'm wrong about Him, that He truly loves me, and that I can trust Him."

"Chance, faith is *active*, not passive; it's the substance of things *hoped* for, the evidence of things *not* seen, and Scripture says in Hebrews 11:6, without faith, it's impossible to please God because anyone who comes to Him must believe He exists and that He is a rewarder of those who diligently seek Him.

"This kind of faith is like one person says, walking to the edge of all the light you have, then taking that first step into the dark unknown and trusting that God will be there to support you and teach you how to soar.

"You've got to surrender completely, letting go of your fears, your insecurities, your misconceptions, and your doubts. You have to willingly accept that God is a *good* father, standing always within reach to encourage, advise, comfort, and console you and that He's there in times good and bad, helping you, strengthening you, and urging you to live an abundant life—one with purpose, meaning." Daniel leaned closer. "God loves you, and He doesn't want you wandering alone and lost, in darkness, anger, unforgiveness, pride, or confusion. He wants you home, in His family, under His authority and protection."

"I'm not ready. Maybe I'll never be."

Daniel stepped back and pulled his hand away. "God is patient—longsuffering—but He won't force you to come to Him or receive salvation through His Son, Jesus. That choice is yours entirely."

"You're right, Pastor. This is my choice—not anybody else's." Chance reached down into his own pocket and removed the letter and envelope his father had given him. It was time for the truth—the real reason he was here. "I need to talk to you privately. Do you have time?"

"We can talk in my office." Turning, he led Chance from the sanctuary to a spacious office crammed with books on shelves and Bible verses framed on the wall. "Have a seat." He pointed Chance toward a sofa, then sat beside him. "What's on your mind?"

"You."

Daniel's eyebrows drew close. "What do you mean?"

"You're my assignment," he said. "I've had you under surveillance for the past week."

Daniel palmed his hands in his lap. "Who hired you, and why exactly am I under investigation?"

"No one hired me. The investigation isn't official either. It's personal, and I'm here on behalf of Nathan and Leah Dearling, my adoptive parents."

"Why are your parents interested in me?"

"These documents explain everything." Chance handed him the letter and the envelope and watched as he opened the envelope first, the one from Richard Williams containing legal documents and a baby photo.

Wordlessly, Daniel scanned the legal document; then he read the Dearlings' letter. Waiting for a response—a reaction—Chance raked rough fingers through his hair and tapped his booted heel on the floor in agitation.

Finally, Daniel raised round gray eyes to his. "I have a twin—a sister! That's unbelievable!" He grabbed Chance's arm, his grip tight. "Where is she?"

His sister? Really? Chance tugged his arm from Daniel's hold. "Your sister's all you care about?"

"She's family—part of me. I want to meet her."

Chance frowned, his face suddenly warm. He had expected more from Daniel—some genuine interest in Nathan and Leah—some show of familial concern, even disbelief or anger. He hadn't expected this indifference.

Daniel didn't care that his birth parents had been robbed of a life with him for thirty-six years and that they were searching for him—seeking an opportunity to build a relationship with him. Disappointment settled like a weight in Chance's chest. *Who was Daniel, really?*

Chapter Six

Search me, God, and know my heart;
test me and know my anxious thoughts.

Psalm 139:23 (NIV)

Increasing Faith Worship Center
Sunday, June 19

*D*aniel couldn't believe it. At age thirty-six, he had a sister—a twin. "Tell me about Leisha."

"Her name's pronounced LAY-SHA, and at the time of her adoption, her parents lived in Corinth, Texas. My brother Victor is there searching for her."

Leisha. Dropping the letter, Daniel laced his fingers on the desk. He had always wanted siblings—brothers, sisters. Now, he had one. "Have you heard anything from your brother yet?"

"Not since he first arrived. He's supposed to phone today, giving an update."

"I'd appreciate any news on my sister."

"What about Mom and Dad—your birth parents?" Chance's dark blue eyes were penetrating and scolding. "I'm primarily here for them, not to reunite you with Leisha Laurence. You've read the letter and you've seen the document, so you know Mom and Dad didn't consent to the adoption, that they've only recently learned that you were alive and want to meet you, yet you haven't made inquiries about them. Aren't you curious?"

He was, but not enough to disrupt his life. "I sympathize with the Dearlings, what they endured all these years, but I don't want to revisit the past, reopen a door that's been shut for three decades. I have parents, the Winwards, and my life and family are here in Sutton, Georgia, not in Crossland, Texas."

"Mom and Dad aren't trying to replace your parents. They merely want you to come to Crossland so they can introduce themselves and have a chance to get acquainted with you."

Daniel shook his head, his decision already made. "I can't."

Chance struck his knee, flashing those blue daggers at Daniel. "Why not?"

"I have a full life and obligations. I can't drop everything, just to go with you to meet two strangers."

"They're not strangers; they're your parents."

"The *Winwards* are my parents. Besides that, I don't have time to spare."

Chance's face was cherry red with emotion, frustration. "You can't sacrifice two or three days?"

"Ministry is full-time for me. So no, I don't have time for distractions."

"You're not the only person whose life has been disrupted. I have a life and obligations, too, yet I dropped everything to honor my parents' request—to go on this quest to find their long-lost son."

Daniel felt a prick in his conscience. "I'm sorry you wasted your time. But this isn't a good time in my life for a drive down memory lane."

"This isn't the best time for me either, yet I've made sacrifices, and I haven't complained once."

"The Dearlings are your family, not mine."

"Still, you have a chance to exercise that faith you're so fond of; to demonstrate that love of God, yet you're closing your heart, putting up roadblocks."

"I'm sorry."

"That's not good enough. I believed in you—thought you were a man of valor—integrity—like my father. *Your* father."

Daniel saw the disillusionment and fatigue on Chance's face, in his eyes, and he wished he could restore that faith, but he couldn't, if it meant traveling to Crossland to meet his birth parents. He had his own reasons for steering clear of the Dearlings, and he wasn't obliged to share them with a man he barely knew.

"What really galls me is that I've been open and receptive to you, sharing my past, my struggle with faith, and my feelings about God. I've sat through your lessons and sermons, keeping an open mind, and today, you almost got me. I almost surrendered, walking toward that altar, toward you."

"You were drawn to God, ready to commit to Him?"

"I considered it."

"What stopped you?"

"Fear, doubt, guilt, shame."

"Chance—"

"Don't even go there, Pastor. You're really ticking me off right now because I'm missing my parents' thirty-third wedding anniversary *today* because of you—the firstborn son."

Chance's anger was palpable, and Daniel couldn't blame him for venting. After all, he was the cause—the stone wall. "I'm sorry if I've misled, slighted, or even offended you."

"You seemed genuine—honest, caring, compassionate, friendly. Was that all for show—a ruse to get me into your spiritual net?"

"I'm not a liar, Chance. That's not my style."

"Still, you got me with that spiel about forgiveness and freedom, especially from bondages of the past." He laughed drily. "But you're a hypocrite, like everybody else. You call yourself a man of God, a man of valor, but you won't meet or fellowship with the people who gave you life."

Daniel felt compelled to defend himself. "It's not merely a matter of breaking bread together, Chance. We're talking about a thirty-six-year-old secret—a scandal in the making—involving an unwed teenage mother who's currently a music minister, an older man who's a renowned minister, and a single father who put his daughter's twins up for adoption while she was in a coma. The situation is delicate, extremely complicated."

"Why don't you admit the truth, at least to yourself: You're afraid of being in the spotlight, of making the headline news."

Daniel sighed. "This isn't only about me. Other people I respect and love would be affected too if this *secret* involving not one, but three, well-known ministers got out."

"My parents are strong, *fearless*; they can handle their own affairs."

"Still, Nathan Dearling, a preacher's kid, was three years older than Leah, who was only sixteen when she gave birth."

"They were young, in love, destined to be together." Chance rubbed his chin, his eyes never wavering from Daniel's. "Anyway, I don't think you're as worried about my parents' shame as your own. You were raised here, in the South, the Bible Belt, and you're a charismatic preacher people flock to and seek counseling from.

"You take pride in your good reputation and your greeting-card family. You're afraid all of that will be tainted if people find out you were born out of wedlock—that you're illegitimate—a lovechild."

"That's not even true!"

"Prove me wrong, then. Come to Crossland and meet your birth parents."

"I can't!"

"You mean you won't." Chance rubbed his temples. "To think I almost turned back to God, trusting your righteousness, your words of wisdom—faith."

Daniel felt the weight of Chance's words pressing his heart, and he felt convicted. "Don't put your faith in me, Chance. I'm just a man who'll let you down, disappoint you. Put your faith in Jesus, *God*. Trust Him and His Word, because He's the only one who can save you and redeem you."

Chance lowered his hand to his lap. "I expected more from you—empathy, compassion, forgiveness, *love*."

"I'm not heartless or unsympathetic. I care about people, including you."

"Then, give me a good reason why you won't meet my parents—why you won't open your heart, giving them a chance to win it."

"I've always known I was illegitimate—born outside of marriage—and for years I *was* ashamed. My parents told me I was adopted when I was eleven, and I always grappled with that sense of rejection, insecurity, shame.

"I believed my birth parents didn't want me, that something was wrong with me, that I wasn't good enough or worthy to be loved or raised by them. I didn't know my family history—my roots—so I always struggled to find my rightful place in life, my real identity."

Even though his adoptive parents had lavished Daniel with love, at times he had still felt like an outsider, a castoff, and the more the Winwards tried to validate him, telling him that he was special and that they wanted him, the more rejected he felt by the people who had brought him into the world. Thankfully, as an adult, he had gained more security in himself, in God.

"Nathan and Leah didn't reject you. They thought you were dead, lost to them. So shouldn't that news set you free from whatever's binding you?"

"I'm just not ready to confront the Dearlings or exhume the past. I'm not opposed to meeting my sister, but my birth parents are another story. I don't need the drama."

"Mom and Dad are good, godly people. You'd learn that about them if you'd soften your heart toward them a bit. It's like you said before, sometimes, courage comes when you allow yourself to be vulnerable, when you surrender control and let God take the wheel in your life, while you sit in the passenger seat, going wherever He takes you."

Daniel's own words slapped him, making him feel a hypocrite. "This isn't easy for me."

"If I've learned anything, Pastor, it's that life isn't always easy. It's complicated, sometimes messy." He palmed his hands. "I was abused, remember? My life was hell on earth, and I didn't think I'd ever escape it. I was so broken in body and spirit that I thought death was better than living with Ray Brayden.

"I was so traumatized that I thought about suicide when I was six years old. One day I saw a car coming, and I ran into the street, hoping the driver would hit me and put me out of my pain, my misery." Chance's voice was dry and emotionless, but his dark blue eyes shined with tears.

Drawn to him, Daniel reached out and touched Chance's hands. "What happened?"

"My mother saw me and screamed; she ran toward me and knocked me out of harm's way. The car swerved, just missing her. Afterward, she hugged me, just clinging to me, like she knew what I had been thinking, and she kept crying, begging me to stay with her, to live. For her. For God. But it's ironic that I promised to live for her, but she died just one year later, leaving me alone."

Daniel could imagine how lost Chance had been if he, at age six, had considered ending his life. "I'm sorry."

Chance pulled away from Daniel. "I don't need your pity. I survived the abuse, even my mother's death. All I need from you is consideration, compassion, and cooperation.

"It's not fair for you to discount Mom and Dad, ignoring them and disregarding their feelings. They were told that you had died, and they grieved you for years. Now that they know that you and your sister are alive, they feel like God has blessed them with a second chance. I'm not robbing my parents of their blessing. I'm not disappointing them again, nor am I leaving Sutton without you. That's a promise."

Daniel saw sincerity on Chance's face, in his eyes. He was determined, and he wouldn't be denied. Although Daniel admired his devotion to his parents, he still didn't know if he could grant Chance's wish. "You've come in faith, sharing the truth and presenting your case, and I appreciate your candor. But I need more time and counsel, and I won't be pressured into making my decision today."

"How much time do you need?"

"A few days."

"Okay. I'll wait." He removed his wallet from his pant pocket, then pulled a business card from it. "Got a pen?"

"Always." Daniel grabbed one from his desk, then handed it to Chance who scribbled on the back of the business card.

"Here's my contact information." He returned the pen to the desk and pressed the card into Daniel's hand. "I'm staying at the motel if you need to reach me." He stood and towered over Daniel, his keen eyes measuring him. "There's no mountain separating you from Crossland, nor any charge against Mom and Dad that would make you hate and reject them. You share their DNA and their faith, and you already have their love. What else do you need?"

"Confirmation, peace."

"Well, if you're half the man Nathan Dearling is, you'll make the right choice and come with me."

"Let me pray on it."

"Do that then." Chance walked away, leaving Daniel alone, reflecting on Chance's words and delving into the recesses of his own heart.

Chapter Seven

A man of too many friends may come to ruin,
But there is a friend who sticks closer than a brother.

Proverbs 18:24 (NASB)

Blessings' Bed and Breakfast
Sunday, June 19

*F*or the past four days, Victor had waged a rose-and-verse campaign, reminding Leisha Laurence of his resolve to her and his cause.

On Wednesday, he sent her a yellow rose, with a corresponding card explaining its symbolism: devotion, friendship, new beginning, and remembrance. Attached on a card was also the verse James 1:17: "Every good and perfect gift is from above, coming down from the Father of heavenly lights."

On Thursday, he gave her two roses, one white and red entwined, signifying unity, beauty, courage, and respect, with the verses Ecclesiastes 4:9–10: "Two are better than one, because they have a good return for their labor: If either of them falls down, one can help the other up."

On Friday, he had the florist deliver six white roses representing purity, reverence, and humility, with verse 1 John 3:18: "Dear children, let us not love with words or speech but with actions and in truth."

On Saturday, he sent a bouquet of pink roses representing appreciation, admiration, grace, gentleness, and gratitude, with Proverbs 3:5–6: "Trust in the LORD with all your heart and lean not on your own understanding; in all your ways submit to him, and he will make your paths straight."

Victor had yet to hear from Leisha, but he wasn't discouraged, and he wasn't giving up and returning home. He would keep praying that the

Lord would touch her heart, turning it to her birth parents, and he would start a new campaign.

Sitting on a window seat, he stared into the night, toward a bright moon, his mind wandering from Leisha to his parents. When he had phoned earlier wishing them a happy anniversary, they had sounded fine, and they were still optimistic about a reunion with their twins.

They had been greedy for news of Leisha, asking Victor to share his first impression of her. He had been honest, describing her as lovely, intelligent, and spirited. He hadn't mentioned his attraction to her. Instead, he had told them he would stay until he made some progress.

Now, he needed to call Chance. They hadn't spoken in a week, and Victor was anxious to find out what headway Chance had made with Daniel.

Grabbing his phone, Victor punched in his brother's number.

Chance answered on the first ring.

"Hey, *hermano*. What's happening?"

"We're missing Mom and Dad's anniversary."

"They know we love them."

"Neither of them mentioned Mom's test results. For all we know, they could be keeping secrets."

"Stop worrying, Chance. They probably don't know anything yet." Victor could imagine his brother in Georgia stressing over their mother's health. He had already lost one mother, and he was afraid of losing another. "Mom is strong. She's a fighter. She'll be fine. Now, tell me what you've been doing in Georgia."

"I've been in church."

As far as Victor knew, Chance hadn't attended church since he had turned eighteen and moved out of their parents' home. At that time, he had severed all ties to God, preferring to live life on his own terms. "Is God reeling you in?"

"Don't get excited. I'm still a work in progress."

"A snail's pace is better than no pace." Victor was grateful but curious. "What's drawn you in?"

"Daniel is the Associate Pastor at Increasing Faith Worship Center, and I've been his shadow all week." Chance laughed. "The man lives and breathes ministry and spends most of his time at the church."

"You learning anything?"

"About God or Daniel?"

"Both."

"Plenty."

"Like what?"

"I don't hate God. But He and I still aren't best friends."

"What about Daniel?"

"Everybody loves him. They call him Pastor Win because he's all about winning souls."

"What's your impression of him?"

"He's a good man, a smart, compassionate, charismatic leader. He could almost pass for Dad's twin. But he's stubborn and more concerned with his public image than his birth family."

"He doesn't want to meet Mom and Dad?"

"He asked for more time, so I'm playing the waiting game, hoping he'll change his mind."

"That's the response I got from Leisha."

"What's she like?"

"Bright, passionate, spirited—a woman of faith, too."

"Does she favor Mom or Dad?"

"She has Dad's backbone and shares his passion for helping kids."

"What about her family?"

"She's single and childless, and her parents died four years ago in a car accident."

"Does she work?"

"She's a family lawyer." Victor stared out his window. "She's strong and independent, not easily broken or manipulated, and she speaks Spanish, too."

"You like her, don't you?"

"Enough to send her roses and verses. But she's been ignoring me, shutting me out."

"Is she attractive?"

Victor imagined her in his mind. "She's tall, full of curves, and she's got amber eyes, almost like a tiger's. She's confident, classy, and poised, a real lady—stunning, beautiful."

"Has she reeled you in?"

He laughed. "Like a fish."

"You're losing your perspective, Victor—falling for her." Concern laced Chance's voice. "That's not good. For any of us."

"I've just met her."

"If she's hooked you in a week, she's too lethal. Most men send roses as a gesture of love for mothers, girlfriends, and wives, not newly-found sisters."

"We're not related, Chance. So technically, Leisha is not my sister."

"She's not an ideal contender for your heart either. She's six years older, and her parents are yours, too."

"You don't have to remind me."

"Apparently, I do."

"I didn't say I was in love with her."

"Because you're either hiding the truth, or you're confused yourself."

"I'm not withholding anything."

"I'm your friend as much as your brother, Victor. I won't betray your confidence, nor will I judge you. Just be honest and admit you have feelings for Leisha Laurence."

Victor clutched his silver cross necklace, the one his grandmother had given him on her deathbed. "All right! I'm attracted to her."

"Don't confuse attraction with love," Chance said. "Eight years ago, you *were* in love with Shayna Riven, and you almost proposed to her."

"What's your point?"

"You've dated women, but you've only let one woman get that close, that deep into your heart, and you've never gifted any woman other than Mom with roses or verses. But Leisha Laurence, in a mere week, has woven her way into your heart and mind, and that's unfortunate.

"You're not there to fall for Leisha nor romance her like some boyfriend. You're there to get her to come home with you so she can meet Mom and Dad. Period."

Victor sighed. "I'm not offering her marriage."

"But you're romancing her, just the same. She's a woman, like any other, and she could get the wrong idea about you and think you're interested in having a real relationship with her. I guess the real question I have for you is this: Why are you interested romantically in this woman— Leisha Laurence?"

Victor didn't know how he could explain to Chance what he didn't understand fully himself. "She's the hidden pearl, the one I wasn't looking for but found anyway."

Victor rubbed the silver cross dangling over his heart. Since Shayna had left him, he had been guarding his heart as fiercely as Chance had been guarding his. That's why he was surprised that Leisha had managed to slip so easily past his defenses.

"She's not a pearl, Victor. She's a thorn that you need to remove before it harms you and causes pain. Neither of us is on this journey for himself. We're doing this for Mom and Dad."

Mom and Dad and their missing twins, Victor thought. *How could he forget any of that? Chance was right. He shouldn't be harboring romantic thoughts about Leisha. He should be paving the way for her to venture to Crossland and commence a relationship with her birth parents.*

"I know the stakes here," Victor said. "I won't jeopardize Mom and Dad's relationship with Leisha either."

"Just slow down; be careful. I don't want you getting hurt."

"Stop worrying about my love life and get one of your own."

"I'm not joking. You're not distracting me either. You need to resolve your feelings for Leisha so they're not a problem."

Victor stared out the window, into the darkness. "I'll take care of my heart if you take care of your soul."

"What's that supposed to mean?"

"You need a Bible."

"I've got a Bible—one from the motel."

"You need your own so you can study."

"I'll consider it."

"Seriously?"

"I always keep my word."

"I guess it's a good time to say goodnight, then."

"Goodnight, Victor."

"Until next time, brother." Victor disconnected, his thoughts running back to Leisha. Regardless of what he had told Chance, he couldn't wipe the woman from his mind, nor did he want to.

If he had learned anything this week, it was this: Leisha Laurence was a woman worth getting to know, a woman worth fighting for.

Chapter Eight

God sets the lonely in families, he leads forth the prisoners
with singing, but the rebellious live in a sun-scorched land.

Psalm 68:6 (NIV)

Wyndham Court
Tuesday, June 21

Leisha lounged against the armrest on her sofa, her legs tucked behind her, her Samoyed Orion resting at her feet, and a greeting card in her hand. Inside the card were the handwritten words, "Let time and chance happen; let your heart find its way home," and the verse, Ecclesiastes 9:11: "I have seen something else under the sun: The race is not to the swift or the battle to the strong, nor does the food come to the wise or wealth to the brilliant or favor to the learned; but time and chance happen to them all." On the coffee table sat the jar of chocolate kisses that had come with the card, a ribbon securing an ivory card with Proverbs 24:26 proclaiming, "An honest answer is like a kiss on the lips."

When she had returned from court to her office this afternoon and had found the card and candy on her desk, she had instantly known the sender, and as she read the verse, her heart had fluttered like an escaped butterfly. Victor Dearling was certainly bold, and he didn't seem the least bit deterred or intimidated like most of the men she had rebuffed.

On Monday, he had charmed her assistant Cassandra Riley into letting him into Leisha's vacant office so he could leave a heart-shaped vessel of candied rainbow hearts on her desk and a large crimson card, with 2 Corinthians 9:7–8 written inside: "Each of you should give what you have decided in your heart to give, not reluctantly or under compulsion, for God loves a cheerful giver. And God is able to bless you abundantly, so that in all things at all times, having all that you need, you will abound in every good work." Beneath the scripture, he had written these inspirational words: "Listen to God, and He'll guide your heart and step. Be strong and courageous. Be an overcomer. Be victorious."

He was challenging her at every turn—invading her thoughts, nurturing her spirit, and laying siege to her heart. In their battle of wills, Victor was definitely a worthy adversary, intent on winning his case. Last week he had romanced her with roses and verses; now he was sending her cards and candy. He was creative, daring, and relentless—more of a threat to her peace than her birth parents because he was a flame of light and passion, and like a moth, she was drawn to him.

The only reason she hadn't gone to him personally, thanking him for the gifts was because she knew for him that would signal her surrender— her agreement to travel with him to meet the Dearlings. As much as she tried, though, she couldn't ignore the man's gifts or fight her awareness of him. He was charming, handsome, faithful, and romantic—as lethal to her heart as her mind.

Victor's pursuit hadn't gone unnoticed by Leisha's colleagues either. The flood of roses, cards, and candy had created a commotion, drawing unwanted attention to Leisha's private life.

Cassandra now teased her about her new admirer, urging Leisha to call him and give him a chance, and after dropping by her office for a conference and seeing the assorted roses in a vase, her law partner Mateo Arrollo had even inquired about her mystery man.

Although Leisha had said Victor was only a new acquaintance, not a suitor, Mateo had grinned knowingly, his brown eyes twinkling. "A new acquaintance doesn't send roses unless his heart is invested. If he's a good guy—one who'll love, respect, and treat you like the lady you are, then open the door to your heart and invite him inside."

He reached across the desk and enfolded Leisha's hand in his. "You're an asset, my friend, and if I wasn't happily married, I'd make an offer for you."

Leisha pulled back her hand. "Stop joking." She and Mateo had met in law school and had been friends for ten years. Not once in that time had he expressed any romantic interest in her. He had always been a confidante, nothing more.

"I'm serious. You're a matchless lawyer, a selfless friend, and a great woman."

"Really?"

"Yes. You deserve a good man, a husband, a family."

"I don't need a man to complete me."

Mateo leaned forward. "You might not need a man to complete you, but you definitely need one to love. For years I've watched you putting on this mask, pretending you're content with being single, yet I've seen those glimpses of longing in your eyes, that expression of sadness on your face when you're surrounded by couples and, especially, those with children. You don't want to be alone, but you build a wall around yourself, pushing everyone away, and if a man gets too close or seems too interested, you find fault with him—an excuse to chase him away."

"That's because most men aren't sincere in a relationship. Most of them play games, trying to overcome a challenge or add another notch on their belt."

"All men aren't rotten apples. Some actually want more from a woman than another conquest; some want a life-long commitment—that forever kind of love with a wife, a home, a future, a family."

"I'm not interested in more family. I have Orion and Salena."

"Orion's a dog, and Salena is only a friend."

"She's my *best* friend."

"Still, she's no substitute for a husband—someone to love, hold, and cherish—or a child—someone you can love, nurture, and protect." Mateo grabbed her hand again. "You're thirty-six years old. If you want a family of your own before it's physically impossible, you need to open your heart now and make yourself emotionally available."

"I'm fine!"

"You're stuck in a classy but confining apartment with your dog. You're lonely, but you won't admit it, and you're scared, but you won't show it."

"What do I have to fear?"

"Love. Vulnerability. Dependence. Heartache."

Leisha's face burned beneath his gaze, and she felt as though he held the Mirror of Truth before her, exposing all that she fought to hide. "You're wrong."

He searched her face. "Why do you sabotage relationships? Why do you limit your chance at love, rejecting every good man that comes?"

"I don't."

Mateo frowned, the desk a barrier between them. "You're either lying or living in denial."

Leisha felt uncomfortable beneath his scrutiny. "I don't want to argue, Mateo, so let's table this theme and discuss the Sanchez case." She removed her hand from beneath his. "Hector Sanchez is suing his daughter-in-law for sole custody of his grandson, Nestor."

"Don't change the subject. We're—"

She shoved a file into his hand and interrupted, launching into the legal nuances of their latest case. Expelling his breath, Mateo conceded defeat and sat back in his seat with his arms folded, listening as she rambled, giving him no opportunity to backtrack.

The doorbell sounded, intruding on her thoughts, and Leisha dropped Victor's card beside the jar of candy, and she rose and walked toward the door. Glancing through the peephole, she saw Salena Blake, her best friend.

Salena Kyleen Blake, whose mother was a candid Catwoman fan, was always vibrant—pulsing with life—and she could rival any professional model with her statuesque height, intense brown eyes, and long sun-red hair which cascaded like rivulets over her shoulders. Usually, her clothes matched her mood—bright colors for good days, muted for sedate, and dark for somber. Today, she wore a scarlet pantsuit, with a matching purse slung over her shoulder, and she held a black folder in her hand.

Leisha smiled and opened the door. "Come in." She hugged Salena, then stepped aside, letting her enter. "I've been waiting for you."

"Sorry I'm late." Salena sat on the sofa. "I was at the TV station when we got news that the parking lot rapist has struck again."

Leisha shut and locked the door, then entered the living room. "What parking lot rapist?"

Salena's jaw dropped. "Haven't you been reading the papers or watching the news?"

"I've been swamped with work."

"That's no excuse for living in a bubble of ignorance."

"Just tell me about this rapist."

"He's some black-hooded man who's been targeting parking lots. In the past month, he's assaulted four women and killed three, stabbing them. This last victim is the only survivor, and the police are waiting for her to regain consciousness so they can get more information on this guy before he finds another victim."

Leisha twined her fingers. "There aren't any leads, any clues to his identity?"

"None."

"That's a travesty. His victims need justice, and he needs to be caught and caged so he can't hurt or terrorize another woman."

"So far the man's been elusive, seemingly one step ahead."

"Well, I'm praying his luck runs out before his next victim, and he makes that one mistake that will get him arrested and locked away for life."

"Until he's caught, be careful and vigilant."

"I'm not defenseless."

"You're not invincible either. And you're not Wonder Woman."

"This guy still won't have a chance against me."

"Don't invite trouble, Leisha. You took that self-defense class years ago. We were still in college. Promise you'll take precautions when you work late."

Leisha knew if she didn't allay Salena's fears, she wouldn't get any peace for the duration of Salena's visit. "All right, I will!"

"Thank you." Salena leaned down and rubbed Orion who lay expectantly at her feet. "How are you tonight, boy?"

Orion barked twice in response, his white tail swishing through the air.

"I have another gift for you." She opened her purse and removed a lime-green rubber bone, then tossed it across the room, and on cue,

Orion leaped to his feet, chasing it. Within seconds, he lay in a corner in his favorite basket, chewing contentedly on his rubber bone.

Leisha laughed. "Every time you visit, you bring a treat or a toy. You're spoiling him."

Salena shrugged. "As your friend, my job is to spoil your baby. In this case, though, the baby just happens to be an adorable canine."

Leisha nodded toward the black folder on the table. "Is that the dossier on the Dearlings?"

"Yes." Salena lifted the folder and handed it to Leisha. "Inside is everything I could find on such short notice."

"Thank you." Leisha opened the folder and removed several documents, news clippings, and photographs. As she perused them, Salena gave a brief summary.

"Nathanial Jacob Dearling and Leah Moraine Hamilton were teenage sweethearts, and they just celebrated their thirty-third wedding anniversary. His parents were the late Reverend Isaac and Rebecca Dearling, and hers were the late Laban and Etta Hamilton, a businessman and a housewife respectively. Nathan has family in Heaventon Hope, Texas, some cousins in ministry named the Caresons, and Leah has some relatives in Rosehaven, Texas, by the name of the Worthings. Neither Nathan nor Leah has siblings, though, so their immediate family consists only of two adopted sons, Chance Brayden and Victor Ortega, ages thirty-two and thirty respectively. The couple founded a church in Crossland, Texas, called Kingdom Family Christian Center in February 1990, and it's been thriving since then. Nathan is the presiding pastor and his wife is the minister of music, and both are heavily involved in outreach programs and community work, especially involving kids."

Leisha held a candid photo of the couple embracing, Leah Dearling smiling with her right hand pressed over her husband's heart. They looked happy, in love. "Are they as perfect as they seem?"

"I've dug beneath the surface, and I haven't found any dirt or skeletons, scandals or abuses, vices or lawsuits." Salena brushed a strand of red hair from her ivory-white forehead. "The Dearlings are godly, good—salt of the earth. They're well respected, charitable by nature, and they live to serve others."

"What about their sons?" Leisha dropped their photo and lifted one of Chance and Victor circled by children at a charity picnic for foster kids.

"Chance is the eldest, graduating from Heaventon Hope University as a Criminal Justice major, later enrolling in the police academy. He was an officer in the Dallas Police Department for eight years before he resigned and became a private investigator. He's single and apparently a loner, which is odd to me because the man is gorgeous—definitely a lethal temptation with those ocean-blue eyes."

Leisha noted Salena's bright eyes and flushed face. "You like him, don't you?"

"I was born a country girl, remember? I like rugged cowboys, and I can't help but admire one as good-looking as this one."

Leisha rolled her eyes. "Aren't you the one who says, don't judge a book by its cover?"

"Unless the cover has a G.O.A.T. on it—someone who's the greatest of all time."

"Don't be so quick to faint over a handsome face. You don't know Chance Dearling; he could be selfish and conceited."

"I seriously doubt that." Salena swiped the photo from Leisha's hand and consumed it with her eyes. "There's a compelling story in this face, and the man behind it is strong and honorable, selfless and good. He's got character, plenty of it."

She likes him. "I can't believe this!" Leisha shook her head, shocked. "You haven't met the man, but you're crazy about him."

Salena lifted glowing eyes. "He's someone I'd like to meet, maybe marry, raise some kids with, and possibly spend a lifetime dancing with."

"That's not likely to happen, friend. He lives in Crossland, and you live in Corinth."

"Distance is supposed to make the heart grow fonder."

"All you know is he's not married. He might have a girlfriend."

"Stop bursting my bubble."

"I'm just giving you a pinch of reality."

"I can still dream."

"Enough about Chance. Tell me about Victor."

"He's a Spanish teacher at Kingdom Family Academy and a volunteer at Hope Recovery, a teen rehab facility. Despite his high-profile parents, he's relatively low-key, spending most of his time in the shadows, away from the limelight."

"Is he involved with anyone?"

"Not that I could find. He hasn't been photographed or associated with any particular woman, at least not recently."

"Has he had any legal problems or brushes with law enforcement?"

"He's clean."

"Is that all?"

Salena folded her arms. "What else do you want?"

Leisha sighed and slipped the photo into the folder and dropped it back onto the coffee table. "Peace. What am I supposed to do with this?" She motioned toward the folder. "I'm Leisha Denise Laurence, not Leisha Denise Dearling, and I don't need my whole life uprooted."

Salena unfolded her arms and grabbed Leisha's hand. "Maybe this shakeup—this encounter—with the Dearlings is just what you need to move forward. For the last four years since your parents' deaths, you've become an ice castle—one that's enchanting on the outside but cool—frigid—inside, especially to any stranger attempting to cross that moat into your heart."

Salena's words pierced Leisha, and a tear slid down her cheek because she knew Salena spoke the truth. Since her parents' accident, she had withdrawn into herself, building impenetrable fences to keep unwanted visitors out. She had done so partly out of guilt. If she hadn't argued with her parents that night, maybe they wouldn't have driven away upset—maybe they wouldn't have encountered that teenager who was more concerned with texting her boyfriend than driving responsibly. Loneliness seemed to be Leisha's penance. After all, she hadn't mended fences with her parents while they lived. Instead, she had wasted time, taking it for granted, and her parents had died believing that they didn't matter to her, that she didn't love them.

"Maybe God's giving you an opportunity for family again."

Leisha swiped the tear away. "I had a family—the Laurences."

"Well, maybe the Dearlings can give you what the Laurences never could—unconditional love, a peaceful home, and a sense of belonging."

She had survived years of criticism from her adoptive parents because of her independence, her profession, her marital status, and her faith. She couldn't endure more with her biological parents. "What if I disappoint them too?"

"You can't live in fear, friend. Sometimes, grief is the price we pay for loving others. In order to find the good, sometimes you've got to risk the bad. You've got to step out in faith."

"I don't want to get hurt again."

"There's no guarantee you won't, but you shouldn't bury your head in the sand, hoping the Dearlings will disappear. Instead, you should meet with Victor, find some common ground, and discover for yourself who exactly the Dearlings are. I can only supply you with cold facts; Victor can reveal to you their true hearts."

Leisha breathed deeply. "If I contact Victor, he won't give me a moment's peace. He'll pressure me to leave with him."

"You can't hide from the man forever. Besides, you've got a twin brother out there. You should find out whether Victor knows his location. Even if you don't bond with Nathan and Leah, you can begin a relationship with your twin."

Her twin. She had forgotten him. Leisha had been so focused on protecting herself from the Dearlings that she had pushed thoughts of her brother aside. She hadn't given him much thought since she had learned of his existence. She'd been too shell-shocked and self-involved. "Am I being too stubborn—too self-centered?"

"Stubborn, yes, self-centered, no." Salena smiled. "You're the least selfish person I know. You're compassionate, loving, and giving, and you're more than a good lawyer; you're a great friend."

Leisha hugged her. "Thank you."

"You're welcome." Salena pulled back, her eyes focused on the card and jar of candy on the coffee table. "Who are those from?"

Leisha groaned. "Victor."

"It's not your birthday, so why is he sending you a card and candy?"

"He wants me to go home with him."

Salena reached forward, lifted the card from the jar, and read the verse aloud: "An honest answer is like a kiss on the lips." Dropping the card, she pinned Leisha with those keen brown eyes. "Is this a love note?"

Leisha's face flamed like fire. "It's a verse from the Bible."

Salena's eyes grew round. "Is Victor *courting* you?"

"With the Bible?!"

Salena massaged her forehead, her eyes flitting toward the greeting card and the chocolate kisses. "Is this the only gift he's sent?"

"No."

"You've been keeping secrets, from me, of all people." She lowered her hand. "What's really happening here?"

"Nothing."

"If he's sending gifts with cards like these, your relationship is more intimate—personal—and that would explain your curiosity about his love life earlier."

Leisha knew she had to explain before Salena drew her own conclusions. "Victor's only using the gifts to soften my heart so I'll go with him to Crossland to meet his parents."

"What else has he sent?"

"Roses and verses last week. Cards and candy for the past two days."

"If they're innocent gestures, why hide them from me?"

"I knew what you would think."

Salena crossed her arms. "What?"

"Victor's acting like an infatuated suitor, not like an adopted brother."

"Isn't he?"

"No, he isn't."

"Then, answer three questions."

"Go ahead. Ask me."

"Do you enjoy receiving the gifts—the roses, verses, cards, and candy?"

"They're thoughtful and inspirational."

"Intimate and caring, too?"

"Yes."

"My next question: Do you like Victor Dearling?"

"He's a good man—intelligent, compassionate, and attentive. Like me, he's passionate about kids and dedicated to helping them."

"So, he's smart and kind, and he likes kids?"

"Yes."

"Those are all qualities of your dream man."

"What are you talking about?"

Salena rolled her eyes. "Your Prince Charming list from college, remember?"

Leisha waved her hand. "That was years ago when I was young, with a head full of fairy tales, rainbows, and butterflies. Now, I don't indulge in such fantasies, and I don't need a prince riding to my rescue."

"Maybe you're not seeking a prince but a Boaz. Maybe that's why you're fantasizing about Victor Dearling."

"I am not fantasizing about him."

Salena pinned her with those intense brown eyes. "So, he hasn't invaded your thoughts?"

"The man's sending me gifts. Of course, he's on my mind."

"Are you attracted to him?"

"Salena, we've had one face-to-face conversation, and that only lasted an hour."

"But it was a memorable encounter, wasn't it?"

"The man dropped a grenade in my hands, revealing my adoption." Salena was worse than a firing squad with her rapid questions, and Leisha barely had time to think or even censor her answers. "Since Victor's arrival, I haven't known a moment of peace."

"Because of your birth parents or because of *him*?"

"A month ago, my life was normal, even predictable. Now, the Dearlings are a reality, and Victor, in a couple of weeks, has insinuated himself into my life, becoming a thorn ever present." She laced her fingers. "Even though he's hijacked my life and shattered my world, uprooting my family tree, and he's intent on gift-wrapping me for his parents, I still like and admire him as a loyal and loving son. He is a great guy, and I would love to know more about him."

"Okay." Salena unfolded her arms and clapped her hands tightly on her lap. "This is my final question, and I want you to be completely honest."

Leisha swallowed hard. She had already revealed more than she had previously intended. Now, she felt emotionally raw, exposed. "What is it?"

"Is Victor a man you could love?"

"He's a stranger. I barely know anything about him."

"Answer my question, Leisha. Can you love him?"

"Yes!"

Salena sank back against the sofa and shook her head. "My friend, I don't believe falling for Victor is in your future; I think it's a current event, and you need to pray for wisdom, guidance."

"Why?"

"You're heading for a collision, and you're going to crash head first and suffer massive heart damage."

Chapter Nine

But the Lord is faithful, and he will strengthen
and protect you from the evil one.

2 Thessalonians 3:3 (NIV)

Golden Heights
Thursday, June 23

Leaving the car in the driveway, Chance walked to Daniel's front door and rang the doorbell. Then, he stuck his hands in his pockets and waited. A clap of thunder sounded, followed by a streak of lightning flashing against the black-blanketed sky. *Maybe I should leave. I barely know the man, yet I'm standing on his doorstep at night. He's probably not even home. If he is, what reason do I have for coming? He'll think I'm here to badger him about Crossland. He'll resent my intrusion—my nerve. I should go.* Chance turned and walked back to his car and pulled out his key.

The front door opened, and Daniel called his name.

Chance turned, facing him.

"Why are you leaving?"

"I made a mistake in coming. I don't even know why I'm here."

Daniel left the threshold and moved onto the front porch. "Well, whatever your motive, you're here now and welcome to stay."

"Isn't it too late for visitors?"

"Not at all. Have you eaten?"

"No."

"Come dine with me and Taryn."

"I don't want to intrude, especially if you're on a date."

"You're not, and I'd like you to meet my fiancée. She's anxious to make your acquaintance." He beckoned Chance forward. "Until she arrives, you and I can chat."

"Are you sure?"

"Come inside; be my guest."

Chance pocketed his key and stepped forward. He followed Daniel over the threshold, into the foyer, then through the living room. They stopped in a large kitchen, where the sweet smell of vanilla wafted through the air and dishes of food were spread across the counter: baked chicken, mashed potatoes, green beans, squash, and banana pudding. He sat on a stool at the counter and watched as Daniel removed a plate of deviled eggs from the refrigerator and added them to the counter. "You cook?"

Daniel sat beside him. "Mom taught me the year before I left for college. She's a bit overprotective and didn't want me starving or always depending on some other woman to feed me. Even though I scorched more than a few meals at first, even smoking out her kitchen, Mom didn't give up on me. Her efforts eventually paid off, and now I love cooking. It's my labor of love, and it allows me to serve others."

"For me, it's a chore. Bad memories."

"Bad memories?"

"Of my mother and Ray. When it got really bad and Ray was bingeing on drugs and alcohol, he beat Mama, so much so that she couldn't leave bed. Most times, I got a front-row seat; often, Mama would make me hide so I wouldn't get hit next. After Ray stumbled out, probably looking for another fix, I would nurse Mama as best I could. Often, I would traipse into our kitchen, raid the refrigerator or climb onto a chair to reach the pantry, then fix whatever I could feed her so she'd regain strength—so she'd heal.

"Usually, I'd fix nothing more than peanut butter sandwiches or a bowl of cereal topped with fruit. She'd thank me and eat it as though it was a feast, never complaining. Eventually, when she felt better, she'd return to the kitchen, preparing me a better meal." He frowned, his memory souring.

"Like clockwork, Ray would always reappear, apologizing and acting as though all was fine, as though he hadn't done anything seriously wrong. We'd have days of calm, possibly a week, and then the cycle of bingeing and violence would begin again."

"Didn't you say the abuse ended when you were six?"

"Ray came home, packed a bag, then left. Without a word. Mama waited for him, but he never returned. After a month, she finally told me he wasn't coming back."

"Has he ever contacted you?"

"Why would he? He never loved me. For all I know now, he's dead." Chance's world wouldn't be shattered if he were. After all, Chance had wished him dead for years. If there was any justice in the world, Chance's wish had been granted, and Ray Brayden was buried six feet deep in a graveyard.

"Have you ever forgiven him?"

"No."

"Why not?"

Chance tossed his hands up. "The man beat my mother and ruined my life! He doesn't deserve any compassion, respect, or forgiveness."

"That's exactly why you should offer all of it to him. Until you do, you're not likely to find peace or closure."

"I can't!" How could he forgive a man who had despised him and made his life hell? How could he overlook all the grief, suffering, and heartache Ray had caused his mother?

"Forgiveness is a choice, and giving it doesn't mean that you're condoning Ray's abuse. Forgiveness is for your benefit—for your healing."

Chance tucked his hands in his pant pockets. "You're not telling me anything Dad hasn't already. He's been urging me to forgive Ray for years."

Daniel palmed his hands. "Maybe it's time you listen and act—breaking the hold Ray has over you."

"Have you forgiven Mom and Dad, even Granddad who separated you from your sister?"

Daniel rubbed his chin. "Yes, I have."

"So, you're coming home with me?"

"No."

"You haven't changed your mind?"

"I'll meet them eventually but not this week."

"When—next week, next month, next year?"

"I'm not sure."

Chance tamped the frustration simmering inside of him. "Have you talked to your adoptive parents?"

"Dad believes I should at least meet the Dearlings. My mother opposes that idea because she doesn't think they have a place in my life." He sighed. "I've spoken to Taryn and Dr. Joseph too. They urged me to pray and let God lead me."

Chance leaned forward. "What is He prompting you to do?"

"Meet with the Dearlings and move forward."

"What more do you need—an arrow from God, pointing directly to Crossland?"

He folded his arms. "I'm not rushing into a reunion after a few days' notice. Now, tell me about Leisha."

"She still lives in Corinth, and she practices family law."

"Is she married or have any children?"

"No."

"What of her parents? Are they still alive?"

"They died four years ago."

"Any other brothers or sisters?"

"No."

"What kind of person is she?"

"Intelligent, passionate, a woman of faith. According to Victor, she's also stubborn and dragging her feet about meeting her birth parents."

"It's a big decision, not to be made in haste. After all, what we decide today will change our lives. Forever." He glanced at his watch, then frowned. "Taryn's late."

"Aren't all women?"

"Not my fiancée."

"If she was in trouble, wouldn't she call?"

"Yes."

"Then, don't worry. She'll be here, safe and sound."

Daniel massaged his forehead.

"How long have you two been engaged?"

"Two years."

"When's the wedding?"

"We haven't decided."

"Does she have cold feet or do you?"

"I've been busy."

Chance tilted his head. "Too busy to get married?"

Daniel got defensive. "Yes."

"Taryn must be some saint." He doubted a busy life was the only reason Daniel had prolonged the engagement. Likely, the good minister had some commitment issues he had to resolve.

"She's an angel, too good for me."

A smile tugged on Chance's lips. "Probably."

The doorbell rang, and Daniel sprang from his stool, practically jogging to the front door. He returned within minutes smiling with his fiancée, a petite woman dressed in a dark pink blouse and skirt. Her brown eyes shone with light, and dark black hair curled inward, framing her oval face. "Chance, this is Taryn Kirkland, my fiancée." Daniel stepped aside so the two could shake hands.

"Nice to meet you."

She smiled. "You, too."

"Daniel invited me to dinner. You don't mind, do you?"

"Of course not." She turned to Daniel. "Where's Mercy?"

"In her dog house in the backyard."

Taryn faced Chance. "We rescued Mercy from an abusive family about four years ago, and storms scare her. Her previous owners starved and beat her mercilessly. They even chained her to a tree, with little care, love, nourishment, or protection, so it's amazing that she's as affectionate and happy as she's been living with Daniel. He's been great with her—so patient and tender. She's not the same wounded animal he brought home."

Chance listened in silence, not surprised that Daniel had taken in a homeless, abused dog. The man seemed to make a habit of befriending the needy, lonely, damaged, or lost. He definitely lived up to his name, Pastor Win.

After Taryn planted a kiss on Daniel's cheek, Daniel excused himself, and soon he was darting in and out, carrying covered dishes from the kitchen. When Taryn and Chance offered to help, he assured them he was fine and intent on serving them tonight. "You two get better acquainted." He walked out with a dish.

Taryn smiled at Chance. "From what Daniel has told me, your parents are good people. He's always been curious about them, his family's roots and heritage. Now, he can finally learn the truth."

"Why don't you convince him to come home with me? So far, I've been hitting my head against a brick wall."

She touched his arm. "Be patient. He'll come around. He just needs time."

Chance looked at her engagement ring. "He's put you and the wedding on hold, too. Why don't you cut your losses and leave?"

"I love Daniel, and I'm content to wait."

"How long?"

"A lifetime, if necessary."

Even if Chance ever loved a woman, he didn't believe he could wait on her indefinitely. "You have a lot of faith in him, don't you?"

"I trust Daniel, and I believe in him, yes. However, my faith—my hope—is first and foremost in God. His promise is that all things will work together for good because I love Him, and I'm called according to His purpose."

Chance could see the love and dedication gleaming in her eyes, and for a second, he was envious, wondering if any woman would ever love him that faithfully or feel just as passionate. He doubted he would ever encounter such a woman, though. After all, his life had a landfill of debris, and he couldn't envision a woman daring enough to risk her heart loving him.

Daniel returned and slipped Taryn's hand in his. "We can eat now." He escorted her to the dining room, and Chance followed, his eyes roaming over the framed scriptures and the large silver cross hanging on the wall with numbers 3:16 beneath it at one end of the table.

As Daniel sat down, with Taryn on his left and Chance on his right, a song called "Simply Redeemed" played softly. Daniel requested that they bow their heads; then, he gave thanks for their food. After he concluded with "Amen," they raised their heads and loaded their plates with food.

"Chance, are you seeing anyone special?"

He looked up, then across the table at Taryn. "I'm single. There's no wife, fiancée, or girlfriend—no one to disappoint or hurt."

"Why would you disappoint or hurt a woman?"

"My birth father ruined me for any good woman, so I'm not interested in inflicting myself on one or even passing Ray's genes on through any children."

"That's a lonely life."

"That's my choice."

"Have you ever been in love?"

"No, and I'm not holding my breath, waiting for it."

"You're missing out on one of God's greatest gifts."

"That suits me just fine. I'm not really interested in any gift from God. For the majority of my life, He hasn't been my Advocate or Friend."

Taryn frowned. "God *is* with you and for you, Chance. He's not your adversary."

Daniel nodded. "She's right. God loves you, even when you don't love Him."

"Some love! He wasn't there when I needed Him most."

Daniel leaned forward, his hands palmed above his plate. "He *was* there—carrying and consoling you, strengthening and protecting you—and you've been too blinded by hurt and anger to see Him."

"Neither of you understands. I can't trust God—to love, protect, or even hear me."

"It's not really about whether you can trust God but about whether He can trust you, my friend. He's fulfilled His promises; He's been faithful, never leaving you nor forsaking you. He even gave His Son Jesus for you, and Jesus is your guarantee for love, acceptance, protection, healing, and deliverance. He's your answer—all you need." Daniel clapped one hand on Chance's arm. "God has given you His best gift—His Son—and He's offering you an escape from all that's binding you and holding you back from your best life. Why won't you invite Him into your heart, making Him a part of your family?"

"He'll have all the control, and I'll need Him for everything."

"That's right where He wants you, under His protection—His authority." Daniel pulled his hand from Chance's arm. "Let Jesus be Lord of your life, Chance. Give Him your heart, your soul, your mind, and your strength. If you surrender and follow Him, He will direct your path, reveal your purpose, and lead you into your destiny."

"I'm not ready." He closed his eyes and let the music wash over him. Suddenly, an image of a bloodied cross rose before his mind's eye, and he saw himself nailed there, writhing in agony, hanging over a pit of fierce, angry flames that licked his feet, then clawed his legs. The man on the cross looked at him with soulless black eyes, then he screamed in blood-chilling torment. Gasping, Chance opened his eyes and stared up at that silver cross, his mind reeling. *What was that? Was it real?*

Daniel leaned over, his hand on Chance's arm. "What's wrong?"

"Nothing." He pushed his chair from the table, then stood, his heart pounding madly against his chest. "I'm sorry. I've got to go."

"So soon?"

He nodded at Taryn. "It was nice meeting you." He turned to Daniel, the car key already in his hand. "Thanks for dinner. Goodnight."

"I'll walk you to the door."

"Don't! I'm fine. Really." Before Daniel could stand, Chance turned, then left the room, running as much from that soulless image of himself as from that ever-mocking cross hanging on Daniel's wall.

Chapter Ten

There is no fear in love. But perfect love drives out fear, because fear has to do with punishment. The one who fears is not made perfect in love.

1 John 4:18 (NIV)

Golden Heights
Thursday, June 23

After Chance left, Daniel and Taryn cleared the table, washed, dried, and shelved the dishes, then settled into a comfortable embrace on the back-porch wooden swing. They listened as rain danced on the tree leaves and ground. Mercy lay quietly at their feet, her head resting on Daniel's shoe. Daniel's chin rested against Taryn's head. "What's your thought on Chance?"

"He's wounded, lost, and sad."

"He's trying to escape his father Ray and God." At their first meeting, Daniel had sensed restlessness—unease—within Chance. Then, after he had learned of Chance's past—the abuse and resentment—Daniel realized that Chance needed guidance—some godly counsel. "His defenses are weakening, but he's still boxing God. He doesn't realize he's fighting a losing battle."

"He seemed troubled."

"He was afraid."

"Of what?"

"Surrendering. That's not easy for a proud, self-reliant man." Daniel was beginning to understand Chance, and what was most disconcerting to him was that he and Chance had more in common than the Dearlings. They were both allowing childhood experiences to prevent them from moving forward in the present. Abuse, grief, and anger were Chance's demons; rejection, fear, and paralysis were Daniel's. His parents were right. His childhood pain—that sense of rejection from his birth family—had left him doubting his worth as a son, as a man—and even now, he suspected that Chance had been right in his charge that Daniel feared further discomfit and, possibly, rejection when everyone discovered the truth— that he was the illegitimate son of Pastor Nathan Dearling and his First Lady, Leah. Maybe this was his own test of faith.

Daniel lifted Taryn's left hand, pressing it to his lips; then, he shifted on the swing so he could see her face clearly. In her brown eyes, he saw an abiding love, and he was deeply humbled. "Chance isn't the only stubborn one." He cupped her face in his hand. "Tonight I realized that I'm just like him, crippled and clinging to fear and the wounds of the past."

Lines creased Taryn's forehead. "You were never abused."

"Still, I used to cry myself to sleep believing that my birth parents tossed me aside like trash, that I was merely an inconvenience to them. Even today, knowing the truth and accepting the authority that I have in the Lord, I've felt inadequate—unwanted, unloved, and rejected."

Taryn pressed her hand to his heart. "That's only the enemy trying to ensnare you and steal your joy. Don't believe the lies. You're more than adequate, you're wanted, and you're definitely loved."

Daniel sighed. "I know that in my heart, but my mind is where the battle exists. Chance's visit, his past, and his words have just brought these feelings to surface. He's helped me realize that I haven't moved forward, that I've been grounded in self-doubt, burying my pain and pretending that all is fine." He caressed her cheek. "I've been skirting this meeting with the Dearlings because I remember that childhood rejection, that shame."

"Honey, they're not to blame."

"I know, but it's hard to erase what's been in my head for thirty-six years. My birth parents didn't protect me or fight for me when I was a defenseless baby. They accepted another man's lies, without verifying the truth, and now, after I've lived three decades in their absence, they want a relationship with me. Despite my walk with the Lord, it's not easy for me to readily accept Nathan and Leah Dearling in the spirit of a son, with untainted love."

"You have a good heart—a pure and noble one. You just need time with the Dearlings. After you've met them, your heart will correspond as it should."

Daniel caressed her cheek. "Maybe I'm rejecting them before they do so to me."

"That's not the kind of man you are. You're compassionate, loving, and selfless."

He kissed her forehead, strengthened by her words, her trust. "I've hurt you the most, putting our relationship on ice, the wedding on hold. How can you so passionately defend me?"

"I love you, and I know you love me. You'll marry me when the time is right—when you've found peace."

Daniel lowered his hand from her face, covering her hand over his heart. "With regard to you, God has given me peace. He's also given me love in you—and I've been taking you for granted for the past two years. I've allowed fear, rejection, shame, and insecurity to derail me, and I've denied both of us happiness as husband and wife. I've never really felt worthy of you. I've never felt I deserved you."

Tears welled in Taryn's eyes. "Daniel Michael Winward, you're worthy—more precious than rubies, diamonds, and pearls—and you deserve a family, with a wife and children who adore you."

"Tonight I truly want that. I want all God has promised me—the marriage, the wife, the children, even the grandchildren. I want you as my wife and my friend, my partner and my helpmate. I love you, Taryn, with everything within me. Will you marry me?"

Taryn laughed, tears spilling down her cheeks. "As many times as you propose, my answer will always be yes, I'll marry you."

"Thank you." Daniel lowered his head, kissing her. He felt as though a weight had been lifted from his chest, as though he were suddenly free. He withdrew, giddy and smiling. "We've been engaged long enough. Let's set a wedding date."

Her eyes glowed as bright as a full moon. "Are you sure?"

"Positive."

"When?"

"This year."

Surprise registered on her face. "Really?"

He nodded. "Yes."

"When?"

"December."

"In six months?"

"Yes."

Fresh tears flooded Taryn's eyes, and she could barely compose herself. "My birthday is December 8."

He grinned. "If we marry in December, you'll have three celebrations— your birthday, our wedding anniversary, and Christmas."

"I'd love that."

"So would I, and I can't wait another year for you to be mine." Daniel hugged her, then stood, tugging her to her feet. Silently, he led her back into the house, into the kitchen and straight to a wall calendar. He flipped the pages, stopping at the month of December. After skimming the days, he turned, facing her. "What about Christmas Eve?"

"It's perfect." Taryn hugged and kissed him. "I love you."

"I love you, too, and I can't wait to make you Mrs. Daniel Michael Winward."

Taryn snuggled closer, content to remain in his arms. "We're finally getting married, and we owe Chance Dearling for stoking the fire and shaking us awake tonight."

Daniel agreed. "I pray he finds what he needs here."

"What's that?"

"God."

Chapter Eleven

For it is with your heart that you believe and are justified,
and it is with your mouth that you confess and are saved.

Romans 10:10 (NIV)

Midnight Motel
Sunday, June 26

At nine o'clock Chance lay in bed, staring silently at the Bible beneath the bedside lamp. He was debating picking it up, flipping its pages, and rereading the verses he had jotted down from Daniel's morning sermon, "Righteous Love, Redeeming Grace." Even now, he vividly recalled sitting through the service, Daniel's words resounding through his head. His text, Zephaniah 3, portrayed God as angry with sin but just and righteous in His actions.

Daniel had stood majestic before the congregation, his Bible clutched in his hand, pressed over his heart, and he urged those who had turned from following God, those that neither sought God nor inquired of Him, and those living irreverently, irresponsibly, and complacently to take heed and repent. He had extended his hand, raising the Bible. "Harden not your heart. Let God's love abide in you, lay aside every weight, and come."

Again, Chance had been compelled to leave his seat, to move forward, and answer that invitation—that call—yet he had remained paralyzed, firmly planted in his seat.

His cell phone rang, and his eyes fell from the Bible. He lifted the phone from the bed, and he saw that the caller was his father. "Hello, Dad. How are you?"

"Fine, son. I'm sorry to phone you so late." He sounded weary, worn, somber.

"What's wrong?"

"Your mother."

Chance bolted in bed, clutching the phone in a death grip. His heart pounded fiercely against his chest as he imagined the worst. "What's happened?"

"She has a malignant brain tumor."

A malignant brain tumor? As his father's words registered, tears stung Chance's eyes, tightness gripped his chest, and he fought to breathe, to speak. His birth mother, Eileen, had died of a brain aneurysm; now his adoptive mother had a brain tumor. "Mom could die?"

"If it's her time, yes. Leah's adamant, though, that all will end well, that she won't die until she's old and gray, surrounded by all of her children."

"I'm coming home."

"Don't let fear bring you back, son. Your mother's fine so far, and the oncologist and her team of doctors are already devising a plan of treatment. Your mother will undergo chemotherapy and radiation therapy to shrink the tumor. If that goes well, she'll be prepped for surgery. Besides that, we're praying and trusting God to carry us through this test. So don't worry."

He wiped tears from his eyes. "I can't lose Mom. I won't."

"She needs prayer, son. She needs *our* faith, not our doubts or fears."

Chance bobbed his head, his eyes darting to the Bible at his bedside. "Haven't you always claimed God to be a healer?"

"Yes. He is."

"Mom needs a healer. She needs God."

"We all do."

"You still trust Him, even with Mom's diagnosis, the possibility of her death?"

"Yes, I trust Him, with not only my life but with Leah's."

"How can you?"

"I love Him, and He loves me. And I've learned that every adversity comes with two responses, son. It either draws a person closer to God, or it drives that person farther away. I choose to run to God, not away from Him 'cause peace for me is always found in His presence."

He doesn't blame God for Mom's tumor. He still believes in Him even though there's no guarantee that Mom will survive. He hasn't lost his faith. Chance rubbed his chin, deep in thought. Like his birth mother, his adoptive parents implicitly trusted God, believing the best in Him and leaning on Him, even in times of adversity. They found joy and strength in Him; they felt His love, even in midst of sorrow and pain, and they rejoiced in Him—worshipping Him with abandon—freedom. *Was it possible that he had been wrong all this time—that his perception of God was distorted?* Chance couldn't deal with that, so he pushed it away. "Have you told Victor yet?"

"He's next."

"He'll want to return, too."

"I'll tell him what I'm telling you: God has your mother covered."

"I wish I had your faith."

"You do. You just haven't exercised it."

"You really think so?"

"You believed once, you can again."

"I'm not a child anymore."

"In God's eyes, you are, son. Now, tell me: How is Daniel?"

"He and his fiancée set their wedding date for this Christmas Eve."

"I'm happy for them."

"He still hasn't committed to a meeting with you and Mom any time soon, but now that I know about Mom's condition, I'm more determined to make her dream reunion a reality." He knew the greatest gift and ray of hope he could offer his parents was their firstborn son, Daniel Winward.

"If he won't come, don't force him. Your mother and I knew it was possible that neither Daniel nor Leisha would welcome a family reunion. Both you and Victor have done your best, more than we even expected, and we're grateful. We may just have to content ourselves with living on the fringe of Daniel's and Leisha's lives, taking comfort in knowing that they're both healthy and happy."

Nathan Dearling wasn't a quitter; neither was Chance. "Don't toss in the towel yet. I haven't given up on Daniel; neither should you."

"All right. I'll wait before speaking to Leah and dashing her hopes."

"Thank you."

"Don't you give up on God. He loves you, even more than I do."

"I can't imagine that."

"He does. Trust me."

"I do, Dad. Trust you."

"Then, increase your faith and run to God, not away from Him. If you draw near Him, He'll draw near you. He won't let you fall, and He'll never leave you or forsake you. Ever. When you choose Him as your Lord, He'll be with you and live in you, and He'll be your strength in weakness and your comfort in sorrow. He'll fight for you and never willingly let you go. And when you finally accept Him as your Father, He'll love you as His son. For eternity. That's God's love—everlasting."

His father's words echoed all that he had heard from Daniel and Dr. Joseph. They all spoke as though they were privy to a secret that he had yet to uncover. Maybe it was time for him to take that first step into the unknown and trust that he wouldn't fall and drown. "I'll consider it, Dad. I love you."

"I love you, too."

"Kiss Mom for me."

"I will. Goodnight."

After he disconnected, Chance tossed the cell phone on the bed, then raised his head heavenward. Sermons of the past week, including this morning's, flooded his mind, and once again he envisioned himself wounded and bloody, hanging on a cross above fierce flames, and he felt compelled to surrender, to rise and walk forward. "What am I supposed to do?"

Two words dropped like rain in his spirit. *Pray, Chance.*

His heart thumped his chest. "What?"

Share your heart.

Chance scrunched his face as a distant memory tickled his mind. Before he could grasp it firmly to the present, though, one church popped into his head, and he recalled his father's advice that he increase his faith, that he run to God. Lowering his head, he turned and grabbed his car key. After hastily collecting his wallet and cell phone, he left the room, got in his car, and drove directly to Daniel's.

At ten fifteen, he stood on Daniel's doorstep, with his heart thumping madly and tears blinding his eyes. One hand was jammed in his jacket pocket, the other was trembling as he pressed the doorbell.

In a pair of jeans and a white T-shirt, Daniel opened the door, clearly surprised by his late-night visitor. "What's wrong?"

"I need transportation and access."

"Where?"

"The church."

"Tonight?"

"Tonight." He swallowed hard. "I listened. I heard it all—about God, His love—and I finally got the message. I only have two options: run to Him or from Him; love or hate Him; accept or reject Him."

"Have you made a decision?"

"I'm ready."

"So be it." Daniel touched Chance's shoulder and drew him inside, over the threshold and into the foyer. "After I grab my keys, we'll leave."

Chance nodded, unable to speak anymore. Inside he was quaking, and more tears were threatening to fall. He'd never felt more exposed, like a scaled fish, and even now, doubts and fears were crowding his thoughts. He fought them, though, recalling that verse that Daniel had first mentioned: "Be strong and courageous. Do not be terrified; do not be discouraged, for the Lord your God will be with you wherever you go." Tonight, he needed strength and courage; he needed God to be real, to be with him, to fight for him.

As Daniel disappeared down the hallway, Chance glanced around, his eyes falling on a framed scripture, Proverbs 3:5–6: "Trust in the LORD with all your heart and lean not on your own understanding; in all your ways acknowledge him, and he will make your paths straight." Those words fed his hungry spirit, and he lowered his head, remembering one bedtime prayer that his mother Eileen always recited with him: "Now I lay me down to sleep. I pray the Lord my soul to keep. Guide me safely through the night. Wake me with the morning light. Amen."

That night Mama smiled at him, tears in her eyes. "Trust in God, Chance, and always say your prayers. If you put your heart, soul, and life in God's hands, He'll protect you. Always. That's how much He loves you, how much Jesus loves you."

At age five, Chance had turned his head sideways. "Does Jesus love us, Mama, really?"

"Yes, He does."

"Even when Daddy hits us, even when he hurts us and makes us cry?"

Mama had bobbed her head, tears spilling from her eyes as she tightened her grip on him. "Yes, baby. Jesus loves us, especially when we're hurting."

"Why doesn't He stop Daddy?"

"Your daddy doesn't believe in Jesus like we do. He's hurting too, but he won't even listen when Jesus tries to speak to him. He doesn't think Jesus can help him or us."

"Is Jesus mad at us? Did we do something bad? Is that why He lets Daddy hit us?"

"No, baby. He loves us."

"Why doesn't He take the hurt away?"

Mama cried, then hugged him tighter. "He did, baby. A long time ago, He took away our pain, shedding His blood on a cross. He died for us, but He didn't stay dead. He rose to life again, just to save us, to get us right, with His Father, God. That was His gift—healing, hope, forgiveness, and love."

"But Daddy doesn't love us, Mama."

"Yes, Daddy does, Chance. He's just too sick and confused to know it."

"He's mean and scary, and he always beats us. Why won't Jesus hurt him back or make him go away?"

"Jesus loves your daddy too, Chance."

"Daddy's a bad guy."

"Ray wasn't always like this, baby. Once upon a time, he was a doctor and he loved me and he loved you. Back then, he helped make sick people better, and he even smiled and laughed a lot. He was a good guy."

"Do you love him, Mama?"

"I love the man I married, and he's trapped in there somewhere."

"I hate him, Mama."

"No, you don't, Chance."

"I really do."

"Baby, we don't hate people; we love them." She kissed his forehead. "I'm sorry your daddy and I made a mess of this marriage. I'm sorry we haven't been the best parents or the most loving. Sometimes we don't always accept Jesus's love or His help. We get afraid and run away from Him. Then, we don't always act as we should, and we don't love each other anymore. We just get angry and mean, and we behave badly, and sometimes, that's what happens to Daddy and me. We forget about Jesus, and we don't think He loves us, that He can save us." She pressed Chance's head against her heart. "Don't hate your daddy, Chance, and don't blame Jesus for Daddy's and my mistakes. Don't let us spoil your faith in God. You just love Him, let Him love you, and pray every night, sharing your heart. If you keep that heart pure and give it to Jesus, He'll always take care of it."

"How do I keep my heart pure, Mama?"

"By forgiving and loving others, inviting Jesus inside your heart, and asking God to clean it. Can you do that?"

"Yes, ma'am."

"Will you choose love over hate?"

"Yes, ma'am."

"Will you pray and share your heart?"

"Yes, ma'am."

"Promise?" She raised her little finger, waiting for his response.

"I promise." Chance curled his little finger around hers. "I love you, Mama."

"I love you too. Now, let's say our prayers so we can go to sleep." She kissed his forehead, ruffled his hair, then lowered him to the floor so he could kneel beside her.

Pray and share your heart. Those had been his mother's words.

Suddenly remembering that night, those words, and *his* promise to Mama, Chance lowered his head, choking back sobs. He had pushed that memory into the recesses of his mind, and he had conveniently forgotten it, especially after his mother's death. He had allowed his hurt and anger to control him, turning him away from God—from Jesus. "I'm sorry, Mama." He squatted and cried. "I'm sorry I failed you and broke my promise."

Daniel returned with his keys and put his hand on Chance's shoulder. "Are you okay?"

Chance stood, swiping tears from his eyes. "I'm fine."

"Follow me then." Daniel escorted him through the house to the garage, then to his silver four-door truck. After he had unlocked the door and he and Chance climbed inside, Daniel told him that he had christened his truck the Faith mobile.

Chance strapped the seatbelt across his chest. "Why call it that?"

"It's another prayer closet, a place where I can exercise faith." Daniel put the key in the ignition, turned it, then eased from the garage.

They rode in silence for a few minutes, and Chance leaned his head against the passenger window, just peering into the darkness, watching a blur of lights stream past, and allowing the music from the radio to wash over him.

"If you want to talk, I'll listen."

Chance turned, facing forward. "I've loved two women in my lifetime, both of them my mothers. One, Eileen, birthed me from the womb; the other, Leah, birthed me from her heart. Both of them in their own way fought for me—for my life, my soul. My birth mother's prayers kept me alive through Ray's beatings, and my adoptive mother's prayers protected me through my years in law enforcement, even until today.

"When I lost my birth mother to a brain aneurysm, I felt helpless, lost. After I was adopted, I was afraid I'd lose my second mother, too. Now, I could." Chance audibly exhaled, tapping his fingers against his leg. "Dad phoned earlier, telling me she has a malignant brain tumor. She's scheduled to undergo chemotherapy, radiation therapy, later surgery."

"I'm sorry."

Daniel's words caused a dull ache in Chance's heart. Leah was Daniel's mother too, yet he considered her a stranger. The possibility of her death didn't even seem to register with the man, and that bothered Chance. A lot. He turned, confronting Daniel. "Mom could die."

Daniel spared him a look. "She could also live, so have faith."

"By nature, I'm a doubter, but tonight I realized Mom is on the brink—facing life or death—and I can't fight this battle alone, not in my own strength, with my own resources. I need help. I *need* God."

"For yourself or your mother?"

"Both."

"You can't bargain with God for your mother's life. That's not how He works. All you can do is pray that His will be done and that He strengthens you so you can accept the outcome—His answer."

Chance clamped his hands together and faced forward, pondering Daniel's words. Total surrender, that's what he would have to give God. He'd have to relinquish the control that he'd fought so hard for and offer everything, withholding nothing.

When they arrived at the church, Chance sprang from the truck, trailing Daniel.

After Daniel disarmed the security system, he unlocked one side door, then turned on the lights, illuminating the corridor. Together, they strode with purpose toward the sanctuary.

Chance breathed deeply, advancing, his eyes straight, toward the altar. Although the journey took less than fifteen minutes, it felt like a lifetime, and the closer he got to the front, the less weight and stress he felt. It was as though his worries were bubbles floating farther away. He stopped before the translucent podium, beneath the large lit cross hanging overhead. He just stood for a minute, his eyes resting on that cross. Finally, he had the sense that he had arrived in the right place at the right time—his appointed time—and this cross wasn't mocking him but inviting him forward and Godward. "Here I am, God—all of me—depleted, lost, and broken. I don't have any other options. I need You." He lowered himself to the carpeted floor, kneeling. "Guide me. Fix me. Help me. Change me." He bowed his head, waiting patiently for something profound—for God's response.

"Would you like to be alone?"

Chance raised his head to Daniel. "Stay and tell me what I need to do."

"Are you here to accept Jesus as your Lord and Savior?"

"Yes. I'm ready."

Daniel smiled and rested his hand on Chance's shoulder. "Are you certain?"

"I am." Chance palmed his hands. "I've been angry and drifting for years, and this emptiness inside is like a gaping hole, sucking the life and joy out of me. Tonight, after Dad called, I realized I need a ray of hope in the darkness. I need rest, peace, God." He lifted his eyes to Daniel. "Where do I begin?"

Daniel kneeled beside him and bowed his own head. "With Romans 10:9–10, which says, 'if you confess with your mouth, "Jesus is Lord," and believe in your heart that God raised him from the dead, you will be saved. For it is with your heart that you believe and are justified, and it is with your mouth that you confess and are saved.'"

"Confess and believe?"

"God's gift is freely given, Chance. But you've got to repent of any wrongdoing or sin and then acknowledge the gift, sincerely receiving and accepting it." He smiled. "Salvation doesn't come through reciting a specific prayer; it comes through your submission to a specific Person, Jesus Christ. The prayer is just your confession of faith in Jesus as your Lord, Savior, Healer, Redeemer, and Deliverer—your acceptance of all Jesus did for you on the Cross at Calvary. So then you're saved by *God's* grace through your faith, not by any works or good deeds that you've done. Do you understand?"

Chance nodded. "Yes. I'm ready."

"All right, if you will, pray after me."

Chance closed his eyes, bowed his head, and repeated the prayer, acknowledging his sins and inviting Jesus into his heart and his life.

After a minute of silence, Daniel gently tapped his shoulder, and Chance opened his eyes to see him standing, with tears flooding his gray eyes.

"Congratulations, Chance! There's a party in heaven tonight, just for you, and there's rejoicing in the presence of angels."

"Why?"

"Because he who was dead is alive again, and he who was lost is found." He drew Chance to his feet and hugged him. "Give thanks, brother in Christ, because tonight your name is written in heaven in the Lamb's book of life."

As they embraced, Chance looked beyond Daniel toward that lit cross, and for the first time he didn't envision himself hanging there but Jesus, and within his own spirit, he heard a still, small voice whispering, *Welcome home, Chance. Welcome home.*

Chapter Twelve

The Lord will keep you from all harm—he will watch over your life; the Lord will watch over your coming and going both now and forevermore.

Psalm 121:7–8 (NIV)

The Bridgewater Building, Sheridan Suite A
Monday, June 27

At five-thirty, Leisha returned to her office, securing folders under her left arm and clutching her briefcase in her right hand.

Her purse tucked under her arm, Cassandra greeted Leisha at the door. "I've left today's messages on your desk beside the phone."

"Thank you." Leisha entered, dropping the folders and briefcase on the desk. She slid into her cushioned chair, kicking her high-heeled shoes off. "Any pressing news?"

"Victor Dearling phoned repeatedly."

Leisha groaned, massaging her forehead. Her plate was full with her heavy caseload, and she didn't have time to spare for Victor or his parents. However, the man was tenacious, not easily defeated. "What does he want?"

"You to contact him immediately. He's been relentless on the phone, so I'm surprised he hasn't camped outside your office."

That's exactly what I don't want—another personal visit. I still haven't recovered from our first one. Leisha mentally tucked Cassandra's message away, then grabbed her other phone messages and skimmed them.

"Are you listening?"

Leisha looked up. "What?"

"The man's not giving up on you, so what are you going to do about him?" Cassandra cocked her blonde head to the side.

"Nothing." Maybe if she continued to ignore him, he would eventually leave. After all, he couldn't stay in Corinth indefinitely. He had a life, a family, and responsibilities back in Crossland.

"Return his call, Leisha. He might have important news."

Leisha dropped the messages, confronting her assistant. "I doubt it." Likely, he wanted to see what progress he had made with the gifts. Leisha's desire for self-preservation had overridden any curiosity she had regarding her twin brother. That's why she had been steadily avoiding Victor.

Cassandra chattered, letting her imagination run wild. "Maybe he fell in love with you at first sight, and now he can't bear to go another day without hearing your voice."

Leisha rolled her eyes. "Those romance novels you've got stashed in your desk have made you delusional. Victor is not in love with me, and he's not interested in romancing me."

Cassandra folded her arms. "How can you know that with certainty if you keep avoiding the man? If he weren't at least interested in you, he wouldn't be sending gifts every week, and if he weren't invested in you personally and emotionally, your frosty attitude would have chilled his affections already."

"I haven't been frosty."

"You've been as cold to this man as icicles on a wire in December, and I'm sure he hasn't done anything to warrant such a reaction. You and I have been friends for five years, and this is the first time that I've seen you behave so out of character—so *deplorably*."

"What have I done to Victor that's so horrible?"

Cassandra raised her index finger. "You're treating him like your enemy or some stalker. You haven't acknowledged any of his gifts or even expressed any gratitude for his consideration. You won't accept any of his calls, usually citing busyness as your excuse even when you are available, and you've even used Jonathan the security guard to foil his attempts to visit your office again." She lowered her hand. "For you, that's not normal behavior."

Leisha felt a prick in her conscience. Since Victor's arrival, she *had* been acting out of character. She couldn't help herself, though. The man had stoked a fire within her heart, making her long for what she had been denied for years—the unconditional love of a family and the enduring love of a good man.

"Are you afraid of Victor?"

"No."

"Then why are you avoiding him?"

"I don't want to speak to him."

"Or see him. Why not?"

"My relationship with him is complicated."

"You only met with him once, a couple of weeks ago. How complicated can it be?"

"He wants me to do what I'm unwilling to."

"What?"

"It's private, personal."

"Not if he's pressuring you to do something immoral or illegal."

"He's not."

Cassandra lowered her arms, her forehead crinkled. "I'm confused."

"Join the club. I've been confused since I met the man." She brushed a stray curl from her face. "Now, is there anything else I should know before you leave?"

"I'm only the messenger, so don't get angry with me. Mateo wants you to use the security escort service. And he said it's not a request but an order."

A security escort? Leisha bristled at Mateo's audacity. She was an adult, independent, too. She didn't need her law partner issuing orders like she was his wife or one of his children. "Why?"

"You've been staying past eight and walking alone through the rear parking lot."

"I don't need an escort. I'm not afraid or defenseless."

"He knows you're not, but he's worried because you're usually the last to leave the office, and he's heard all the news about the parking lot assaults."

Leisha recalled Salena mentioning those assaults recently. The police only had a vague description of the attacker. He was a black-hooded man who raped, then stabbed his victims to death. Of the women assaulted, only one had been found alive. "Cassie, the likelihood of the attacker targeting our parking lot is slim, so don't worry. I'll be fine."

"This isn't a joke, Leisha. The threat is serious, and both Mateo and I would feel better if you allowed Jonathan to escort you to your car."

Leisha sighed. "I'll consider it. Now, stop fretting and go home to your husband and children." She waved her away.

"You're as stubborn as a rock."

Leisha smiled. "I'll take that as a compliment."

"It wasn't one."

"Goodnight, Cassie."

"Be safe, Leisha. Goodnight."

After she left, Leisha opened her briefcase, removing a set of legal documents, then she turned on her computer and logged in. Soon, she became so engrossed in working that she lost track of the time. At nine, however, her office phone rang, and she jerked, startled. Glancing at the display, she saw that the caller was Victor, and she debated answering. Only after the fourth ring did she finally decide to pick up.

"Leisha?"

"Yes."

"I've been trying to reach you all day."

"I'm busy, so what do you want?"

"It's late, so why are you still at the office?"

"I'm working on a case."

"Can't you work from home?"

"Where I work is none of your business." She heard the frost in her own voice but still didn't soften her tone. Victor wasn't her boyfriend or her husband, yet he had insinuated himself into her life. If she didn't establish some boundaries, he would take control, consuming her completely. "Now, is there a reason for this call?"

"I really need to talk to you tonight."

"Well, you've got me, so talk."

"Not over the phone. In person. What time are you leaving the office?"

Leisha rolled over her wrist, glancing at her watch. "In fifteen minutes."

"I'm already en route, so I'll meet you there and escort you home."

"I don't need an escort or a bodyguard. I'm quite capable of taking care of myself and getting home safely. I've been doing it for years."

"Accepting help isn't a sign of weakness, even for an independent woman. It's a sign of wisdom."

"I'm tired, and I don't want to argue with you."

"We won't argue. I promise."

"We will if you're set on me traveling to Crossland."

"Have you been praying?"

"Every day."

"What's God prompting you to do?"

Trust you and walk in faith. She knew if she confessed that to him, he would wonder why she wasn't being obedient. Even Salena was frustrated with her stubbornness. "I can't chat with you now, Victor. I need to finish my work so I can go home, eat, and relax."

"If traffic permits, I should be there soon. Wait on me."

First, Mateo; now, Victor. Why did men always order women around? She didn't respond well to orders, especially from men who thought they knew better than she what was best for her. "I told you I don't need a protector."

"Humor me anyway and tell me where you parked."

Recalling Cassandra's charge about her deplorable behavior, Leisha held back the sarcasm. "The rear parking lot, near the west end."

"All right, I'll be there. Just wait in the lobby until I arrive."

"Victor, I really don't—"

"See you soon." He disconnected.

Exasperated, she dropped the phone in its cradle and glared at it, muttering. "Men!" She turned her eyes toward the computer screen again, but she was too flustered to resume working. Finally, after staring at the same document for five minutes, she saved it, then logged off the computer, slipping her feet into her blue high heels. She returned the legal documents to her briefcase and within ten minutes, she was ready to leave.

After locking the office, she walked through the deserted and dimly-lit lobby toward the elevator and punched the button, descending to the ground floor. Jonathan Murray, a muscular, navy-clad security guard, greeted her from his station. "It's pretty dark out there, Ms. Laurence, especially in that rear parking lot. Would you like an escort?"

"No, thank you." She dismissed Mateo's command and Cassandra's warning. "Someone's meeting me outside. He's probably waiting already."

"I don't mind walking out with you, just to make sure he's there."

"I'll be fine, Jonathan. Don't worry."

"I'd feel better if you let me escort you, ma'am. In case you haven't heard, there's a rapist at large who's attacking and killing women in secluded lots."

"I doubt he's lurking in our parking lot."

"Still, it doesn't seem right for me to let you venture out alone."

"I won't be alone. There's a friend outside, waiting to escort me home."

"If you say so, miss."

"I do. Now, stop fretting and let me go."

"Okay, Ms. Laurence." Jonathan frowned, clearly uncomfortable. "Be careful."

"I will." She waved, then strode forward, pushing against the glass door and exiting the building, her purse draped over her shoulder and her briefcase in her hand. She turned the corner, walking briskly toward the rear parking lot where two light poles spilled pools of light along the east and west ends. Away from the building, the back south side of the lot was dark and shadowed, clothed in bushes and grass. Three cars were still in the lot: Leisha's silver four-door car at the far west end, a black pickup truck midway, and a white van with an oval orange logo on the side, near the Bridgewater building.

Leisha quickly scanned the lot but didn't see Victor or anyone else. Relieved, she high-clicked it past the white van. She was midway, near the black pickup in a darkened area when she heard the crunch of footsteps on gravel, and she sensed a shadow drawing near.

She froze, thoughts of the parking lot predator fresh on her mind, and she became apprehensive, furtively glancing back and holding her briefcase defensively. When she didn't see anyone following her, she berated herself for letting Mateo, Cassandra, and Jonathan's worry frighten her. "I'm being silly. Nobody's here but me." She drew a deep breath, then advanced, her eyes fixed on her car sitting near the west-end light. All she had to do was walk another twenty feet, climb into her car, lock the doors, and wait for Victor to arrive. After that, she could go home, eat, deal with Victor, send him back to his lodgings, and then remove her blouse and skirt, slipping into a pair of comfortable silk pajamas.

Finally arriving at her car, she sighed, sitting her briefcase on top of the trunk while she dug her hand into her purse, fishing for her key. Pulling it out, she depressed the button, unlocking the doors. Next, she lifted the briefcase and tossed it into the backseat. Afterward, she opened the driver's door, removed her purse, and leaned down, dropping it onto the passenger seat. She was about to slide into the driver's seat when someone roughly grabbed her waist from behind and dragged her from the car. *No!* Instinctively, she struggled, trying to escape, but she was pressed tightly against a dark, strong wall of muscle. *It's him—the parking lot rapist!* Before she could scream, a black-gloved hand clamped over her mouth, muffling any sound, and she felt a knife prick near her cheek.

"Resist me or even scream, and you die faster. Got it?"

I'm dead even if I do comply. If that's your plan, you pervert, you picked the wrong woman. I'm not making this easy for you, and you're not touching or killing me without a fight. Quickly, she devised a plan. *God, give me strength, courage.* She knew if he got her away from the lights and those two cameras mounted near the building and into those darkened bushes, her chances of survival were limited. *I can't waste time. I've got to get free! Now!* She jerked her head until she got her mouth free, then clamped spiked teeth into his gloved hand, biting mercilessly into his flesh while stomping her sharp-heeled foot into his shoe and jabbing her elbow into his body.

Startled, the man grunted, then fell back, dropping the knife and releasing her. Leisha swiftly turned and aggressively attacked, giving him a hard knee to his groin before she kicked off her shoes, racing barefoot toward the building, screaming as though a thousand hellhounds were chasing her. She knew if she could make it to those cameras or the front door, Jonathan would see her, and she would be safe. "God, help me!" She heard an enraged curse from behind, then the fast, harsh crunch of gravel, getting closer, closer, closer.

She had just reached the black pickup truck when the attacker yanked her hair, pulling her backward. "No!" She screamed, kicked, and fought even as he hooked an arm around her waist and dragged her beside the black truck, throwing her on the ground, then looming over her. "Stop!" she screeched, but he raised his left hand, striking her with his fist till her right jaw exploded in pain, in burning fire.

"Shut up!" He flashed the knife, pressing it against her throat, then angrily ripped her blouse and tugged on her skirt with his free hand.

Leisha sobbed. "Jesus, help me." The man's hand touched her skin, and she screamed again, her cry piercing the silence of the black night.

"Quiet!" He curled his hand into a fist, and Leisha flinched, turning her face to avoid another blow.

An engine sounded, then a door slammed. Suddenly, a dark-haired man in a white shirt and jeans hurled himself into the attacker, knocking him away from Leisha.

Paralyzed by fear, she stayed on the ground, trembling and holding the torn pieces of her blouse together—watching helplessly as her rescuer valiantly fought, straddling the attacker, yanking the hood from his head, and pummeling him without mercy or restraint. Only when the attacker fought back, gaining release and barreling into the rescuer, shoving him back into the light did Leisha recognize her rescuer as Victor Dearling.

The attacker, a white man with long greasy blond hair and dark, malevolent eyes, butted Victor with his head, then punched him ferociously till they were both back on the ground, struggling for an advantage. Just as Victor got the attacker's legs pinned, the man roared in anger, grabbing his knife and jabbing maniacally at Victor until he cut him, slicing his upper, left arm.

"No!" Leisha screamed, finding her voice again as Victor clutched his arm, and the attacker commenced striking blows to his head. Weakened, Victor collapsed on the ground, and the attacker faced Leisha again, advancing with the bloodied knife still in his left hand.

"Your turn." The attacker hovered over her, ready to strike a death blow, and Leisha saw pure evil in his eyes. *God, help me. Please.*

The knife descended.

"Drop your weapon! Now!" Jonathan ran toward them with a flashlight and a baton, even as a siren sounded in the distance, and the attacker turned on his heels, running in the opposite direction. Jonathan finally stopped at Leisha's side. "Are you all right?"

She nodded, still shaking, in shock.

Jonathan lowered his baton. "He won't escape this time. That's a promise. We got his face on camera, and I've already called the police." As Jonathan placed a gentle hand on her shoulder, Leisha dissembled, sobbing. "I'm sorry, Ms. Laurence. I came as fast as I could."

"Thank you."

"You're welcome, miss. But the real hero is that guy who showed up and fought him, giving me time enough to come."

Victor! Leisha scrambled to rise, to reach him. "He got cut badly, then struck in the head." She led Jonathan to Victor who lay motionless, crimson blood staining the sliced arm of his white shirt. Afraid, Leisha shook him. "Victor, open your eyes."

"I'll call for an ambulance." Jonathan lifted a cell phone from his pocket and punched 9-1-1.

Leisha leaned over Victor, caressing his bruised face. "Look at me, Victor. Help is on the way. Hold on." She lowered her hand, covering his wound to stop the blood's flow, but she knew it wouldn't be enough. Victor needed medical attention. Immediately.

His eyelids fluttered, and pain was written in his green eyes.

"Thank God!" Leisha gently kissed his forehead before withdrawing to caress him with her eyes. Even swollen and battered, he was beautiful, almost angelic.

He weakly raised his right hand to her throbbing face. "You okay?"

"I'm fine. Thanks to you." She kissed his hand. "Now, save your strength and you'll be fine."

"It hurts all over."

"You got cut, then hit. Hard." Her heart ached for him—for his pain, his suffering. "This is my fault."

"No, it's not."

"You're hurt because of me—my stubbornness."

"I don't blame you."

"I've been horrible to you, so you should."

"I don't." He lowered his hand, gently drying her tears. "You're loved, Leisha. Loved."

"What?"

"I love—." His hand fell, then he closed his eyes.

"Victor?" Fearing he was dead, Leisha sobbed uncontrollably, raising his head to her heart. "Please, don't die. Don't give up on me."

Chapter Thirteen

Though one may be overpowered, two can defend themselves.
A cord of three strands is not quickly broken.

Ecclesiastes 4:12 (NIV)

Corinth Medical Center
Tuesday, June 28

At six in the morning, Leisha sat forlornly in an ICU waiting room, in a fresh mint-green blouse and blue jeans, her head bowed and her hands palmed in her lap. At mention of her name, Leisha raised her head and saw Salena subdued, dressed in a gray shirt and matching slacks, her fiery red hair tamed in a ponytail. Standing, she rushed into Salena's arms, sobbing on her shoulder and releasing all that fear she had been bottling since the assault.

After five minutes, Salena escorted her back to her seat, sitting beside her and holding her hand. "I'm sorry for not coming last night. I was stuck at the news station, and after I got home, I went straight to bed without checking my voicemail."

"You're here now. That's all that matters."

"I heard the police caught the man—Devilon Fox."

"I had to file a report and identify him at the police station." Tears streamed down her cheeks as she recalled all he had done to her and Victor. "If Victor hadn't arrived when he did, Devilon Fox would have raped and killed me."

"Thank God for Victor, then. He's a true hero. How is he?"

"Under observation. That's all they'll tell me since I'm not family."

"Have you contacted the Dearlings?"

"No."

"He's been knifed and struck in the head, Leisha. His family should be here."

"I know, and I even have his cell phone." Leisha removed it from her pocket. "I just don't know who to notify."

"You should call his parents—*your* birth parents."

"No!" Leisha shook her head. "I can't meet them here, under these circumstances. They'll blame me for Victor's injuries, and they'll hate me if he loses his arm or suffers any brain damage."

"The Dearlings won't hate you, nor will they blame you. Neither the assault nor the stabbing is your fault. Devilon Fox is the only culprit in both cases."

"Still, I can't phone them and announce I'm their missing daughter, that I was almost raped and killed tonight, and that Victor had the misfortune of saving me. That's too much for an introduction."

"You can call his brother then—Chance. Talking to him might be easier."

"Maybe you're right." Leisha looked down, scrolling through the contact list on Victor's phone until she found Chance's name. She highlighted his number, then pressed the dial button and raised the phone to her ear.

A man drowsily answered. "Why are you calling this early?"

"Chance Dearling?"

"Who are you, and why do you have my brother's phone?"

"I'm Leisha Laurence. I'm at Corinth Medical Center."

"Where's my brother?"

"Last night he was cut in the arm and struck repeatedly in the head. He was rushed to the hospital, and he's currently under observation. Other than that, I don't know the extent of his injuries."

"Why was he cut and beaten?"

Leisha closed her eyes, raking her fingers through her curls. "He was defending me. Last night after I left work, a man assaulted me in the parking lot, and he would have raped and murdered me if Victor hadn't shown up and fought him. A security guard alerted the police, then came outside, preventing the attacker from doing any more damage to Victor or me."

"Did the police catch the guy?"

"A few hours ago."

"Good."

"I wasn't ready to phone your parents, so I called you."

"You made the right choice. I'll tell our parents."

Leisha exhaled. "Thank you." Fresh tears stung her eyes. "I'm sorry. For everything. If Victor hadn't been meeting me, he wouldn't have been hurt."

"I'm not blaming you, nor will Mom and Dad."

The tears fell down Leisha's cheeks. "Thank you."

"Now, tell me: How are you?"

"Bruised and shaken, but I'll survive."

"I know it's hard right now but get some rest—relax."

"I wish I could, but every time I close my eyes, I relive it all. I see that hooded man—Devilon Fox—and I feel that knife against my face and his hand on my skin."

"In time the memory will fade."

"I pray so." She dried her tears. "Are you coming to Corinth?"

"I'm in Georgia, but I'll schedule a flight from here to Texas today. I'll have to rent a car and drive to Corinth, so it might be late when I arrive. Do you mind keeping an eye on Victor?"

"I don't mind."

"Thanks. I'll see you soon."

"Goodbye." Leisha disconnected, then lowered the phone.

"How did he seem?"

"Nice. Caring. Concerned."

"What did he say?"

"He's coming."

Salena covered her heart with her hand. "Are you sure?"

Leisha glanced at her, noticing her bright eyes and flushed face. "Yes. He's coming from Georgia."

"Oh, Lord! Oh, Lord! Oh, Lord!" Salena raised her hand, feverishly fanning herself.

"What's wrong with you?"

"My dream's coming true."

"What dream?"

"A meeting with my future husband–Chance Dearling."

Increasing Faith Worship Center
Tuesday, June 28

"I love you, too, Taryn." Daniel lowered the phone to its cradle and glanced up to see Chance standing in the doorway of the office, his leather jacket draped over his left arm. Daniel smiled, then rose from his chair. "Come in, Chance. Have a seat."

"I'm not interrupting, am I?"

"Not at all."

Chance entered, and Daniel leaned forward, shaking his hand, then hugging him. After Chance sat down, Daniel sank back into his seat. "What can I do for you?"

"Come with me."

"To Crossland?"

"Corinth. I got a call this morning. My brother's been cut, badly beaten, and he's in the hospital. I'm leaving today so I can check on him."

"How severe are his injuries?"

"I'm not sure." Chance brushed a lock of hair from his forehead. "I know you're busy, but I'd appreciate your company."

"Wouldn't I be intruding?"

"You'd actually be a comfort."

"Won't your parents be there?"

"They don't know yet. I'll tell them after I've spoken to Victor's doctor."

"He's their son, and he's hurt. I'm sure they'll want to be with him."

"Of course, they will, but Mom's health is an issue. She doesn't need more stress and worry; she needs rest, peace. That's why I'm going to convince her and Dad to let me handle this situation."

"I'm still not family. Why do you want me there?"

"We *are* family, brothers in Christ. Aren't we?"

"I'm not ready to go to Texas."

"You're not interested in meeting Leisha?"

Daniel's heart sped at the thought. "She's with Victor?"

"She's the one who called me. She was attacked last night, and Victor was hurt fighting her attacker."

"He saved her."

"Yes."

Daniel digested the news, his mind reeling and his heart aching. His sister—his twin—had been in danger, and he hadn't been there to help or console her. It didn't matter that they had never met; Leisha was still his sister, and she needed him. He definitely needed her. "How is she?"

"Bruised, shaken, and guilt-ridden but surviving. Victor rescued her from rape and certain death."

"He's a hero." Victor Dearling had done what Daniel was unable to do—protect his own sister from harm. "Was the attacker apprehended?"

"He's in police custody."

"That's a relief!"

"It is." Chance stood. "I still have a few errands to run before heading to the airport. If you're interested in taking up my offer, I'll leave a ticket for you with your secretary. The earliest flight I could find leaves at four, so you'll have plenty of time to drive home, pack, and meet me at the gate."

Daniel was conflicted. He wanted to see his sister, yet he didn't know if he could leave on such short notice. He was a minister, one with many obligations—responsibilities. "I don't know, Chance. I—"

"If you're coming, include some family photos in your luggage. They might break the ice with your sister and with my parents if you choose to continue to Crossland." Chance extended his hand, and Daniel gripped and shook it. "In case this is our farewell, it's been a pleasure."

"Likewise." In the short time that they had known each other, Daniel had grown to like Chance, to care about him.

"Thanks for the new Bible."

"Study it and use it wisely."

"I will." He waved. "Till next time."

"Till next time."

After Chance closed the door, Daniel lifted his phone, redialing Taryn's number. Quickly, he explained.

"If God's prompting you to go, listen. Obey. I can't go with you. Still, I'll be here praying for you."

"Thank you. I'd better hang up so I can call my parents, then speak to Dr. Joseph."

"Do you know how long you'll be gone?"

"Not really."

"Are you going to Crossland?"

"I don't have any more excuses for staying away. Besides, I owe that much to Chance. He's put his life on hold just to find me, and he's remained here with me even though his parents need him at home." Also, since Chance had shared news of his birth mother's brain tumor, Daniel had been praying earnestly for her healing and recovery. Over the past weeks, he had become more inclined to meet the Dearlings. After all, they seemed like good people and loving parents to have raised such devoted and courageous sons as Chance and Victor. "Before I make a final decision about Crossland, I want to meet Leisha and talk to her first."

"Well, take all the time you need. I'll be here, waiting for your return."

"I love you."

"I love you, too."

Daniel disconnected and called his parents. His father wished him well, but his mother expressed some reservations about him leaving. In the end, both his parents left the decision to him and agreed to board and feed Mercy while he was gone. After bidding them farewell, Daniel rose from his seat and strode to Dr. Joseph's office. Succinctly, he told him the situation and requested a leave of absence. A friend as much as his spiritual mentor, Dr. Joseph assured Daniel that he had his blessings, and he told Daniel to take as much time as he needed. Then, he prayed with Daniel and wished him a safe journey.

Next, Daniel stopped by his secretary's desk, requested his plane ticket, and left the office, anxious to pack his bags and begin the journey to Texas.

At the airport, he found Chance sitting and waiting at the gate, his head bowed and the blue Bible opened in his lap.

Daniel dropped his carry-on bag next to Chance's foot and plopped down in the vacant seat beside him. "What's so fascinating?"

Chance glanced up with surprised blue eyes, and a smile tugged at his mouth. "Matthew 21:22: 'If you believe, you will receive whatever you ask for in prayer.'"

"That's a good verse. Another is Matthew 7:7, which says, 'Ask and it will be given you; seek and you will find; knock and the door will be opened to you.'"

"I'll remember that one." Chance closed the Bible. "I didn't expect to see you again. What made you come?"

"Partly your loyalty, your devotion." Daniel tapped his own chest. "God's also been pursuing me about the Dearlings as faithfully as He's been pursuing you about your soul. I've just been dragging my feet and being obstinate because I don't want my life changed."

"How do you feel now?"

"Change is inevitable. Sometimes it's even good."

"Will you meet Mom and Dad?"

"After I meet my sister, I'll give you an answer."

"That's fair. I'm just glad you're here and that you're seriously considering a reunion. I can almost believe anything is possible."

Daniel tapped his arm. "If you exercise your faith, Chance, and dream the impossible, then anything *can* happen, and all things *are* possible."

Chapter Fourteen

Two are better than one, because they have a good return for their work:
If one falls down, his friend can help him up.

Ecclesiastes 4:9 (NIV)

Corinth Medical Center
Tuesday, June 28

As they sat in the hospital cafeteria, Leisha quietly nibbled on a turkey sandwich and Salena sipped iced tea. Finally, Salena broke the silence. "How did Mateo take the news of your attack?"

"He was upset and concerned. He told me to take as much time as I needed to recuperate. He and our other partner Alexander will oversee all my current cases until I return. He made me promise to forget about work, to rest and heal."

"You do need to relax."

"I can't until I know Victor is all right."

Salena raised her eyes, tapping a fingernail against her cup. "Are you concerned as a close friend, an adopted sister, or an enamored woman?"

"I'm not his sister." Leisha had been fighting an attraction to Victor since their initial meeting, and it hadn't diminished. Instead, it had blossomed, more so since he had endangered himself. For her. "I care about him, even though we're not truly friends."

"You've only known him for two weeks."

"Still I care." In mere weeks the man had endeared himself to her, and that gift campaign hadn't turned her heart toward her birth parents but toward him instead.

"What makes him so different—so heart-worthy?"

Leisha laced her fingers on the table. "He's selfless and genuine, loving, giving, and kind. He's a gentleman—charming and courageous—and he's intelligent and godly."

Salena leaned in. "He's also young, single, and sinfully good-looking."

"He's not unattractive."

"He's a walking temptation, a threat to your heart."

"He's not a threat."

"You're falling in love with him, so he is."

"I'm not in love with him!"

"Are you trying to convince me or yourself?" Salena reached across the table, covering Leisha's hands. "Be careful, friend. You're headed for heartache."

"I'm not in love with Victor, and he's not going to hurt me."

Salena rolled her eyes. "Stop lying, Leisha. We both know the truth: You've fallen for your adopted brother, and you're afraid to admit it."

Leisha snatched her hands from Salena's. "I'm not lying, and Victor's not my brother, adopted or otherwise. We're not blood relatives. We're not even remotely related." She tugged on her sleeve, exposing her arm. "In case you've forgotten, he's Puerto Rican, and I'm Black."

"He's still family."

"No, he's not!" She lowered her sleeve and retracted her arm.

Salena raised her hands. "Okay! I get it. You're in denial. Stop glaring at me, too. I'm only warning you because I love you, and I don't want to see you get hurt."

"Caring about Victor won't hurt me."

"He's the first man you've ever cared deeply about, Leisha. The first to wage a well-planned war against your heart, and now that he's sent a stream of gifts and has put his life in danger to save yours, your head is stuck in the clouds, and you're seeing rainbows and butterflies everywhere."

"You're exaggerating!"

"I'm looking out for you, trying to be your friend. Any love affair you have with Victor will come with complications."

"I'm not rushing into an affair. I'm only *attracted* to the man."

Salena cocked her head to the right. "Attraction is the first step to love, and you've already confessed how easily you could fall for him." She stood, lifting her cup, and Leisha rose as well.

She grabbed her empty paper plate and followed Salena first to the trash bin then into the corridor. "I like Victor." Leisha turned right with Salena, stopping in front of the elevator. "I admire him, and I'm even grateful to him. But I'm not in love with him." The elevator door opened, and she and Salena stepped inside.

Salena pressed the button for the third floor, then turned to Leisha, disbelief in her eyes. "You're deluding yourself, friend. You're not as immune to Victor as you want me to believe. You're just in denial, and you fail to realize that he and your birth parents are a packaged deal." She folded her arms, looking forward as the elevator ascended, and Leisha remained quiet, staring blindly at the red numbers on the overhead panel. *Maybe Salena's right, and I'm swimming in the Lake of Denial. Loving Victor would be so easy. He's practically a prince, and I'm already drawn to him by those kind gestures, inspiring words, and that act of heroism. No other man has made me feel as cherished or protected. No other man has defended me so passionately or stayed around this long. No other man has tempted me as much.*

The elevator stopped on the third floor, and the door slid open. Leisha and Salena exited and turned left, headed for the Intensive Care Unit waiting room. As they passed the Nurses' Station, they both noticed two tall, well-built men lounging there with a petite dark-haired nurse: one man was white, with thick waves of brown hair and dark blue eyes, dressed in a blue shirt and jeans; the second man was dark brown with eyes as gray as an overcast day, and he was dressed in a pale orange shirt and beige pants. After they had passed the men, Salena glanced back, doing a double-take, then tugged hard on Leisha's arm. "What is it?"

"That's him! Chance Dearling!"

Leisha looked back. "Are you sure?"

"I never forget a face, especially one with such beautiful deep blue eyes." She looked at the man again, this time her eyes lingering. "He's more gorgeous in person, and that lock of hair curling on his forehead just begs a woman's hand to brush it aside." She sighed and swished her hand in front of her face. "That man is made for good loving and sweet kissing, and he's definitely worth a concerted effort."

"What's wrong with you?" Just moments ago Salena was warning Leisha against pining after Victor; now she was lusting after Chance.

"Nothing." Salena pulled off the gray band securing her ponytail, and as her sunset hair cascaded freely down her back, she combed fingers through it, then wet her lips. "How do I look?"

"Like Rapunzel dropping her hair to lure an unsuspecting prince up the tower." She had never seen her friend this enthralled with a man before, even her college sweetheart and fiancé, nor had she witnessed her preening to please a man. In the past, she had adamantly refused to change for any man, and she often dared them to accept her for the forthright, uncompromising woman she truly was.

Salena laughed. "Am I that obvious?"

"Yes." Leisha pulled her into the waiting room, then gently pushed her into a cushioned seat before plopping down herself. "Calm down and stop ogling the man." Even as she spoke, Leisha's own eyes were drawn to Chance Dearling's companion. "Doesn't his friend seem familiar?"

"Yes. But I can't place him."

"Neither can I."

As they watched, the men left the Nurses' Station, entering the waiting room and sitting beside each other only three rows in front of Salena and Leisha. The friend leaned forward, grabbing a magazine from the table and flipping absently through the pages. Chance removed a blue book from his pant pocket, clutched it in his right hand, and bowed his head over it.

"Should I introduce myself?"

"Yes, let him know you're his adopted sister."

Leisha cut her eyes at Salena. "We're not related."

Salena pursed her lips and rolled her eyes. "Go talk to the man."

"I will." Leisha stood, ready to face Chance, but a pink-faced, middle-aged doctor appeared, striding toward Chance and his friend.

"Mr. Dearling?" The doctor's pale eyes shifted between Chance and his companion.

Chance raised his head, rising to his feet. "I'm Chance Dearling."

"I'm Dr. Lee Davis, your brother's physician." He extended his hand, shaking Chance's.

"How's Victor?"

"Stable."

"Were you able to repair the knife damage and save his arm?"

"Fortunately, yes."

"Any brain injury?"

"We've run tests but haven't found any evidence of swelling or hemorrhaging. However, we're keeping your brother under close observation, so we can monitor his condition for the next twenty-four hours."

"He'll recover, won't he?"

"We're optimistic that he will."

"That's a relief!" Chance shook his hand again. "When can I see him?"

"Shortly. He's already been moved to a private room."

After Chance had questioned the doctor further about Victor's condition and his recovery time, Dr. Davis nodded, then excused himself before leaving. Chance turned to his friend, exhaling audibly. "Thank God I don't have to call my parents with more bad news."

His friend stood, patting Chance's shoulder. "God's good, remember?"

Silently, Leisha gave thanks for Victor being out of danger, then she walked toward Chance, her heart dancing in her chest. "Excuse me." She waited as his blue eyes seemed to consume her in a glance, finally stopping at her face. "You're Victor's brother, right?"

"Yes, I'm Chance Dearling." His stare was direct and intense. "You're Leisha Laurence, aren't you?"

She offered her right hand. "Yes."

Smiling, he firmly shook her hand. "Nice to finally meet you."

"Likewise."

Salena joined them, practically gluing herself to Leisha's side.

"This is Salena Blake, my best friend."

Chance leaned over, reaching for Salena's hand. "It's a pleasure, Ms. Blake."

"Call me Salena."

"Nice to meet you, Salena."

"You, too, Chance." Salena flashed her brightest, most cheerful smile before removing her hand from his. "Who's *your* friend?"

Stepping aside, Chance beckoned the man forward. "Pastor Daniel Michael Winward." He faced Leisha. "He's your brother."

Leisha's jaw dropped and her eyes fastened on Daniel. "*You're* my twin?"

Daniel nodded, brandishing the sunniest smile. "Yes, and you and I have thirty-six years to catch up on."

Speechless, Leisha could only gawk, with tears welling in her eyes. *Here was her brother, her own flesh and blood, her own family, and he was a complete stranger.*

Chapter Fifteen

Now it is God who makes both us and you stand firm in Christ. He anointed us, set his seal of ownership on us, put his spirit in our hearts as a deposit, guaranteeing what is to come.

2 Corinthians 1:21–22 (NIV)

Corinth Medical Center
Tuesday, June 28

At eight, Chance suggested everyone leave and get some rest, and Daniel was surprised when Leisha offered him a guestroom in her apartment. He hadn't expected her to invite him into her home—her haven—especially after their initial meeting. Since then, she had been relatively quiet and firmly attached to her friend Salena's side, occasionally glancing his way.

Chance faced Daniel. "I'll unlock the car so you can get your bags."

"Thank you."

Chance pulled the car key from his pocket, then addressed Leisha and Salena. "Do you mind if Daniel and I escort you to the parking garage?"

Salena stood and grabbed her purse. "Of course not."

Leisha smiled, first at Chance then at Daniel. "You're both kind. Thank you."

Chance nodded. "No problem."

Salena looped her arm through Chance's, leading him from the waiting room to the elevator, and Daniel walked in silence beside Leisha, still getting used to his sister's presence. In the elevator, Salena kept the conversation alive, and Daniel thought she had a very expressive and inviting personality. Unlike Leisha who'd been relatively quiet, Salena rarely seemed at a loss for words.

In the parking garage, the group separated.

Salena kissed and hugged Leisha, bade farewell to Chance and Daniel, then trotted toward a cherry-red convertible. She slid into the driver's seat, then drove away with the black top down and her red hair wildly dancing in the wind.

At his rented car, Chance pressed a button to open the trunk. Daniel hoisted his own large black suitcase out and onto the cemented ground and draped his carry-on bag onto his left shoulder. Chance closed the trunk and leaned over, hugging Daniel. "Thanks for coming and for offering support."

"You're welcome. Get some rest. Okay?"

"I will."

"Phone if you need me. The time doesn't matter. Just call, and I'll answer."

"Thanks. I will." Chance turned to Leisha. "Take care of yourself and get a good night's rest."

"I'll try."

Chance waved, then turned, heading back toward the elevator.

Leisha turned to Daniel. "Are you ready?"

He waved his right hand. "Lead the way, sis."

When she walked away, then stopped beside her car, Daniel chuckled.

She looked up, her forehead creased. "What's funny?"

"The color of your car."

"I don't get it."

"It's silver. So is my truck."

"So, we both like silver. It's just a coincidence."

"I believe in God, not in coincidences." He put his luggage in the trunk, then opened the passenger door, sank into his seat, and fastened his seatbelt. He turned to Leisha who was already in the driver's seat, her hands on the steering wheel. "I wonder what else we have in common."

"You're a minister, right?"

"An Associate Pastor at a church in Sutton, Georgia."

"How long have you been preaching?"

"Since age twenty, so about sixteen years."

"How'd it happen? Was it a choice?"

Daniel laughed. "Teaching was my first choice. But God had other plans, and He called me into ministry before I even graduated high school."

"So, He courted you?"

"In a manner of speaking. I was nine when I accepted Jesus as my Lord, Savior, and King, seventeen when I gave my first sermon before a congregation, and twenty when I officially accepted the call to preach. Throughout my life, I've always felt the presence of God and His hand covering and guiding me. But my most vivid sense of Him happened one night when I was nineteen and driving home from college. It was extremely dark and wet, and my car hydroplaned on the rain-slick road. I lost control, and the car slid into the other lane, then went careening into the tree line. All I knew to cry was, 'God.' I gripped the wheel and pounded the brake. Time slowed for me, and seeing death ahead, I squeezed my eyes shut, waiting for the end."

They stopped at a traffic light, and Leisha turned, looking at him, her eyes wide. "What happened?"

"God's grace. The tires got stuck in the mud. When I opened my eyes, all I saw were those trees straight ahead and all I heard was the chorus of a gospel song blaring from my radio: 'By and by when the morning comes.' I was shaken but alive, safe. I knew then God was really with me. He'd spared my life; *He'd* saved me. Since then, He's been my Rock—my foundation—and the Captain of my soul. And His will and mission have become my own."

The light turned green, and Leisha faced forward and drove through the intersection. "You're passionate about Him, aren't you?"

"I take Deuteronomy 6:5 seriously, loving the Lord completely, with all my heart, soul, mind, and might."

"I'm no minister, just a lawyer, but I know God has a purpose for me, too. He's given me a desire to help families, children."

"Do you want a family of your own?"

"Eventually."

"What's stopping you?"

"I haven't met the right man. Most of the ones I know don't care about marriage or kids. They're more interested in their careers, money, or sex."

"Have you looked in the right places?"

"I'm not looking at all. I don't date. I don't need the hassle of babysitting a man or stoking his ego. My life's fine as it is, and my job fulfills me."

"God created you for more than work, sis. He created you to love and be loved. You're fearfully and wonderfully made—a daughter of the King of kings—and I doubt you're meant to be alone for a lifetime."

"I'm not Ruth. Maybe I'm not meant to find then marry Boaz."

"Sounds like you've already given up on love."

"I don't want to make a mistake, giving my heart to a Bozo."

"There's a difference between being cautious and being fearful. One protects your life; the other paralyzes it, crippling you. If you let fear control your life, it'll take over, robbing you of a blessed life and every good gift God wants to give you."

Leisha sighed. "Maybe I'm the problem. In college, a few guys even called me Ice Princess."

"That must have hurt."

"I never let them see that."

Daniel's heart ached for her. She was a beautiful woman, yet some part of her was wounded, hurting, reserved. She needed healing, encouragement, love. "Are you still wearing a mask, still protecting yourself?"

"I'm a lawyer, and perception is everything. I can't always express what I feel, especially if it makes me look insecure or worse, weak."

"It's hard to make a genuine connection with a man if you don't occasionally risk your heart—if you don't let him get close enough to love you."

"Haven't you been listening? I don't want to get hurt."

"You won't ever be happy hiding, running away, or living in isolation, sis. I know that from experience. It gets old and lonely. Life is meant to be shared and enjoyed, preferably with someone who understands and complements you. Have you ever met such a man—someone who's tempted you, making you dream of marriage, kids, your own family?"

"In the past, no."

"What about recently?"

She glanced at him. "There's one man. He's managed to slip past my defenses. But he hasn't gotten far because I've done nothing but run from him."

"Why?"

"We're strangers. And I'm not ready to risk my heart on him, especially if he doesn't love me."

"If you give him a chance, you might discover he's the *right* man—your Boaz."

Leisha shook her head, her eyes looking forward toward the dark road ahead. "He's a great guy, but he's not a good investment for my heart."

"Why not?"

"He's younger."

"How much?"

"Six years."

"That's not a problem, sis. A man doesn't have to be older than the woman he loves."

"That's not all. He comes with complications, extra baggage."

"He has kids?"

"No."

"Addictions?"

"Not likely."

"A criminal record?"

"He's a good guy—law-abiding—and he who works with kids."

"Sounds like he's a prize worth fighting for."

"He's forbidden."

"Married or engaged?"

"No."

"With another woman?"

"He's single."

"An unbeliever?"

"He's a Christian."

"What exactly *is* the problem, sis? Why can't you be with this man?"

"It's complicated."

"You can speak freely. I won't judge you."

"I'm just confused myself, trying to sort through my feelings for the man."

"How long have you known him?"

"About two weeks."

"Is it about lust or attraction, or is it about something deeper, something more?"

"I care about him. A lot. And with him, it's about admiration and affection, fairy tales, hearts, candy, roses, and romance. That scares me most. He's my dream man—someone I can actually love."

"Does he feel the same?"

"We haven't really talked, at least about love or our feelings."

"Maybe you should so you both can openly confront and resolve your feelings."

"That's a conversation I'm not ready for."

"Then pray and trust God for an answer. If this relationship is meant to be, He'll open a door for you and this man. If it's not His will, He'll shut the door and you'll know that He has someone else for you, someone who'll bless and not burden you."

Leisha remained quiet, and Daniel knew she was mulling over his words. As he turned, staring out the passenger window, he silently prayed that she found the courage she needed and the comfort, love, and companionship that she so obviously desired.

A fluffy white dog greeted Leisha and Daniel in the living room of the apartment, jumping on Leisha and licking her hand, then turning to Daniel, sniffing him. After dropping his suitcase beside the sofa and lowering his carry-on bag to the carpeted floor, Daniel leaned down, running fingers through the dog's fur. "Who's this guy?"

"Orion." Leisha watched as the dog licked Daniel's hand, his ivory tail swishing merrily. "He likes you."

Daniel laughed. "Good. I'm a dog lover."

"How many dogs do you have?"

"One named Mercy. She's a Golden Retriever rescued from an abusive home."

"Any problems?"

"No. She's a good dog—lovable and friendly." Daniel sat on the sofa, his hand resting on Orion's head. "How long have you had Orion?"

"Four years." Leisha sank into a beige recliner on his right. "Salena brought him to me after my parents died. Like her, he's become family."

"In time, I hope you'll consider me family as well." Daniel earnestly desired a closer relationship with Leisha. He knew one night wouldn't override thirty-six years of separation and that they had a long road to travel, but he still cared about Leisha and her well-being. In his heart he had already claimed her, considering her family. Now, he prayed she would view him as the same and permit him a permanent place in her life.

Leisha smiled and tucked a curl behind her right ear. "This is strange for me. I've never had a brother, and I don't even know how I'm supposed to act around you."

Daniel raised his hand from Orion and leaned over, touching his sister's arm. "We're in the same position. For thirty-six years I've been an only child. I've always dreamed of having a sister—someone to love and protect—and now I have you." He gently squeezed her arm. "Don't worry because of me and don't act out of the ordinary. I want to get acquainted with the *real* Leisha Laurence."

"I want to learn more about you, too."

He leaned back, relaxing with Orion at his feet. "Ask me then."

"Are you married?"

"Engaged."

"What's her name?"

"Taryn Kirkland, and we're getting married this year on Christmas Eve."

"Congratulations!"

"Thank you."

"What's your fiancée like?"

"Sweet and lovely, full of goodness and kindness."

"I'm happy for you." She smiled, but it didn't quite reach her eyes.

Daniel leaned forward and reached for her hand. "Your day for love will come, too, sis. Wait and see."

"Waiting is all I do."

"Then don't get discouraged. God doesn't forget His children or His promises."

"I'm thirty-six years old and getting older every year. Soon, it might be too late for me to have my own children." She pulled her hand away from his. "In my life, I've dreamed of having four things: my parents' love, my own law firm, a loving husband, and healthy children. I've got the law firm. But my parents are dead, so that first dream is lost. And with every year that passes, the rest are fading fast."

"Age isn't a problem for God; your doubt is. If you truly trust Him, then don't waste your time and energy worrying. All things will work together for your good in His timing. Have faith."

"Are you always this optimistic?"

"No. But I'm always prayerful, and I trust God, believing that with Him, all things are possible. Do you think you can muster that much faith for yourself?"

Leisha nodded. "I'll try." Leisha stood, then lifted his carry-on bag from the floor and hoisted it onto her right shoulder. "Follow me, and I'll show you to the guest room."

Daniel stood, grabbed his suitcase, and trailed her down the hallway to a spacious room with a cherry wood sleigh bed, a bureau, a glider, and a bookshelf filled to capacity. She dropped the carry-on bag onto the bed, then gave him a quick tour before returning to the doorway.

"When you're finished in here, come to the dining room."

"I will, and thank you again for letting me stay."

"You're welcome." Leisha stepped back and closed the door.

Daniel kneeled beside the bed, bowing his head. *Heavenly Father, thank You for grace and mercy, for provision and protection, for comfort and compassion, love and forgiveness, health and peace, and thank You for today's blessings, foremost this introduction to my sister. Please, grant her courage and wisdom, and guide her to a place of love, hope, and happiness. In Jesus' name I pray, Amen.*

After he had unpacked, Daniel left the guestroom and found Leisha in the dining room, sitting at a three-leaf table, with a plate prepared for him.

She pointed toward the vacant seat across from her. "Have a seat."

Daniel looked appreciatively over the meal, a true Southern feast: broccoli soup, meatloaf, mashed potatoes, green beans, yellow squash, cornbread muffins, and chocolate fudge for dessert. "You didn't have to cook for me."

"I didn't." She offered him a fork and napkin. "Those are leftovers."

"Well, it looks delicious, and I can already predict it'll taste even better."

"Do you mind giving thanks?"

"Not at all." He lowered his head, thanking God for the food, for Victor's healing and recovery, and for his and Leisha's meeting. Then, he raised his head, lifted his fork, and ate with pleasure, devouring everything. After he finished, he smiled and flashed Leisha a thumbs-up sign. "That meal was excellent, simply divine."

She smiled. "I'm glad you enjoyed it."

Daniel studied her face, his eyes drawn to that bruised right cheek. "Chance told me about the assault. How are you coping?"

"I really haven't had time to deal with it. I've been busy waiting for news on Victor." She brushed a stray curl from her face. "To be honest, I only invited you home because I didn't want to be alone tonight."

"Well, I'm here and grateful, just the same."

"You're not upset?"

"No. I'm just glad we're spending time together. Regardless of your motive."

"Devilon Fox is behind bars, and he can't hurt me. But I still feel unsettled and insecure, not quite myself."

"It's not unnatural what you're feeling." He reached across the table, covering her hand with his. "In time, you'll recover, you'll feel safe again, and you'll get your life back."

Tears shimmered in her eyes. "That's my prayer. Even though he didn't rape me physically, he still violated me and left me feeling dirty and beaten, worthless and weak. I blame myself for giving him that power—that opening—that opportunity."

"The assault was his fault, not yours."

"That's what Salena and my friend Mateo said, but I still feel responsible. Everybody warned me; the security guard even offered to escort me to the car, but I was proud and preoccupied. I didn't want to admit that I needed anyone's help, that I needed a man's protection."

"You didn't ask to be attacked, and you didn't deserve it, regardless of any mistake you made. Forgive yourself, sis."

"Forgiving is hard."

"Do it anyway."

"Is that an order?"

"Yes."

"I hate taking orders, especially from men."

"And why is that?"

"I'm not that submissive. I'm not some weak woman who needs a man controlling her thoughts and actions."

"Who are you, then?"

She dried tears with her right hand. "I'm a fighter. I'm independent, educated, and successful. I'm not some man's trophy, doll, or puppet, and I'll never be any man's beggar, servant, or slave. I don't need a man hijacking my life and ordering me around. Not Devilon Fox or anybody else."

"All men aren't bad, sis. They're not all control freaks, predators, or puppeteers."

"That's debatable."

Daniel rubbed her left hand. "Good men exist, Leisha, and the most faithful of them is waiting for the chance to love and marry you and make your dreams come true. For that man, submission isn't a weapon for abuse and control but a gift of love, trust, and respect."

"Seriously—submission is a gift?"

"According to God's plan, yes."

"That's a lot for me to digest. Especially tonight."

"At least think about it and pray for insight, wisdom."

"I will." She stared at him, her eyes shimmering in the light. "Thank you."

"For what?"

"Helping me relax."

"You're my sister, and I have thirty-six lost years to make up for."

"Am I stuck with you now?"

"Like a bad penny. Now that I've found you, I'm not losing you again."

Leisha stared at their bound hands, fresh tears gathering in her eyes. "That's good. Because I may not need a controlling man, but I do need a big brother—one who'll hold my hand through the storm, who'll offer me comfort after my darkest night, who'll walk in faith with me and never let me go."

Daniel rose from the table, drawing Leisha to her feet and around the table into his arms, his embrace. "I'm here, sis, and you can lean on me.

Always." He kissed her forehead, then gently placed her head on his right shoulder, letting her tremble and cry and release all those emotions she had been storing—hiding—since the attack.

Chapter Sixteen

Love does not delight in evil but rejoices with the truth.

1 Corinthians 13:6 (NIV)

Corinth Medical Center
Wednesday, June 29

*V*ictor opened his eyes and found himself in a hospital bed, sore, with his left arm bandaged and in a sling, and Chance sitting beside him, his head bowed and a Bible opened in his hands. "If you're really reading that Bible, I must be dead."

Chance glanced up, a smile of relief on his face. He closed the Bible and leaned over, gently hugging Victor. "Good morning, sleepy head." He ruffled Victor's hair. "You scared me, playing hero the other night. When I heard you were knifed in the arm, beaten, and struck in the head, I was afraid for you."

Victor met his eyes. "As you can see, I'm alive and well. I've got Jesus, plus those heavenly angels watching over me."

"For that, I'm thankful." He sat down. "How do you feel?"

"Like my whole body's been rammed through a meat grinder. How's Leisha?"

"Fine. She's just shaken and sporting a bruise on her face."

"Her attacker?"

"In police custody."

"Thank God."

"Why were you in that parking lot?"

"I was meeting Leisha so I could tell her about Mom's tumor." He closed his eyes, recalling that night. "When I arrived, I had the window down and the radio off. I heard a scream that sent chills through me; then, I saw a black-hooded man straddling a woman on the ground. I didn't think or plan. I just jumped from the truck, knocking him away from her. Then I struck him. I knew the woman was Leisha after she yelled my name." He opened his eyes and found Chance frowning.

"First, you romanced her with gifts, and now, you've risked your life for her." Chance looked at him closely. "You, the self-proclaimed peace-keeper, actually fought for her."

"She was in trouble."

"Are you in love with her?"

"I barely know her. She's an unsolved mystery."

"But you care about her anyway?"

"Yes. She's stubborn, but she's strong and brave. She's not selfish either. She stayed by my side, comforting me until help arrived. That night, she was one of my earth angels."

"Sounds like you love her."

Do I? That's the thousand-dollar question. Victor searched his own heart. "Since I've met her, she's never been far from my mind, and I pray for her daily, asking that God would guide her, bless, protect, and comfort her. In her presence, I'm happy and content. I feel electrically charged and spiritually inspired, and I want to make her smile, forget her worries, relax, and laugh. I want to protect her, take care of her, and save her from all hurt and harm. If all of that defines love, then I love her."

"After one meeting?"

"Yes."

Chance rubbed his forehead. "Are you going to tell her how you feel?"

"I don't want to blindside her or chase her away, especially if she doesn't feel the same."

"I hate to rain gloom and doom, brother, but you've got to consider more than yourself and Leisha. Think of our parents. Leisha is their biological daughter; you're their adopted son. You two are related—family. A romantic relationship between you would be taboo."

"Leisha and I are not blood relatives. So, there's no incest involved.

And if we were to fall in love, Mom and Dad would accept us as a couple. They'd want us both to be happy. Together. Because they love us. Period."

"That's a rosy, romantic view, not a guarantee, and you're setting yourself up for disappointment, grief, and heartache. That's why you need to nip whatever blossoming feelings you have for Leisha now before your heart gets any more involved."

"You've never been in love."

"Why is that relevant?"

"Love defies logic, and it's not a faucet you can easily turn on and off. The heart loves whom it will, for better or worse." His failed relationship with Shayna Riven had taught him that much.

"You're entering the danger zone. Be careful."

"Don't worry. I'll be fine. I know how to protect myself."

A knock sounded on the door, then Leisha peeked inside. "You're awake!"

"Come in." Victor beckoned her forward and then drank plentifully as she walked toward the bed, wearing a melon pink blouse and dark green slacks, with her thick, brown curls clamped in a barrette. The only blemish he saw was the round, bluish-black bruise on her cheek.

Chance nodded. "It's good to see you again."

Leisha smiled. "You too."

"Did you have a peaceful night?"

"I did."

"I'm glad." Chance turned to Victor. "I'll leave so you two can talk privately."

"Daniel's waiting outside if you want some company."

Victor leaned forward. "Daniel's here?"

"He came with me yesterday. He spent the night at Leisha's."

Victor turned to Leisha. "What's he like?"

"Kind, considerate, loving, and protective."

"I can't wait to meet him."

"He's a good guy. He even stayed up with me until eleven last night, just letting me unload and cry."

"I'm glad he was there, that you didn't spend the night alone."

Chance coughed discreetly, getting Victor's attention. "I'll be outside with Daniel. I'll check with you later."

"Okay. See you." He watched Chance leave, closing the door. Then, he devoted his full attention to Leisha. "Have a seat." He motioned toward the chair Chance had vacated.

Leisha sat down, then removed his black cell phone from her purse and handed it to him. "This is yours. You dropped it in the parking lot, during the fight."

Victor accepted it, his fingers brushing hers. "Thank you." He laid the phone on a nearby table. When Leisha grabbed his right hand, folding it in hers, he was pleasantly surprised and definitely content. He lifted his eyes, drawn to the depth of concern he saw reflected there.

"Thank you for saving me."

"You're welcome." Victor raised their hands, then kissed hers. "Are you okay?"

"Other than being a little scraped and bruised, I'm alive, with my virtue intact. I owe you."

"No, you don't. I'm just thankful you're safe."

She looked toward his arm. "Are you all right?"

"I'm sore but better, now that I've seen you."

"Why were you so anxious to meet me that night?"

"Sunday night I learned Mom has a brain tumor."

Leisha gasped, and her eyes grew round. Without hesitating, she leaned over, carefully hugging him. "I'm sorry to hear that. I know how much you love your parents. Is the tumor operable?"

"Dad only shared the diagnosis. After he told me, though, I wanted to call you."

She leaned back. "Why didn't you?"

He stared deep into those amber eyes, mesmerized. "It was late, and

I didn't know if you would welcome my call or even pick up. After all, you've been avoiding me and giving me the silent treatment since our first meeting."

She bowed her head, averting her eyes. "I've been busy."

Victor raised her chin. "Work is a convenient barrier for you, Leisha. I work and have obligations, too, yet I don't barricade myself in the office until nine o'clock. I take time to relax, and I definitely make time for family and friends—the people who matter most."

"I can't afford distractions."

"Is that what I've become?"

"My life hasn't been normal since I met you."

"Neither has mine, but I don't regret meeting you or infiltrating your life over the past two weeks. I want you to trust me even though I make you uncomfortable, even though I've shattered your illusions about your family, and even though you're afraid of meeting your birth parents. I've put my life on hold for two weeks. For you. Now, it's time for you to make a decision: Come with me or stay here."

"Why now?"

"I'm going home after my release from the hospital. I need to be there. For my family. For Mom. Because for me, love is selfless, not self-centered."

Tears glistened in her eyes. "I understand: your family matters."

"Yes, family is important to me." He lifted his hand, pressing it to his heart. "I don't want to go home alone. When I leave, I want you to come with me."

"For your parents?"

"For you, too. This reunion could heal my parents and you."

"I'm fine."

"You're hurting and you're closing your heart instead of opening it to love and family. But it's time for you to take a chance—on this new family and this new friend."

She dried her tears. "You?"

"Me."

She laughed. "Even when I'm stubborn and disagreeable, you don't give up. Do you?"

"If it's a worthy cause, about God, or even a matter of heart, I'll fight for it."

"I get it: You're a man of conviction, and you only fight for what you believe in. Your parents are lucky to have you."

"I'm willing to fight for you too, Leisha. In case you haven't noticed, I care about you."

"You do?"

"Yes."

She frowned. "I'm not family, I'm not your sister, your responsibility. So, why?"

"You're my friend, Leisha."

"You really consider me a friend?"

Victor smiled. "Yes."

"All right! I'll be your friend."

"Will you come home with me?"

Leisha sighed. "You're like a broken record, stuck on one song, aren't you?"

"Give me a good answer, and I'll stop asking."

"I'll talk to Daniel about it. Then, I'll give you my final answer."

"I'll give you one day to make a choice. After that, if all's well medically, I'm going home, even without you."

"I understand." Leisha removed her hand from his. "I'll leave so you can rest."

"I'm glad you came. Really. Your visit means a lot to me."

"I couldn't stay away, especially after what you did for me. I'm thankful you're alive and recuperating. God answered my prayers."

His heart somersaulted, thumping his chest like crazy. "You prayed for me?"

"Constantly, since the attack."

"I've been praying for you too, since our first meeting."

Her eyes pierced his own. "You care that much?"

"Yes."

"I care about you, too."

He grabbed her hand. "Trust me then."

"You're asking a lot. And I don't know if I can trust myself with the right decision." She pulled her hand from his and retreated to the door.

"If you won't trust me and you can't trust yourself, trust God, Leisha. He won't fail you."

She silently bobbed her head, then opened the door and walked away.

Victor stared blankly at the door, keenly feeling Leisha's absence. More than anything he wanted to call her back, wrap his arm around her, and kiss all that sadness and hurt away. That was dangerous territory, though. Because if he ever held her in his arms or kissed her from the depth of his heart, he knew he'd never let her go. Ever.

.

Chapter Seventeen

Delight yourself in the Lord and he will give
you the desires of your heart.

Psalm 37:4 (NASB)

Corinth Medical Center
Wednesday, June 29

*I*n the waiting room, Chance asked Leisha how her visit went.

"Fine. Victor's going home after his release. He asked if I would go with him. Home. To Crossland."

"Are you?"

"I need to talk to Daniel first."

Chance glanced from one twin to the other. "I'll leave then." He turned and stepped away, but Leisha grabbed his arm and stopped him.

"Salena invited us to dinner at Escape tonight. You're included. I'd love for you to come too. Also by then, Daniel and I should have our decision made."

"Okay. I'll come."

"Thank you." She opened her purse, pulling a pen and a scrap of paper from it, then she jotted down the address and handed the paper to him. "We'll be dining at eight."

"Formal or casual?"

"Formal."

"I'll see you there." Chance hugged her, then clapped Daniel on the back. "Bye." He turned, then strode toward his brother's room.

From his bed, Victor looked up. "What's new, *hermano*?"

Chance closed the door. "You're being released on Friday, and I've agreed to a dinner date tonight with Leisha, her friend Salena, and Daniel."

"That's great news! On both counts. So, where are you guys going?"

"Some fancy place called Escape."

"You buying a suit?"

Chance shuddered. "I hate suits."

"That's better than wearing Ol' Faithful, that leather jacket you got with your first real paycheck. Rain or shine, winter or summer, you wear it, like a rebel. Like it's your trademark. You've had it since your rookie year as an officer. Said it suited you, expressed your attitude, and made you stand out as different in a uniformed, cookie-cutter world. Even told me it was your fist raised against God. If you ask me, it's an eyesore, nothing more than a symbol of pain and pride, and it's time for you to bury it or burn it." Victor fixed steady eyes on Chance, then suddenly scrunched his face.

"What's wrong?"

"You're not wearing the jacket."

"No, I'm not."

"Where is it?"

"In my suitcase. I've retired it."

"After all this time, why?"

"The jacket's old—worn and tattered—a tribute to a rebellious past. In the last two weeks, I've changed and moved on. I'm not the same man. I'm a new creature in Christ, and I don't need that jacket as an expression, a shield, or a curse anymore. I have Jesus, and He's enough."

Victor's face lit like a match. "You're a believer? Really?"

Chance nodded and grinned. "Yes. Really. I surrendered my life Sunday night at approximately ten forty-five."

"Wow! What a gift! You're saved." Victor hugged him, then pulled back, with tears in his eyes. "You've got to tell me, *hermano*: What happened?"

Chance leaned back and sat down on a chair. "I stopped running, and I sat still long enough to listen. The more I learned about Daniel, the more I learned about God. Even the sermons made sense and seemed just for me. Dad even said I had two choices: run to God or away from Him. After he told me about Mom's tumor, I had nowhere to turn but to God. Alone I couldn't save Mom or myself. I sought Daniel's help, and he led me through the confession of faith. He even gave me a Bible, and I've been reading it."

"Here's an answered prayer, Chance. Mom and Dad will love it too. They've been praying for you. For years. Even when we were kids."

"I know, and I'm grateful."

"So, where are you staying?"

"At a motel two blocks from here."

"You don't want to be late tonight. You should leave, get everything in order."

He glanced at his watch. "I've got time."

"No, you don't. You've got to buy a suit. Or at least a new jacket and dress pants."

Chance groaned. "For me, this is hell—shopping."

"It's for a good cause."

"It's another headache."

"If you stop complaining and being stubborn, you might actually enjoy yourself."

"I'd rather call Leisha and cancel."

Victor shoved a finger in his face. "Don't you dare!"

"I could camp out here and keep you company."

"I'm not a kid anymore. I don't need a babysitter."

"You don't want me to stay?"

"Stop stalling, Chance. Leave the fortress, get out, and socialize."

He folded his arms. "I'm not a suit-and-tie guy."

"Well, we're changing your script tonight, and the jeans and boots are out. You're buying a suit and some new shoes, too, then you're going to relax and have fun. You're even going to let down your guard and show Leisha, her friend Salena, and Daniel that there's a lighter side to your personality."

"I'm not making any promises."

"At least make an effort." Victor waved his hand. "Now, go."

Reluctantly, Chance lowered his arms, stood, and walked to the door. "I'll call you later."

"Good, 'cause I'll be waiting for an update."

Later, Chance arrived at Escape, wearing a trendy black jacket, dress pants, and a white shirt. The hostess led him to the back of the restaurant where Salena Blake sat alone. Chance nodded to her, then sat down, for the first time really noticing the woman elegantly draped in a ruby-red knee-length dress, with long, dark red curls spilling over her shoulders. Diamond teardrops dangled from her earlobes, and crimson lip gloss drew his eyes to her plush upturned lips. "Hello."

"Hello, Chance." She studied him. "You look handsome. Especially in that suit."

"Thanks. You look nice, too."

Salena wrinkled her nose. "Only nice?"

"Are you fishing for compliments?"

She laughed. "Obviously. You're supposed to say I'm breathtaking, even striking."

"I stand corrected. You look great, positively stunning."

Salena preened. "Thank you."

"Are the twins here?"

"On their way. Leisha called and said they'd be here in fifteen minutes. So make yourself comfortable." Salena motioned for a waiter. "I don't drink wine, so I'm ordering ginger ale. What's your preference?"

"Ginger ale is fine."

The waiter took their orders, then left menus before leaving.

"How long have you and Leisha been friends?"

"We were dorm mates our freshman year in college."

"Are you a lawyer too?"

"A news reporter at KTCN."

He wasn't surprised. Where else would a tall, gorgeous woman be but in front of someone's camera? The dark red hair was her best feature, almost like sunset or sunrise, depending on the mood, the setting. "How long have you worked there?"

"Since I was twenty-three, so about twelve years."

The waiter returned and placed their drinks on the table in front of them. Salena thanked him, then said that they would order when their friends arrived. After he left, Salena concentrated on Chance. "What else would you like to know?"

"It's your life. You tell me."

She smiled enticingly. "Okay. The essentials. I'm single, and I'm a Christian. My birthday's May 26, and I'm thirty-six. My parents are A.R. Wallace and Ruthanne Blake, a farmer and housewife, and I have nine siblings—five brothers and four sisters."

Ten kids? Chance recalled the old nursery rhyme about the old woman who lived in a shoe and had so many children she didn't know what to do. "Your parents really have ten kids?"

"I'm the seventh. Until I left for college, I lived and worked on the family farm in rural east Texas."

"So you're a small-town farm girl?"

"Born and raised. We had a rooster, some chickens, and a few pigs. But Dad mostly grew fruit and vegetables. And everybody pitched in, doing his or her part."

Chance tried to imagine Salena Blake caked in dirt, tending pigs, but he couldn't reconcile those images with the woman sitting across from him. "What was it like, living in a house with eleven people?"

"Noisy but never dull. Having privacy was hard, though."

"That, I can imagine." Chance was thankful for his own small family and for all the personal time his parents had devoted equally to him and Victor. He and Victor might joke about their parents having favorites, but neither of them had really felt any lack, especially in the love department. "From farming to journalism is quite a leap, isn't it?"

"Farming was my father's passion, never mine. I could never devote my life to it because I craved excitement, freedom, travel, adventure. I thrive on action. And I love playing detective and solving mysteries, just like you."

Chance tilted his head. "What could you possibly know about me?"

Her eyes gleamed. "More than you can imagine. Your birth name is Chance Holden Brayden, and you were adopted before your tenth birthday, which is July the fourth. Your favorite color's blue, your favorite sport is football, and in every game, you always cheer for the underdog. You're a private investigator, formerly a police detective. You've got a college degree, a clean record, and good credit. You're thirty-two years old, a bachelor, and you've lived with your brother Victor since your return home from Dallas. And, apparently, you're discreet and keep your girlfriends hidden because you've never been seen or photographed with one."

Chance folded his arms. "How do you know so much?"

"I'm good at my job."

"Still, why dig up dirt in my backyard?"

"Leisha's my friend, more like a sister, and she's had a rough life. Especially since her parents' accident. Anything I can do to protect her, I'll do, even investigate her birth family, the Dearlings. That includes you and Victor."

"My parents are both ministers. Good people. All they do is give and love, help and encourage. They're not manipulative, underhanded, or dangerous, and they're no threat to Leisha. Neither am I."

"What about your brother?"

"He's harmless, more gentle than violent. And he got hurt saving her. That alone should speak volumes."

"Okay. He's a good guy—heroic." She leaned forward. "So, answer me this: Why aren't *you* married?"

He shrugged and unfolded his arms. "I'm not interested. Never have been." He leaned in, his face inches from hers. "What about you, Ms. Blake?"

"I haven't found a man yet who could match me or hold my attention."

"So you're a challenge, difficult to please?"

"I'm independent and selective. Some men even call me aggressive, intimidating."

"Are you?"

"Depends on the man, even more on the situation. I'm honest, confident, and fearless. Some men can't handle that in a woman."

She had piqued his interest. "How fearless are you?"

"I like skydiving, bungee jumping, exposing criminals, and flying helicopters."

"You're a thrill seeker?"

"More like an adventurer. I don't run from a challenge. I don't stay home twiddling my thumbs or clicking a remote through TV channels. I don't hide from danger or life. I get out, meet new people, listen to their stories, and explore wherever the Lord leads me." She pinned Chance with intense brown eyes. "I'm rarely passive, and I'm more than a pretty face in front of a camera, talking about newsmakers. I get involved, get my hands dirty, and try to make a difference. On my job and in the community. And in my twelve years at the news station, I've survived tornadoes, hurricanes, fires, floods, politicians and criminals, all without flinching or running away."

Chance eased back in his seat. "Unusual, that's what you are."

"Is that a compliment or criticism?"

"A compliment."

She smiled, then snapped her fingers. "Firecracker."

"Firecracker?"

"My nickname. What's yours?"

"Don't have one."

"I've got a perfect one, just for you."

"What?"

"Blue Eyes."

"Not that original, is it?"

"It's appealing, and it suits you. Are you interested?"

"In the name?"

"In me, Detective."

"I don't date."

"You just haven't met the right woman."

"You think you're the *one*—Ms. Right?"

She leaned forward, covering his hand on the table with hers. "Is that so inconceivable?"

"Yes." He pulled his hand from hers. "I have doubts."

"What? Are you afraid of me?"

"If you're delusional, I should be."

Her eyes grew wide. "You think I'm crazy?"

"Aren't you?"

"Of course not! My mind's completely sound."

"Then you must be lonely and desperate."

"I'm neither."

"You did a background check on me, and you think you're my soul mate, even though we're strangers. That doesn't inspire much trust or confidence on my part."

"We're not strangers, and I never said we were soul mates."

"You implied it."

"You're a great catch, Blue Eyes, and I'm casting my net tonight. Just for you. So stop struggling, surrender, and let me reel you in."

"I'm not a fish. I'm a man."

"And I'm a woman." She raised a brow. "Haven't you noticed?"

"I don't want to be caught."

"Then, toss your rope, Blue Eyes, and try to catch me."

Pursue her? Really? His heart rammed against his chest. "Absolutely not!"

Her eyes twinkled like they were laughing at him. "Aren't you even tempted, just to find out whether you can handle a firecracker like me without getting burned?"

He wouldn't tell her that those Fourth of July and New Year's fireworks had always thrilled him or that as an adolescent he'd always been fascinated by sparklers and firecrackers. They didn't scare him, because he knew how to handle them. Not once had he ever been singed or burned. Not once had he been afraid of fire. Salena didn't need to know everything about him. Especially that. "No, I'm not tempted."

She tilted her head. "Why not?"

"You're not a blonde, you don't have blue eyes, and you don't have dimples."

Indignation shone on her face, in her expressive eyes. "Seriously?"

Chance laughed. "No. I'm not that shallow, and I don't have a preference."

"But you do have a sense of humor."

"Occasionally." He grew sober. "You're an attractive woman, gorgeous even, but I'm not interested in dating. Even you. Period."

"Can't you feel the sparks, the chemistry between us?"

He crossed his arms. "Not really."

She frowned, staring him down. "You're lying, Blue Eyes. But even though you won't admit it, I will: I'm attracted to you and I'd like to spend more time with you. Alone."

Chance had never met a woman as bold as Salena Blake—one who placed every card on the table and didn't hide anything. The woman *was* a firecracker. Although she intrigued him, he still couldn't envision dating her or any other woman. He had to get himself straight, and he couldn't afford any distractions.

Leisha and Daniel arrived and offered apologies.

Leisha sat beside Salena, across from Daniel. Makeup skillfully hid the bruise on her right cheek. "Have you two ordered yet?"

"We were waiting on you." Salena raised her hand, getting their waiter's attention; then, she requested two menus.

Chance sipped his ginger ale, wondering why Salena had suddenly set her sights on him. As far as he knew, he hadn't sent her any signals that he was available or interested. If anything, he'd been polite but distant. He was getting his life in order now, and he wasn't ready for a committed relationship, for love. And from what he had learned already, Salena wasn't a woman a man could trifle with or ignore.

The waiter returned and they all ordered. After the food arrived, they enjoyed both a delicious meal and lively but light conversation.

After he had finished his dessert, Daniel palmed his hands over his plate, his eyes on Chance. "My sister and I are going home with you and Victor."

"Seriously?"

"We're ready, and we'd like to meet your parents."

"This is great! Thank you!" He couldn't wait to share the good news, letting his parents know that their children were finally coming home. "Mom and Dad need this. They need *you*."

Leisha waved her hand. "Don't get excited. We're only staying a few days. We're not guaranteeing a lifelong commitment."

"At least you're taking this first step. From here forward, we'll just pray for the best and take one day at a time." Chance excused himself, then escaped to the secluded balcony so he could phone his brother. "How are you?"

"Bored. You?"

"Better than you, and I've got good news."

"Let me guess: The Fortress of Solitude is gone, you've finally met the woman of your dreams, and you've fallen in love."

"Wrong!"

"Then what's your news?"

"Leisha and Daniel are coming home with us."

"Praise God! Mom and Dad will be ecstatic."

"Yes, they will. Now, get some rest. I'll see you tomorrow."

"See you later, *hermano*. Goodnight."

After Victor disconnected, Chance slipped the phone into his pant pocket and glanced toward the dark, boundless sky, his eyes settling on a brilliant moon. Closing his eyes, he silently prayed, asking God to strengthen his family, to favor them all and make this family reunion a joyous one. A gentle hand on his shoulder startled him, and he jerked, opening his eyes. "Salena?"

"If you want solitude, I'll leave."

Solitude? Am I really a fortress—an iceberg—keeping others away? Is that the kind of man I want to be—cold, distant, boring, hard? Maybe it's time I let somebody in. Maybe it's time to thaw that ice from my heart and really change. For the better. Maybe it's time I take a risk and let down my guard. "Stay, please."

"Thank you."

Chance knew he wasn't as handsome, charming, or compassionate as his brother, nor did he have Daniel's wisdom, faith, or charisma. So, he was curious. "Why me?"

Salena folded her arms. "You're genuine—honest and real. Except when you're confronted about your feelings and you lie." She smiled. "I'll forgive you and offer you another chance, though." She lowered her hands, placing one on her hip. "Are you interested in me? Do you find me attractive?"

Chance raked rough fingers through his hair. "I'm a new believer. I've never been in a relationship, and I'm returning home Friday." He stared deep into her eyes. "Honestly, tonight's all you and I have together. Once I go home, I doubt our lives will ever cross again. So, whether I'm interested in you or not doesn't matter."

"You're not running from me so easily, Chance." She stepped forward and looped her arms around his neck. "I'm bold and fearless, and I don't run from challenges, remember?"

Her perfume danced beneath his nose, and he had no choice but to steady himself, with both hands firmly on her waist. Surprisingly, she felt natural in his arms, like she belonged there.

"You like me, don't you?"

He sighed. "Against my better judgment, yes. I like you."

She snuggled against him, invading his space. "Enough to kiss me?"

"No."

She stepped back, frowning. "More than anything, I hate lies, Chance. I'm a journalist, and my mission is always to uncover the truth. Also, I'm a smart, passionate redhead, not some gullible, placid blonde. So, lie to me once, and I'll forgive you. Lie to me twice, and I'll pray for you. Lie to me again, and I'll distrust you. Keep lying and this firecracker will flare up and burn you. Quite literally."

"I'm not afraid, Salena."

"Prove it. Kiss me."

The woman was tenacious. "You do like playing with fire."

"As long as I don't get burned."

"Why do you want me to kiss you?"

"So you'll enjoy your first kiss."

"I'm not some thirty-two-year-old virgin. I've kissed a woman before and done more than that, even later."

Salena's eyes grew wide. "Really?"

"Yes."

"Who was she?"

"A fellow officer."

"Was she your girlfriend?"

"She was my partner."

"Were you in love with her?"

"I cared about her. As a friend."

"What about her? Did she love you?"

"She thought she did."

"How long were you together?"

"Four years."

"If you didn't love her, why would you stay? Kiss her? Have an affair—"

"Why do you even care?"

"I already told you: I like you. I'm curious, too."

"Be honest, Salena. You're just nosy and jealous."

"I'll admit it; I am. Now, tell me what happened to the woman."

"A month after I resigned and left the police department, she was killed in the line of duty. She was only twenty-nine, a year younger than me." For two years Chance had blamed himself for Dana Santoya's death, first because he had taken advantage of her and second because he hadn't been around to protect her. After all, for four years, their lives revolved around each other. They had been partners, friends, and more. Even if he hadn't been in love with Dana, he had cared about her and loved her in his own imperfect way.

"Have you been with any women since her?"

"I'm not prowling the streets, Salena. I'm no womanizer, playboy, Don Juan, or Casanova. What you see in me is what you get—a bachelor."

"So you haven't kissed a woman lately?"

"Sorry to disappoint you, but I've been busy. I haven't completed this year's random-woman kissing quota."

She laughed. "Seriously, are you going to kiss me or not?"

"Not."

"Let me kiss you then." Before Chance could object or pull away, she lowered his head and planted a soft, tantalizingly sweet kiss on his left cheek. A kiss so gentle but strong it left an imprint, warming both his skin and his heart. She stepped back, with her eyes glistening and her left arm resting on his shoulder. She raised her right hand and gently brushed the stray lock from his forehead, before combing her fingers through his hair. Just like his mother—Eileen.

Chance jerked like he'd been singed. "What was that?"

Salena lowered both arms to her sides, a contented smile on her face. "A love note, Blue Eyes—something for you to remember me by." She raised her hand again, thumbing a smear of lip gloss from his cheek.

"Why did you do it?"

"You're irresistible, and I couldn't waste the moment."

"Why not a real kiss?"

"I'm not a thief or a kissing bandit. Stealing kisses from an unwilling partner is not what I do. Not who I am. I only take what's freely given. So, when you're ready, we'll kiss."

Salena was a mystery, a contradiction, and she left Chance confused. "Who are you, really? The virgin or vixen?"

"I'm the best woman you'll ever meet—your equal—your match."

"You know hard facts, Salena. You don't know the real me."

"I'm willing to learn. But are you willing to teach?"

"This isn't a classroom. This is my personal life. And I'm not giving you a crash course in Chance 101."

"Why are you fighting me?"

"I'm not."

"Then, what are you running from?"

He crossed his arms, tired of her digging and probing. "Nosy stalkers who kiss strangers."

"I'm no stalker, and you know it."

"But you do kiss strange men, don't you?"

"You're the *second* man I've been interested in or even kissed. I'm not promiscuous, and I don't give my heart, my time, or my kisses to every man I meet."

Chance lowered his arms. "You're beautiful and smart, funny and bold. You could have any man you want. Why set your sights on me?"

"You're a special breed of man, and for some reason, I'm drawn to you."

"I'm no different than any other man. So, why?"

She sighed. "When I look in your eyes, I see glimpses of the man behind the mask. A good man, full of integrity, courage, loyalty, love, kindness, humor, and strength. Someone I could love. But you apparently don't see all that in yourself. And you won't share any of it, at least not with a woman like me. Because you're afraid, and something's holding you back, keeping you isolated, alone. And I've seen something else in your eyes and heard it in your voice. Sadness. Resignation.

"Since I've met you, you've been more serious than relaxed, more closed off than open. Polite but distant, physically present but emotionally absent. Almost as hard and thick as a stone wall. That bothers me. Because you're a man made for laughter and smiles, love and happiness, friends and fun. But it doesn't seem like you've had those in your life. At least not on a regular basis. And that makes me sad.

"Because in you I see hope, a future, potential, and even how great you could be as a husband and father if you would just share your heart and invite the right woman into your life."

Tears glistened in her eyes, then streamed down her cheeks. "You need more fire, passion, and adventure in your life alongside tenderness, comfort, and calm. You need someone who'll encourage and pray for you, who'll love and counsel you, who'll even tease and tickle you just so you don't take yourself so seriously. You need someone like me. A firecracker. And that kiss was more for you than me; it was meant to crack that stone wall, shake you up, and spark your interest so you'd actually see the woman standing in front of you and realize she's worthy of your notice, your respect, your heart."

Chance reached out, brushed the tears from her face, then lowered his hands. "Since I walked in, I've noticed you, Salena. I respect you, too. I'm just not ready to offer my heart or my time. To any woman, not just you. I'm not a closet romantic, and I've never believed in love at first sight."

She looked up, her brown eyes shimmering. "Do you believe in love?"

"Yes."

"And marriage?"

"Yes."

"God?"

"I do."

"Then anything is possible, and you're worth my time."

"I'm not Mr. Right."

"You're more than that, Chance. You're a prince, and you don't even know it." She dried tears with her fingers. "If you don't know who you really are, you'll never find that place you're meant to be or that life you're meant to have. That's the real difference between us: I have an identity in Christ; you haven't found yours yet."

Identity in Christ? What's that supposed to mean? Chance was moving into unchartered territory, and he didn't know how to navigate around a woman as direct and determined as Salena Blake. For some reason, she had latched on to him, and he didn't know how to disengage her. "Where do we go from here—from the kiss?"

"Dancing." Salena grabbed his arm, twined her fingers with his, and pulled him from the dimly-lit balcony toward the twinkling lights inside. On the dance floor, she wrapped her arms around his neck, lifted her face, and smiled, with sadness in her eyes. "No need to be afraid of me, Blue Eyes. I'm smart enough to read the clues you keep dropping. So we'll dance the night to its conclusion, and before the clock strikes twelve, our fairy tale will come to its scripted end: the daring princess will go on her adventures, the lonely prince will return to his castle of stone, and their happily-ever-after with each other will be as distant as the heavenly stars."

Salena's words should have pleased Chance, but they didn't. He wasn't elated; he was disappointed. And as he held her in his arms, and he and she danced through one song, then another, he wondered whether rejecting Salena had been his best decision or his worst mistake. Would she fade in his memory and be easily forgotten? Or would memories of her pursue him, following him all the way home?

Chapter Eighteen

Whether you turn to the right or to the left, Your ears will hear a voice behind you saying, "This is the way; walk in it."

Isaiah 30:21 (NIV)

Texas Highway
Friday, July 1

As Chance drove and Victor sat in the front passenger seat of his truck, Leisha and Daniel rode in the back seats, each looking out of the window as gospel music drifted from the radio during the four-hour journey.

Daniel leaned forward, his hand on the back of Victor's seat. "What kind of place is Crossland?"

"The heartland, about three hours from Heaventon Hope, known for its fruit production, but the business district is thriving, and the historic district is a tourist haven. Even the railway that cuts west of town adds to the old hometown feel."

Daniel imagined the town as Victor described it—a little-known treasure. "It sounds like a great place."

"It's the best, especially during the holidays. It's a deep Southern experience with turkey legs and baked beans and deviled eggs around Resurrection Sunday, barbecue brisket and potato salad during Memorial Day weekend; fireworks and patriotic anthems during Independence Day; food, family, and fellowship during Thanksgiving; and carols, giving, and goodwill during Christmas. It's all about family, love, home."

"You really love it, don't you?"

"I do. The people are friendly too. Both you and Leisha will get to experience that hospitality on the Fourth of July. Usually, our family goes to the fireworks show at Hope Park and camp on the grounds with other families, eating chili dogs, barbecue chicken, turkey legs, and hamburgers."

Daniel eased back in his seat. "Are you still living with your parents?"

"Chance and I have our own house, about four blocks away."

"Where will Daniel and I stay?"

"At our parents' house. Chance and I will be there too. Is that a problem?"

"Seems overcrowded and complicated."

"The house is large enough for us all, Leisha, and you don't have to worry about your personal space either. Mom and Dad won't invade your privacy or force a relationship. They'll give you time and space."

"Wouldn't a hotel be better?"

"You and Daniel need time to bond with Mom and Dad. That won't happen with you staying across town in a hotel."

"How are we going to be introduced to others?"

"As extended family."

Leisha leaned forward. "What do we call them? Mr. and Mrs. Dearling seem too formal, Nathan and Leah are too informal and disrespectful, and Mom and Dad are not even options."

"Pastor and La' Dear."

"La' Dear?"

"Short for Lady Dear. Any more questions?"

"Not at the moment."

Daniel smiled reassuringly at Leisha, then gently squeezed her hand, lending his support. She had more reservations about this reunion than he did.

"What if they don't like me or I don't bond with them?"

"Don't worry, sis. Everything will be fine."

"How can you stay so calm?"

"I'm resting in the Lord, letting Him guide me."

"I've got butterflies waging war in my stomach."

"Stick with me, and you'll be fine."

"Sure about that?"

"Positive."

They crossed the city line into lush greenery dotted with vibrant flowers of orange, yellow, red, white, and blue, and Daniel saw a "Welcome to Crossland" sign. Soon, they left the highway and rode through quaint neighborhoods until they reached an open gate with two bronze guardian angels on either side of Holly Drive. Chance drove around a circular driveway with a three-foot angel at its center with an uplifted hand above a pool of water. As they passed the fountain, a gray and maroon bricked, three-story house with golden lamps lit on either side of the front door came into view.

Chance stopped in the driveway. "We're home."

Daniel and Leisha exchanged looks, then released hands. "You ready, sis?"

"As much as I'll ever be."

"Then, let's go meet the Dearlings."

Chapter Nineteen

Before they call I will answer;
while they are still speaking I will hear.

Isaiah 65:24 (NIV)

Holly Drive
Friday, July 1

They were finally home.

As Chance hoisted luggage from the trunk, Victor advanced toward the front door, Leisha and Daniel side by side, following him. Both were quiet—subdued—Leisha dressed in a white blouse and lavender pantsuit, with her thick curls bound in a barrette, and Daniel in a gray shirt and navy pants. Even though he had tried to allay their fears about meeting their birth parents, Victor knew they were still nervous. He figured they would have to meet the Dearlings for themselves to realize that they were genuinely kind, good-natured, and loving people—incapable of inflicting harm.

Finally, they all reached the front door, but before Victor could ring the bell, his dad opened it, with Mom at his side, and they both had hundred-watt smiles on their faces as they drank in the company outside—their returning sons and newfound twins.

"Welcome home!" Dad stood tall and commanding, gold-rimmed glasses over his piercing eyes, and Mom, at his side, seemed petite and delicate in a fuchsia blouse and black skirt, silky brown hair brushing her shoulders. Together, they presented a united front.

For a moment, everyone froze in silence, just exchanging glances, and Victor could imagine that his dad saw a reflection of himself in Daniel and that his mom saw embers of her own beauty in Leisha. After all, these, indeed, were their children, the fruit of their love.

Dad traded glances with Mom whose eyes brimmed with tears, and he pulled her closer, into a protective embrace. Then his eyes alighted on Victor, Leisha, Daniel, and Chance. "Come in." He stepped aside with Mom so everyone could enter.

Victor led Leisha and Daniel through the foyer to the spacious living room.

As soon as Chance and his parents entered the room, Victor grinned, walked forward, and hugged his parents. He pulled back so he could see their faces. "Did you miss us?"

"Of course, we did, son. We're glad you're back home, safe and sound." Dad looked Victor over, his eyes searching. "How are you feeling?"

"Better than I look. There's no substantial injury to my left arm, and I don't have any cerebral damage. I'm supposed to take my medication, rest, and schedule an appointment with my own doctor to discuss further treatment and therapy."

Mom placed a firm hand on his shoulder. "God spared your life. I hope you take the doctor's advice seriously and slow down enough to let your body heal."

"Don't worry, Mom. I'll behave."

"Good."

"Now that you've finished fussing over me, Chance and I would like to introduce you to the twins." Victor turned, motioning Daniel and Leisha forward.

Chance stood beside Daniel, his hand on his shoulder. "Dad, this is Daniel."

Daniel offered his right hand. "Nice to meet you, sir."

"You, too, Daniel." Dad firmly gripped his hand and shook it.

Daniel pulled away and looked toward Mom, and she returned his stare, her light-brown eyes glistening with tears. "It's a pleasure to meet you, too."

"You'll have to forgive me, but I'm a hugger and a mother." She extended her arms and patiently waited until Daniel's composure slipped, and he walked forward, hugging her. "God is good, God is just, and God is love." She kissed Daniel's forehead, then stepped back. "He can work all things together for our good, can't He?"

Daniel nodded. "Yes, ma'am."

"I hope you'll let Nathan and me get to know you."

"I'm willing."

"We're blessed then."

Victor smiled. "Mom, this is Leisha."

She looked up, her eyes focusing on Leisha beside him.

"Hello, ma'am."

"Call me La' Dear."

"You have good sons, La' Dear. You must be proud of them."

"I'm proud of *all* of my children, even the ones I didn't raise." She opened her arms. "Will you permit a hug?"

Leisha nodded, then stepped forward.

Mom wrapped secure arms around her, then brushed fingers over her dark-brown hair. "Thank you for coming, and thank you for taking this first step." She pulled back, smiling and wiping tears from her own eyes; then, she turned and faced the others. "I hope everyone's hungry because I've spent the day preparing a feast of soul food, and I don't intend for any of it to lay wasted."

"Mom, you shouldn't overwork yourself. Save your strength."

"I'm not an invalid, Chance, and it won't compromise my health to cook a meal for my family. Now, stop fretting, grab those suitcases, and show Daniel and Leisha to the blue and gold guest rooms upstairs. They'll need to freshen up because dinner will be served at seven."

"All right. You win." Chance followed her instructions, retrieving the luggage, then heading upstairs with Daniel and Leisha.

Victor faced his parents. "So, what do you think of the twins?"

"They're more than we expected or dreamed. Daniel could be *my* twin, except he's inherited those clear eyes from my grandmother Callie."

"He seems warm, reverent, and approachable."

"What about Leisha?"

Dad frowned. "She's quiet, uncomfortable, and distant, like a turtle hiding in its shell. It's likely going to take some time to get her to relax and be herself."

Victor turned to his mom. "What's your impression?"

"She's polite and well-disciplined, not that emotional."

"She's just protecting herself because she's nervous and doesn't know you well. Once you spend more time with her, her demeanor will change, and you'll discover she's warm, caring, and lovable."

Mom raised her eyes. "You've gotten to know her that well?"

"Well enough."

"Has she shared anything about her parents or her past?"

"Not much, but there's some pain involved. Leisha didn't seem surprised that her parents kept her adoption a secret, and it doesn't seem like they were close."

"Sometimes, parents keep secrets to protect their children and lessen their pain. At least that's what Daddy claimed he was doing."

"Are you shielding Chance and me, Mom?"

"No, I'm not."

"Are you really okay?"

"I feel well today, and the treatments, though invasive, have eased some of my pain."

"What about side effects—nausea, fatigue, sores, hair loss?"

Mom absently ran fingers through her hair. "I won't complain, especially when I'm blessed with days like this when I can be with all my children."

Victor hugged her tightly. "I love you, and I don't want to lose you."

She caressed his face. "I feel the same about you. I was scared when Chance phoned, telling us that you'd been cut and beaten, and I felt helpless because you were hurt and I couldn't protect or comfort you. It took all of my strength not to hop in the car and speed to Corinth while you were hospitalized. Nathan alone convinced me that it was best to remain here, lifting up fervent prayers and trusting God for your safety and healing."

Dad placed a warm, strong hand on Victor's right shoulder. "You're not upset we didn't visit, are you?"

"Mom's health is top priority. Besides that, I'm fine, on the mend."

"For that, we're grateful."

"If you don't mind, I'm going upstairs to rest. I'm tired, and my arm is aching."

"Do you need me to tend to you?"

"I have some pills for the pain. I'll be fine."

"Are you sure?"

"I'll see you at dinner." He kissed her forehead, bade his father farewell, then turned, heading for the staircase. As he ascended, he wondered how Daniel and Leisha were faring. Like his parents, they had some adjustments to make. Now that the twins had met the Dearlings, Victor prayed they had no more reservations about making the couple a permanent part of their lives.

Chapter Twenty

As iron sharpens iron, so one man sharpens another.

Proverbs 27:17 (NIV)

Holly Drive
Saturday, July 2

At three the next morning, Daniel woke up and, unable to return to sleep, he climbed from his bed, donned a green robe, and walked barefoot downstairs to the kitchen for a glass of warm milk or hot chocolate. He had just washed his glass, putting it in the dish tray when a noise broke the silence, and he decided to investigate.

He crept from the kitchen through the dining room to the hallway leading to Pastor Dearling's study. A stream of soft, golden light spilled from the partially-opened door, inviting Daniel forward, so he pushed the door open, stepping inside.

Nathan Dearling sat in his pajamas behind a desk, with a Bible spread open before him, a glass of milk and a plate of peanut butter cookies at his fingertips. At Daniel's entrance, he glanced up, smiling. "Daniel!"

"Excuse me, sir. I'm intruding."

"If you're here, there's a reason." Nathan raised his hand, urging him forward. "Come and have a seat."

"You don't mind?"

"No, I don't."

"All right, then." Daniel stepped forward and sat down on a cushioned chair, facing the towering minister. Nathan's presence filled the room, and, even though Daniel had only met the man, he already respected him as a man of God and the spiritual head of this household.

"What's got you up this early?"

"I couldn't sleep, so I thought a glass of milk would help. And you?"

"This is the hour the Lord tends to meet me, sharing scripture and pearls of wisdom."

"Then, I am intruding."

"No, you're not. If anything, you're an unexpected blessing." He raised the plate, offering it to Daniel. "Share some homemade cookies with me. They're my wife's special recipe, passed down from her grandmother Samantha."

Daniel graciously accepted one. "Thank you." As Nathan returned the plate to the desk and grabbed a cookie himself, Daniel quietly chewed, savoring each morsel and glancing at the family photos on the desk and walls. Earlier, after dinner, when Chance had given him and Leisha a tour, Daniel had only gotten a cursory glimpse of this room. Now, he could study the portraits of his birth father's life at leisure.

In one photo Nathan beamed proudly, his arms wrapped around teenagers Chance and Victor, both in baseball uniforms. In another Nathan, Chance, and Victor stood in front of a white and blue boat, all of them holding fishing rods. A final snapshot caught Nathan and Victor, Leah and Chance together on a rollercoaster, their hands raised heavenward and their faces reflecting happiness, love, freedom, and joy.

"You're an active parent, an attentive father, aren't you?"

"I'm involved, yes." Nathan dusted his hands of crumbs. "I believe in parental responsibility, in fostering a child's dreams and helping him or her realize his or her potential and purpose."

"You and your wife have done a great job raising Chance and Victor."

"They were both good boys. They just needed some love, stability, and encouragement."

"From what Chance has told me, he had a troubled childhood—an abusive one."

"If he shared that much, he must really trust you. Six months passed before Leah and I could get him to open up, discussing his father Ray's abuse or his mother Eileen's death. Both were tough subjects, and both left him angry, dispirited, and rebellious. He couldn't rage against Ray, so he pitted himself against God. Now, he blames the Lord for all that bad in his life, and he doesn't believe he needs Him. He refuses to relent or invite Jesus into his heart." Nathan exhaled, shaking his head. "My deepest regrets are letting Chance fall astray and failing him as a spiritual father."

"You didn't fail him. Chance is covered by the Blood."

"What do you mean?"

"He accepted Jesus as his Lord and Savior."

Tears fell from Nathan's eyes. "When?"

"Last Sunday night. He and I prayed together."

Nathan clapped, then lifted his head toward heaven. "Thank You, God! You've answered my prayer." Drying his tears, he looked back down at Daniel. "Thank you, too."

"You're the one who sowed the seed of faith."

"But God chose you to reap the harvest."

"I'm merely a vessel serving the Lord."

"Well, I'm grateful you were at the right place at the right time for Chance's breakthrough."

Daniel felt uncomfortable beneath Nathan's penetrating eyes, his effusive praise.

"Was Victor as difficult as Chance?"

"Not necessarily, but Leah and I had to labor with him, too."

"How so?"

"Victor lost his parents young and later lived with his grandmother in extreme poverty. It got so bad for them they were left homeless. After she died, fear had a firm grip on Victor, and he had a tendency to cling tightly to those he loved, namely me, Leah, and Chance. For months after we adopted him, he barely let us out of sight. We were his only family, and he was afraid we would die or one day abandon him like everyone else in his life. He required a lot of time, patience, love, and counseling, but he overcame his fears and made it through."

Daniel couldn't reconcile that poor, fearful boy with the confident man he had previously met—the one who had courageously defended Leisha. "He and Chance seem extremely close, like real brothers."

"They are real brothers. Each would sacrifice his own life for the other; that's how close they are." He laughed. "They'll tell you Leah and I saved them, but the truth is those boys are our blessings from God, and it's always been a privilege and pleasure for us to raise and love them. Both have brought such happiness to our lives, and Leah and I are thankful they've accepted us as parents."

Daniel saw genuine love written on Nathan's face, especially when he mentioned his sons, and he fought to crush that bit of envy he felt. Here was a good father—one most boys dreamed of having, one who would sacrifice his own life for his children and would do all within his power to make them happy, one who wouldn't willingly give his children to another unless he had no alternative. Daniel grappled with his emotions, willing the tears stinging his eyes to stay away. "What's my place in this family portrait? What are your expectations for me?"

Nathan met him eye to eye. "You're my firstborn son, and like Chance and Victor you have a place in my heart, and I'd like to have a personal relationship with you. I'm not demanding that you recognize me as your father, nor am I trying to usurp Elec Winward's place. I'm just seeking a place at your heart's table—some part in your life, even as just an intimate friend or a spiritual mentor. Is any of that possible for us?"

"Maybe. Over time." He discreetly rubbed tears from his eyes. "As a child, I often wondered why my birth parents rejected me, why they gave me away."

Nathan leaned forward. "We didn't reject you. Neither Leah nor I were given a choice to raise you—to be your parents in truth."

"After meeting you in person, I understand that."

"Yet you won't invite us into your life or your family?"

"I need time, Pastor. More than one weekend."

Clearly disappointed, Nathan sank back in his chair. "I admire your honesty, Daniel, and I won't try to force myself on you. I never expected a week away from your own home, family, and friends to change your whole world or mindset." He rubbed his chin, seemingly lost in thought. "You alone have to decide whether or not you can love Leah and me—whether we can exist in your world."

Daniel sensed his sadness. "I'm not trying to hurt you intentionally by withholding my heart—my love. I'm just grappling to make sense of this situation and to do what's right for everybody involved."

Nathan waved his hand. "Don't worry. I understand, and I'll grant you the time you need." He raised his glass of milk, then stood, leaving behind the plate of cookies. "I'm off to bed, but you're welcome to stay as long as necessary. Feel free to eat the rest of those cookies, too, because I have a feeling you and God have a conversation pending." He walked around the desk, placing a firm hand on Daniel's shoulder. "Goodnight, son."

"Goodnight, Pastor."

After Nathan left, closing the door behind him, Daniel bowed his head, palmed his hands, and prayed for guidance. *Lord, open the eyes of my heart and teach me how to see beyond the shame and pain of the past to the real hearts of these people. Show me how to love this family with a sincere heart.*

Chapter Twenty-One

Many a man claims to have unfailing love,
but a faithful man who can find?

Proverbs 20:6 (NIV)

Holly Drive
Saturday, July 2

That afternoon Chance prepared a cookout in the backyard near the patio and pool. As his father and mother sat with Daniel and Leisha at the table poring over photo albums, those of the Dearlings and those that Chance had suggested the twins bring from home, Victor supervised Chance at the grill.

Chance lowered the spatula in his hand. "Daniel has softened considerably since last night. He's more at ease."

"Leisha's making an effort too."

"Where do you two stand now?"

Victor met his eyes. "What do you mean?"

"You confessed to loving her. Does she feel the same?"

"She cares about me. Beyond that, I have no idea."

"The best thing for you to do is forget about her, at least in a romantic sense."

Victor tilted his head. "Since when did you become Dr. Love?"

"Since you started courting Leisha. I'm no expert on love, women, or relationships, but I am acquainted with you. Leisha fascinates you, and you've labeled what you feel as love. However, she could just be an appealing woman that you fancy—nothing more."

"Chance, until I met Leisha, I never realized how complacent I had become." Victor glanced over Chance's shoulder. "She inspires me like no other woman, and since I've met her, I've been happier and more driven than ever. Even within me, I've felt a renewed flame of hope, life, love, passion." He pressed his right hand over his heart. "Seriously, I haven't felt this connected to a woman in eight years."

Chance put his hand on Victor's shoulder. "There's a major difference between Shayna and Leisha. Your relationship with Shayna progressed over years, especially since you dated throughout college. If she hadn't chosen that job in New York over you, it's likely the two of you would be married." He frowned. "I could never understand why you just let her walk away."

"I loved her. But all her dreams were centered in New York. By keeping her here, I was stifling her, forcing her to live a life she didn't really want in a place she didn't like. So, rather than let her live in Crossland with regrets and resenting me, I did the only honorable thing I could and let her go."

"But you loved each other."

"Still, that wasn't enough for us to build a life or a future together."

"If she returned, what would you do?"

"Wish her the best. She's married now and has a four-year-old daughter."

"How do you know that?"

"She called and told me."

"And you didn't tell me?"

"I didn't want you or anyone else feeling sorry for me."

"Aren't you angry?"

"Honestly, no. Shayna and I had our moment, and we just weren't meant to be. If we were, no obstacle would have separated us, driving a wedge between our hearts."

"So, you're really over her?"

"Yes, I've moved on."

"To Leisha?"

Victor stole another glance at her. "We haven't spent much time alone. All I know with certainty is that she and I have a connection—an awareness of each other."

"Fight it. If you don't, you'll only complicate an already complex situation."

"Love isn't a complication but a blessing, especially if it comes from God."

"You think it's God's plan for you to fall in love with Leisha?"

"That's not what I said!"

"You implied it."

Victor confronted him. "Why are you against her?"

"I have no problem with her as a sister. I object to you romancing her and perceiving her as a girlfriend or a potential wife, especially since you've known her for less than a month. If you're ready to date, find another, more suitable woman—someone from church or work. Just leave Leisha alone and let our parents pursue a relationship with her."

"You're asking me to give her up before I've even gotten her?"

"Yes, Victor. I'm asking you to make a personal sacrifice—to put our parents' needs before your own. Dad's putting on a brave front, but he's juggling a lot with Mom's tumor and his church obligations. Mom pretends she's well, but she's under siege, fighting for her life. Let's not add more stress or turmoil to the equation. Let's not rock the family boat." Chance looked toward their parents. "Mom and Dad need us united." He confronted Victor again. "You care about Leisha, right?"

"Yes."

"Then don't confuse her or distract her. Give her time to bond with her birth parents."

"Deny my feelings for her?"

He gently squeezed Victor's shoulder. "Can you do that—for Mom and Dad?"

Victor breathed deeply, audibly. "Yes."

Chance hugged him. "I hate having to ask this of you."

"Don't worry. I'll survive." Victor pulled back, a sad smile on his face. "Besides, there's no guarantee she loves me."

"You're a good son."

"So are you." He playfully punched Chance in the arm. "You see the big picture, not just one snapshot." Victor nodded toward their parents. "They seem happy, don't they?"

"Yes, they do."

"Let's not spoil the reunion then. Let's finish these beef patties so everyone can eat."

"You okay?"

"I'm fine."

"You know I love you. I'd never intentionally hurt you either."

"You haven't, so lose the guilt."

"All right. Let's finish this." Chance returned to the grill, his thoughts still on Victor and Leisha. In his mind, he was confident he had made the right decision, but in his heart he felt like he had just crossed a line, dashing Victor's dreams and crushing *his* heart. It was that seed of doubt that kept Chance from being content. If, indeed, he had counseled Victor wrong, he prayed that his brother could one day forgive him. More than that, Chance prayed he could forgive himself.

Chapter Twenty-Two

May the Lord direct your hearts into
God's love and Christ's perseverance.

2 Thessalonians 3:5 (NIV)

Holly Drive
Saturday, July 2

Leisha listened avidly as Nathan and Leah shared family stories and humorous tales of Victor's and Chance's youthful exploits. Both she and Daniel had spent most of the meal laughing. Afterward, Chance grabbed a ball and proposed a friendly game of volleyball.

"Dad?"

"Count Leah and me out. We know how competitive you are, so we'll just sit here, enjoying our lemonade."

Chance turned to Daniel and Leisha. "Either one of you in?"

"Sorry, Chance. I prefer basketball."

He looked at Leisha. "What about you?"

"I played in college. But I'm rusty and out of shape now."

Victor laughed. "You'll be fine, Leisha. Have some fun and get some exercise. Once you start playing the game, everything will come back."

"I'm a lawyer, not an athlete."

His eyes gleamed, and he grinned. "Sure you're not afraid of losing to a younger, more seasoned champ like Chance?"

"Of course not!"

"No need to get upset. If you're afraid of a challenge, you should bow out gracefully. We wouldn't want you to get hurt or be embarrassed."

Have some fun. Get some exercise. Bow out gracefully. Leisha bristled. She was only four years older than Chance, six years older than Victor. *Did Victor seriously consider her too boring, fat, and old? Did he think she was a coward—too afraid to compete against a man? Well, if that was what he believed, he didn't know her at all.* "I'm not afraid, and I'm not a loser. I'm a competitor. I know how to win, especially against *immature* opponents with *inflated* egos."

Victor traded glances with Chance. "That sounds like a challenge, *hermano*."

"Indeed, it does." Chance looked at Leisha. "Does that mean you're playing?"

Fired up, she pushed her chair back, then stood, her hands extended. "Throw me the ball."

"Game on, then." Chance tossed her the ball, then jogged toward the volleyball net.

Victor smiled, then winked at Leisha. "Be careful. Chance is beyond competitive, and he's fierce in battle. He won't be gentle or gracious, even during a friendly game. He's relentless, regardless of his opponent's gender, and he's liable to embarrass you, then take your head off."

"I'm not scared of him or you, Victor. You shouldn't underestimate me either. Now, more than ever, I plan on winning."

Victor grinned. "A fearless woman besting Chance—that, I'd like to see."

"Keep your eyes on the ball, and you will." She strode away, the ball tucked beneath her right arm. She was determined to win so she could wipe that smirk off Victor's face. In the end, he would be the one embarrassed—the one apologizing to her.

Daniel jogged after her, stopping her at the volleyball net. "Slow down, sis."

Still upset, she snapped. "Why are you following me?"

He raised both hands in surrender. "I came to give you a pep talk, but now I see you may need some brotherly love instead."

"I'm fine, and I'm sorry for the harsh tone."

"What's wrong?"

"Nothing."

"Then why snap my head off?"

"At times, I overreact, taking criticism too personally."

"What criticism?"

"It doesn't matter."

He studied her face. "Apparently, it does. You and Victor seemed pretty intense together, smiling and joking one minute, then like flint and sparks the next. There's definitely some tension between you. Did he upset you?"

"I'm fine."

"Did something happen in Corinth between you and Victor?"

"No."

"Is he the guy you were telling me about—the one who comes with baggage?"

Leisha shook her head, praying her face didn't betray her. "Victor and I are just two passionate people."

"Are you sure that's all?"

"Yes."

His eyes bore into hers. "You can trust me, Leisha. With anything, including your secrets."

"There's nothing to share."

"So, there's nothing strange or romantic happening between you and Victor?"

"No! Now stop the interrogation."

"All right, I won't pry anymore." He clapped a hand on her shoulder. "So, what's your game plan against Chance?"

"Strike the ball across the net and win."

"That's it?"

"Pretty much."

"Sounds good to me." He smiled, giving her a thumbs-up sign. "Stay confident and know I'll be cheering for you on the sidelines."

"Thank you." Daniel's encouragement pleased her, and it made her feel good to know he believed in her and stood in her corner. She smiled and watched him return to the others, then she got into position on her side of the net.

Chance whistled. "Ready?"

She gripped the ball. "Yes!"

"Let's play ball then!" On the other side, Chance positioned himself—his stance challenging.

As they commenced, Nathan and Leah cheered diplomatically, alternating between Leisha and Chance, while Daniel rooted loudly for her, and Victor remained surprisingly silent and neutral. As play progressed with Leisha slamming the ball directly at Chance, a lively battle ensued between the two of them, with both plowing the ball rapidly and mercilessly across the net. Finally, Leisha saw an advantage and took it, whopping the ball behind Chance. Giddy, she crowed, holding up her right index finger. "My point!"

"Enjoy it. You won't get another so easily."

"You don't intimidate me, Chance. Bring your best game."

He sopped sweat from his face with the hem of his shirt. "I always do."

They resumed play, alternating leads, and during a water break, Daniel hugged Leisha, laughing and shaking his head. "I thought you two were supposed to be playing a friendly game for fun."

"We are." Leisha turned to Chance who was squatting on the grass, dousing his head with the bottled water that Victor had handed him. "Aren't you having fun?"

"I'm also getting a great workout, thanks to you." He wagged his finger accusingly at her. "You're one tough lady."

"If that's a compliment, thanks; if it's criticism, watch your back. This tough woman's got some sharp claws, even sharper high heels."

Chance laughed. "Seriously, it's a compliment."

"Thank you, then. Now I can scratch your name from my payback list."

Chance lowered his finger. "You're misleading."

"How?"

"Since I've met you, you've been calm and quiet. Now, I'm seeing another side of you—the competitor—the warrior. You must be a terror in the courtroom."

Leisha laughed. "I have my special moments and my battle gear. And more than anything, I hate being predictable, ordinary."

"Sis, after today, I'd say Chance knows you're both unpredictable and extraordinary."

"You're amazing, a puzzle—that's what you are," Victor said.

Leisha looked at Victor. "A puzzle, huh?"

"Yes—one I hope to solve this weekend."

"Really?"

He smiled. "I like mysteries, and you're full of surprises."

Chance rose to his feet, stood between them, and handed Victor his empty bottle. "Leisha and I have a game to finish. And Mom and Dad don't need you delving into Leisha's life anymore. Anything they need to know about her, they can ask her for themselves."

Leisha squashed waves of disappointment and sadness. She had thought she meant more to Victor than a consolation prize for his parents. Apparently, she was wrong.

Daniel touched her arm. "What's going on?"

"Nothing." She turned her back on Chance and Victor. "I'm just tired."

"Do you have enough fuel in the tank to win?"

"I can beat him. I can win."

"Then do it, sis." He caressed her face. "I believe in you."

Tears stung her eyes. "Really?"

"Yes."

She hugged him, holding on tight. "Thank you."

"Enough chatter! Let's finish this game." Chance clapped his hands on his thighs, spurring them all to action, and Leisha stepped from Daniel's arms, jogging to her side of the net. Daniel and Victor returned to the sidelines with Nathan and Leah.

Leisha thought she could overpower Chance, but within ten minutes of resuming play, Chance, with renewed vigor, won decisively. Afterward, Leisha walked graciously over to him, thanking him for a good, spirited game; then, she walked back to her side of the net, with her hands over her head, exercising her legs and regaining her breath.

"You okay, sis?"

She looked up and saw concern in her brother's eyes. "I'm fine, and I've conceded defeat."

"You have nothing to be ashamed of, you know. You held your own against Chance."

She flashed a genuine smile. "For an old, fat, weak woman, I did, didn't I?"

"You're anything but old, fat, and weak. You're unique and rare, quite like that water Jesus turned to wine. I'm proud of you, Lady Fearless."

She laughed. "Thank you. I needed to hear that."

"You ready to join Pastor and La' Dear at the table?"

"Not yet. Give me a few minutes. Okay?"

"You got it." He blew her a kiss, then returned to the Dearlings.

Five minutes later, Victor pulled her aside, offering her a fresh towel so she could dry her face. "You played impressively—with passion and heart. You're truly a competitor. And you've got some great skills and the heart of a champion."

"Thank you." Leisha glanced down at the sweat stains, dirt, and grime on her blouse and shorts, then confronted Victor, her face scrunched. "I look a fright and smell worse! Why didn't you tell me?"

His eyes scanned her. "You look beautiful, and you smell authentic—real."

"You need your eyes and nose checked. I'm dirty and stinky, and I need to shower and change." She excused herself from the others, returning to the house and walking upstairs to her bedroom.

As Leisha kicked off her shoes, discarded her soiled clothes in the laundry hamper, and sashayed toward the bathroom, garbed in a rose-pink robe and slippers, she hummed, relaxing her mind and body. Later, after she had showered, she returned to her bedroom and turned on the radio beside the bed, listening to the soothing sound of worship music as she put on a purple shirt and slid into a pair of denim jeans. She was trying to clasp her silver heart-shaped necklace around her neck when a knock sounded on the door. With the necklace still clutched in her right hand, she traipsed barefoot to the door and opened it, her left hand resting on the knob. Seeing her visitor, she swallowed hard, fighting the urge to fan herself.

In his green shirt and blue jeans, Victor stood at her door, his black hair damp and tousled, and he looked simply gorgeous—suave and divine. "Mom sent me to collect you. Daniel's in his room, and Dad and Chance are busy attaching Deliverance to the truck."

She composed herself. "Deliverance?"

"The boat we're taking out to Lake Haven this evening. Daniel's already agreed to come, and I'm here to see whether you're interested, too."

"I've never been boating before."

"It's an exhilarating experience."

"What kind of boat is it?"

"A motorboat. You'll love it. I guarantee it."

"Thank you for inviting me."

"It wouldn't be any fun without you." He lowered his eyes. "Do you need help with your necklace?"

She looked at his left arm, bound in a sling. "Thanks for the offer, but I believe you're presently disabled."

"I'm right-handed."

"Still, it'll be difficult for you to fasten my necklace with one hand."

"Together we can manage. Besides, you'd be amazed what a motivated man can do with one hand."

"Really, Victor, it's no problem. You're not obligated to help me."

"I want to, and I wouldn't have offered if I was incapable of doing it."

"Victor—"

"Stop arguing, turn around, and hold the necklace in place."

"Are you sure you can do this?"

"Yes."

Leisha turned around with the necklace pressed against her neck, and when his fingers touched her neck, then he brushed her hair aside, she shivered.

"Are you cold?"

"No."

"Are you sure?"

"Positive."

"Then, why are you shivering?"

"I'm not."

Instead of contradicting her, he quietly fumbled with the clasp, working diligently.

"Are you having trouble?"

"No."

"Are you sure?"

"Positive. Now, be still and let me work."

"If you can't do it, all you have to do is admit it. I won't think less of you."

"Leisha."

"Yes?"

"Mission accomplished." Slowly, he turned her around, then lifted the necklace, caressing the cross at its center.

"Thank you."

"You're welcome." He studied the necklace. "It's an exquisite piece. Where did you get it?"

"Dad gave it to me for my twelfth birthday. He was a cardiologist, so he thought it was the perfect gift." Absently, she covered Victor's hand with hers, pressing it over her own heart. "I've always cherished this because it's a reminder of a special time in my life—a time when my dad and I actually got along, when he loved me and was proud that I was his daughter."

"What ruined it?"

"I stopped being Daddy's Little Girl and became a young, independent woman—one who continually disappointed him with my choices."

"What about your mother?"

"She spent more time planning social events with her friends than spending quality time with me. We lived under the same roof but had very little in common."

"Were they Christians?"

"They were the lukewarm, bench-warming kind. They only attended church on Easter and Christmas. The rest of the time in our household, Sunday was just another day, and Jesus really wasn't included in the family plans."

"When did you become a follower?"

"My freshman year in college. Salena invited me to church, and it was there that I found Jesus for myself."

"Then what happened?"

"My life changed dramatically. I was on fire for Jesus, ready to share the Gospel. But my parents thought I'd been brainwashed, and they didn't appreciate my attempts to 'save' them. Life at home became tense and unbearable, and at times, it felt like God was the only one who truly understood or even loved me. Sometimes, it still seems that way."

"God isn't the only one who loves you."

"Salena makes two."

"That's not all."

"Who else?"

"Mom, Dad, Daniel."

"They barely know me."

"Yet they love you."

"Do you love me?"

His jaw dropped, but no words came out.

She frowned. "Did you hear me?"

Victor remained silent, just staring into her eyes, his hand covering her heart. "Of course!" Then, as though awaking from a dream, he jerked, visibly withdrawing, and removed his hand from beneath hers. "I'm sorry, Leisha, but I've got to go." He backed away. "I'll meet you downstairs." He left, shutting the door behind him.

Was that a yes or no? Leisha stared at the closed door, her hand clutching the necklace. *Was I wrong about him—his feelings for me? Is he only interested in being my friend?*

Chapter Twenty-Three

Do not withhold any good from those who
deserve it, when it is in your power to act.

Proverbs 3:27 (NIV)

Holly Drive
Sunday, July 3

The next morning, Leisha woke early, showered, then traipsed downstairs to the kitchen, prepared to surprise everyone with breakfast. As she scrambled eggs, she turned on the radio, humming as she leaned over the oven with a pan of fluffy homemade biscuits in her hand.

Leah walked in, still in her peach robe, a pleasant smile on her face. "You cook?"

"Not often." Leisha placed the pan on the countertop. "I live alone, so it doesn't make sense to cook elaborate meals for one. Usually, I pop a meal in the microwave."

Leah grabbed a red-and-white checkered apron from the pantry door. "What would you like me to do?"

"Relax." Leisha removed the apron from her hands, then escorted her to one of the stools at the counter. "You've been fluttering around, tending to our needs. Today, I'm serving you."

"Are you sure?"

"Yes." Leisha returned the apron to the pantry door, then removed a glass from the cabinet. She sat it in front of Leah and poured milk from the refrigerator into it. "Drink and enjoy."

"Thank you." As Leah sipped the milk, Leisha cooked, and soon, they fell into a comfortable silence.

After fifteen minutes, Leisha glanced up and found Leah watching her. "Thank you for yesterday. I enjoyed our time at the lake. It was peaceful, and that sunset was amazing. Even the stars over the water were breathtaking."

"Give God credit. Everything He created is a masterpiece." She tapped the stool beside her. "Have a seat so I can share my favorite love story."

Leisha accepted the invitation, settling on the stool. "Who's it about?"

"Nathan and me. At the time I was fourteen and quite mature for my age, and Nathan was seventeen, tall and handsome. We grew up in the same town, but our lives never intersected until one Sunday in July when he attended my church. He was an usher and the visiting preacher's son, and he won my heart that night, just like a fairytale prince."

"What happened?"

"I dropped my handkerchief, just to see if he would pick it up and return it. When he did, I almost fainted. The boy smelled as good as he looked, like a fresh, cool sea breeze sweeping through the summer heat." She fanned herself dramatically. "That boy was handsome, every girl's dream. He found me in the parking lot after church and asked my name. After I told him, he introduced himself, then asked if I had a boyfriend. I confessed I was only fourteen and my daddy wouldn't let me have a boyfriend. Nathan wasn't deterred, though. He promised friendship and said we'd see what happened when I turned fifteen; then, he grinned, scribbled his name and phone number on a church program, and made me promise to hold on to it. Afterward, he walked away. Whistling."

"What did you do, then?"

"Stood there like some statue, pressing that program to my heart and praying for that boy to be mine one day."

"You fell in love?"

"Completely. Nathan fell for me too."

"How did your relationship work, with him being three years older?"

"Surprisingly, well. We had the same values and liked the same things, and we mostly held hands and talked, sharing our lives, our hopes, our dreams. Nathan was always a gentleman—caring, respectful, and protective. He didn't pressure me for intimacy, a physical relationship. In fact, the only kissing we did was on each other's cheeks."

"Holding hands and kissing cheeks don't leave girls pregnant at age sixteen. Something happened."

"The week before Nathan left town for college, we let fear and passion make us forget ourselves and our resolve to remain pure before marriage. We knew what we were doing was wrong, but we did it anyway. And we paid the consequences later. Quite dearly."

Leisha clenched her hands on the counter. "You regret getting pregnant?"

Leah covered Leisha's hands with hers, and she stared directly into her eyes. "You may have been a surprise, but you were never a mistake. I don't regret giving birth to you and Daniel, but I do wish Nathan and I had been married, that we'd had the opportunity to raise you and watch you both grow into the man and woman that God destined you to be. Before you were even born, I loved you. I wanted you. And in spite of how you were conceived, you were never my mistake or my sin; you were always my blessing, my gift, my daughter."

She loved me. She wanted me. Leisha felt tears stinging her eyes. "Why didn't you fight for us—for me?"

"I thought you had died, Leisha. I was young and naïve, too, and I trusted my father's word. I never imagined that he would deceive me, that he would hurt me so cruelly. But he did; he betrayed me. In the worst way."

Leisha blinked tears away, and Leah raised her hand, caressing Leisha's face. "I've missed so much of your life, and there's no way I can reclaim those years, but I'd like a fresh start with you. I'd like to make memories that you and I can share." She lowered her hand, then raised Leisha's necklace. "I'd like a place in your heart."

Why now when you're sick, possibly dying? Leisha pulled back, creating more space between them. "I heard about the brain tumor, that it's malignant."

Leah released the necklace. "Who told you?"

"Victor." She breathed deeply, meeting Leah's eyes. "I've already lost a mother and a father, and now, you want me to risk my heart again—only to lose you too."

"This tumor doesn't decide my fate; God does, and He promises Life, not death."

"You're certain you're going to survive?"

"No, but I have faith that God will heal me. I also have a loving family, an awesome ministry, and much to live for, and I don't believe I'm done yet."

"Aren't you scared?"

"Not for myself, mainly because fear has no place in me, and sickness has no authority over me. This tumor is not cheating me out of an abundant life. And don't you let it cheat you out of a relationship with me."

"I may not be as strong or as faithful as you." Even in the face of death, Leah Dearling was courageous. She was an inspiration—a fighter and a survivor—a woman Leisha could respect and love.

"My strength is the Lord, my faith is in Him too. As long as you carry Him with you, you're strong enough and your faith will hold. Just trust Him, and He'll sustain you, supply all your needs. Don't give up on Him."

"I won't."

"Don't give up on me either."

Leisha hugged her. "I've been praying for you. Even before I met you."

Leah tightened her grip. "Thank you, sweetheart. I welcome prayer, but right now I need this hug from you. I need you."

"I'm here." Leisha enjoyed the comfort and security of Leah's embrace a few more minutes before pulling back and standing up. "You'd better call the guys before the food gets cold."

Leah laughed, drying her eyes. "Nathan doesn't need a wake-up call when food's on the table. He has the nose of a hound, and he's likely awake, ready to trample the boys just to get the first plate." She rose to her feet. "I'll wake the others though and give them a heads-up." She touched Leisha's arm. "Thank you. Again." She smiled, then turned and walked away.

Leisha set the dining room table, her mind still on Leah—her faith and optimism. If she could still hope, dream, laugh, love, and trust, even in the face of adversity and death, maybe Leisha could be brave enough to conquer her fears, open her heart, and welcome Leah inside. After all, didn't she have more to gain than lose?

Chapter Twenty-Four

But may the righteous be glad and rejoice before God;
may they be happy and joyful.

Psalm 68:3 (NIV)

Kingdom Family Christian Center
Sunday, July 3

As Nathan sat at his desk in his office, Leah, Chance, and Victor relaxed on a sofa, and Daniel and Leisha sat in two cushioned chairs. The patriarch looked distinguished in his chocolate-brown suit, crisp white shirt, and mustard-yellow tie, and he complemented Leah in her yellow dress and gossamer jacket.

Glancing around, Daniel thought they all made a fine family portrait, wearing their Sunday best. He had dressed comfortably in a pale pink shirt and dark blue pants while Leisha wore a powder blue shirt, with a purple jacket and skirt, her thick curls unbound. Even Victor looked fashionable in a white shirt, smoky gray jacket and trousers, and Chance seemed relaxed in a royal blue shirt and denim jeans.

"Did you hear me, Daniel?"

Daniel turned to find Nathan's eyes on him. "Excuse me?"

"I'd like you to sit with me and the other ministers during the service."

Daniel shook his head. "I appreciate the courtesy, but I'll sit with the family. This way, you and I won't have to field questions about our relationship. I'll also be able to relax and enjoy the service without being conspicuous."

Nathan grinned. "You notice our resemblance, then?"

"Yes, Pastor. If I sat beside you on a platform, so would everyone else."

"The truth can't stay hidden forever. You're my son, and I'm proud of that. I'm not ashamed to claim you. Even here. Before the congregation."

"Pastor, this weekend is personal, just for immediate family. I respect you, but I'm not ready for full public disclosure, the revelation that I'm your biological son. I don't want to be thrust into the limelight and have my life dissected. I don't want photos of me splashed across newspapers or television screens. And I don't want to be the hottest topic or gossip on the talk shows, in beauty and barber shops, or around town. My life is my own, and I've got a family, a fiancée, and a ministry waiting for me in Sutton, Georgia. I won't jeopardize any of that or my privacy and peace. Even for you."

Nathan frowned. "That's fear, not faith, talking, Daniel. You're letting it control you—your thoughts and your actions—so it's getting the best of you." He sighed. "You're a minister, a man of God, so more than most, you should know that perfect love casts out fear and that fear has to do with torment." He palmed his hands and leaned forward, his eyes never leaving Daniel's. "I love you, and you're my son—my hope, my pride and joy. I'm not afraid of gossip, scandal, or public opinion because I've already been forgiven for my sins, and I'm right with God. And He's more than able to work all things together for my good because I love Him and I'm called according to His purpose." Nathan eased back in his seat. "My prayer is that one day you'll trust God like I do and believe that He'll work all this out in *your* favor and help you cast off that fear and shame and be able to love and accept me and your mother in the spirit of a son, regardless of any price." Nathan motioned toward Chance and Victor. "And chat with your brothers sometime. They're veterans—preacher's kids and Dearlings to the core—and they can tell you what it's like to be a son of mine and still have privacy, individuality, and peace."

Nathan's words rang in Daniel's ears, reprimanding him, and he wondered if he would ever be able to acknowledge the truth of his birth without worrying about a scandal. He knew he couldn't maintain a relationship with the Dearlings or Leisha indefinitely without their relationship being questioned, and like Nathan said, the truth wouldn't stay hidden forever.

Leah rose, then walked toward Nathan and kissed his cheek. "It's time for us to leave."

He smiled at her. "You're welcome to stay."

She shook her head. "This is your time with the Lord, and we're not intruding on it."

"Thank you. I love you, dear."

She kissed his forehead. "I love you more."

"Then I'm blessed."

"We both are." She put her hand on his shoulder, then bowed her head with her eyes closed. "Heavenly Father, bless this man of Yours this morning with a ready word for Your people, fill him with Your Spirit, and give him power and authority, and fill him with love, strength, and fire so he's able to stand mightily before those assembled today wielding the Sword of the Spirit, which is Your Holy Word, for edification, enlightenment, and encouragement. Grant him peace and wisdom, knowledge and understanding, and courage and protection so that he might serve You faithfully, rescuing those being led away to death, holding back those staggering toward slaughter, and drawing those wandering or lost back home, into Your flock and kingdom. Let him walk out in faith, speak truth in love, and preach the uncompromising Word under the anointing of Your Holy Spirit, and let him humble himself and act according to *Your* will so he can fulfill the Great Commission, his purpose, and his calling. In Jesus' name. Amen." She opened her eyes, then hugged Nathan. "Be blessed and loved, and let God use you today."

"I will, and thank you, dear."

Daniel was deeply affected by the scene, Leah Dearling praying for her husband—pouring her love over him. She was a strong, virtuous woman who knew her husband's worth and her own. She was incredible, quite the Proverbs 31 woman.

Leah turned toward the rest of them, smiling, then walked from behind the desk and roused them from their seats and the office into the large sanctuary.

They trailed Leah to their seats: Chance, Daniel, Leisha, and Victor, in that order. As they got comfortable, several members stopped by, greeting and hugging Leah. Before any of them could inquire, Leah took the initiative, introducing Daniel and Leisha merely as family. A few did double takes, and they remarked on Daniel's uncanny resemblance to Pastor Dearling, but in each case, Leah merely beamed, saying, "They're like twins, aren't they? Isn't it amazing how God works—leaving His handprint on a family?" Then, she politely but masterfully redirected the conversation.

It was evident from their words and actions that everyone adored First Lady Dearling, and she doted on them, too. She not only knew their names but their families, professions, and interests. She even made the newcomers she was introduced to feel appreciated and welcome. No one seemed a stranger, and all received smiles and hugs and left cheerful.

Daniel was impressed with her, and he leaned toward Chance. "Your mother is remarkable."

"That's no secret. She genuinely loves, and she inspires it, too."

As the musicians commenced playing and the choir and worship leader entered the sanctuary and took their places in front, Daniel stood with everyone else, prepared to usher in the Lord. He clapped and sang through four songs, then later worshipped reverently with his hands uplifted during a soul-saving rendition of Donald Lawrence's "II Chronicles," inspired by one of Daniel's favorite promises from the Bible, 2 Chronicles 7:14.

Afterward, Nathan approached a transparent podium, thanking the worshippers, then flipping his Bible open and commencing his sermon. "Today, we're visiting the Lost Son, known as the Prodigal Son from Luke 15:11–32, but we're not focusing on him or even his brother, the son who remained home. Instead, we're studying the father, a forgiving, patient, and loving man so reminiscent of our heavenly Father, and our lesson today is titled, 'The Father's Heart.' These words found in Luke 15:32 which the father uses to justify his actions in welcoming his repentant son home are particularly appropriate today to any father who's ever lost a son, to any parent who's ever been reunited with a missing child: 'It was meet that we should make merry, and be glad: for this thy brother was dead, and is alive again; and was lost, and is found.' This father's heart is full, brimming with love, joy, peace, happiness, and compassion; it's pure, bearing no grudge, resentment, or stain from sins of the past; and it's open, ready to welcome and to bless with the abundance therein. This father's heart mirrors God's, and his relationships with his two sons, the sinful but repentant youngest and the faithful but unforgiving elder, reflects our relationships with God, the heavenly Father."

Daniel listened attentively as Nathan weaved a lesson of forgiveness and mercy—one of amazing grace, heartfelt gratitude, and selfless love. As Daniel recalled their late-night chat in Nathan's study and even this morning's conversation in his office, he couldn't stop the tears from welling in his eyes and falling down his cheeks. Like that father from Luke 15, Nathan had been patient, understanding and kind, full of wisdom, strength, and faith, and he had welcomed Daniel into his home, his family, and his life, without fear or reservations but in joy and gladness, with open arms and a loving heart.

Daniel sniffled, and Leah silently pressed a handkerchief in his hand. He accepted it and dried his eyes.

Later, Nathan extended the Invitation, welcoming those in need toward the altar—toward home. "Whether you're the wanderer or the faithful, a sinner or a saint, your heavenly Father is awaiting your homecoming with a feast prepared. Come and sup with Him. Come and let Him heal your hurt, romance your heart, ease your pain, and claim your soul. Come, casting your cares on His altar, and kneel before His throne of grace. Come, even in your brokenness, sickness, oppression, fearfulness, doubt, and sin. God loves you, and He wants to heal, deliver, and save you. He loves you so much He gave His only Son to suffer and die for you on Calvary's Cross, and Jesus, with His life and His blood, with His death and His resurrection, took your punishment, your penalty, and He paid in full the price for your sins—*your* debt. So you could be free, so you could come home and spend eternity with Him. This is the Father's heart for you: redemption, salvation, forgiveness, and reconciliation. So, stop running, come home, and find peace—all that you need in the arms of a loving Father, a matchless King. Today's your day, and this is your hour. Choose God, follow Christ, come." He stepped down from the podium, his hands open, his arms extended.

Chance stood, with his blue eyes pools of tears. He pushed past everyone, then ran up the aisle and threw himself in his father's arms. "I'm sorry, Dad. Forgive me."

"Always, son. I love you." Nathan held him at the altar, his own eyes glistening. He pulled back and kissed Chance's forehead, then he cried,

"Hallelujah! Thank you, Lord. Hallelujah!" He hugged Chance again, pressing him against his heart. "Welcome home, son. Welcome home."

Leah and Victor raced to the front and joined Nathan and Chance, and the four of them stood together, hugging and crying, praising and rejoicing in the Lord—all of them united—all of them a family.

Daniel glanced at Leisha, and he saw that she, too, was equally affected, with her hands palmed before her mouth and tears streaming from her eyes. She seemed forlorn even though she was surrounded by a crowd of people, so without hesitation, he turned and hugged her, letting her know that she wasn't alone, that he loved her and hadn't forgotten her, that she had family, too—him.

After the service, Daniel told Leah that her husband was anointed and truly gifted. "I felt the Holy Spirit at work within him."

"Preaching is in his blood. Nathan's father and grandfather were both ministers, and even his mother was an evangelist. That's why I'm not surprised that you were called into ministry. Evidently, God knows He can trust the family with His Word and His flock." She smiled. "You really are your father's son, Daniel. There's no escaping that."

An elderly Hispanic woman stepped in front of them, and at her side a younger woman with long black cascading hair and honey-gold eyes, wearing a white ruffled blouse and matching skirt. "How are you doing, Lady Dearling?"

"Better, Sister Avalos. Who's this young lady with you?"

Sister Avalos smiled. "Alessia de la Cruz, my youngest granddaughter. A child psychologist too. She just moved here from San Antonio, and she'll be working at the Hope Recovery Center. Most people know her by her professional name, Dr. Alessia de la Cruz."

"Nice to meet you." Leah leaned forward, hugging her.

"It's a pleasure to meet you, too, Lady Dearling. Granny Avalos loves you and Pastor Dearling, and she raves about you so much, I feel like I'm part of your family too."

Leah hugged her again. "That's so sweet."

"Since Victor works with kids and volunteers at Hope Recovery and he and Alessia are around the same age, I had hoped they could spend some time together. Away from work."

Leah's eyes sparkled. "That's a great idea, Sister Avalos. I'll definitely have to invite her over for Sunday dinner so she and my son can get better acquainted. I'm sure they'll have a lot in common. Wouldn't it be great if they became good friends?"

Sister Avalos beamed. "Great minds think alike, Lady Dearling. That's exactly what I've been telling my granddaughter, that your Victor is a good, respectful, and godly young man, and he and she would make great friends."

"Well, let me officially introduce her to everyone." She waved toward Victor and Chance. "Alessia, these are my sons Victor and Chance." She pointed out Daniel and Leisha. "These two, Daniel and Leisha, are family as well, and they're spending the weekend with us."

"Nice to meet you." Alessia shook their hands.

"I'd love for you to visit the house next week. Maybe if we're both nice, we can even convince Victor to escort you through town."

Alessia glanced at Victor, smiled at him, then blushed. "I don't want to impose."

Leah turned to Victor. "She wouldn't be, would she?"

"Not at all. I'm here to serve."

Chance touched Leah's arm. "I hate to interrupt, Mom, but we need to leave for lunch. Dad's already waiting on us."

Leah bade Alessia and her grandmother farewell. After they left and the group began walking through the corridor toward Nathan's office, Victor jockeyed for a position next to his mother. "I can't believe you did that, Mom."

She looked at him, her forehead creased. "What?"

"Embarrassed me."

She stopped walking, and so did Daniel, Chance, and Leisha. "How did I embarrass you?"

"You just set me up on a blind date."

"I only suggested you spend some time with Alessia, showing her around Crossland. As a friend. You're a grown man, you can choose your own dates."

"I'm glad you realize that."

Leah raised innocent eyes. "But Alessia *is* lovely, don't you think?"

"I just met her."

"I fell in love with Nathan at first sight."

"Alessia isn't you, and I'm not Dad."

"She's sweet, and she works with kids like you."

Victor rolled his eyes, then looked toward Daniel and Chance, who were both smothering their laughter. "This isn't funny."

"Of course it is, *Prince* Charming."

"Don't start that again, Chance. I'm not in the mood."

"Honey, Alessia might be the right woman for you. But you won't know until you give her a chance."

"Mom, listen. I'm not—"

She clapped her hands, cutting him off. "If you and she fell in love, got married, and had children, I'd be the happiest mother in the world. And I'd have the most adorable grandchildren—little dark-haired boys and girls."

"Slow down, Mom! Alessia and I are strangers. We're not getting married; we're not having kids; we're definitely not dating each other."

Ignoring him, Leah turned to Leisha. "Don't you think Victor and Alessia are compatible, that they'd make a great couple?"

"I'm a lawyer, not anybody's love expert."

"You're a smart woman, Leisha, so I'm sure you have an opinion."

"Not one I'm willing to share."

Victor clamped his hand on his mother's arm. "Mom, this is family business, just between you and me. Leave her out of it."

"Leisha's family, too. Or have you forgotten?"

"Of course not! But this isn't about her. It's about you forcing Alessia de la Cruz on me."

"I'm not forcing her on you."

"Feels like it."

"She's sweet, pretty, and intelligent, and she comes from a good family—a godly one. Why don't you like her?"

"It's not that I don't like her. My problem is this: She and I only met five minutes ago, and you're already pairing us together and giving us kids. I know she's attractive and nice and loves kids and she's the grand-daughter of a good family friend. And I know you'd love to have a daugh-ter-in-law to enjoy and some grandkids to spoil. But please, stop playing matchmaker, at least for me. I'm fine." He released her arm and pointed at Chance. "There's the confirmed bachelor. If anyone needs a love match, it's Chance. So push Alessia on him."

Chance raised his hands, shielding himself. "Don't get me involved. I've got enough problems getting myself straight with God. I don't need distractions or a child psychologist messing with my head. I definitely don't need her as a girlfriend or wife."

Victor frowned, then turned to Daniel. "What about you?"

"I'm a visitor, and I'm engaged, so count me out."

Victor sighed, shook his head, and grabbed the cross on his necklace. "God, protect me from a loving but meddling mother."

Daniel chuckled. "A better prayer would be: 'God, protect me from sweet but tempting Alessia.'"

Leah folded her arms. "I don't see what all the fuss is about, Victor. Alessia is a gift, a blessing, and God's put her right in your hands. Instead of complaining and rejecting a good gift, you need to be thankful and receive the gift with gladness. Besides, Alessia is a good investment, and you might not find a woman more suitable—one more complementing. That's why you need to accept her, while she's interested and available."

"I don't want to *accept* a woman, Mom. I want to really love her.

What if I settle for a safe, suitable woman, then find out later there's a more perfect love—a more amazing woman—meant for me?"

She lowered her hands and raised her eyes to his. "But is there a more perfect love, a better woman meant for you?"

"Only God knows, Mom."

She smiled, then patted his arm. "Then keep an open heart and don't give up on Alessia."

Victor sighed. "I'm not making any promises."

"Will you at least give her a chance—as a friend?"

"All right, Mom. You win. I'll—"

Leisha doubled over, coughing, her hands covering her eyes.

Daniel rushed to her side and put his hand on her back. "You okay, sis?"

She raised her head and looked at him, her eyes swimming in tears. "Dry throat. I need some water."

"Is that all?"

She stood straight and bobbed her head. "Yes."

Victor stepped to her side, concern on his face. "There's bottled water in Dad's office. I'll get it for you."

She coughed again. "I'll go to the restroom. There's a fountain outside of it." She turned from him and grabbed Daniel's arm, her grip firm. "Walk with me."

"Of course."

"Do you need me, sweetheart?"

Leisha looked at Leah. "No, La' Dear. Daniel's with me, and he'll take care of me."

She glanced from Daniel to Leisha, her eyes shining with tears. "I'm a mother, and I hurt when my children hurt. That includes you and Daniel." She touched Leisha's arm. "You can trust me. Always. If you need me for anything, I'm here too." She pulled her hand back and dried the tears from her eyes. "You're both my children, the joys of my heart, and I don't mind taking care of either of you, in sickness and in health. I love you. Always. Remember that."

Daniel nodded. "We will, La' Dear, and we'll see you in a few minutes."

"All right. I'll let you go then."

Chance stepped in and gently pulled his mother aside. "Let's go, Mom. Dad's waiting." He glanced at Victor, who lingered near Leisha. "You coming, Victor?"

"Sure." Silently, Victor joined Chance and his mother, and the three of them walked away.

Daniel escorted Leisha to the nearest water fountain, then he waited outside the Ladies' Room while she went inside. As he waited, he wondered what was really going on with Leisha. One minute she was fine, the next she was in tears.

Earlier that morning, she had been enjoying herself, even worshipping during the service. She hadn't become silent and distant until they had met Sister Avalos and her granddaughter. Until La' Dear had gushed over the girl and had welcomed her with open arms into the Dearling family. Was it possible? Could his sister be jealous? Five minutes later, she stepped from the restroom, her face fresh and clean, devoid of all tears and all traces of sadness. And his first thought was, she's got her mask back on. "You all right?"

"I'm fine. Thank you."

He gently grabbed her arm, pulling her to one side, away from the flow of traffic. "I've got three questions for you, sis, and I want you to trust me enough to be *real* and honest."

"I'll try."

"Do you like it here, being with the Dearlings?"

"Yes."

"Do you like Alessia, for a new friend?"

She met his stare, her amber eyes direct—unwavering. "No."

"Why not?"

"Is that your third question?"

"I'm just curious."

"I'd rather not answer it, then."

"All right, sis. I won't pry. But here's my final question: Are you ever going to tell a certain young, heroic man that you like him, that you might even love him, as more than a friend?"

A single tear slid down her cheek, and her mask finally cracked. "No, I'm not."

Chapter Twenty-Five

Let the beloved of the LORD rest secure in him, for he shields him all day long, and the one the LORD loves rests between his shoulders.

Deuteronomy 33:12 (NIV)

Holly Drive
Sunday, July 3

That night Nathan found Leisha sitting alone on a wicker bench on the back patio, her face uplifted as she stared at the stars shimmering in the sky. He held two popsicles in his hand, one grape and the other orange. "Do you mind some company?"

"No, I don't." Leisha shifted left on the seat.

"It's a little warm out here, so I thought you'd appreciate a cool treat." Nathan eased down beside her and extended the popsicles. "Choose your favorite."

Leisha smiled and selected the grape-flavored. "Thank you." She tore the wrapper. "I haven't eaten one of these since I was a kid." She lifted the popsicle to her mouth with enthusiasm, then savored every bit of it—enjoying the sugary sweetness even as it melted in her mouth.

"I love them, so Leah always stocks two boxes of them in the freezer." Nathan unwrapped his, then merrily bit into it, his eyes on Leisha. "So, tell me: What's your favorite color?"

"Purple."

"Is there a reason?"

"It's the color of my birthstone—amethyst."

"Your favorite singer?"

"CeCe Winans."

"She's good." He laughed. "But I've actually got four: James Cleveland, Shirley Caesar, Andraé Crouch, and Richard Smallwood." His eyes twinkled. "For a favorite song, though, I'm partial to Vanessa Bell Armstrong's 'Peace Be Still.'"

"There are three songs I like most: Andraé Crouch's 'Bless His Holy Name,' Lionel Ritchie's 'Jesus is Love,' and Myrna Summers' 'Uncloudy Day.'"

"Do you have a favorite choir?"

"Love Fellowship."

"Mine is Mississippi Mass. I favor those sermonettes they include. I was raised in church, so there's nothing better to me than listening to good gospel music and a powerful sermon."

"At my church, I like the music more than the sermons. Don't get me wrong: I love Pastor Derbey as a preacher and teacher, and his sermons are good and practical. But praise and worship is what really moves me spiritually, connecting me to God and helping me *feel* His presence. Does that make me a bad Christian?"

Nathan chuckled. "Goodness, no! Every sermon may not be for your benefit specifically; there may be others who need to glean from that message. However, when the sermon *is* meant for you, God will definitely tug on your heart, get your attention, and draw you in so you're in the right spirit to hear, receive, and act on His Word."

She relaxed. "Really?"

"Yes. If you think about it, too, praise and worship is the only part of the service devoted exclusively to God, for His glory and to usher in His presence. When we worship in spirit and truth as God desires, we're looking Godward and we're exalting Him above all things, including ourselves. The rest of the service is usually about us satisfying or supplying our individual needs—the spiritual, emotional, physical, or financial."

"I never thought of that." Leisha finished her popsicle, then sighed. "It's peaceful here, very relaxing. I'll miss all this beauty and serenity when I go home tomorrow."

"You're only four hours away, so you don't have to be a stranger. You can return any time, and you'll always have a place here."

Leisha turned, facing him. "Pastor, this weekend was nice, but I don't know if I can offer more or be the daughter you want—that baby girl you lost thirty-six years ago."

"You don't have to be anyone other than who you are, Leisha. I don't expect you to fit into some mold just to please me. I'm only asking that you be at ease around me and that you be yourself."

"Revealing the real Leisha Laurence hasn't always been easy."

"From what I've seen this weekend, you're one remarkable young woman. You're strong, smart, spirited, giving, kind, and gracious." He laughed. "You're a good cook, too, almost in Leah's league, and she's one of the best."

His praise warmed Leisha's heart and brought tears to her eyes. Her adoptive father had rarely relaxed with her, just to eat a treat, nor had he ever sat her down, enumerating her good qualities. He had been more preoccupied with work than her, especially after she had stopped chasing after him, trying to win his love, attention, and approval. After she had become a teenager, he had often been critical, focusing on what he perceived were her weaknesses—her flaws—her fluctuating weight, her single status, and her unwavering faith. Now, here was her birth father, who had only known her a couple of days, investing quality time in her and seemingly seeing beyond the cool façade she had worn for years straight to the woman within.

"You don't need to reinvent yourself; you only need to accept that others can love and appreciate you for who you truly are."

"I don't want to disappoint you or La' Dear. I had a habit of doing that with my parents, the Laurences. They had plans for me and my life, but I rebelled, choosing my own path and cutting them out of the picture. After college, I left home permanently, and we barely spoke without arguing. Eventually, we let distance, hurt feelings, and silence separate us. They died before I could ask for forgiveness for the disrespect, before I could tell them that I loved them, or even try to mend the rift between us."

Nathan covered Leisha's hand with his. "Regardless of what transpired between you and your parents, you should take comfort in knowing they did love you, even if they didn't always express it in the way you desired or could readily understand. Remember, they personally chose you for their daughter. Out of all the babies in the world, the Laurences wanted you." Nathan smiled, then raised Leisha's chin with his index finger. "Sweetheart, you were loved, and you *are* precious—one of a kind."

His words spoke to her heart, yet she couldn't forget the past—that pain she had carelessly inflicted. "I made so many mistakes with my parents. I disappointed them, and I judged them because they weren't living as I thought they should."

"Did you love your parents?"

"Yes."

"Were they perfect?"

"No."

"Are you?"

"Of course not!"

"Then know as humans we all make mistakes—sometimes big ones we can't always correct, but that doesn't mean we're beyond hope or that all is lost. You can't continually punish yourself for what you didn't do or say while your parents lived. What you *can* do is honor them by living a full life, by giving love and sharing it, by fulfilling your purpose while you're alive to do so." He gently squeezed her hand. "You've got to forgive yourself and even your parents, then move forward in joy, hope, and peace. And never forget: you're not alone. You have us, the Dearlings."

Leisha raised tearful eyes to his. "I'm not a Dearling, Pastor. I'm a Laurence."

Nathan took the popsicle stick from her hand, then discarded it with his before confronting her again, taking her hand in his. "Regardless of who raised you, you're my daughter, and I love you."

"You don't know me. Not really."

"I know enough, and I'm willing to learn more if you'll let me."

"I'm not some princess or ideal daughter." She lowered her eyes, gathering courage to expose the worst part of herself, her flaws. "I'm a loner who usually chases people away. And until recently my only family has been my friend Salena and my dog Orion. I don't date because it's hard for me to trust people with my heart, and I don't know if there's a man out there who can really love me as flawed as I am. I'm too stubborn, independent, and proud at times, and it's hard for me to stay quiet, be weak or submissive or even accept criticism and love. Likely, I'll never get married and I'll die a spinster—childless and alone."

Nathan's forehead creased. "Do you believe God loves you?"

"Yes."

"Have you accepted Him as your heavenly Father?"

"What do you mean?"

"God knows the plans He has for you, plans to prosper you and not to harm you, plans to give you hope and a future. If all you expect to get from Him in this life is loneliness, unhappiness, and disappointment, then you don't understand His concept of love, and you don't trust Him to treat you as His beloved daughter." Nathan caressed her hand. "Honey, He's good, more faithful, patient, and loving than I am or your adopted father ever was, and He wants you to trust Him with your whole heart, soul, mind, and strength, with every part of your life, the good and the bad, including your flaws. And like a Good Father, He's ready and willing to bless you and give you good gifts, to love and protect you, to sustain and guide you, to comfort and counsel you, to encourage and correct you, and to supply all your needs, even give you the desires of your heart, when you ask according to His will."

"I'm used to being on my own—making my own dreams come true, not letting down my guard or trusting many people. Especially with my heart." Leisha exhaled. "I love God, but sometimes, it's hard for me to see Him as Father—my parent. I don't know why, but maybe it has more to do with how I was raised than any fear I have about God hurting me."

"Did your parents ever tell you they loved you?"

"When I was younger, all the time. After I turned thirteen, not so much. I became their problem child—ungrateful and rebellious."

"What was significant about age thirteen?"

"I thought my parents cared more about public perception than me, and I stopped trying to please them. They wanted a perfect child—a replica of themselves—and I could never satisfy them because I was so imperfect, so different from them. I didn't trust them, and I didn't think they could love me for the person I was, mainly because every time I did reveal my heart to them, they would pound on it, like they wanted to break it.

After a while, I got more disappointment, criticism, and shame from them than love, kindness, encouragement, or respect, so I rarely felt comfortable, even in my own home. I became distant and shut down emotionally, almost to the point where I didn't feel anything, good or bad. I was a rebel, cold and reserved, even during my first semester in college, and that's why some of the guys I rejected started calling me the Ice Princess. After that, nobody bothered me much, except Salena Blake, my dorm mate. That first semester I was horrible to her, not friendly at all. I was either silent and frosty or sarcastic and rude. I didn't trust her; I didn't trust anybody." She looked up and was surprised to see compassion, not pity, reflected in his eyes. "So, you see, giving my heart is a matter of trust, and that's been a major problem for me."

Nathan pulled her closer, into his warmth. "Let me tell you a story called 'Little Heart.'"

She frowned. "How's a story supposed to help me?"

He smiled and patted her arm. "Listen, and you'll find out."

She sighed. "All right, I'm listening."

"Once upon a time there lived a family: a father, mother, and daughter. The father adored his daughter, calling her Little Heart, and he lavished her with an abundance of love and gifts and spent much time with her, hugging her close and holding her tight so he could protect her. Soon, the time came when the father had to release that daughter's hand, slowly letting her go—first to school, then into the world. He still loved her fiercely, but he wasn't always present to protect her. Since he couldn't embrace or protect her forever, he entrusted her to God.

"When she was eight, she returned home with dirty clothes, a bloody face, and scraped arms and legs, and she cried, 'Daddy, I fell from my bike, and I got hurt.' He hugged her, gently picked her up, and cleaned her, tending those wounds with ointment, bandages, and love. She rewarded him with a bright smile and a warm kiss, saying, 'Thank you, Daddy. I'm all better now. I don't hurt anymore.'

"When she was sixteen, she fell into his arms inconsolable, sobbing, 'I'm ugly, Daddy, and the boy I like doesn't like me.' He dried her tears, pulled her in front of a mirror, and stood behind her, saying, 'You're beautiful, Little Heart, fearfully and wonderfully made in love, in the image of God—His very likeness. You were conceived in God's heart, fashioned with hair like glorious silk, cascading gracefully to your shoulders, with eyes as deep and colorful as pools of precious water, with lips shaped like a heart, full and smiling, and skin, soft and unblemished formed from the best of God's good earth. You're extraordinary and precious, more valuable than rubies, emeralds, diamonds, or pearls, and in time the right boy will come along and discover that you're God's best treasure, and he'll appreciate you, just as you are.' The daughter saw herself through her father's eyes, and she swirled, looping her arms around his neck. 'Thank you, Daddy.' She beamed brighter than the noon sun. 'Instead of ugliness, I see beauty in me.'

"After her eighteenth birthday, the daughter stomped into the father's study and threw a rejection letter onto his desk, declaring, 'I'm a failure, and nobody wants me. I didn't get into my first choice for college.' The father stood, extending both arms, and she walked into that consoling embrace. 'You're a survivor—an overcomer,' he said, withdrawing and studying her tear-streaked face. 'You're victorious, too—not easily defeated. If God has closed the door to that college, then He has another opened to the college that's more suited to your gifts and talents. Don't count this one rejection as a lifetime failure, a comment on your ability or potential; instead, look at it as a gift, a stepping stone toward your destiny, your calling, your ministry—your purpose.'

He turned, lifting a second letter from his desk, then handed it to his daughter. 'This came in the mail for you last week, but I forgot to give it to you.' He watched in anticipation as she scanned the return address, then ripped into the envelope. Her face lit like sunshine breaking through clouds after a storm, and he knew she had received good news. 'What is it?' he asked. She leaped into his arms, laughing and crying. 'I got in, Daddy! My third choice accepted me! This was my dream college—the best one, the most expensive and the most competitive—and I didn't even expect a reply—yet, they've chosen me, and they're offering a four-year, full academic scholarship.' She danced in her father's arms, smothering him with kisses. 'Thank you, Daddy, for believing in me, even when I get discouraged.' The father kissed her forehead and said, 'You're blessed, Little Heart. Thank God for His favor. Your last choice was His first, His best for you.'

"When the daughter was twenty-two, she returned from college heartbroken, telling her father, 'I'm destined to be single, to live and die alone. Nobody loves me.' He wrapped secure arms around her, saying,

'Your mother loves you, for she carried you beneath her heart for nine months, lavishing you with songs and promises, speaking Life into you and spinning dreams around you. Then, she labored for hours bringing you into this world. I love you, too, with a love as high as mountains stretching toward heaven, as deep and wide as oceans spanning this globe. But, as much as your mom and I love you, God loves you more. He gave His only Son for you so you could be reconciled to Him and enjoy eternal life, and that Son loves you beyond boundaries and imagination, and His love lives and abides in you. You're not alone, Little Heart, for God is always with you. You're loved. Never forget that.' The daughter dried her tears, pressed her hand over her father's heart, and said, 'I love you, Daddy. You see love in me.' He smiled, then winked at her, saying, 'Little Heart, Jesus is Love, and I see Him in you.'

"Finally, when the daughter was thirty years old, she raced into her father's arms, dressed in a bridal gown with tears of happiness glistening in her eyes. 'Daddy, you were right. God sent the right man, just for me. He's my Boaz, my prince, my friend, and the man in all my dreams. I love him, Daddy, but more than that, he loves God, and he loves me. He says he wants to be my husband for a lifetime and the father of every child I ever have. Oh, Daddy! I'm so happy, so grateful. Thank you for praying for me, blessing me, always protecting and encouraging me, and for seeing the best in me, even when I saw only the flaws—the imperfections.' The father pressed her hand to his heart, then kissed her cheek, telling her, 'Thank you, Little Heart. It's been an honor and a privilege to be your father, to watch you grow into this beautiful, caring, and loving woman of virtue, faith, love, and joy.

'Today, with gladness I'll escort you to your future husband and entrust you into his care, for I know he's the man God has chosen for you, the one meant to love, cherish, respect, and protect you from this day forward. However, never doubt I'm always here when you need me, ready to battle any adversary, to climb any mountain, to cross any ocean, or to offer any consolation. I'm releasing you today, giving you to another man, but I'm never releasing you from my heart. You're my daughter, and you forever will be my precious Little Heart. I love you.'

The daughter lifted her face and kissed his left cheek. 'I love you, too, Daddy. In every lesson and through every trial you've shown me the heart and love of God.' The father dried her tears, tucked her arm beneath his, then proudly escorted her up the aisle to the man she loved. When the minister asked, 'Who gives this woman away,' the father stood beside his wife and declared, 'We do—her mother and I.' Then, he sat down and watched with a full heart as his only child—his daughter—before him and God pledged herself to another. And with a grateful heart, he silently prayed: 'Thank You, Father, for the precious gift You gave me. Once again I give my Little Heart back to You. May You bless her and keep her and make Your face shine upon her and be gracious to her; may You lift up Your countenance upon her, and give her peace. In Jesus' name, amen.'"

Tears streamed down Leisha's face. "That's a beautiful story."

"It's a love story between a father and his daughter." Nathan pressed his and Leisha's combined hands over his heart. "It's *our* story, Leisha—the missing chapters—my hopes and dreams deferred for thirty-six years. Today, at this moment, though, I'm making a declaration: you're my Little Heart, my precious daughter, and I want you."

She saw the love in his eyes but was hesitant to trust it. "You really want me?"

Nathan nodded. "Yes, sweetheart, I do. I've always wanted a daughter, and you're just the daughter I've dreamed of—a gift from God." He caressed her face. "I'm a man of faith, and I believe God has brought us together after all these years so we can love each other." He kissed her forehead, then pulled back, his eyes shimmering. "I accept you, and I love you, just as you are."

Leisha bridged the gap and hugged him, and Nathan held her close—lovingly and protectively. "Thank you, Pastor." She snuggled against him, inhaling his peppermint scent. "Thank you."

"You're welcome, Little Heart." He gently rubbed her hair and pressed another kiss atop her head. "Will you give me a chance to love you?"

She bobbed her head, her arms secure around him. "Yes, sir. I will."

"I thank you, and I thank God for softening your heart toward me and for giving me a new chapter in your life." He pulled back and cupped her face in his hands. "I love you. Don't ever doubt that." He kissed her forehead again, then stood, pulling her to her feet. "It's getting late, and Leah wants us to play Bible Bingo before heading to bed, so we'd better go inside now."

As they walked side by side, his arm still draped around her, Leisha felt cherished, loved, and protected, and being with Nathan felt natural, right. For the first time, she felt like she mattered, like she really belonged, and she wasn't as eager as she had previously been to return home to her empty apartment and her lonely life.

Chapter Twenty-Six

Let love and faithfulness never leave you; bind them around your neck, write them on the tablet of your heart. Then, you will win favor and a good name in the sight of God and man.

Proverbs 3:3–4 (NIV)

Holly Drive
Monday, July 4

"*H*appy Birthday!"

Chance's mother and father surprised him in bed with hugs, kisses, and a white-frosted birthday cake with red, white, and blue sprinkles and candles on top.

"Thanks, Mom and Dad. With everything going on, I didn't think we'd be celebrating."

His mother frowned. "Of course, we'd celebrate your thirty-third birthday. You're our son, and we love you."

"I love you guys, too."

His mother pushed the cake forward. "Now, blow out these candles. Then, shower and get dressed. We've got a full agenda today. We're having a family breakfast, watching a movie, letting you open your gifts, driving to Hope Park at six, then returning here so Leisha and Daniel can collect their luggage for their trip home."

"Are you sure you're up for all of this?"

"Yes. I'm fine."

"Don't overexert yourself, Mom."

"Stop worrying about me and enjoy your birthday." She leaned forward and ruffled his hair, then she kissed his forehead. "Blow out your candles!"

"All right. You win." He took a deep breath, then blew.

"Did you make a wish, son?"

"Yes, Dad. I did." He had wished for his mother to get well and cele-brate more birthdays with him.

"Let's hope it comes true." Chance's mother handed his father the cake, then hugged Chance again. "We'll put the cake in the kitchen and cut it after lunch." She stood, moving beside his father.

"Have a blessed day, son."

"Thanks, Dad. I will." He watched them leave, then he climbed from bed, heading for the bathroom and a quick shower.

Downstairs at breakfast, Victor, Daniel, and Leisha greeted Chance with hugs and an impromptu serenade of "Happy Birthday," and his mother plied him with healthy servings of his favorite breakfast food: scrambled eggs, buttered cream of wheat, turkey bacon, and buttermilk biscuits with peach jelly—all of which he washed down with a tall, cold glass of milk. Later, they paired into teams and played a board game, then settled in the living room with soft drinks, popcorn, and nachos, and they watched an inspirational film.

That evening at Hope Park, they all found a vacant spot on the grass and set up camp, pulling out their assorted red, white, and blue portable chairs. As patriotic music pulsed through the air, Chance's parents held hands, chatting with passersby and pointing out people and attractions to Daniel and Leisha. Later, they encouraged the twins to get up and explore, enjoying themselves with Chance and Victor.

After enticing Daniel and Leisha to loosen up and participate in some of the group games, Chance and Victor led them toward the food stands so they could sample Crossland's best in holiday fare. In the spirit of the occasion they all stuffed themselves, then ventured through the park, greeting other families and admiring the firework displays. Eventually, they returned to their mother and father so they could watch the colorfully majestic and orchestrated fireworks finale.

Leisha clapped. "That was spectacular."

Chance's mother leaned over and hugged her. "I'm glad you came."

"So am I, La' Dear. This has been a great weekend."

She pulled back, her eyes shifting from Leisha to Daniel. "I pray it's not the last we spend together. As a family."

Chance's father stood. "It's getting late, so we'd better head home."

They all packed up their belongings, then walked toward the parking lot. When they arrived at their vehicles, they separated—Daniel and Leisha following Chance's parents to their black car and Chance and Victor striding toward Chance's blue truck. Twenty minutes later, they arrived back at Holly Drive.

After Daniel and Leisha collected their luggage, both came downstairs to the living room and exchanged hugs with Chance's parents, telling them that they were glad to have finally met them and that they had had a fun, memorable visit.

"Phone us and let us know you got home safely."

Leisha nodded. "We will, La'Dear."

"You've got our contact information, so stay in touch."

Daniel smiled. "Yes, ma'am."

"Grab your mother's digital camera, Chance. I'd like for us to take a family photo."

"Okay, Dad." Chance brought out the camera and a tripod, letting everyone get positioned, his parents sitting on the couch in the center, Daniel and Leisha on their left and Victor on their right. He adjusted the camera on the tripod, then joined Victor as the camera began its countdown. When it flashed, everyone was smiling.

As his parents, Daniel, and Leisha admired the photo, Chance pulled Victor aside. "Since you're still recovering, you can stay here. I'll drive Leisha to Corinth and Daniel to the airport."

"Don't pamper me. I can handle a road trip."

"What about Leisha?"

"Not a problem. You and I started this together, so we'll finish it the same."

"We'd better leave then." He rounded up the twins and their luggage, then led Daniel and Leisha to the driveway with his parents trailing behind, tears already in their eyes. As Chance hoisted Leisha's and Daniel's bags into the back of his truck, then secured them, Victor offered Daniel the front passenger seat, and he climbed in back beside Leisha.

On the road, Leisha dozed, and Victor and Daniel chatted, often drawing Chance in to keep him alert as he drove. But for the final hour, everyone was quiet, and the fourth hour seemed to fly as swiftly as the progressing songs on the radio. When they passed Corinth's population sign, Leisha tapped Chance's right shoulder. "I need to pick up my dog Orion from Salena's. I phoned her before we left, so she's waiting for us."

"No problem." He followed her instructions, and within thirty minutes, they were pulling into a gated community and advancing through winding streets. Finally, they reached a two-story brick home surrounded by tall trees and colorful flowers.

As they pulled into the driveway, Salena and a white dog sprang from the front door, and as soon as Chance stopped the truck, Leisha opened the passenger door and leaped down, hugging Salena who wore a white blouse and red slacks, then the dog who jumped into Leisha's arms, barking.

Salena walked toward the truck, her eyes bright, her smile winsome, and her face radiant, and Chance rolled down his window, surprisingly glad to see her. "We meet again, Blue Eyes."

"I guess so."

She peeked inside the truck and greeted Daniel and Victor, and they both returned the salutation. Then, her eyes focused on Chance. "I'm two hours late, but 'Happy Birthday!'"

"Thanks."

"I've got something for you." She pulled a small box from her pocket and offered it to him.

"What is it?"

"A birthday gift, a token of remembrance."

"You didn't have to buy me a gift."

"I wanted to. Don't return it either. It's yours. No strings attached."

"Thanks."

"You're welcome." She smiled, then touched his arm. "Open it when you're alone, thinking of me. I'm sure you'll like it."

"When did you buy it?"

"The day after we danced, after our first kiss."

His eyes met hers. "How could you be certain I'd come back, that you'd have a chance to give it to me?"

She pointed up, toward heaven. "I have a divine connection." She stepped closer, her face inches from his. "Now, I'll give you my last surprise—a *real* kiss." She leaned over the window, pressed soft lips against his, and kissed him so thoroughly she left him speechless, breathless, warm. Finally, she pulled back, brushed the hair from his forehead, then stepped away from the truck. "Drive safely. Enjoy your gift."

"I will."

She smiled, then strutted back inside her house, with Leisha and the dog at her heels.

"*Hermano*, have I missed an update?"

"No, you haven't." Chance slipped Salena's gift into his pant pocket.

"Why didn't you tell me you had kissed Salena?"

"It was personal, none of your business."

"Are you two an item?"

"We're not dating, we're not a couple."

"That kiss looked pretty intimate. Didn't it, Daniel?"

"Definitely."

"Do you think Chance is holding out on us?"

"He and I met Salena the same day, yet he's the one she danced with all night, the one she nicknamed Blue Eyes, the one she gave a gift, the one she's staked her claim on and branded with a decadent kiss."

Victor laughed. "That was some kiss, all right! It was so blazing hot I thought we'd hear fire alarms blaring."

"I'm in the front seat," Daniel said. "And it was so sizzling, I almost got burned. So intense, I had to cover my eyes."

"That's enough, guys." Chance got enough teasing from Victor; he didn't it need from Daniel too. "It was only a kiss, nothing more."

"I can't see from here, Daniel. Is my brother's face red?"

Daniel flicked on the overhead light, then looked at Chance. "Like an apple."

Chance reached over and turned the light off. "What does my face have to do with anything?"

"If it was an innocent kiss, *hermano*, you wouldn't be blushing."

"I'm not blushing!"

"Of course, you're not! I still can't believe you didn't tell me about that first kiss. We're brothers, friends even."

"There's nothing to tell. We dined together with Daniel and Leisha, and later on the balcony, Salena kissed my cheek. Afterward, we danced. That's all."

"Congratulations! You finally have a girlfriend."

"She's not my girlfriend."

"Then why'd you let her kiss you?"

"I told you: She kissed my cheek."

"If that kiss was tame, this second was fierce. And you didn't seem to mind either. Looked like you were enjoying it. A lot."

"You've had your fun, Victor. Let it go."

"Since you're getting sensitive, I will. For now."

"Thanks."

Leisha returned with Orion on a leash, and she climbed back into the truck, settling the dog between her and Victor. After Chance heard her seatbelt click, he turned the key in the ignition, shifted into reverse, and left Salena's driveway.

Thirty minutes later, they arrived at Wyndham Court Apartments.

Victor, Chance, and Daniel each got out to escort Leisha to her apartment. Daniel volunteered to carry her luggage, and Victor held Orion's leash while Leisha fished inside her purse for her key. She inserted the key in the lock, but before she could twist the doorknob, Chance covered her hand, offering to enter first and make sure all was safe and secure.

"I appreciate your concern, but it's not necessary. These apartments are gated, they have twenty-four-hour camera surveillance, and there's a policeman on the premises. I'm safe here."

"Humor me."

She released the knob and stepped back. "Be my guest, then."

Chance opened the door, flicked on the lights, then surveyed every room. When he was satisfied all was well, he returned to the front and called the others. "All's clear." He stepped aside so Leisha, Daniel, and Victor could enter.

As Victor removed Orion's leash, Daniel carried Leisha's luggage to her bedroom, and Chance took a bathroom break, then returned and sat on the sofa, twirling his key around his index finger as Victor ventured to the bathroom. When they were all together again, Leisha asked whether any of them wanted food or drinks.

Chance shook his head. "I'm still stuffed from all we ate on my birthday. And we really don't have the time. We've got two more hours of driving to get Daniel to the nearest airport in Heaventon Hope. His plane leaves at six forty-five, so we need to get back on the highway."

"Chance is right, sis. We've got to go." Daniel hugged her. "Now that I've found you, though, don't think I'm losing you again." He cupped her chin in his hand. "Call me anytime for anything."

"I will." She hugged him again. "I pray you all have traveling grace."

"Thank you." Daniel raised his head and kissed her forehead. "Stay safe and be blessed."

"Likewise." She pulled away, with tears in her eyes, turned, and hugged Chance. "Thank you for playing the chauffeur this weekend and for helping us get acquainted with Pastor and La' Dear."

"You're welcome."

Leisha stepped back and dried her wet eyes. "You're a good son, a good person. I don't know if, in your position, I would have been as gracious or accepting. You welcomed Daniel and me into your family and your home with openness and love, and for that, you have my respect and appreciation."

Chance grinned. "You and Daniel are good people, too, so it wasn't a hardship to welcome you home. I've known Daniel longer, but I've gotten to know you better this weekend, and you've grown on me, too." He laughed. "At times, you've been soft and tender; at others, you've been tough and competitive, and it all works in your favor." He jabbed her shoulder. "You're okay for an older sister."

She smiled. "And you're all right for a little brother. Thank you. For everything."

"You're welcome."

Leisha exhaled, then turned to Victor. "May I hug you?"

"Anytime." He wrapped his right arm around her and pressed her against his chest, his eyes closed.

Leisha stepped back, and he opened his eyes. "Thanks for finding me, for telling me the truth, and for saving my life." She raised her head and kissed his forehead. "Take care of yourself."

He smiled. "You too, Leisha." He tucked a brown curl behind her ear. "I enjoyed spending time with you this weekend, getting to know the great woman behind the good lawyer. In case this is it, I want you to live, laugh, and love. More than anything, I want you to be happy."

"I will."

"Goodbye."

She looked at him, fresh tears in her eyes. "Not goodbye. Goodnight, Victor."

"Goodnight." He turned, walked away from her, and motioned to Chance. "Come on, brother. It's time to go."

Chance saw tears in his eyes and knew it was too late to stop him from careening over a cliff. Victor had already fallen—hard. He was in love and had already given his heart away. Unfortunately, to the wrong woman. Mindful of his brother's promise—his sacrifice—Chance hastily bade Leisha farewell; then, he ushered Victor and Daniel out of the apartment door. When he glanced back, he saw Leisha standing over the threshold, watching them. Silently, he waved, then faced forward and walked away.

Two hours later at the airport in Heaventon Hope, he and Victor said goodbye to Daniel, exchanging hugs and handshakes with him.

"I appreciate all you two have done," Daniel said. "I know this wasn't easy on either of you—tracking me and Leisha down, spending weeks away from home and work, and then being forced to share your parents with us."

"We weren't forced," Chance said. "We acted freely."

Daniel clapped his hand on Chance's shoulder. "All I can say is, thank you. It's an honor to call you both brothers—family—and if you ever need anything, you can count on me. Just pick up a phone and call, and I'll answer. Always." He hugged Chance, then Victor again. "Till next time, be blessed." He waved, then walked away, disappearing in a sea of people.

Chance turned to Victor. "Do you think they'll come back on their own? For Mom and Dad?"

"I hope so." He clapped his right hand on Chance's back. "You've earned some rest, so I'll drive home."

"Nice joke, but that's not happening."

"I can drive."

"With one hand?"

"I can try."

"No, thanks. I'm not ready to die."

"Aren't you tired?"

"I'm fine."

"Are you sure?"

"Positive. Now, let's go home."

They returned to the truck and rode in silence most of the journey home. After two hours, they stopped at a convenience store for gas and snacks.

As Chance sat outside in the truck waiting for Victor's return, he removed Salena's gift from his pant pocket. He flicked on the overhead light, lifted the box lid, and removed a folded note and a gold pocket watch. Turning the watch over, he saw that it was engraved on its back with Ephesians 2:10, and the word *DARE*, and inside the watch lid was a round photo of Salena smiling. On the note, Salena had written the verse, Ephesians 2:10: "For we are his workmanship, created in Christ Jesus unto good works, which God hath before ordained that we should walk in them." Beneath it was written her personal challenge: *Dare to dream, Dare to love, Dare to live, Dare to dance.*

Chance folded the note again and returned it to the box, but Salena's words burned within his mind and heart. He turned the light off. He closed the lid on the watch, palmed the watch in his right hand, and pressed it against his heart.

Victor climbed into the passenger seat, a plastic bag looped around his right arm. He put the bag on the floor, then shut the door. After fastening his seatbelt, he looked at Chance, his eyes drifting to Chance's right hand. "Is that Salena's gift?"

"Yes."

"What is it?"

Chance turned from him and stared ahead, his eyes fixed on the long, lonely highway stretching before him. "A watch and a dare."

Chapter Twenty-Seven

And he has given us this command:
Whoever loves God must also love his brother.

1 John 4:21 (NIV)

Corinth, Texas
Saturday, September 3

At six o'clock, Leisha returned home from her workout at Lakeland Fitness Center, and she tossed her purse and purple duffel bag onto the sofa, calling Orion. After he came bounding from her bedroom toward her, his tail swishing, she leaned down, running her fingers through his fur; then, she hugged him. "I've had my exercise; now it's time for yours." She grabbed his blue leash from the table and fastened it onto his matching collar. Next, she removed the apartment key from her purse, zipped it inside a black pouch, then snapped the pouch around her waist. "We're ready!" She stood and escorted Orion from the apartment and along the walkway circling the spacious grounds.

They walked thirty minutes and were traipsing over a footbridge when a well-built man with a clean-shaven head, wearing a gray shirt and navy shorts, approached them smiling, a German Shepherd plodding beside him. Leisha recognized him as her neighbor from apartment 390, but she couldn't recall his name. In the two years he had been living at Wyndham Court, she had seen him countless times but had only conversed with him once. Then, she learned that he was from Richmond, Virginia, and had been in law enforcement.

Instead of passing Leisha, the man stopped, his golden-brown eyes bright as though he were pleased to see her. "We finally meet again, Leisha Laurence from apartment 377."

"Apparently." Leisha mentally flogged herself for forgetting his name. "You're from 390, right?"

He grinned. "You don't remember me, do you?"

"Sometimes I'm better with faces than names. Sorry."

"We haven't spoken in two years, so I understand." He extended his hand. "The name's Bennett Ford."

Leisha shook his hand, smiling. "Nice to see you again, Bennett. I apologize for the memory lapse."

"You're forgiven." He released her hand but kept staring at her. After she stepped back, trying to escape the intensity of those eyes, he looked down and pointed. "Who's your friend?"

"Orion. And yours?"

"Lady." He leaned down and rubbed his dog. "She's my best girl, and we've been together for three years. Before then, she was a search and rescue dog for the police department. She's like family, and I love the old girl dearly."

"I feel the same about Orion. That's why I feel guilty about leaving him alone so often when I'm working. He's an active dog and hates being cooped up for long."

"Lady and I have the same problem." His gaze shifted from Leisha to Lady and Orion who were standing obediently but were eying each other with curiosity. "Maybe you and I should consider setting up some play dates for these two."

"Seriously?"

"Both would benefit from the fresh air, exercise, and companionship, and you and I would have time to become better acquainted." He fastened those bright eyes back on her. "Are you interested?"

"Give me some time to consider." She hardly knew the man, so she wasn't about to make any hasty decisions or leap blindly into an unknown situation.

Bennett flashed a brilliant smile. "How about you give me your answer over dinner next weekend?"

Leisha's eyes widened. "You're proposing a date?"

"I'd like to spend time with you, just talking and sharing a good meal."

"Why?"

"You left quite an impression on me the first time we met, and since then, I've been waiting for another chance to talk to you." He laughed. "To be honest, I've thought of nothing more than dating you. Exclusively."

Leisha frowned. "You want to date me?"

"It would be an honor."

Leisha placed a hand on her hip. "Why do you assume I'm available?"

"I've never seen you with a man, a boyfriend. You're either with your red-haired friend or you're alone."

"Maybe I'm discreet."

"Then, pardon the assumption. Are you involved with anyone?"

"I'm single, but I don't date. What about you? Is there already a girl-friend or fiancée lurking in the shadows?"

He laughed. "I'm not a man who plays the field or juggles women, so there's no competition. I'm single and monogamous, and my last relationship ended three years ago before I left Richmond." He raised his finger. "I've never been married or divorced, and I don't have any children, in or out of wedlock."

Leisha had seen other female tenants ogling Bennett, so she was curious why some woman hadn't already snatched him up. "You've been here two years. Why aren't you involved with anyone yet?"

"I have a demanding job, and it doesn't leave much time for romance."

"You're a police officer, right?"

"A police helicopter pilot."

"Really?"

"I've been flying for twenty-one years, beginning when I was sixteen."

Leisha quickly calculated. "You're thirty-seven?"

"I celebrated my birthday the twenty-second of August."

"Happy belated birthday."

"Thank you. Now, for future reference, when's your birthday?"

"February, the twenty-first."

His smile broadened, and he tapped his forehead with an index finger. "You were born in the month of Love. I'll definitely remember that." He lowered his hand, appraising her again with those appealing eyes. "So, now that you know I'm single, sane, and safe, will you have dinner with me next Saturday night?"

"Didn't you just say your job prevents you from dating?"

"I'm available next weekend, and I'd enjoy spending that time exclusively with you."

"I'm flattered, Bennett, but I'm really not interested in dating." She touched his forearm, trying to lessen the rejection. "Thank you for the offer, but I can't accept it." She pulled back her hand.

"I'll accept your refusal this evening, mainly because I blindsided you. However, I'm not giving up so easily. I'm a patient man, and you're definitely one woman I don't mind waiting for. When you're ready to move forward and trust me, I'll be here. Just knock on my door, let me know you're interested, and I'll welcome you inside. Until then, good evening." He tilted his head toward her, then walked away whistling, with Lady at his side.

Leisha returned to her apartment, her encounter with Bennett Ford still on her mind. Her second meeting with him reinforced her first impression that he was a nice, attractive man. However, she wasn't ready to commit to a serious relationship with him, especially when her thoughts and her heart were still plagued by Victor Dearling.

After Leisha removed Orion's leash and fed him, she undressed and soaked in a nice, warm bubble bath. Later, she donned a gray shirt and shorts, warmed herself a plate of baked chicken and snap beans, and silently ate, mulling over Bennett's parting words again—his invitation. Bennett was genuinely interested in her, and he hadn't been shy about sharing his feelings—unlike Victor.

For the past two months, Victor had been silent and invisible, rarely around the few times Leisha had visited the Dearlings, nor had he even called, just to check on her. Leisha had even learned from La' Dear that Victor was often in the company of his new friend, Alessia de la Cruz, the seemingly sweet, dark-haired angel Leisha had been introduced to from church. Although she and Victor weren't officially a couple, La' Dear thought them perfect together, a match made in heaven.

Naturally, Leisha had been disheartened by the news. Although Victor hadn't declared his feelings for her or even hinted that he loved her, she had assumed he felt more than friendship and affection. Now, she wasn't certain. If he could forget her and turn to another so easily, maybe she should do the same. Maybe she should stop putting her love life on hold and waiting for Victor to make his intentions clear. After all, he was the one who had urged her to live, love, and laugh more. Maybe it was time for her to do so.

After washing her plate, Leisha collapsed on the sofa and dug through her purse until she found her cell phone. She was anxious to phone Salena and get her thoughts on Bennett Ford, the bold neighbor from apartment 390.

Instantly, she saw the notification that she had a voice message and several missed calls from Chance Dearling. *Something's wrong.* She punched in her security code. *Chance wouldn't be this frantic to reach me unless he had bad news.* She clutched the phone and pressed it against her ear.

In the message, Chance said that he urgently needed to speak to her about his mother and that Leisha should contact him at her earliest convenience. Her heart thumping hard against her chest, Leisha dialed his number and waited impatiently to hear his voice.

"Leisha?"

"What's happening?"

"Mom collapsed, and she's been hospitalized."

No! Leisha's heart sank. "Is she all right?"

"Dr. Camm wants her to have surgery next week. Until then, she'll remain at Crossland Memorial."

Leisha sank back against the sofa, covering her mouth. "She's having surgery next week?"

"Yes."

"Is she strong enough?"

"We're praying she is."

"Does Daniel know yet?"

"Victor phoned him earlier."

Leisha tried to process all that Chance had told her. La' Dear was in the hospital fighting for her life, and she had a risky surgery on the horizon. What he hadn't said but she intuitively knew was that there could be complications and La' Dear could die, and that thought caused a tremendous ache in Leisha's heart. Now that she personally knew and loved La' Dear, she couldn't imagine losing her. "Do you need anything?"

"All we need is love, faith, hope, and prayer."

"You've got it all, then." She swiped tears away with her fingers. "Are you at home or the hospital?"

"At my parents' house. Victor and I are taking shifts, commuting between here and the hospital. He's there, and I'm here, house-sitting while Dad is camped at Crossland Memorial with Mom." He sighed, sounding exhausted. "I figure with Mom facing surgery next week, Dad doesn't need to worry about anything else."

"Well, I won't hold you longer. Thank you for calling and notifying me."

"You're family, so you have a right to be informed." He yawned. "I'm going to catch a few hours of sleep before heading back to the hospital to relieve Victor, but I'll keep you updated."

"Thank you."

"Goodnight."

"Goodnight, Chance." She disconnected, then dropped the phone and massaged her temples. Now that she knew about La' Dear, she couldn't pretend that all was well, that her life was as normal as it had been minutes ago. A pebble had forcefully struck the window of her heart, and now it was about to shatter.

Standing, Leisha walked to her bedroom and retrieved her family album from the closet. She returned to the living room with it, then sat down on the sofa, the album in her lap. Turning to the final sheet, she found a copy of the family photo she had taken in July with the Dearlings, and she brushed her finger across Leah Dearling's radiant face. The camera had captured love and joy in that face.

God, strengthen and heal her. Let her sit among family smiling like this again. Let no weapon formed against her prosper. Let her overcome this; let her live victoriously a conqueror through You. Leisha closed the album, then lifted her phone again, calling Salena.

"What's wrong, friend?"

"La' Dear is in the hospital, and she's scheduled for brain surgery next week."

"I'm sorry to hear that. I'll add her and the rest of the Dearlings to my prayer list."

"Thanks. But I had more in mind than prayer."

"What do you need?"

"A big favor."

"Tell me."

"I need you in Crossland with me."

"When?"

"As soon as I can make arrangements."

"All right, I'll go with you."

"Thank you. I didn't want to go alone."

"You're never alone, Leisha. As long as you live, you've got two life-long partners, God and me."

Sutton, Georgia
Saturday, September 3

Daniel sat at his dining room table with his parents and Taryn, and he apprised them of the situation with Leah Dearling in Crossland, Texas. "La' Dear is part of my family now, and she and Pastor need my support. I can imagine how stressful this is for Chance and Victor, both of whom have lost mothers before." He palmed his hands on the table. "I told them they could count on me as a brother, that I'd always be available to them.

I'm needed there, so I'm going back." He turned to Taryn. "I'd like to take you with me this time."

Taryn reached over, covering his hands with hers. "Of course, I'm going with you."

His father clapped him on his shoulder. "I support you whole-heartedly, Danny, and I'll be praying that all works out well."

"Thank you, Dad." He shifted his eyes to his mother—the one who had first opposed his relationship with the Dearlings. "Mom, you've had some concerns in the past—some reservations about me bonding with the Dearlings. How do you feel now?"

"Like God's blessed me with the most wonderful, loving son in the world." She swiped tears from her dark-brown eyes. "If Leah Dearling needs you to stand by her as one of her sons, then you should do so with my blessing." She pressed her right hand over her heart. "I love you, and I'll always want what's best for you. At first, I'll admit I was being self-ish and jealous, thinking you'd come to prefer Leah Dearling over me, especially since you bonded with her and you've kept in touch these two months. I was afraid that I would lose you, that there wouldn't be room enough in your heart for two mothers. Finally, your father and the Good Lord helped me see how wrong and uncharitable I've been."

"Mom, nobody, including La' Dear, will ever replace you, especially in my heart." Daniel pulled his hands from Taryn's, then stood, went to his mother, and pulled her from the seat, straight into his arms. "You're my mother, and I love you completely and faithfully."

His mother smiled through tears. "I know that now. That's why I'm ashamed that I ever let fear and doubt cloud my judgment."

"Do you still have a problem with me accepting Leah as my birth mother and giving her a place in my life?"

"I've mulled it over, prayed about it, and I'm at peace with your deci-sion. It's your life, and you're free to love whomever you will. Anyway, if it wasn't for Leah, I wouldn't have you. She may have had the privilege of carrying you in her womb, then giving birth to you, but I had the joy of raising you all these years. So, you love and honor her as God puts in your heart to do without fretting over me."

"Thank you, Mom. I needed to hear those words, especially from you."

"Love is precious, Daniel, and it comes in different forms. Don't ever take it for granted, and once you find it, don't ever let it slip through your fingers."

"I won't, Mom." He turned from her to Taryn. "Never again."

Chapter Twenty-Eight

For the LORD loves the just and will not forsake his faithful ones.

Psalm 37:28 (NIV)

Crossland, Texas
Friday, September 9

*C*hance was dozing on his parents' sofa when the doorbell sounded. Waking, he glanced at his wristwatch, noting that it was nine o'clock; then, he stood, pulling down his navy blue shirt, and strode to the front door expecting to find Daniel and Taryn. Instead, he opened the door to see Leisha and Salena standing on the doorstep, both with suitcases in their hands. Leisha seemed subdued in a metallic white blouse and burgundy slacks, but Salena flamed like a sunburst draped in an orange shirt and scarlet, pleated pants, part of her dark-red hair spilling over her shoulders, the rest cascading down her back.

What is Salena doing here? Chance was shocked more by Salena's presence than Leisha's. He had thought about the browned-eyed reporter constantly, and he had pulled out her photo countless times over the past two months, but he hadn't been bold enough to contact her. Only now with her standing before him did he realize how naturally beautiful she was and how much he had actually missed her. In those few times he had been with her, she had made his dull life more exciting, and her passion and drive had become addictive.

Leisha lowered her suitcase and leaned forward, hugging him. "I'm sorry I didn't give you any notice. For the past six days, we've been rearranging our schedules so we could come."

Chance stepped back. "Don't worry about it. This is home, and you're always welcomed here." He glanced toward Salena and greeted her with a cursory head nod. "Come inside." He ushered both women through the foyer, to the living room.

"You don't mind that I invited Salena, do you?"

"Of course not." He faced Salena. "You're welcomed here, too, so make yourself at home."

"Thank you. I will."

Leisha lowered her suitcase to the floor. "Are you alone?"

"Daniel and Taryn are coming shortly."

"What about Victor?"

"He'll be back around eleven thirty."

"How's he been?"

"Strong, faithful, stubborn. He's been camping by Mom's side, entertaining her, reading the Bible, and giving Dad some relief."

"He's ever the dutiful son."

"He has a tendency to serve others at the expense of himself, though. He's been so intent on taking care of Mom and Dad that he hasn't been caring for himself." Chance suspected Victor was driving himself to exhaustion so he wouldn't have to confront the possibility of their mother's death or confront his dilemma with Leisha and Alessia. While he was obsessing over Leisha, Alessia was becoming steadily more invested in him, and that put Victor in an untenable position of being trapped between two equally appealing women. For that, Chance felt responsible.

He was the one who had urged Victor to deny his feelings for Leisha, the one who had forced him to choose family over himself, and the one who had counseled him to move on with Alessia. Chance had thought he was protecting Victor and his family, but maybe he was wrong. Maybe he didn't have a right to intrude in his brother's life or the affairs of his heart. If Victor truly loved Leisha, maybe Chance should stop interfering and let Victor and Leisha work out their own relationship.

"Is Victor sick?"

"Fortunately, no." Chance focused on Leisha, noting her concern. Since he had first met her in that hospital after the assault, she hadn't ceased worrying about his brother. She was always attentive to him and worried about him, and that suddenly made Chance wonder whether she loved Victor too. "Victor's being mulish, refusing to come home and rest. He's only coming here tonight because he promised Dad that he'd finally take time for himself to eat, shower, and sleep." Chance leaned down to collect Leisha's and Salena's suitcases. "If you would, follow me, and I'll show you to your rooms."

He led them upstairs, then stopped at the first door on the right, put down Salena's suitcase, and opened the door to the guest bedroom. "Leisha, this is yours." He crossed the threshold and lowered her suitcase onto the carpeted floor. "Salena will be next door."

He left her, then retrieved Salena's suitcase, escorting her to the next room. Once inside, he dropped the suitcase near the bed, then turned to find her close at his heels, a breath from his face. Instantly, their last kiss flashed in his mind, and his heart thumped his chest hard.

Salena raised her hand and caressed his face. "I've missed you. Have you missed me?"

"Too much."

"You had my number. You know where I live. Why not call or visit, then?"

"I'm not ready for romance or a serious relationship."

Her eyes shined. "I am. All I've done is dream about us as a couple. As good as we are individually, we'd be great together. All you have to do is dare to dream and dare to love."

"I'm not some man of valor, Salena. I've been beaten and broken; I've been angry and irreverent, and I'm still in the mending stage."

"Still, you're worth the time and effort, and I'm not giving up on you."

"Why not?"

"I've fallen for you. Hard. I love you."

Chance heard the sincerity in her voice, saw that light reflected in her eyes. *She really loves me.* For years he had thought himself damaged and unlovable, and he had consigned himself to a life of solitude, loneliness. Now, God was dangling love before him like a carrot, and He was transforming the man before the mirror, reintroducing Chance to himself as a new creature in Christ, a man worthy of love, a happy family, a good woman, and a blessed life. All he had to do was be daring enough to act and spirited enough to walk by faith, not fear.

Salena stood silent, just staring at him.

He was clueless; he had never been in love. "What do I say?"

"I don't need a declaration. Especially if you don't mean it. I just thought you should know the truth: You're my guy, and I'm your girl." She brushed the wayward lock of hair from his forehead, then cupped his face in her hand. "You look tired, and these blue eyes are weary."

Chance covered her hand with his, removing it from his face and pressing it against his pounding heart. "I've had a lot on my mind, and I've had some restless nights."

"You've got to take care of yourself. You've got to sleep and guard your mind and heart, even during stressful times like these. If you don't, you could end up in the hospital as well."

"You're concerned about me?"

"I didn't come just for Leisha. I came to comfort you, too, if you'll let me."

"Honestly, I can't offer anything of value right now, Salena—not my undivided attention, my whole heart, or a declaration of love." He wanted to be upfront, letting her know that he wasn't a good investment for her heart. "I like you immensely—your fierce loyalty and indomitable spirit—but I can't commit to you, not in the way you want. Both my head and heart are devoted presently to my family."

"I'm not here to pursue or distract you. I'm only here as a friend, lending support, so you're not obligated to say you love me nor make promises you have no intention of keeping. I merely want you to accept my help and feel comfortable in my presence. I understand your family needs you, but I also know you need someone you can confide in and unwind with—someone beyond family. Will you consider me that person, trusting me enough to lean on me? Will you open yourself enough to let me in?"

Chance pushed fear aside. "Yes."

"Thank you." She kissed his cheek, and when she pulled back, Chance released her hand.

"I'll leave and let you get settled. If you need anything, I'll be downstairs in the living room." He stepped past her, then crossed the threshold, walking into the hallway. He had just gone downstairs when the doorbell sounded again. This time when he answered, Daniel and Taryn stood outside. "Welcome!" Chance hastily ushered them into the living room, exchanging greetings and hugs with them.

Soon, Leisha and Salena descended the stairs and entered the room, and Chance stepped aside as Daniel, surprised to see his sister, enthusiastically lifted her off her feet into his arms. After lowering her to the floor, he turned, introducing Leisha to his fiancée.

"Nice to meet you, Taryn." Leisha reached out for a handshake, but Taryn hugged her.

"It's a pleasure to meet you, too." Taryn pulled back, a smile on her face. "Daniel didn't exaggerate. You're beautiful. I can't wait for us to become family. I've always wanted a sister. Now, I'll finally have one."

Daniel touched Taryn's arm, guiding her from Leisha to Salena. "This is Salena Blake, Leisha's best friend. Since they're inseparable, consider her your second sister."

As Taryn and Salena greeted each other with a hug, Chance stepped forward, lifting Taryn's suitcase from the floor. "Daniel, I've put you in your old room, and Taryn is next door. Is that all right?"

Daniel grabbed his luggage. "That's fine."

"If anyone is hungry, there are leftovers in the refrigerator. You're also welcome to raid the pantry and fix anything you like."

"Salena and I ate before we left home."

Chance looked to Daniel. "What about you and Taryn?"

"We're good. We ate on the flight, then stopped for sandwiches about two hours ago."

"Then, I guess everyone can settle in for the night. If you need me, I'll be down here for another thirty minutes; then, I'll retire to my room, the one on the third floor, at the top of the stairs." Chance bade Leisha and Salena goodnight, then he led Daniel and Taryn to their respective rooms. Afterward, he returned to the living room and settled himself on the sofa, turning on the television. Within ten minutes, though, his eyelids grew heavy, and he was fighting a bout of drowsiness. Surrendering, he finally turned the television off, flicked on the security lights outside for Victor, then ascended the stairs. On his way up, he met Leisha in a lavender robe, coming down. "Do you need anything?" He struggled to keep his eyes open.

"Not really. I'm just not sleepy yet."

He yawned. "You want some company?"

"Thank you for the offer, but no. You're already asleep on your feet. Go to bed. I'll be fine."

"Okay. I'll see you in the morning." He continued up the stairs until he reached his bedroom. After changing into a white T-shirt and gray pajama bottoms, he collapsed on the bed, losing himself in slumber.

Chapter Twenty-Nine

For if our heart condemns us,
God is greater than our heart, and knows all things.

1 John 3:20 (NIV)

Holly Drive
Saturday, September 10

At midnight, Leisha sat at the kitchen table with a covered plate in front of her and two glasses of ginger ale. An engine broke the silence, and she glanced up. *Victor's here!* Her heart sped in anticipation.

Leisha stood listening and heard a door shut; then, she advanced toward the dining room. As she neared the foyer, she heard keys jingling, then the front door opening and shutting. Soon, footsteps fell upon the tiled floor in the foyer.

Leisha leaned against the doorframe, noticing beneath the golden dome of light how depleted and exhausted Victor looked in his wrinkled green shirt and blue jeans. "Hello, stranger."

Victor raised his head, clearly surprised—shocked even. "Leisha, what are you doing here?"

She smiled. "I couldn't stay away. I'm not the only one either. You've got a full house: Daniel, Taryn, Salena, and Chance. The others went to bed a couple of hours ago, but I've been waiting on you." She approached him, then grabbed his arm, leading him through the dining room into the kitchen. "I've prepared a plate for you with baked chicken, green beans, and sweet bread rolls, and there's a glass of ginger ale beside it." She pulled a chair from the table, gently pushed him into it, and uncovered the plate.

"Did you cook all of this?"

"Only the chicken."

"Thank you."

"You're welcome." Leaving his side, she sat down across from him with her glass of ginger ale in her hand. "Now, give thanks for your food and eat."

"You're staying?"

"Do you mind?"

"Not at all." He bowed his head, thanked God for the food, then lifted his fork and knife, cutting into the chicken breast. As he ate, savoring every bite, Leisha raised her glass, silently sipping her drink.

After Victor lowered his fork and pushed the plate aside, Leisha stood, walking toward the kitchen counter; then, she returned with his final treat. "Here's dessert." She slid a slice of chocolate cake with whipped frosting in front of him. "Although I didn't bake this, it still comes from the heart."

"You're spoiling me. I love chocolate."

"Enjoy it then."

After Victor had eaten the last chocolate crumb, he raised his eyes to hers and looked at her with intensity. "You didn't have to stay awake this late or do any of this for me."

"I wanted to. Besides, you rescued me, and I never did repay you."

Victor shook his head, his eyes boring into hers. "I saved you because it was the honorable thing to do, not because I expected anything in return. I don't want you to feel beholden to me."

Here's my opening. Lord, give me courage. She palmed her hands, leaning forward, her eyes trained on him. "How exactly do you want me to feel about you then, Victor?"

He sighed, raking harried fingers through his black hair. "What do you feel for Chance?"

"Affection, warmth, and concern."

"And Daniel?"

"I feel the same but have a closer relationship with him, likely because he's my twin."

"Do you love them?"

Do I? Leisha quickly examined her heart, then nodded. "Yes, they already feel like brothers—like family."

"Do you love me, too—like a brother?"

Lord, let me be honest with him and let him be the same. Her hands clenched, and heat flooded her face. "Not like a brother, no. Do you consider me a sister?"

"I should. After all, everyone else considers you family, and you are my parents' biological daughter. To consider you anything other than a sister would muddy the waters. Mom and Dad love and treat us equally as their children, and even Chance believes we should act as siblings."

Leisha balked at that notion. "We're *not* siblings, regardless of what your parents, brother, or anybody else thinks. We didn't share the same womb, we don't share any genes, and we don't even share the same last name."

"Chance doesn't believe—"

"Forget Chance right now. What do *you* believe?" Leisha sought the truth but feared Victor's response. Already overwhelmed with emotion, her heart was battering her chest.

"Sometimes we have to sacrifice what we want for the good of others, and sometimes love can be expressed in silence, even in selflessness." Victor reached across the table, covering Leisha's clenched hands with his. "It's so easy to love you, Leisha, to be in love with you, but I can't be in love with you. Not here, not now, with everything else happening."

Like knives, his words pierced her heart, and she jolted, even as tears began to sting her eyes. She could see in his eyes and feel in his touch that Victor felt her pain, too. She didn't want any doubt, though; she needed him to clarify his sentiment, to say the words. "You said you can't be in love with me now. Does that mean you're not in love with me or you already are?"

He closed his eyes and when he reopened them, tears glistened in them. "I made a promise. I—"

She pressed him. "Are you in love with me?"

He breathed deeply, audibly—like a bloated balloon seeping air. "Yes, I am."

She prayed her ears weren't deceiving her. "You really love me?"

"Yes. I love you."

A wave of pure joy flooded Leisha's heart. *Victor loved her. Her feelings for him weren't unrequited.* "How long have you felt this way?"

"Since our first meeting."

She was amazed that he'd fallen for her when she had been at her lowest, showing him nothing but her worst—indifference and stubbornness. "Why did you keep silent, especially after the assault?"

"Because our relationship has been complicated since the beginning, and at that time, we were still strangers, and I wasn't sure how deeply you felt about me."

"Why didn't you just ask me?"

"You were avoiding me, screening your calls."

"Not at the hospital."

"That doesn't matter." His voice was low, dry, and emotionless.

"Why not?"

"In these last two months, I've finally made peace with loving you from afar—loving you as family—not like a woman, a girlfriend, a wife."

No! Tears streamed down Leisha's cheeks, but with her hands beneath Victor's, she couldn't wipe them. "I can't be your sister or just family now—not after you've confessed to being in love with me."

He gently squeezed her hands. "I'm sorry. We can't be more."

"If you love me, fight for us—for this relationship."

He shook his head, tears cascading down his cheeks. "I do love you—enough to do what's best and let you go."

Leisha's heart plummeted, and she struggled to make sense of Victor's renunciation of his love for her. *How could he love her if he could so easily give her up? Why was he letting others influence the decisions of his heart?* "I didn't ask you to release me, nor do I need your misguided protection. All I want is the truth, a good reason why you can't love me—why we can't be together."

"A romantic relationship would be complicated, not just for us."

"For whom?"

"Everyone."

She snapped. "I don't accept that! Your loving me isn't a sin, and I'd call anyone a liar who says it is."

Victor removed his right hand from hers, raising it to caress her face. "Letting me go is best for everyone."

"No, it's not! Everyone else, including your brother, needs to get a life and stop interfering in ours. Nothing gives them the right to dictate our hearts."

"I'm sorry for hurting you."

Her anger dissipated. "Then, don't."

Sighing, Victor lowered his hand. "Don't close your heart to loving someone else—someone God has chosen."

Leisha tasted the saltiness of her tears. "You don't think God sent you to me?"

"He sent me to find you and to bring you home. Maybe He's chosen another man for your heart, your love."

"What are you saying?"

"There's a worthy man out there who'll love you passionately, uplift you spiritually, and enrich your life immeasurably. Loving him won't bring sorrow, gossip, scandal, or heartbreak."

She remembered the other woman in his life, Alessia. "You're giving up, and you're rejecting me because *those* are the best options for everybody else?"

"I'm moving on, and so should you. Neither of us will be content to wait and wallow in angst forever, grieving for a love that's not meant to be. You and I will find our chosen mates. We'll fall in love again with the right people, and we'll both be happy."

"Is that wishful thinking or divine insight?"

"That's faith. You have it, and so do I."

"I do have faith—in God and in us, together."

"Leisha—"

"You've had the floor, speaking what you perceive to be true. Now, it's my turn to tell you the truth." She leaned forward, invading his personal space. "You're making a mistake that you'll eventually regret, and you're trying to convince yourself as much as me that your sacrifice is right and honorable. Pure love, the kind that's sent from God, isn't meant to be renounced, bartered, or cast aside for anyone, including family. It's meant to be cherished and protected, regardless of the cost." She raked fingers through her hair, her eyes fastened on his as she leaned back in her seat. "You may have conceded defeat and be content to live a complacent life with someone who's safe, acceptable, and uncomplicated, but I haven't. I love you, Victor, and I'm willing to fight for every drop of love God gives me, even if I have to fight against you, too. Do you understand me?"

"I don't want to fight with you."

"Then, don't because you'll lose."

"I've already lost you."

"You haven't lost me; you're letting me go. There's a difference."

"For what it's worth, I'm sorry."

"I thought you were stronger, more courageous."

"Sometimes, I wish I were." Victor sighed and massaged his temples. "It's been a long day, and tomorrow promises to be even worse. I think I'll retire now." He stood, prompting her to do the same. "Thank you for the food and company."

She dried her face with her hand as he put his dessert plate atop his dinner plate, then lifted both. She removed the weight from his hands. "I'll clean the dishes. You've had a rough day, so you need to get some rest."

Victor paused, his eyes meeting hers again. "Will you be all right?"

"I'm a lawyer. I have tough skin."

"Tough skin usually covers a tender heart."

"I'm strong and spirited, an overcomer."

"I know you are." He leaned forward, caressing her face. Then he kissed her forehead and pressed his against hers. "I do love you."

Fresh tears fell from Leisha's eyes as his words dropped like rose petals in the bower of her heart. "I love you, too."

He leaned back, cupping her face in his hand. "In a perfect world, we'd go on our first date, share our first kiss, get engaged, get married, and enjoy our first child."

She wanted all of that, too; she wanted him. "It can still happen if you really believe in us, and you want me and that life badly enough." Suddenly she dreamed of a lifetime at his side as his friend, his partner, his helper, his wife, his lover—the mother of his children.

"It's only a dream—an unattainable one." He stepped back, thumbing her tears dry. "Be encouraged, be blessed, be uplifted, and be loved." He turned, then walked away, leaving her alone.

Silently, Leisha carried the dishes to the sink, then opened the blinds and stared out the window, lifting and caressing her heart-shaped necklace. As she stood, looking at the star-blanketed sky, she realized that she was, indeed, a dreamer, with stars in her eyes and hope in her heart. She dared to dream the impossible—an amazing future and a happily ever after with Victor Dearling.

Chapter Thirty

A gift opens the way for the giver and ushers
him into the presence of the great.

Proverbs 18:16 (NIV)

Crossland Memorial Hospital
Sunday, September 11

This is love. Victor sat beside Chance at his mom's bedside, watching his father softly comfort and reassure her. As they professed their love—their faith—he almost felt like he and Chance were voyeurs.

His dad sat on his mom's right, caressing her hand as she lamented her baldness—the loss of the glorious dark-brown hair. "You're beautiful, honey, even without the hair." He kissed her forehead. "I love *you*—not what covers your head."

Victor's mom raised her left hand to touch his dad's face. "I love you, too." She studied his face as though memorizing it. "We may celebrate our anniversary in June, but every day that I'm blessed to be with you is worth celebrating. I thank God for choosing you for me."

She smiled. "He knew I needed you—a strong man of faith, integrity, courage, and vision. You're the love of my life, Nathanial Jacob Dearling—and it's been a joy walking in faith with you for the last thirty-three years." She lowered her hand, pressing it against his chest—upon his heart. "Thank you."

Victor's dad's eyes glistened with tears. "You're not saying farewell, are you?"

"No, love." She lowered her hand. "I'm not giving up—on God, our family, or us. I'm just expressing my gratitude. God has been good to me, and He's blessed me with a magnificent husband and incredible children."

Chance leaned forward, gripping Mom's hand. "We're thankful for you, too, and we're not giving you up without a fight."

Mom turned, her eyes on him and Victor. "I'm not planning on dying anytime soon, but if that's the Lord's will for me, I'm not afraid to die." She removed her hand from his so she could caress his somber face. "I have no regrets, no fear." She lowered her hand again, love radiating from her as she captured Chance and Victor in her sight, as though her eyes were camera lenses, snapping a photograph—recording a precious memory.

She's ready to leave us. Victor's chest got tight, and his heart ached. He'd already lost his birth parents and his grandmother. He didn't know if he could recover from losing another mother. *God, please give me strength.* He extended his hand, gently palming his mom's head. "We love you, Mom."

"I love you both, too, and I'm proud of the men you've become. Promise me, though, that you'll continue to walk in faith, trusting in the Lord, even if the outcome of tomorrow's surgery isn't as you hoped."

"I promise." Victor fought for composure. He didn't want his mom severely altered, nor did he want her to die. He wasn't ready to lose her or live without her.

His mom faced Chance whose tears were already bathing his cheeks. "Will you be faithful to God, even if He carries me home to heaven?"

"Yes, Mom. I promise."

"Good, because I'd hate to become a stumbling block between either of you and God. He's our Advocate, not an adversary."

Dad kissed her hand. "Honey, you never cease to amaze me. You're the strongest of us all—our ray of hope and sunshine, even on a cloudy day."

"That's because I'm blessed."

"You are, my love." He gently squeezed her hand. "Are you ready for Daniel and Leisha?"

She rubbed her left hand over her smooth honeyed head. "Are you sure I'm presentable?"

"You look absolutely stunning."

"Let our children in."

Dad released her hand, then stood, opening the door and beckoning Daniel and Leisha into the room. As they entered and stopped at the foot of the bed, Mom's face shined like the sun rising over the horizon, and her smile eclipsed any pain, gloom, or discomfort.

Daniel stepped forward and hugged Mom, then kissed her forehead. "Hello, La' Dear."

"God is good, isn't He?"

Daniel grinned. "Always. He's a healer, too." He raised her hand, pressing it over his heart. "My fiancée, Taryn, is outside. Would you like to meet her?"

"Invite her inside!"

Daniel walked out, then returned with Taryn. "La' Dear, meet Taryn Kirkland, and Taryn, meet La' Dear."

Taryn hugged Mom. "It's an absolute pleasure to meet you, Mrs. Dearling."

"I'm happy to finally meet you, too." Mom folded Taryn's hand in hers. "You've found a prince in Daniel. Love him, pray for him, confide in him, and cherish him."

Taryn smiled. "Don't worry. I will."

Mom looked at Daniel. "You've got a jewel in Taryn. Love her, pray for her, protect her, cherish her, and confide in her, too."

"I will, La' Dear."

She released Taryn's hand. "A good marriage is based on a solid foundation, and it requires effort from both partners. Remember that."

"We will." Daniel grabbed Taryn's hand. "Speaking of marriage, Taryn and I would like to invite you to our wedding on Christmas Eve. Will you come?"

Tears gleamed in Mom's eyes. "God willing, yes! I'll be there."

Daniel then turned to Dad. "Pastor, will you perform the ceremony?"

Dad staggered, then gripped the back of the chair beside him, regaining his balance. "Are you sure?"

"Yes, sir. We are."

"Do your parents—the Winwards—know of this?"

"They're in agreement. That's not all either. We'd like to spend Christmas with the Dearling family in Georgia."

Dad shined a hundred-watt smile at Daniel. "You've blessed me, and I'm profoundly grateful, but are you certain that with our resemblance, you want me standing before you, performing your wedding? Or sharing such an important family holiday with you?"

Daniel's gray eyes met his hazel. "Yes, Pastor. I've accepted that you're my birth father, so you *are* family now, and I'd be honored to stand with you before God and everyone else. Will you stand with me?"

"Of course, I will." He released the chair, pulling Daniel into an embrace. "Thank you for asking, for including the Dearlings among family."

Daniel stepped back, leading Taryn to the foot of the bed.

Leisha, stylish in her purple shirt and brown pinstriped pantsuit, approached Victor's mom, thumbing her own eyes dry.

Victor's heart jolted even as his eyes consumed her. *She's beauty personified. How am I supposed to forget her? How do I blot her from my mind and heart, especially now that I know she loves me, too?*

Since his late-night confession, he had been avoiding her, valiantly trying to honor his brother's request and not intrude on Leisha's relationship with his parents. His attempts to move on though had proven futile. He *loved* Leisha—more so as he continually spent time with her, discovering the different facets of her personality.

"La' Dear, I didn't come empty-handed. I have a gift for you that's actually from both Daniel and me." Leisha removed a black box from her pant pocket, extending it to Victor's mom.

Mom carefully studied the box in the palm of her hand. "What is it?"

"Open it and see."

Mom raised the lid on the box, then gasped loudly, removing a silver heart-shaped locket, with a diamond-studded cross in its center. "This is precious." She turned it over and read aloud the verse engraved on its back, Psalm 113:9: "He settles the childless woman in her home as a happy mother of children. Praise the LORD." She opened the locket, then cried.

"What is it, dear?"

She raised it so everyone could see photos of Daniel and Leisha inside. Then she closed the locket and pressed it against her heart. "I love it."

"I love you, La' Dear."

"I love you too, Leisha." Mom reached both arms forward and pulled Leisha toward her own quaking body. Then she smothered Leisha with kisses on her cheeks and forehead. "Sweetheart, I thank you and Daniel for this wonderful gift. It's perfect, priceless."

Leisha moved back, drying fresh tears. "Enjoy it and keep us in your thoughts, in your heart."

"Of course, I will." She extended the locket to Victor's dad. "Nathan, come and fasten this."

He stepped forward and fastened the necklace, then he smiled, admiring Mom as she pressed the locket to her lips, then carefully placed it over her heart. "This is a day for love and celebration, not fear and sorrow. This is the day the LORD has made, so let us rejoice and be glad in it." He called everyone together, urging them to form a prayer circle around Mom. "Now, let us as a family join hands and hearts, going before the Lord's throne of grace." Dad grabbed Mom's and Leisha's hands, Leisha took Daniel's, he clasped Taryn's, she held Chance's, he grabbed Victor's, and Victor completed the circle, folding his mom's hand in his own. Then, they all bowed their heads and closed their eyes as Dad commenced praying: thanking, praising, petitioning, and glorifying God.

After he had finished speaking, Leisha took the mantle, and prayer spread like a wildfire from one person to the next until last came Victor, and then they all concluded resoundingly with, "Amen"—so be it.

Chapter Thirty-One

So the sisters sent word to Jesus, "Lord, the one you love is sick."
When he heard this, Jesus said, "This sickness will not end in death.
No, it is for God's glory so that God's Son may be glorified through it."

John 11:3–4 (NIV)

Crossland Memorial Hospital
Monday, September 12

After Leah's four-hour brain surgery, she was transferred to the Neurosciences Critical Care Unit, and Dr. Camm met privately with the assembled family—Nathan, Chance, Victor, Daniel, Taryn, Salena, and Leisha—apprising them of her situation. As he assured them foremost that the brain surgery had been successful and that they had effectively removed the tumor, Leisha, sitting beside Nathan clutching his hand, had sighed in relief, offering God a silent prayer of thanksgiving and praise. However, as Dr. Camm warned them that there could still be complications—setbacks—along Leah's road to recovery, Leisha suddenly realized that there was no guarantee that Leah would be the same woman she had been before the surgery, and that thought disheartened her.

"Now that the tumor's gone, will Mom feel better?"

Dr. Camm looked at Chance. "Not necessarily. It's not unusual at first for the patient to feel worse than she did before the operation, and this can be stressful for the patient and relatives." His brown eyes roamed over the group. "For the next few months, Mrs. Dearling will require a lot of time, patience, care, and support. She'll need supervision and assistance until she's well enough to resume her life or return to her usual activities."

"You don't have to worry, doctor. Leah won't confront this alone. She has me, the Good Lord, and the rest of the Dearlings ready and willing to tend to her every need. We won't leave her alone, and we definitely won't lose faith and stop praying for her complete healing—a full recovery. We're conquerors, all of us."

Leisha admired Nathan's faith, his confidence. He refused to concede defeat, believing that the wife he knew was gone. She prayed her faith held as his did and that Leah would overcome every obstacle and come through stronger and whole—completely healthy and victorious.

Victor leaned forward, his hands palmed in his lap. "What exactly can we expect, Dr. Camm?"

"Typically after brain surgery, swelling can cause dizziness, weakness, poor balance and coordination, confusion, personality changes, speech problems, and seizures. These episodes can come and go, but they usually disappear as the patient recovers. Sometimes, this takes only days; sometimes, it takes weeks or even months. Also, in some cases there could be headaches, hallucinations, mood and behavioral changes, vision and hearing difficulties, nausea or vomiting, trouble talking, sensitivity to light, trouble urinating, and difficulty waking up."

With each side effect he listed, Leisha felt an invisible hand clutching and squeezing her heart, and she closed her eyes, blinking away tears. She didn't want Leah to endure any of those. She wanted her healthy, whole, and at peace, with nothing broken and nothing lost. *God, we claim healing for La' Dear—total deliverance and restoration. Jesus bore her sickness and pain on the Cross, so no sickness or disease has authority over her and no room in her brain, in her body. No weapon formed against her will prosper, for she is an overcomer, fearfully and wonderfully made in Your image, Your likeness, and she can do all things through You who strengthen her.* She opened her eyes, her hand still wrapped around Nathan's.

Daniel leaned forward, his hand bound with Taryn's. "A full recovery's possible, isn't it?"

"Yes. For some people, recovery will be complete, and they're able to get back to the same fitness level they had before and return to activities such as caring for themselves and driving and even fulfilling their jobs."

"How long will La' Dear be here?"

"Typically, we keep patients four or five days after brain surgery. After surgery, depending on that patient's condition, she begins recovery in the Neurosciences Critical Care Unit (NCCU), and a team of doctors and nurses trained in neurology and critical care provide around-the-clock intensive care. Once the doctors and nurses have completed their assessment and the patient is stable, she'll be able to see family members. Then, after NCCU, the patient recovers in a neurosurgery nursing unit."

He faced Nathan again. "We're committed to your wife's recovery, Pastor Dearling. In fact, we already have a rehabilitation therapy team in place."

"What's a rehabilitation therapy team?" Salena sat beside Chance, her hand resting on his arm.

"A group of specialists who provide assistance. A physical therapist who assesses the patient's ability to walk safely and climb stairs before being released from the hospital and someone who helps improve the patient's strength and balance. An occupational therapist who assesses the patient's ability to perform activities of daily living such as getting dressed, using the toilet, and getting in and out of the shower and someone who tests the patient's vision and thinking skills to determine whether the patient can return to work, driving or other challenging tasks. And there's the speech-language pathologist who evaluates problems with speech, language, or thinking and may also evaluate the patient for problems with swallowing."

"Is there anything I'll need to know about caring for Leah after she's released?"

"Before your wife goes home, we'll teach you about home care and what to expect during the healing process, we'll provide you with resources, and we'll give you instructions on when to call 9-1-1 or me." Dr. Camm stood. "Do you have any more questions?"

"Is Mom conscious?"

He glanced at Victor. "Not yet. But she'll be ready for visitors in an hour."

"How long will it take her incision to heal?"

"Usually one to two weeks, and the staples are removed about ten days after surgery."

"Will Mom need more treatment?"

"She'll need radiation and chemotherapy, and we'll be monitoring her improvement continuously, following up throughout the year." He glanced at his wristwatch, then told them he had to leave.

"Thank you, Dr. Camm."

"You're welcome, Pastor Dearling. Goodnight."

"Goodnight." After Dr. Camm walked away, shutting the door behind him, Nathan turned to the others, his eyes pensive. "Well, family, we've got a long road ahead of us, but it's not one that's impossible for us to travel."

"Mom's a fighter—a survivor. She'll make it through this. One hundred percent."

Nathan smiled, his eyes on Victor. "Of course, she will."

Leisha squeezed Nathan's hand, drawing his attention to her. "I want to stay and help with La' Dear."

"What about the law firm—your caseload?"

"I've already talked to my partners Alexander and Mateo, and they can cover me for two weeks."

He stared into her eyes. "Are you sure?"

"I love you, and I love La' Dear, and this is where I want to be for the next two weeks—right beside you both, helping you get through this."

Nathan kissed her forehead. "God bless you, honey. I love you, too, and I gladly welcome you back home." He pulled back but didn't relinquish Leisha's hand. "I'm confident that whatever happens with Leah, she's going to have an inspiring testimony to share, and God alone will get the glory."

"You really believe she'll come through, Dad?" Chance's forehead creased, and the weight of all the doctor had unloaded upon them seemed to rest on his broad shoulders. "You're not afraid of Mom suffering through all those side effects Dr. Camm mentioned?"

"My faith isn't shaken, son. I'm yet trusting God and believing in His power, His strength, and Leah's determination."

"What if God doesn't bless her with complete healing? What if He doesn't answer your prayers as you hope, and He allows Mom to live with chronic headaches, nausea, personality changes, or seizures? What if she can't function normally or she can't communicate well, dress, feed, or bathe herself? What if she doesn't remember us or can't talk? What will you do then?"

"I'll love her, pray for her, sacrifice for her, and take care of her—feeding, dressing, and bathing her, cooking her food, washing her laundry, cleaning her vomit, soothing her fears, easing her pain, and reminding her every day I'm her husband, her *helpmate*—the man who loves her beyond her good appearance, hygiene, speech, memory, mood, and health. I didn't vow to love Leah only in good times when it was convenient for me. I vowed before her and before God to love and cherish her in sickness and in health, in good and in bad *faithfully* until death separated us.

"Now, I have faith that Leah and I will overcome the tumor and even the surgery and that within the year, Leah will be one hundred percent healed and cancer free, yet if God *allows* Leah to endure in this trial, I won't question His wisdom, nor will I get angry, feeling as though God has betrayed me. I know without a doubt that God is good, just, and loving, and I'll continue to serve, obey, and worship Him, just as I've always done."

Chance frowned. "How can you stay so calm and confident, especially with the battle ahead of us?"

"First John 4:18 declares, 'There is no fear in love. But perfect love drives out fear, because fear has to do with punishment. The one who fears is not made perfect in love.' The only reason I'm not crumbling now and raging against life and God is because I know *what* and *who* real love is, and I'm clinging to it and Him.

"I could easily give up, admit defeat, and walk away discouraged and depressed, believing that I've truly lost the love of my life—the only woman meant for me—or I can put my faith in action and trust God, believing that anything is possible, even my wife's healing and deliverance from any sickness, pain, or disease.

"If I didn't cling to faith like a lifeline of light in the blackest night, like a thirsty soul beside a well of refreshing water, I would be broken and lost, careening over the edge of a steep mountain into utter darkness and despair."

Leisha swiped fresh tears from her eyes and remained silent, reflecting on his words as the minutes slowly ticked away.

When an hour had passed, they were notified that they could visit Leah.

As Nathan, Chance, Victor, Daniel, and Leisha rose to their feet, Taryn and Salena both decided to remain in the waiting room, giving the family some privacy.

Soon, the group stood in Leah's room, surrounding her bed, all of their eyes fastened on the woman who looked like she had been through a major battle, who seemed so weak and fragile—confined in that bed, with machines beeping and tubes and monitors around her.

She looks different, not like that strong and fearless woman I first met. Have we lost her already? Tears stung Leisha's eyes, and she couldn't control them as they streamed down her cheeks. *God, give me strength. Help me be strong, especially for Pastor. He's the one who stands to lose the most if La' Dear isn't the same woman—the one he fell in love with, the one he married and promised to cherish for a lifetime.*

Nathan edged closer, sitting down beside Leah and gently folding her hand in his. He raised his other hand, caressing Leah's face. "Love, can you hear me?"

Leah's eyelids fluttered, and those beautiful but seemingly blank eyes stared first at Nathan, then at the others who had inched closer around her bed.

Leisha's heart plummeted in her chest. *We've lost her.*

"Honey, you know who I am, don't you?"

Leah swallowed hard, then opened her mouth, but no words came out.

Nathan turned. "Do any of you have a pen and some paper?"

Leisha opened her purse, then removed a lavender notepad and purple pen, extending them to Nathan. "You can use these."

"Thank you." Nathan put the pad in Leah's left hand and pressed the pen in her right. "Write down what you'd like to say, love."

Leah gradually lifted the pen, then pressed it upon the pad and began slowly to write with tears racing down her cheeks. After she was finished, she raised those wet lashes to Nathan, extending the pad to him.

Nathan glanced down, silently reading her message. Then, he removed his glasses, drying tears from his eyes, and leaned over, kissing his wife's forehead. "I love you, honey."

She mouthed four words. "I love you, too."

Chance craned his neck. "What did she write, Dad?"

"A love letter." Nathan put his glasses back on, then read the message aloud: "I know all of you. Nathan, you're the love of my life; Daniel, Leisha, Chance, and Victor are the children of my heart. God is good, God is just, God is love. I'm alive, and I'm going to live my life every day in joy with gratitude because I am a survivor. I am an overcomer. Don't weep for me because I'm not gone; I'm not lost. I'm here, I'm healed, and I already see myself today as God sees me—cancer free and at peace, with nothing broken and nothing lost. God's got me covered. So, don't worry." Nathan lowered the notepad, his eyes fixed on Leisha, Chance, Victor, and Daniel. "As you all just heard, Leah is fine, and she doesn't need your tears right now. She needs your love and your faith. Got that?"

They all bobbed their heads. "Yes, sir."

As Chance, Victor, and Daniel then stepped forward, greeting Leah with hugs and kisses, Leisha stepped back. *Forgive me, Father. I didn't trust You to work this all out in La' Dear's favor, in our favor. I let fear crowd my thoughts, and I forgot You're greater than fear and greater than sickness and disease, even death. With You, all things are possible. Please, increase my faith and guide me so that I can walk in courage and confidence like Pastor and La' Dear, and please help me accept whatever You decide with respect to La' Dear.*

"Leisha?"

She lifted her eyes to Nathan's. "Yes, sir?"

"Leah would like a hug and a kiss from you, too."

Leisha dried her tears and stepped forward, a greeting smile on her face. "I'm coming, Pastor. I'm coming." As she kissed, then embraced Leah, Leisha felt as though a blanket of peace was being spread over her—like everything would work out as it was meant to and that it all would be good. She felt like she was finally coming to a place she hadn't known before but one that she had always been searching for—a place called home.

Chapter Thirty-Two

Above all, love each other deeply, because
love covers a multitude of sins.

1 Peter 4:8 (NIV)

Parkland Place
Sunday, October 9

As he sat in bed, his Bible opened over his outstretched legs and his cell phone beside him, Chance felt nothing but gratitude. For the past month, his mother had been steadily recuperating with no adverse psychological effects, relatively minor physical problems from the surgery, and no evidence of cancer in her brain or in the rest of her body. Although his mother was apprehensive about singing publicly, she *had* regained her voice and could communicate with them again, and she gave all credit to God.

Chance and Victor had become permanent shadows in their parents' home, both anxious to comfort and support. From a distance, even Daniel and Leisha monitored Leah's recovery, making weekly phone calls or in Leisha's case, making biweekly visits on the weekends to spend some quality time with the Dearlings and assist them with whatever they needed.

Indeed, Leisha had become comfortable enough around the Dearlings to let down her guard, revealing more of herself and her past with the Laurences. She had even made the effort to befriend Chance. However, it was apparent to him, if not to his parents, that she was more than polite and cordial to Victor when he wasn't avoiding her.

Leisha cared about Victor. She could possibly even love him, and that revelation bothered Chance, because if Leisha truly loved Victor as he loved her, then who was Chance to stand in the way, imposing his will on them? If Leisha was truly the woman God had created for his brother, then Chance had no moral right to deny either of them an opportunity at love together.

More surprising than his awareness of Leisha and Victor's love and woes was his own correspondence with and burgeoning feelings for Salena Blake. For the last four weeks, she had been phoning him nightly at eleven, sharing the events of her day, inquiring into his, getting updates on his family, and praying for and with him. Salena had become a true friend, and after a month, Chance now looked forward to their bedtime chats. He was gaining new insight into Salena, and he was fascinated by what he learned. The woman was a contradiction, controlled, objective, and professional when reporting horrific, devastating, and traumatic news, yet expressive, passionate, and intimate when sharing her faith, values, and concerns. Like him, she valued family and loved hers tremendously, visiting the family farm often and assisting her parents and siblings as much as she was physically, financially, and spiritually able.

Salena wasn't coy but refreshingly candid, especially about the affairs of her heart. She admitted to saving herself for marriage and told him that she'd been engaged at age twenty-four and that she had been heartbroken when her fiancé had deserted her six months before the wedding to pursue a relationship with a female colleague at his accounting firm. Later, he justified his behavior by blaming Salena—claiming that she was ill-suited to be his wife because she was too blunt and religious. Since then, Salena hadn't been in a serious long-term relationship. She hadn't even been interested in dating or investing her heart in another man—until Chance.

For the past month, Chance had discovered that he wasn't indifferent to Salena either. He enjoyed her company and anticipated her calls, and his icy heart had thawed considerably since that first encounter in Corinth. Salena had invaded his thoughts and his life, and she had him reevaluating his past decisions, even himself.

On cue, promptly at eleven, Chance's phone rang, and he raised it to his ear, a smile on his face and a jolt in his heart.

"Greetings, Blue Eyes."

"Hello, Salena."

"How's your day been?"

"Better now." He envisioned those brown eyes and that long hair, like silky strands of sunlight. "How was yours?"

"Great, inspirational."

"What happened?"

"I was at Redemption House, a church-sponsored homeless shelter, volunteering in the kitchen and dining room when a pregnant woman stumbled through the door, with a battered face, and in full-blown labor, with her contractions coming about two minutes apart. There wasn't time to transport her to the nearest family clinic, and we knew she wouldn't wait until an ambulance arrived."

"What did you do?"

"I prayed, and God answered. One of the diners took charge, finding the pregnant woman a clean, private space, then ordering me and another volunteer into action getting fresh towels and hot water. Before we knew it, he had delivered the woman's baby girl—safe and healthy."

"A random homeless man delivered a baby?"

"He was more god-sent than random. He was a doctor."

"A homeless doctor?"

"That's unbelievable, right?"

"Yes, it is."

"The paramedics touted him a hero, saying both the battered woman and her baby would have died without his quick action. The man was humble, though, with a servant's heart, and he didn't want any fanfare. He just said he'd done enough bad in his life that it was a blessing to do good for once. Then, he walked away, more sad than happy, with tears in his eyes." She sighed. "He's had a tough life and made some terrible choices, but he's changed, for the better."

"Did he tell you that?"

"After the commotion ended. I searched for him, and we had a chance to talk. I found out he was an emergency doctor who lost his job and family because of alcoholism, drug addiction, and abuse. He said he became a monster and destroyed everything that was good in his life until he lost it all—his wife, son, home, and even his own self-respect."

Chance remained silent as Salena shared the homeless man's story, his thoughts spiraling toward his own childhood with Eileen and Ray, and reels of fear-filled, violent scenes began playing across his mind's eye. He, better than anyone, knew first-hand what life with an addict was like. As a child, he had blamed himself for Ray's abuse, believing that he wasn't a good son, that something was wrong with him. As an adult, though, he placed the fault squarely on Ray's shoulders. Ray had been the weak one—the bad husband and father; he had been the monster—the devil. *Why am I still letting Ray get to me? Why can't I escape him?* Chance snapped from the shadows of his past. "What happened to the man's family?"

"He left, then lost touch with them."

"Maybe that was best for everyone involved." Chance recalled his own relief when Ray had finally disappeared. "The man was a threat and probably would have killed them if he had stayed."

"Maybe that's true, but he regrets leaving them like he did. He wants to find his family and beg their forgiveness."

An image of Ray surfaced in Chance's head. "He had his chance, and he wasted it. His family's better off without him."

"He's a good guy, Chance. He's changed, and he's already repented. Now, he's sober, drug-free, and *redeemed*. He deserves an opportunity to make amends for past mistakes. After all, he has nothing left now but faith."

Redemption. Chance glanced down, his eyes settling on the Bible on his outstretched legs, and he suddenly recalled the scriptures he'd been reading before Salena's phone call, Romans 3:22–24: "This righteousness is given through faith in Jesus Christ to all who believe. There is no difference between Jew and Gentile, for all have sinned and fall short of the glory of God, and all are justified freely by his grace through the redemption that came by Christ Jesus."

"Raymond knows he doesn't deserve mercy, but that doesn't mean he shouldn't receive it. He needs our compassion and prayers, not our judgment or—"

Chance jerked, knocking the Bible from his legs. "What did you call him?"

"Raymond."

"What's his last name?"

"Brayden."

"Ray Brayden?"

"Yes."

"This is one cruel joke!" Chance clutched the phone in a death grip, his heart thumping hard. *After all this time, his past was coming back to haunt him.*

"What's wrong? Why are you upset?"

"Ray Brayden is my birth father—the man who beat my mother and me, the one who destroyed our family, our lives."

"I'm sorry. I didn't make that connection. I know you've been angry with him, justifiably so, but he's changed. Really. He wants to meet you, make amends. Won't you forgive him and be—"

Forgive him? Really? How could she ask him that? How could she so easily defend him? Chance felt betrayed. "No, Salena. I won't. Goodnight." He disconnected, dropped the phone, then cupped his face and lowered his head. *Ray's alive, living four hours away, and he wants forgiveness.* "God, why now?" Tears scalded his eyes. "Why let Mama die and Ray live?"

Redemption Fellowship Center
Sunday, October 16

Chance sat quietly on the last pew at Redemption Fellowship Center, the Hispanic minister's sermon washing over his ears as his eyes scanned the congregation for sight of Ray Brayden. It had taken him a week of prayer and counseling with his parents to finally release his anger and get enough courage to come and confront his birth father. For years he had wished Ray dead, and as a child, he had even fantasized about killing him. Now, his flesh and spirit were in conflict, and he didn't know how to meet the man who had violated him and stolen his childhood—his innocence.

The old, worldly Chance hated Ray and craved a pound of flesh, desiring to inflict as much pain as possible upon Ray for the years of misery he had endured at his hands. The new Chance, redeemed by the blood of Jesus Christ, however, was supposed to be gracious—loving and forgiving Ray and even praying for his well-being.

God, how do I forgive him? How do I love him? Chance raised his eyes to the cross hanging behind Pastor Bienvenido, and then his words penetrated Chance's consciousness, compelling him to tune in and listen closely.

"Love is more than some emotion; it's a choice on our part and on God's." The minister's hands rested upon the Bible on the podium. "We choose whom we love, just as God chooses to love us—even when we sin and rebel, even when we grieve and deny Him. The true test of our faith, though, is *our* ability to love in obedience to God those unlovable ones—those who've persecuted, rejected, wounded, and violated us physically, emotionally, even financially." His brown eyes roamed the congregation, seemingly resting upon Chance. "God *is* love, and He forgives faithfully, and He expects us to do likewise. First John 1:9 says, 'If we confess our sins, he is faithful and just and will forgive us our sins, and purify us from all unrighteousness.' So, if God forgives and even forgets the sin, and we call ourselves followers of His, why won't we do the same? Why do we continually bludgeon reformed sinners with their past mistakes, believing we're somehow better? What makes our sins less offensive than theirs?"

His words convicted Chance, and he bowed his head, palming his hands in his lap. *Like Ray, he, too, had sinned, especially against God. He had even overstepped his bounds as a brother, inflicting his will on Victor and forcing him to renounce his love for Leisha. He hadn't assaulted his brother physically, but he had hurt him just the same.*

The minister continued with fire and passion, reciting 1 John 2:4–6: "The man who says, 'I know God,' but does not do what he commands is a liar, and the truth is not in him. But if anyone obeys his word, God's love is truly made complete in him, and this is how we know we are in him: Whoever claims to live in him must walk as Jesus did." He leaned over the podium, extending his right hand and pointing his index finger. "This is my charge to you this evening; when in doubt, walk as Jesus did—obeying, loving, forgiving, interceding, and praying."

Through the altar call and benediction, Chance remained seated with his head down, meditating on the minister's final words—his charge—to walk as Jesus did. *He had to forgive Ray—not for Ray's benefit but for his own. He'd spent too many years hating the man and letting the poison of his childhood infect his heart. Now was his chance to be strong and courageous, a man of valor relying on the Lord's strength and counsel. Now was his chance to walk in faith, not bitterness, resentment, or fear.* Chance raised his head, his eyes toward the altar where one man with silver-streaked brown hair, dressed in a blue shirt and charcoal gray pants, knelt alone, sobbing.

The man's body quaked as he bowed his head and palmed his hands. "Father, thank You for Your Son, Jesus. Thank You for loving me, saving me, and giving me another chance."

That voice Chance remembered. Unconsciously, he stood, his eyes never wavering as he walked up the aisle, toward the altar and the man he hadn't seen in years—his abuser, his adversary, his father—Ray. The cross hung over him, and as Chance walked forward, tears stung his eyes, then fell, washing his cheeks, and the closer he got to that altar and to that man, the freer he felt, like chains were breaking from him, like a weight was lifting from his chest and ice was melting from his heart.

"Thank You for looking beyond the man I was to the one You created me to be. I've sinned, Lord, and I know I'm not worthy of consideration, even love and forgiveness, but I thank You for grace and mercy, especially today."

Chance stopped, towering over him, and he heard the minister's voice in his head again, urging him to walk as Jesus did. Slowly, he extended a trembling hand, lowering it to Ray's shoulder, and he heard himself say, "Ray, I'm—"

Startled, Ray jerked, shaking Chance's hand away; then, he turned, lifting wet blue eyes upon him. "Who are you?"

"Chance."

Ray staggered to his feet, shock on his weary face as he assessed Chance from head to toe. "Is it really you, Chance—my son?"

"Yes."

"Thank God!" He swiped fresh tears from his blue eyes. "How did you find me?"

"Through the reporter you met, Salena Blake."

"You know her?"

"We're friends."

"You live in Corinth?"

"No, I live in Crossland with my family."

"Are you married?"

"No."

"You still live with Eileen, then?"

"Mama died of a brain aneurysm shortly after you left." Chance watched the play of emotions on Ray's face at the news of his wife's death, and he searched for a trace of the man he had been. All he saw, though, was a flood of tears in his blue eyes.

"Eileen's dead?"

"Yes."

"I'm sorry." Ray cried, then pressed a hand over his chest. "She was a good woman, a faithful wife, and she didn't deserve the misery and heartache she got from me." He focused on Chance, his eyes intense. "After she died, what happened to you?"

"I was placed in foster care until a preacher and his wife adopted me."

"How long were you in foster care?"

"Two years. I got adopted when I was nine."

Ray shook his head, more tears welling in his eyes. "I'm sorry, Chance, for Eileen and for you. Back then, I was self-destructive, spiteful, and plain evil. I didn't love myself and couldn't love your mother or you properly, at least not without hurting you. You must hate me."

"I did, as recent as last week. But I finally realized that hating you wouldn't change the past or bring Mama back. All it did was poison my heart, making me miserable."

Ray raked fingers through his hair. "I know about poison. I let it destroy my career, my family. Now, all I have left is regret."

"How long have you been clean?"

"Ten years, and I've been a believer for three." He looked earnestly at Chance. "After I got out of rehab, I went back to our old house, but the people who lived there had no recollection of you or your mother. Even the old neighbors who remained were suspicious of me and wouldn't tell me anything. I finally gave up, figuring you and Eileen had moved on and were likely better off without me."

Chance mulled over Ray's words, surprised that he had actually returned, trying to contact them. "You were a doctor. How did you end up here in a homeless shelter?"

"Through a series of bad choices and misfortune. After I got clean, I was blessed enough to get hired at a medical clinic. But years of insufficient funds led to it finally being closed. A lot of good people lost their jobs, not just me. But with my known history of addiction and multiple stints in rehab, nobody would risk hiring me, and soon the money ran out, my car got stolen, and I had no place to live."

"Don't you have friends?"

"No one willing to offer financial assistance or shelter. No one I trust that much."

"Are you still seeking employment?"

"Yes. Pastor Bienvenido is involved, too. He's arranging an interview for a position at a non-profit hospital affiliated with this church. If all goes well, I should be practicing medicine again."

"Good luck, then." Chance took no pleasure in Ray's misfortune. He actually hoped he did turn his life around and find some measure of peace. Like Salena said, the man deserved some compassion and prayer, not judgment. Chance glanced at his wristwatch, then back up at Ray. "I've got a four-hour drive back home, so it's time for me to leave." He had turned around, his back to Ray when he felt a firm hand on his shoulder.

"Wait!"

Chance faced him again. "What is it?"

"I don't deserve it, but can you forgive me?"

In his spirit, Chance distinctly heard a still, small voice say, *Walk as Jesus did*. He nodded, his mind set—his decision made. "I forgive you."

"Thank you."

"Goodbye." Chance turned again, prepared to walk away with a clear conscience and a clean heart, but Ray stopped him again, his hand back on his shoulder.

"They're serving dinner. Won't you stay an hour, just so we can talk?"

Chance faced the door—his exit. "About what?"

"You—your new life and this family of yours. I'm not asking for a place in your life—just one hour with you—breaking bread and fellow-shipping in God's House. Please?"

God, I'm trying to walk as Jesus did. But how much am I supposed to give this man? What am I supposed to do?

Share your heart.

Chance heard that small voice in his spirit and turned, confronting Ray. He saw hope gleaming in those blue eyes so like his own. "All right. I'll dine with you."

"God bless you." Ray smiled as he and Chance left the sanctuary together, each of them seeming to close the book on the past and walk in faith, with purpose to a better place—one of forgiveness, healing, closure.

Chapter Thirty-Three

Listen to advice and accept discipline,
and at the end you will be counted among the wise.
Many are the plans in a person's heart,
but it is the LORD's purpose that prevails.

Proverbs 19:20–21 (NIV)

Kingdom Family Christian Center
Wednesday, October 19

During Chance's dinner with Ray, they mostly talked about Chance's life after his mother had died, first in foster care and then with the Dearlings. Other than apologizing for the abuse and the hell that he had put Eileen and Chance through, Ray hadn't been forthcoming about himself or the path that had led him to the alcohol, drugs, and violence. Neither at the time had Chance been that interested in hearing his personal story. After all, he was still grappling with his emotions, trying to separate the man of Christ before him with the monster who had mercilessly beat him for three years. Even though he had genuinely forgiven Ray, he still couldn't completely forget the past and readily trust Ray.

In the end, after dinner, Chance had wished Ray well and had driven from Corinth, still with more questions than answers and still believing that his path would never cross Ray's again. However, later that night as he lay in bed, he tossed and turned unable to rest in peace, and those unanswered questions plagued him: *Did Ray have a family of his own—parents, brothers, or sisters? If he did, where were they—those unknown Braydens? If Ray was a skilled doctor—someone dedicated to saving lives and helping those sick and in pain, what had driven him to abuse alcohol and drugs, to inflict pain upon those weaker than himself—his wife and son? If he had really loved Eileen, why did he viciously turn upon her, beating her over the smallest thing? Did Ray ever love him? If he did, why didn't he ever say it? Why did he always make Chance feel as though he was weak, worthless, and a nuisance? Why, if Chance resembled Ray so much, couldn't Ray stand the sight of him? Why, back then, didn't Ray trust God or believe in Jesus?*

On Wednesday, after Bible study at Kingdom Family, Chance had broached the subject with his father Nathan in his church office, asking for his advice. "Dad, for years I've hated Ray and wanted nothing more than his death." Chance leaned forward, his hands palmed in his lap. "Now that I know where he is and I've forgiven him and even shared a cordial meal with him, I'm suddenly curious about the man—who he is, where he comes from, and what motivated him in the past. All I know of Ray Brayden is what I experienced as a child; I'm ignorant about every other aspect of his life. I don't even know if there are other Braydens out there carrying on the family name—grandparents, aunts, uncles, cousins, or even brothers and sisters."

"If you have questions about Ray or your family's history, then you should spend more time with him, Chance. You should sit down with him, be honest, and let the Lord lead you." His father leaned forward, his fingers twined on the desk. "You might not realize this, but God has given you a gift—an opportunity to forgive Ray, a second chance to mend what's broken between you and build a better, stronger relationship."

"Ray's not my father; you are, and I'm not sure I'm ready to bond with him, even if he has changed." Sure, he and Ray had had a decent conversation during dinner, but he didn't know if that was a good basis for a closer relationship.

His father pinned him with those hazel eyes, so penetrating and wise. "I imagine Daniel had similar reservations about spending time with Leah and me when you suddenly showed up a few months ago, interrupting his well-ordered life and requesting that he return with you to Crossland to meet a couple of strangers. After all, he considers Elec and Marissa Winward his *real* parents, and for most of his life, he's believed that Leah and I didn't love him, that we rejected and abandoned him."

As his father spoke, Chance recalled that encounter with Daniel when he had first revealed his birth parents' identity, announced that they were interested in a reunion, and had been met with a veritable brick wall of resistance. At that time, Chance couldn't fathom how a man of God and faith could be so indifferent to his biological parents. Now, Chance himself was such a man, and his heart and attitude with respect to Ray Brayden were being put under the spotlight of God's watchful eyes.

"Daniel had no reason to love us or even honor our request. He didn't have to come to Crossland with you, but he did. He didn't have to spend time bonding with us or learning about the rest of the family—the Dearlings—but he did because he let the Lord lead him, he opened his heart, and stepped out on faith. Now, in these short months, both Leah and I have a better relationship with Daniel, one that promises to get stronger in the coming years. We have a place reserved in Daniel's life and in his heart, and all of that happened because of faith, prayer, forgiveness, love, and trust."

"Are you telling me to trust Ray?"

His father sighed. "I'm telling you to open your heart and trust God. Sometimes in the physical, the only way you know that a wound or a sore has healed properly is when the bandages and even the scab are removed, and what's been hidden underneath is finally exposed to the air and sun.

"In the spiritual, you're truly healed and have a real breakthrough when all that rubbish—that garbage and waste—the fear, pain, anger, resentment, bitterness, and hatred—have all been uncovered and cast off, and that psychological protection has been removed so that the hidden wound or sore is finally exposed beneath the healing, restorative blood of the Son, Jesus Christ, and through the transformative power of the Holy Spirit, and then you don't realize that the wound is there or even feel its potent sting anymore. Even though it might leave a scar and become a part of you, it doesn't define who you are, nor does it have the power to hurt you anymore. You accept it as a part of your past, and you move forward—Godward."

Chance sat there in silence, pondering his father's words. In his spirit, he knew his father spoke the truth and that it was time for him to release the past—to truly let go and let God work within his life, especially with respect to Ray. "I've forgiven him, Dad. What more would God have me do?"

"Love him and pray for him. In Matthew 5, Jesus says, 'But I tell you, love your enemies and pray for those who persecute you, that you may be children of your Father in heaven. He causes his sun to rise on the evil and the good and sends rain on the righteous and the unrighteous. If you love those who love you, what reward will you get?'"

"None."

"That's right. Accept that Ray isn't your enemy anymore and that, like you, he's been redeemed and forgiven." He unlaced his fingers and covered the Bible on his desk with his right hand. "What I'm about to tell you might not sit well with you, but it's true: You can't do less for Ray than God has done for you."

"What does that mean?"

"You're not to hold a grudge against Ray, using his past or his mistakes against him as a weapon, especially now that he's confessed his sins before God. You're not to sit in judgment of Ray or to condemn him."

"Seriously, that's in the Bible?" He had been judging and condemning Ray for years. He had even equated the man with the devil, believing he deserved to roast in hell. Now, his father was exposing another sin Chance hadn't even been aware he was committing.

"Read Matthew 7 and Luke 6. God doesn't show favoritism, even among the saved and righteous. We all have sinned and fallen short of His glory, and we all need to be forgiven of something. But God is gracious, merciful, patient, loving, and *true*. He loves us even when we don't deserve it, yet He gives us ample time to make the right choices, turn our lives around, and surrender to Him."

"All right, Dad. I'll ask Salena to contact Ray."

His father smiled. "I'm proud of you, son. It takes courage to confront someone who's hurt you and do so in a spirit of love."

"Don't praise me yet. I'm only meeting Ray. I can't make any guarantees about loving him."

"You'll get there. Just be willing to follow where God leads you."

Chance stood, feeling more at ease. "Thanks for the advice, Dad. Once again, I'm indebted to you."

His father smiled, looking at him with such compassion in his eyes. "Son, haven't you learned yet: there's no charge for godly advice, nor is there a price on a true father's love? I love you, and anything I have, including wisdom, is yours, freely given."

Tears swelled in Chance's eyes, and even his heart was overflowing—quite full. "Thanks, Dad. For everything."

"You're welcome. Now, walk in faith, paying God's love forward."

Chapter Thirty-Four

But whatever were gains to me I now consider loss for
the sake of Christ. What is more, I consider everything a loss
because of the surpassing worth of knowing Christ Jesus
my Lord, for whose sake I have lost all things.

Philippians 3:7–8 (NIV)

Corinth, Texas
Saturday, October 22

At seven o'clock at night, Chance found himself sitting across from Ray in a booth beside the window at an all-night diner, treating him to a Southern meal of cheeseburger soup, chicken fried steak smothered in white gravy, mashed potatoes, green beans, and a glass of sweet, pink lemonade. Since they had arrived, Ray had been courteous and inviting, not only to Chance but to their waitress, a short, curvy dark-skinned, platinum blonde woman in a pink and white uniform with an angel's halo and wings as the logo on her right shoulder.

Within minutes of their arrival, Ray had introduced himself and had begun conversing naturally with the ever-smiling woman, learning that her name was Diane Brant and she was a thirty-year-old breast cancer survivor who had recently moved to Corinth and had been church hopping but hadn't really found the right church home—one where she could be plugged in to the pulse and purpose of God and get in the trenches, serving those in need. Immediately, Ray had begun talking enthusiastically with her about God, the Great Commission in Matthew 28, and telling her about Redemption Fellowship Center and its leader, Pastor Antonio Bienvenido.

Chance merely watched the interaction between them, silent and surprised. Ray wasn't ashamed to admit that he was homeless and unemployed, and neither was he ashamed to talk openly about Jesus, sharing his faith with a stranger. The father Chance had known as a child couldn't tolerate the mention of God, especially Jesus. He had always called faith a crutch for weak-willed and simple-minded people. Now, Ray was one of God's cheerleaders. *Who, but God, could have foreseen Ray Brayden's conversion—his transformation?*

Before Diane left to check on their order, she thanked Ray for the recommendation, grabbed his hand, and offered a sincerely heartfelt prayer that God would open a door for him to find a good job and a permanent home, and then she hugged him, promising to visit Redemption Fellowship Center on Sunday.

After they received their food and Diane left, Ray was the first to bow his head, palm his hands over his plate, and give thanks for the nourishment and the fellowship. "Thank You, God, for this special reunion with Chance. May it bless both of us and be all that You would have it be." He lifted blue eyes toward Chance and offered a smile, then raised his fork. "We should probably eat before this food gets cold."

"You don't want to talk first—about all that we both let slide last Sunday?"

Ray sighed. "That's a lot of dirt and debris to wade through, and I'd rather enjoy a good meal with you first. We'll have plenty of time to revisit sins of the past."

"All right." Chance chose to be patient. He would graciously share a meal with Ray; then, he would probe, hopefully discovering the man's identity and finding out why Ray had made Chance's childhood utter hell. Raising his fork and knife, Chance cut into the steak.

Later, when their plates were nearly empty, Ray shared stories from his life on the road and from testimonies he had heard at Redemption House. "We all have our personal stories—our triumphs and trials, our good times and bad, our successes and mistakes, our celebrations and tragedies. Sometimes, the roads we take and the travelers we meet on the journey lead us to God, and sometimes, they take us straight to hell." Ray palmed his hands over his plate, and his eyes fixed firmly on Chance. "Those of us who reach an intersection on that road to Damascus like Saul and have a profound and true encounter with Jesus can't help but change everything about ourselves, including our purpose in life and even what we call ourselves—our names. We can't continue on that path of destruction because we know that God loves us and has a greater purpose for us."

"What does any of this have to do with our history—yours and mine?"

"Much." Ray pulled a gold cross necklace from beneath his shirt. "For me, this cross is a symbol of God's love and Jesus' sacrifice, and it reminds me that I am saved by grace through faith, not by works."

"After Mama died, I was angry and lost. I hated crosses. I hated God."

Ray looked at Chance, his eyes focused, his stare direct. "And now?"

"I have faith and love, and I've finally learned to trust God."

Ray caressed his cross. "That's a lesson we all have to learn. Even the Apostle Paul who has his own compelling story. In his duality as both Saul and Paul, he fascinates me. He's someone I can even relate to because, like him, I have a dark past—one that isn't a fairy tale, nor am I a prince, a saint, or a hero for most of it. In it, I'm the lost and lonely one, the broken-hearted, the unloved, the betrayed, the addict, the abuser, and the villain. Like Saul, I was the persecutor, but then I had an encounter with Jesus, and today, like Paul, I'm redeemed and willing to share the love of God. I'm also ready to share my story—my testimony." His eyes pierced Chance's. "Maybe after you hear it, you'll have the answers you need, you'll understand me better, and we'll both find some measure of healing, peace."

Chance leaned forward. "I'm listening, Ray. Tell me your story."

Chapter Thirty-Five

Therefore, since we have been justified through faith, we have peace with God through our Lord Jesus Christ, through whom we have gained access by faith into this grace in which we now stand. And we boast in the hope of the glory of God. Not only so, but we also glory in our sufferings, because we know that suffering produces perseverance; perseverance, character; and character, hope.

Romans 5:1–4 (NIV)

Corinth, Texas
Saturday, October 22

Ray sighed, pushed his plate aside, then raked a hand through his hair. "I was born in New York City, the youngest of two sons, but my parents moved to Houston when I was three. I was raised in church as a young child but turned from God before I turned twelve."

Chance sat silent, amazed to learn that Ray had been raised in a Christian home. His mother Eileen had always led him to believe that Ray didn't believe in God, that he was an atheist. *What happened?*

Ray smiled, seemingly lost in memories. "There were four of us, my mom Meredith, who was a stay-at-home wife and mother, my older brother Timothy, who was four years my senior and very athletic and smart, me, and my dad, Chandler, who was an amazing father, an even better pediatric doctor."

Chance saw a bright light flare in Ray's eyes as he mentioned his family, especially his father, and it was that same light that he had had earlier when he had been talking about God to their waitress, Diane. Now, Chance recognized it for what it was—genuine love. *God, what corrupted Ray, and where is his family now?*

"Everybody loved my dad. He was a great guy—a loving father, a good husband, and the best friend—someone who was a natural leader and commanded discipline and respect but who also had a fun and silly side. He was a brilliant and dedicated emergency pediatric doctor who loved God, his family, and his patients. He never met a stranger, and he always managed to make people feel at ease—comfortable enough to smile, to even laugh—so much so that they could sometimes forget their worries, their suffering and pain. I loved that about Dad. He was my hero, and when I grew up, I wanted to be just like him—a doctor, a healer, a good person—a great dad."

Ray glanced up at Chance with gleaming, wet eyes. "You and I both got the best of Chandler Brayden. He was a handsome man, tall with broad shoulders, an unruly lock of brown hair that would always frustrate my mother because it always curled like a question mark on his forehead, and these infamous Brayden blue eyes that made Dad a magnet for a lot of single ladies, some who were ambitious enough to flirt with him, trying to lure him from Mom. He was faithful though, and Mom, his college sweetheart, was the only woman he loved—the only one he had eyes for."

Ray studied Chance's face closely. "I didn't recognize it when we met Sunday, but when I look at you today, I can see a mirror's reflection of my dad—how he looked at your age when I was a young, precocious boy who was still innocent, safe, and full of goodness, hope, and dreams." Tears slid down his cheeks. "I *loved* my life, my family, and my world back then, but I haven't thought about any of that in years."

"Why not?"

"It always hurt too much to remember—to admit how far from those people and that life I had strayed. When I lost them, I lost everything, my whole identity."

"Where's your family?"

"Gone. I was eight—at home with a babysitter because I was recovering from an illness." Ray absently rubbed the necklace, the cross. "Timothy, my big brother, was twelve and popular, usually busy with school and sports, but he always made time for me, always looked out for me. He loved soccer, and that night he was returning home with Mom and Dad from a soccer competition when they made a wrong turn, venturing into a crime-infested, gang-ridden neighborhood in an expensive car."

As Ray spoke softly with tears continuously falling, Chance could envision the scene as though he was there witnessing the event, and since he had been a police officer in Dallas, he could imagine how the story ended—badly.

"Before Dad could turn around or escape, the car was shot upon and disabled. Dad, Timothy, and Mom were shot and killed at point-blank range. The car was rifled through, and everything of value was taken—stolen." Ray stared at Chance, pain reflected in his eyes. "In one violent night, I lost my family, my security, my childhood, my life. I became an orphan."

Ray's family was murdered. Chance felt his loss, that pain. "Was there anyone left to take you in—grandparents, uncles, or aunts?"

"No one who really cared about me or was interested in raising me. Dad was an only child whose parents were both missionaries and doctors who died of an infectious disease in an African village when he was still in medical school, and my mother came from a poor, broken, and dysfunctional family. Her parents divorced before she turned nineteen, going their separate ways and pretty much tossing Mom out to fend for herself."

"Did she have any siblings?"

"A free-loading stepbrother named Mick Devin. My mother had always warned me to steer clear of Mick when he visited begging for a place to crash or for money, but after the funeral, I couldn't avoid him. He was the only relative alive who would take responsibility for me. The same week we buried my parents and Timothy, Mick moved into our house, became my legal guardian, and began siphoning money meant for my care and making my life hell on earth."

Chance saw Ray's eyes darken. "How did he make your life hell?"

"He turned me from everything my parents had ever taught me—making me forget all that was ever pure and good in my life and destroying any faith I ever had in God." Ray dropped the cross, meeting Chance's inquisitive stare, his eyes red and swollen with tears. "For eight years, Mick beat me mercilessly." He combed trembling fingers through his hair. "He was clever, though, about covering his tracks. He rarely left any visible evidence, and when he did, he'd always have me lie about the bruises, the broken limbs."

"Did you tell anybody?"

"I was a terrified kid, mostly a loner. I didn't trust anybody. Besides, Mick threatened to kill me if I betrayed him, and I believed him."

"Was he ever caught?"

"After I turned sixteen and finally got enough courage to report Mick to the police for funneling my money into his private accounts and for the abuse. By that time, I had gotten wise enough to collect some concrete evidence."

"Did he go to jail?"

Ray shook his head. "Before the police could arrest him, he ran away and committed suicide. He thought I had told the police *everything*—all of his sordid secrets."

"Didn't you?"

"I didn't tell them that Mick forced me to watch pornography, nor did I tell them that he got me drunk on alcohol or high on drugs so he could molest me. I didn't tell anyone, including Eileen, because I was ashamed, and I felt dirty and worthless, like it was my fault and God was punishing me for not being good enough. After Mick died, I buried those secrets and pretended like I was an average teenager, with plenty of money to spare and a bright future ahead."

God, this is beyond dysfunctional! How am I supposed to digest this? Chance cupped his face in his hands, overwhelmed but unable to blot the mental images from his mind or Ray's emotionless voice from his ears. He hadn't expected Ray to unload all of this on him, nor had he expected to feel any sympathy for the man who had himself been prey to a vicious predator. Audibly sighing, Chance lowered his hands, looking directly at Ray. "What happened next?"

"I survived and reinvented myself. I applied myself in school, graduated in the top of my senior class, attended a good college, then med school, and then I met a sweet nurse named Eileen Dorsey, and for the first time I dreamed about having a family again and a marriage like my parents'.

"Eileen and I dated for a year before I actually got the nerve to propose. Although she initially had reservations about marrying a man who didn't attend church or even acknowledge Jesus as the Savior, she loved me and eventually agreed to become my wife. I always figured she thought her love was enough to change me—to save me. Those first few years, I almost believed that myself. We were both relatively young and in love and had a good life together—a happy one. What neither of us realized, though, was that only God can compel a person to change, and only He can cleanse a heart, renew a mind, and mend what's broken."

"What went wrong?"

"Eileen got pregnant, and I got scared, especially when I learned she was having a baby boy. I had two pictures of a father in my head, one of Chandler Brayden, which was good and right, and one of Mick Devin, which was dirty and distorted." Ray looked into Chance's eyes. "For a while, I got past the fear, and when you were born on the Fourth of July, on Independence Day, I thought I was favored, finally free from my past with Mick. When I first held you in my arms, I loved you, as much as I ever loved my parents, Timothy and Eileen. Your mother chose Holden as your middle name, but I'm the one who called you 'Chance' because it was similar to my father's name and you were *my* chance to be a good father, to cast aside the weight of my shame, and to honor the one man I had always loved and respected, my dad—Chandler Hudson Brayden."

Ray had named him, not his mother. He was named in memory of his grandfather, Chandler Brayden. As Chance digested Ray's words, tears stung his eyes. "You really named me in honor of your father?"

"Yes."

"And you loved me?"

"Yes, Chance, even though it's hard to believe. I did, and I still do."

"Even though we're strangers, you love me?"

"You're the best part of me, a true gift from God."

Chance tried to wrap his mind around that thought, but he was struggling to accept it, to receive it. "If you loved Mama and me, why did you beat us? Why did you follow in Mick's violent footsteps?"

"Because inside I was broken, hurting, in pain. For all of my good intentions, I really didn't know how to love you and Eileen because I didn't love myself, and I didn't love God." Ray brushed the lock of hair from his forehead. "By the time you turned three, my past had come back to haunt me with a vengeance, and all that rage inside of me was just waiting for release—for an explosion. I couldn't escape Mick or any of that poison he had planted within me. I started having nightmares, reliving those abusive years, and the more I looked at you, the more I saw myself as that weak, defenseless, and worthless little boy—the one who wasn't good enough for God. I started drinking again, then graduated to drugs, and it got so bad that I gave up on everything. Before I got fired or killed somebody, I quit my job—the one good thing that had linked me to my father, Chandler.

"I was sick and perverted, no better than Mick, and I hated myself and made life miserable for you and Eileen because I didn't care about anyone or anything anymore except getting drunk or high and blotting out all those bad memories from my childhood. Finally, I couldn't stand looking into Eileen's eyes or yours anymore. In them, I saw fear and hatred, and I saw myself—broken and lost.

"Every day that I was home, I could see that love fading from Eileen's eyes and that light and innocence fading from yours, just like mine had during those years of abuse and molestation with Mick. When I saw that and realized that I was corrupting and destroying you both like Mick had done to me, I did the only good thing I could have done. I grabbed my duffel bag and left permanently. If I hadn't, there was a real possibility I would have ended up killing all of us. That's how lost and self-destructive I was."

Ray draped the golden cross over his hand. "There are three lessons that I've finally learned, Chance. The first is sometimes a person has to lose everything, including himself, to find his true identity in Christ. The second is that sometimes a person has to be completely broken so he can be fully healed, and the third is that sometimes a setback is only a setup for God to intervene." He lowered the cross, letting it fall back over his heart. "Today, sitting with you here, I know that my leaving was the best gift I could have given you. I was a rotten father and an even worse husband and man. Before I could appreciate you and Eileen, I had to find God and learn how to love, especially myself. Like Saul the persecutor, I was on the road to Damascus, never suspecting that I was about to have a personal encounter with Jesus."

"Where did you find Jesus?"

"In a dingy motel room when I was lost, dispirited, and broken, ready to swallow a lethal dose of pills and wash them down with as much alcohol as I could guzzle before losing consciousness. Although I had been sober for years, I was willing to give it all up, just to find some peace." He smiled. "God was one step ahead of me, though. Before I could even raise my hand to plop those pills in my mouth, I heard that still, small voice, and it freaked me out, making me spill every one of those pills on the floor."

"What did He say?"

"Turn on the television."

Chance rubbed his forehead. "Turn on the television?"

"It sounds crazy, I know, but I was curious, even desperate. I turned on the television, and at that moment, God saved me. The channel was set on a Praise-a-thon on a Christian network. And, that night, as I listened to those testimonies and got lost in that glorious music, something clicked inside of me. The scales fell from my eyes, the black ice melted from my heart, and I found love and peace. I saw myself as the lost sheep that God, the Good Shepherd, was leading back home, and in that instant, I got hooked on something greater than alcohol and drugs; I got hooked on God, on Jesus Christ, on love. And in that motel room, with only God as my witness, I kneeled before that television screen, I surrendered my life, and even though I've had some hardships and setbacks, my life has never been better or more fulfilling."

"You consider being unemployed and homeless a blessing?"

Ray bobbed his head. "I've had to hit rock bottom and lose everything, including myself, to gain what I need most—what I can't live without—love, God, redemption, and faith. I've had to learn about submission, humility, and forgiveness. Before I could heal completely, I had to submit my whole heart, soul, and mind to God, letting Him transform me; I had to be humble enough to allow Him to use me in whatever capacity He required, and I had to be obedient and merciful enough to forgive Mick, just as God had forgiven me." Ray shook his head. "It took much time, prayer, and counseling with some true men of God before I could sincerely forgive Mick, but in the end, I did it."

Chance combed fingers through his hair. "You really forgave the man who beat you and molested you, the one who got you hooked on alcohol and drugs?"

"Yes. I couldn't live with that hatred and anger anymore, and I wouldn't let Mick control my life from the grave."

At that moment, Chance realized that he and Ray had more in common than a dysfunctional childhood and a family resemblance. They both had taken detours, straying from the purpose and will of God, and they both had been pursued by Him and had been compelled to seek comfort, provision, and peace from the One Father who had promised never to leave or forsake them.

Ray reached across the table, touching Chance's hand. "I know you've forgiven me, Chance, and I'm grateful for that, especially considering how badly I treated you and Eileen and how much pain and suffering I inflicted on you. I'd like you to know that I didn't tell you about my past so you'd feel pity or sympathy for me, nor did I do so to excuse my behavior. I was an adult, and I had free will, so I take full responsibility for my actions and all of my mistakes."

"Why did you, then?"

"You deserve the truth, and I'm tired of keeping secrets." He pulled back his hand. "Now that God has blessed me with the opportunity to meet you as an adult, and I've been privileged to learn more about your life and family and the kind of man you've become, I don't want to lose touch with you again."

Diane arrived with their bill, and Chance handed her his credit card, then lowered his head and his voice. "What else do you want from me?"

"A second chance, a monthly meal, and a couple of hours here in this diner. We can talk about God, our lives, or anything else you'd like to discuss."

Again, he surprised Chance. "You want to spend time with me?"

"Yes."

"In this diner?"

"If you're willing. The food's good, the employees are great, and I love the name—*Angel's* Diner. It's got a heavenly sound to it."

Diane came back and returned Chance's card.

Ray smiled at her, then refocused on Chance when she left. "Do you think you can tolerate me long enough for us to get reacquainted?"

"That depends."

Ray's smile faded. "On what?"

Chance relaxed, deciding to walk in faith, paying love forward. "Who's paying?"

Ray chuckled, shaking his head. "I'm between blessings—homeless and unemployed—so you'll have to pay until God opens the next door for me."

"You think He will?"

"Yes, I do. He's the Head of my life now, the Author and Finisher of my faith." Ray raised those intense blue eyes back to Chance. "I don't doubt God anymore. After all, I had already depleted my resources and given up hope, believing both you and Eileen lost to me, but this past Sunday, God showed up again and did what I thought was impossible— He reunited us and gave us a rare opportunity to fellowship as men—a once prodigal father with his firstborn, his only son.

"Even if you decide against seeing me, I won't be disappointed. I'll still be happy, favored, and *blessed* because I've spent this precious time becoming reacquainted with you, sharing my story, remembering my own family, and getting a glimpse in you of the father I haven't seen in years—Chandler Hudson Brayden. He was a good man—the best—and you inherited more from him than from me."

This isn't the Ray I grew up with; this man seems different, humbled, changed. Maybe it's time I put my faith into action and extend an olive branch, the right hand of fellowship. At that moment, Chance made his decision. "When would you like to meet?"

Sunlight shone in Ray's eyes. "Every third Saturday about seven o'clock, if we're both available and it's not a holiday."

"I'll have to check my calendar, but if I'm free, I'll be here."

His eyes grew round. "Really?"

"Yes." It was like his father Nathan had said, sometimes you had to remove the bandages and the scab so you could expose the wound and discover whether it was truly healed.

"Thank you."

"You're welcome." Chance was glad he had come. Now, he knew

more about Ray than he had previously, and he had a better sense of his family history. The next time he and Ray dined, he would find out more about the Braydens, especially Dr. Chandler Brayden, a man who had already piqued Chance's interest. Who knew he came from a family of doctors and missionaries?

Ray glanced at his watch. "It's late, and you've got to drive back to Crossland, and I've got to make curfew at Redemption House." He rose to his feet, extending his right hand to Chance. "Thank you again, Chance. I enjoyed myself."

Chance stood, accepting his handshake. "It was only a meal."

"It was more than that. It was a blessing, and I'm not taking it or you for granted anymore." He smiled, then leaned over. "Don't forget to leave Diane a tip."

"I've got it covered." Chance removed his wallet, pulling a hundred-dollar bill out and placing it on the table.

Ray smiled again. "You've got a good heart and a giving spirit, Chance, just like my dad." He clapped his hand on his shoulder. "I'm glad you found me, even gladder you forgave me. Eileen would have been proud of you—the good man you've become."

"I'm no saint. I had to learn that *all* have sinned and fall short of the glory of God and that I can't ask God to do for me what I won't do for others."

"Those were tough lessons for me, too. Some days they still are."

On their way out the door, they saw Diane again and waved to her, bidding her farewell.

She returned their waves. "Come back anytime!"

"We will, every third Saturday at about seven o'clock." Ray smiled, then walked out with Chance, with a youthful spring in his steps and hope shining in his eyes.

Chapter Thirty-Six

Love must be sincere. Hate what is evil; cling to what is good.
Be devoted to one another in love. Honor one another above yourselves.
Never be lacking in zeal, but keep your spiritual fervor, serving the Lord.
Be joyful in hope, patient in affliction, faithful in prayer.
Share with the Lord's people who are in need. Practice hospitality.

Romans 12:9–13 (NIV)

Crossland, Texas
Saturday, October 29

As they dined at Marciano's, Chance looked around the table, his eyes alighting on each person present: Victor, Alessia, Salena, his father, and his mother. This was his mother's first public appearance outside of church since the surgery, and she had only come tonight because Victor had invited her, refusing to accept her excuses.

Still self-conscious about her baldness and the scar from the surgery, she fastidiously covered her head with scarves. Tonight, she had donned a peach scarf to complement her white blouse and peach skirt, and Chance thought she looked as lovely as ever. His eyes left her, returning to Salena, his date, and as she chatted and laughed with his father, Chance gazed upon her with adoration and pride. Like always, she was gorgeous, draped elegantly in a royal blue dress, with her red hair bound in a thick, round braid, with long tendrils framing her face.

Sensing his gaze, she spared him a glance, blessed him with a radiant smile, then grabbed his hand beneath the table, folding it in hers before she resumed the conversation with his father. *She truly loved him, and he felt and recognized it—in her smile and even in her touch.*

Since his reunion with Ray, Chance had firmly latched on to Salena, relishing what he had long denied himself—intimacy, romance, love. Now, in the past week, he and she had become more than friends; they had become partners, a couple. Chance trusted Salena, and he had no problem sharing his past with her. Hopefully, one day he could even return the depth of her feelings and be courageous enough to say those three words he hadn't uttered to any woman but his two mothers: *I love you.*

Victor raised his knife, clinking it against his glass, and Chance, along with everyone else, glanced his way. He traded a silent glance with Alessia, and after she smiled and nodded at him, he lifted his eyes toward their parents. "Mom and Dad, I didn't just invite you here to celebrate Mom's recovery."

"Then, why did you, son?"

He took Alessia's hand into his. "Alessia and I wanted to share some news."

Chance's mother clapped, bouncing in her seat in excitement. "You're getting married, aren't you?"

"No, Mom! We're officially dating. We're a couple."

The revelation that should have excited Chance dropped like a stone in his heart. He'd spoken to Victor about his relationship with Alessia last month, and his brother hadn't been in love with her then. He'd been pinning his heart and hopes on Leisha. Now, suddenly, he was announcing a commitment to Alessia. Chance didn't know if Victor's feelings had changed that drastically over the past month or if Victor was still enamored of Leisha but finally taking his advice and moving on with another woman. If Victor didn't love Alessia but was settling for her, then he was making a colossal mistake, and Chance blamed himself.

"Well, I'm still happy for you." Chance's mother calmed down and smiled sweetly at the new couple. "Congratulations!"

"Thank you, Mom."

"Welcome to the family, Alessia."

"Thank you, Mrs. Dearling." Alessia leaned her shoulder against Victor's.

Chance's father chuckled, winking at Alessia. "If all works well, this time next year we may be dining here again, celebrating an engagement."

Alessia's eyes twinkled. "We just might, and if we do get married, I'd love for you to officiate the wedding."

As Chance's parents chatted with the couple, Salena tensed beside Chance, pulling her hand from his. She clutched her purse, then politely excused herself. When she rose, Chance saw that she was crestfallen, with unshed tears in her eyes. Concerned, he stood and followed her, catching her arm before she entered the women's restroom.

She snapped at him. "What do you want?"

He pulled her aside, away from the flow of traffic. "What's wrong?"

She thumbed tears from her eyes. "Nothing."

"Why are you crying?"

"I'm a woman. Sometimes, we cry."

"Be honest."

She sighed, staring into his eyes. "I've got to phone Leisha."

"That doesn't explain why you're tense and upset, with tears in your eyes."

"Victor's announcement caught me unexpectedly."

"Still, that's not a valid reason for tears."

"It is when the news will be the final nail in someone else's heart."

"Stop talking in code and say what's bothering you."

"Leisha's in love with Victor."

Her words punched Chance in the gut. "Really?"

"Yes. Since he confessed to loving her last month, she's been holding out faith that they would eventually get together, as a couple."

"You're sure Leisha loves my brother?"

"Absolutely. All this time, she's been faithful, too, praying earnestly that Victor would change his mind about renouncing his love and letting her go. Now, with tonight's news, she'll finally have to accept his decision—his choice to be with Alessia, not her—and she's going to be devastated."

Chance raked fingers through his hair. "This is a complicated mess, and it's all my fault."

"How is any of this your fault?"

"I'm the one who discouraged Victor from loving Leisha, from pursuing a relationship with her. I pulled the family card, convincing him that their relationship would upset our parents and cause more harm than good. Now, he's only with Alessia because of my counsel—my interference—and I'm not even sure he genuinely loves her."

Salena reached out, touching his face. "Don't blame yourself for your brother's lack of loyalty or faith. Victor's an adult, capable of making his own decisions, and he alone is responsible for the fallout of his actions."

Chance heard the accusation in her voice and again felt guilty. "Don't be angry with him. Victor *is* a good guy, and he is faithful and loyal, just primarily to this family."

Salena lowered her hand, her eyes shining with flames. "If he really loves Leisha, he should be fighting for her, not placating other people or dating another woman. If he can forget Leisha so easily, maybe he's not the one for her. Maybe he's not worthy of her heart."

"Of course, he's worthy. He's better than I am, and when he loves, he does so deeply and wholeheartedly, without reservation. Walking away from Leisha hasn't been easy for him."

Salena scoffed. "He doesn't seem heartbroken tonight. He's pleasantly sitting beside Alessia, smiling and committing to an exclusive relationship with her."

"Likely, he's pretending."

"Then, why live the lie? If he's a true man of God, why can't he be courageous enough to walk in faith, even if it means walking against the opposition, including that from his own family?"

"He's lost a lot of people in his life—his birth parents, his grandmother, and his first love. Now, he may be trying to protect those he still has."

"That makes no sense. Leisha isn't a danger, nor will Victor loving her be catastrophic for the Dearlings. All after, Leisha is their daughter, and they already love her. Why wouldn't they want both her and Victor to be happy together, if they're in love?"

"Maybe Victor is misguidedly trying to please Mom. She's expressed interest in having Alessia as a daughter-in-law, and she's been pushing the two of them together for months."

"If Victor told her the truth, confessing his love for Leisha, I'm sure Mrs. Dearling would stop plugging Alessia and urge him to follow his heart. From what I've seen, she's reasonable and empathetic. She loves Victor, and she wouldn't willingly cause him harm or guide him toward a woman he didn't love—one who wasn't meant for him. All he has to do is be honest with her and with his father."

"That's not likely now that he's made a commitment to Alessia."

"Then, he doesn't deserve Leisha, and she's better off without him." Salena brushed past Chance and entered the restroom, her purse tucked under her arm.

Chance exhaled deeply, shaking his head. *What do I do? I've already interfered once in Victor's love life, and now he's dating Alessia. Do I backtrack now, apologizing and telling him I was wrong, that he has a right to follow his heart—to be with Leisha? Or do I mind my own business, praying for the best and letting You work all of this out for everybody's good?* Silently, he returned to his family's table and sat down.

Chance's mother looked at him. "Is Salena okay?"

"She had to make an important call."

She smiled, her eyes bright. "I like her. She's a good woman—intelligent and engaging. You and she make a beautiful couple—the *forever* kind."

Chance groaned. "Don't start planning our wedding. This is only our first official date."

"Still—"

"Enough, honey." Chance's father covered her hand with his. "If Chance and Salena are meant to be, they'll be, and if not, then they'll figure that out."

"Thanks, Dad." Even though he was happy with Salena, Chance didn't know what the future held for them. Presently, he was grateful that she loved him in spite of his flaws, and he was content to take one day at a time.

Chapter Thirty-Seven

Come, let us sing for joy to the LORD; let us shout
aloud to the Rock of our salvation. Let us come before him
with thanksgiving and extol him with music and song.

Psalm 95:1–2 (NIV)

Holly Drive
Thursday, November 24

Excited about sharing her first Thanksgiving with the Dearlings but nervous about overseeing her first major holiday dinner, Leisha fluttered around the kitchen like a butterfly, stirring, seasoning, baking, and tasting, with Salena often at her side, lending a hand and urging her to slow down and take a break, and Alessia, at the kitchen table, first preparing a fruit salad, then adding whipped frosting to a rectangular white cake.

Leisha was working so tirelessly because this was her gift to the entire Dearling family—her labor of love—and she wanted the dinner and day to be memorable—perfect—even though Daniel was in Georgia with the Winwards. She also wanted to honor her birth parents, especially La' Dear. That's why Leisha, Salena, and Alessia had commandeered the kitchen for the day, banishing Leah to the living room with the men.

Leisha was still amazed at how fast the time had flown. Five months had passed since she'd first learned that Pastor and La' Dear were her biological parents, and all of their lives had changed irrevocably since then. What was truly astonishing was that they had bonded despite the thirty-six years that had separated them, and over five months, new friendships and relationships had developed.

Since September, Salena and Chance had drawn closer, first as friends, then as partners, a couple, and now they made sense together and complemented each other. Salena inspired Chance to laugh, joke, take risks, and be spontaneous and not be so solemn, and Chance inspired her to relax, find joy in peace and quietness, to be tame, more reserved, and not so fiercely independent. These days it wasn't unusual for the two of them to commute the four hours between Corinth and Crossland to spend time together.

Another budding but painful romance for Leisha was that of Alessia and Victor's. They had been dating for the past month, and Alessia had become a frequent guest in the Dearlings' home, often invited to dinner. Their relationship and Alessia's presence had become a constant thorn in Leisha's heart, and she tried valiantly to pretend that nothing was wrong and her heart wasn't breaking, but being around Alessia and Victor together tested both her faith and patience. The younger woman hadn't just endeared herself to Victor; she had captivated his family as well. She had even opted to spend Thanksgiving with the Dearlings instead of at her uncle's house with her grandmother.

From the onset, Alessia had made bold attempts to befriend Leisha, but Leisha had remained guarded and aloof. She was polite and cordial to Alessia, treating her respectfully, but she didn't extend herself trying to become one of Alessia's friends. After all, Leisha wasn't perfect like Jesus; she didn't see Alessia as a sister in Christ but as her rival for Victor's heart—the woman he had ultimately chosen over her.

At six, Salena clapped a hand on Leisha's shoulder. "Everything's done: the food is finished, and the table is set. We're ready."

"Thank God, and thank you two." She hugged Salena but bobbed her head at Alessia. "I couldn't have done any of this alone." She smiled. "Now, let's see if everyone is ready to eat."

When they entered the living room, they found the television off and Nathan, Chance, and Victor all sitting, their heads turned toward the corner where Leah sat comfortably at the piano, her fingers poised above the keys. Leisha had heard that Leah was an anointed musician with a heart for worship, but in the months since they had met and become acquainted, Leisha hadn't yet been privileged to witness her using her gifts. Now, as Leisha silently studied her, she saw pure love and rapture on Leah's face, and Leisha was drawn even closer to her.

When Leah commenced playing "The Lord's Prayer" and her fingers danced nimbly and masterfully across the keyboard, she commanded everyone's attention, their respect; however, when she began singing with that dynamic voice and ingeniously interpreting the song, she lifted spirits and captured everyone's heart. After she sang the last soulful note, everyone applauded, immediately requesting an encore. Leah then blessed them with a heartfelt rendition of "His Eye is on the Sparrow," and as Leisha listened and recalled all that God had brought her through, she bowed her head, with tears falling from her eyes, and she thanked Him for His provision, protection, faithfulness, and love.

If Salena hadn't taken charge, herding them all into the dining room, they all would have gladly stayed in the living room, worshipping with Leah.

Soon, however, the smell of food encouraged everyone to find their seats around the dining room table: Nathan and Leah sat in places of honor at both ends of the table; on Nathan's right were Salena, Chance, and Alessia; and on Leah's right were Victor and Leisha.

Nathan requested that they bow their heads; then, he lifted his voice in prayer and blessing. "Lord, thank You for letting us assemble here on this day of thanksgiving to give You all honor, glory, and praise. We thank You for health and strength, for family, and for love. We also ask a special blessing for Daniel and the Winwards, that they may enjoy in peace the bounty of this day. Finally, thank You for this food that has been so graciously prepared. Bless the hands of those who have prepared it. In Jesus' name. Amen."

Everyone lifted their heads, and Nathan grinned, eying the plump, golden-brown turkey on the platter before him. He wet his lips. "Now that we've thanked the Lord, let's eat!" He lifted a knife near the platter, then smoothly carved the turkey.

Soon, everyone else served themselves, courteously sampling the turkey, cornbread dressing, mixed greens, black-eyed peas, potato salad, deviled eggs, broccoli and rice casserole, fruit salad, candied yams, and squash. Then, as they ate, the table exploded with appreciation, conversation, and laughter, and Leisha, Salena, and Alessia received many compliments, first from Leah, then from the men.

The praise continued through dessert after Alessia, Salena, and Leisha paraded before everyone sweet potato, chocolate meringue, then pecan pies, a German chocolate cake, followed by a whipped-frosted white cake, and finally bowls of banana pudding and peach cobbler.

After he had demolished two slices of chocolate meringue pie and had spooned a bowl of banana pudding empty, Nathan pushed his bowl away, sighing in contentment. "Bless the Lord, and bless the cook. If you don't believe I ate, just come and look." He patted his stomach; then, his eyes went first to Salena, then to Alessia, and finally, they rested on Leisha. "Ladies, I commend you on an excellent Thanksgiving dinner. You definitely put your hearts into every dish, and I thank you for it. Everything was delicious."

Leisha, Salena, and Alessia exchanged looks and smiled beneath his praise. "Thank you, Pastor."

Next, Leah tinkled her fork against a glass, garnering everyone's attention. "Like Nathan, I also want to express my gratitude to you three for making this a memorable occasion. I loved the food, but I love all of you more." Her eyes fell upon Leisha. "I especially want to thank you for your love, labor, and selflessness. You did well, as I knew you would, in hosting this dinner in my stead. Thank you for being here and for a job well done."

Leisha felt the touch of Leah's love, and her words went straight to her heart. "I'm glad you and Pastor enjoyed the meal. I truly wanted this to be the Dearlings' day to be pampered and loved, and I wanted everything to be perfect."

Leah looked at Leisha with such an expression of maternal love that tears stung Leisha's eyes. "Sweetheart, this day wasn't perfect because of the food; it was perfect because you were here with us, sharing in our love—our family. As much as I enjoyed the dinner, I'm most thankful for my family: Nathan, Chance, Victor, Daniel, and you. I love you."

"I love you, too, La' Dear." Leisha palmed her hands over her plate, her heart like her stomach full and singing with thanksgiving, in rejoice.

Chapter Thirty-Eight

The faithless will be fully repaid for their ways,
and the good man rewarded for his.

Proverbs 14:14 (NIV)

✞

Kingdom Family Christian Center
Wednesday, December 14

After the Wednesday night Bible study concluded and most of the attendees had left the sanctuary, Victor remained sitting on the first row in front of a lit cross on the wall, his hands palmed, his head bowed, and his heart heavy and conflicted. For the past two months, he had been deluding himself and living a lie—pretending that he could forget Leisha so easily and commence a new life with Alessia. His feelings hadn't changed, corresponding to Alessia as he had hoped, even prayed. He loved Alessia, but he was in love with Leisha. Victor wasn't doing Alessia any favors either by deceiving her, letting her believe that he would eventually propose marriage, that they had a future together. Each time she looked at him with eyes lit with love and trust, he felt dishonest, corrupt, a fraud.

His fear and cowardice had cost him—love and self-respect. Even Leisha. She was dating a neighbor, some helicopter pilot named Bennett Ford. Since learning the news this morning, Victor's mom was already excited, speculating whether love would blossom and the courtship would end in marriage.

Victor had assumed he would be happy for Leisha, pleased that she had taken his advice and moved forward with another man; however, in his heart, he felt grief, pain, sorrow. Now, he knew a fraction of what Leisha must have felt regarding his relationship with Alessia.

His faithlessness had robbed him of the love of one good, godly woman, and his dishonesty would rob him of the respect and love of another—Alessia. Once he confessed the truth, she would be disappointed and feel betrayed, and she'd likely hate him for taking advantage of her and exploiting her feelings. Both she and Leisha deserved better. They deserved an honorable man—one who was faithful and didn't hide from the truth. Tonight, he would be transparent, and he would bare his soul and heart, first to Alessia, then to his family. He couldn't stomach any more lies—any more pretense.

Victor raised his eyes to the cross. "Lord, forgive me for giving in to fear and rejecting the gift of love. Please, give me courage and the right words to say and work this all out." He lowered his head, then pulled out his cell phone, calling Alessia and requesting that she meet him in the sanctuary before she left the church.

She arrived fifteen minutes later, greeting him with a kiss and a hug. She pulled back, her forehead creased. "You look upset. What's wrong?" She sat beside him, her hand on his arm.

"I'm wrong." He faced her directly. "You've been honest about loving me, but I haven't been as upfront with you."

She slid her hand back. "I don't understand."

Please, forgive me. He sighed, willing himself to continue. "Alessia, you're a great woman, worthy of any man. But I'm not in love with you."

Tears glistened in her eyes, and she sniffled, brushing the tears with her fingers. "Maybe you're just nervous about taking the final step with me. Maybe your heart needs a little longer than mine." She smiled weakly. "We've only been dating two months. There's plenty of time for us to grow as a couple, to think about marriage."

Her faith shamed him, and he hated having to hurt her, but he couldn't pretend anymore. He couldn't smother his own feelings and deny what was truly in his heart. That wouldn't be fair to Alessia or him. "I don't need more time, Alessia, and my heart won't change because it's already engaged."

She covered her heart with her hand. "What does that mean: Your heart's already engaged?"

He had to be honest; he couldn't sugarcoat the truth so he would come out unscathed. "For these past six months, I've been in love with another woman."

Alessia gasped, pulling inward as though he had physically punched her, and he saw that hurt, betrayal, and anger in her eyes. "Who is she?"

"A name doesn't matter."

"Of course, it does!"

"I've lost her. To another man."

"I hope you don't expect me to feel sorry for you."

"No, I don't."

Her eyes struck him like daggers. "If you loved this woman, why did you even agree to date me?"

"Because I was weak, a coward. I couldn't pursue a relationship with her, so I let her go. I thought I could move on with you. I cared about you, Alessia, and I prayed that my heart would correspond to yours. As more than a friend."

"So, I was your second choice, a standby, or some consolation prize?"

"It wasn't like that. I cared about you; I still do."

"You used me and took my love for granted." She swiped more tears from her flushed face. "This entire relationship was a lie."

"I'm sorry. I never meant to hurt you or to abuse your friendship, your love." He reached out for her hand, but she shrank from him, spurning his touch.

"You should have been honest. At least then, I would have been forewarned, and I could have protected myself better. Instead, you've been toying with me for the past two months, raising my expectations toward a future with you—toward love and marriage."

"I sincerely apologize. I know it'll take time, but I pray you'll forgive me."

Alessia sniffled again, then rose regally to her feet, her head held high, even as she dried her face with her hand. "I don't hold grudges, so I'll forgive you one day. Just not tonight or even this year. You're not the man I thought you were; you're definitely not the one I need. Goodbye, Victor." Turning, she strode away, leaving him alone.

Victor collected himself, then stood and left the sanctuary, striding toward his dad's office where he knew he would find his parents and Chance. He knocked softly on the door, then entered after he heard his dad's invitation. He found his dad seated comfortably at his desk and Mom and Chance sitting side by side on the sofa. Instead of taking a seat, Victor remained standing, his right hand curled around the cross on his necklace.

His mother looked up first. "You look agitated, Victor. What's wrong?"

"Alessia and I just ended our relationship. We're not a couple anymore."

She stood and rushed to his side and pressed a hand on his arm. "What happened?"

"I told her I didn't love her as deeply as she loved me and that I've been in love with another woman for the past six months."

His mom dropped into the nearest seat, her eyes wide and her mouth open. "You didn't!"

"For once, I was completely honest." He saw the disappointment and confusion written on his parents' faces, and he steeled himself, resolving to forge ahead with the truth. He was tired of keeping secrets, and now he only wanted to unburden himself, sliding from beneath the weight of secrecy.

His dad palmed his hands on his desk. "I'm deeply troubled, son. What's gotten into you? Why all the deception?"

"Apparently, I'm no perfect son nor am I Prince Charming. I'm sorry for lying—for deceiving you all."

"Why would you commit to Alessia if you were in love with someone else?"

Chance stood and walked toward Victor. "This is my fault, Dad. I urged Victor to forget this other woman. I didn't think she was suitable, and I didn't believe you and Mom would condone his relationship with her. I'm also the one who advised him to move on, pursuing Alessia." He clapped his hand on Victor's shoulder. "I was wrong to interfere, dictating who you should love, and I had no right to use your love for this family against you. I've done what I always promised myself I wouldn't do—hurt you and betray your trust. Can you forgive me?"

Victor saw love, sincerity, and regret in Chance's eyes, and he knew his brother hadn't meant to intentionally harm him. Chance had only been trying to protect him, as he had done ever since Victor was eleven years old. Besides, Chance wasn't the real culprit. Victor was an adult now, and he alone was the one who had renounced his love for Leisha and had left Alessia broken-hearted. "Yes, I forgive you." He released his necklace and hugged Chance. "I accept your apology, too."

Chance pulled back. "Thanks."

"Who's the mystery woman?"

Victor looked at his mom. "I've lost her. So it doesn't matter anymore."

"Did she die?"

"No."

"Is she married?"

"No."

"An unbeliever?"

"No."

"Have we met her?"

"Yes, Mom." Victor sighed. "I hurt her badly, especially when I chose Alessia over her. She may not forgive me or even want me anymore, and I can't even blame her."

"Who is she, son?"

"Tell them, Victor. It's time."

He looked from his mom to his dad, then he exhaled. "I'm in love with Leisha, and before I broke her heart, she was in love with me."

Chapter Thirty-Nine

The purposes of a man's heart are deep waters,
but a man of understanding draws them out.

Proverbs 20:5 (NIRV)

The Harlington Hotel
Sutton, Georgia
Saturday, December 24

At seven thirty, Chance and Salena met at the hotel elevator, then arrived together at the breakfast room that Daniel had reserved for the family on his wedding day. Chance's parents were already seated, chatting amiably with Elec and Marissa Winward at the covered table, and Daniel stood at the buffet table, putting food on his plate.

Upon seeing them, Chance's father leaned back in his seat. "Good morning, you two."

"Good morning." Chance hugged him, then turned to his mother, kissing her before stepping aside, letting Salena greet them with hugs and kisses.

"Where's Victor?"

Chance looked at his father. "Upstairs getting ready."

"I still can't believe he waited six months to confess his love for Leisha. Why didn't he trust us or seek our counsel?"

"He didn't want to put us in an awkward position, honey. He wanted to protect and spare us, and that's why he kept silent. I should have been adept at reading the signs, though. I've raised Victor since he was eleven years old, and I've seen him give his heart away, only to have it broken.

"For eight years I've watched him coast through life, occasionally dating but never really getting serious about any particular woman. However, that time in Corinth with Leisha changed him. When he came home with her, he was a different man, especially around her. As his mother, I should have been privy to that love, and I shouldn't have been so eager to foist Alessia on him."

"The signs were there, but we both missed them." Chance's father sighed, rubbing his chin. "I love Victor and Leisha, and I'd give anything to protect both of them from hurt. I'm their father, and I want the best for them, even if that means having them together, loving each other. It hurts to know that Victor didn't readily trust me, that he was afraid that I would disapprove of his relationship with Leisha, and that he thought I could be happy when he was miserable. I'm not that selfish or that heartless." He shook his head. "I always promised that I would never do to my children what your father tried to do to you and me—discount our love, deceive us, and tear us apart."

"You're nothing like Daddy." Chance's mother covered his hand with hers. "Victor was just confused and misguided. But now he knows we're not against him."

"Mom's right. Both Victor and I were acting out of fear, not faith."

Chance's father shook his head. "Victor is miserable and alone, and Leisha is dating some man we know nothing about. So, what can we do?"

"Pray, my love. Only God knows what's best for Victor and Leisha, so we've just got to have faith that He'll work out their relationship."

Chance's father exhaled. "I'm a praying man but not a passive parent. I'll try to release the reins this time. But it won't be easy."

"They're adults, Nathan. They don't need our interference."

At that moment Victor walked through the door and advanced toward them. He greeted Chance and Salena, then turned to his father. "Hello, Dad."

"Hello, son." Chance's father embraced him, holding him slightly longer than necessary.

Finally, Victor pulled back, facing his mother. "How are you feeling, Mom?"

"Like the most blessed mother in the world." She raised her head and kissed his cheek, then pulled back, beaming. "I'm content because I'm alive and well, surrounded by my three handsome sons."

Chance smiled, with Salena's arm resting on his waist. "We're content, too, Mom."

"If I were vain, I'd be jealous of you, Mrs. Dearling," Salena said. "You look radiant today, outshining even me."

Chance's mother laughed. "Thank you, Salena. You're a sweetheart, and I can't wait for my son to get smart and snatch you up permanently."

Salena winked at her. "If he's too slow, I'll snatch him up. How about that?"

"Perfect!" Chance's mother waved her hand. "Now, you all stop dawdling over here with us and go fix your plates. We'll have plenty of time to talk later." She shooed Salena, Chance, and Victor toward the buffet table.

After piling his plate with food, Chance returned to the table, sandwiching himself between his mother and Salena, and as Salena engaged Victor in conversation, he fixed his attention on Daniel and his parents.

"Are you enjoying yourself, Pastor?"

"Immensely. Thank you for the family breakfast. It gives us an opportunity to break bread and fellowship with you and your parents."

"I knew the wedding reception would be hectic and crowded with family, friends, and church members, all vying for our attention, so you and my parents wouldn't have time to relax, becoming acquainted."

"Well, God definitely led you in the right direction, and I appreciate you and Taryn inviting us to your house tomorrow to celebrate your first Christmas as newlyweds before you leave for that Caribbean honeymoon."

"Family matters to me, so I wouldn't dream of celebrating my marriage or the birth of my Savior without including all the people I love and cherish."

Chance's father spoke to Marissa and Elec. "You should be proud as parents to have such a gracious, honorable son—one after God's own heart."

Elec grinned. "The four of us do, Nathan."

"Let us praise God, then."

Marissa smiled. "Amen."

"Leisha's here." Daniel directed everyone's eyes toward the door where Leisha stood with her date, Bennett Ford.

Since his back was to the door, Victor couldn't see the couple, but Chance saw his reaction to the news of their arrival. His head dropped, and his eyes fell.

Chance's father leaned over to Daniel. "What do you think of Bennett?"

"He seems like a good guy—honest, likable, attentive."

"Do you believe your sister is serious about him?"

Daniel shrugged. "With Leisha, it's hard to tell. She holds her heart close at times, so it's difficult to know exactly what she's feeling. I have no doubt Bennett cares deeply for her, though. All he did last night when we spoke was rave about her. He's crazy for her, and he's just waiting for her to give him a real chance."

Leisha and Bennett approached the table, walking around to greet Chance's parents.

"Good morning, sweetheart. Bennett." Chance's mother kissed and embraced Leisha before offering Bennett a friendly hug.

"Good morning, Mrs. Dearling. How are you?"

"Blessed and highly favored."

"Praise God." He greeted everyone else before escorting Leisha back around the table to the vacant chair across from Leah. "You relax and enjoy yourself." He settled Leisha into her seat. "If you tell me what you want, I'll prepare your plate and bring it to you." After Leisha told him what she wanted, he kissed her forehead, then left for the buffet table.

Chance's mother leaned forward. "Are you and Bennett a serious couple?"

"We're not a couple. We're just friends who enjoy each other's company. That's all."

"Well, take care with your heart and his, too."

"I will, La' Dear."

She reached across the table, grabbing Leisha's free hand. "I'm here if you need me. Always. Okay?"

"Yes, ma'am."

Chance's mother pulled back, her eyes darting between Leisha and Victor, both of whom had yet to speak to each other, and Chance could tell she wasn't pleased with what she saw. However, she remained silent, merely observing.

Bennett returned with two plates, lowering one in front of Leisha and putting the other beside it; then, he sat down, a buffer between Leisha and Victor.

"God is good." Chance's father looked around the table. "He brings the lost home, makes a way out of no way, and makes all things work for our good."

"Amen to that, Pastor." Daniel stood on his feet. "God is definitely good, and for that, I'm grateful." He looked over those assembled, smiling. "Thank you all for coming today and for sharing this, my wedding day, with me. I'm, indeed, blessed and honored. Now, if you would, please bow your heads and join hands as I give thanks for this food." Everyone complied, and after Daniel finished then sat, they raised their heads, lifted their forks, and commenced eating.

Soon, the room was abuzz with conversation, laughter, and camaraderie, and Chance just sat back watching, his eyes as precise as a camcorder, capturing and recording the scene, the faces, the family, the joy, the love. Everyone seemed happy and exuberant except the two sweethearts divided—Victor and Leisha.

Chapter Forty

"Honor your father and mother"—which is the first
commandment with a promise—"that it may go well
with you and that you may enjoy long life on earth."

Ephesians 6:2–3 (NIV)

The Harlington Hotel
Saturday, December 24

After the meal ended and everyone sat chatting, Daniel beckoned
Leisha away from the group so she could stand beside him in front. Then,
he called again for everyone's attention. "At this time, I'd like to discuss a
private family matter, so Bennett, would you please excuse us?"

"No problem." He said farewell, waved his hand, then walked away.

After the door shut behind him, Daniel nodded to his mother and
father, and they removed two gift bags from beneath the table, one lavender and the other white. Daniel's mother handed the lavender bag to
Leisha, and his father passed the white one to Daniel. Both Leisha and
Daniel then pulled single lavender and white roses from their respective
gift bags. Afterward, Daniel faced Nathan and Leah. "Pastor, would you
and La' Dear please rise and come stand before Leisha and me."

"Of course." Nathan grabbed his wife's hand and led her forward.

"What's happening?"

Leisha smiled knowingly, exchanging glances with Daniel. "Be
patient and you'll find out, La' Dear."

As Nathan and Leah stopped, standing before him and Leisha
respectively, Daniel shifted his gaze from one to the other before commencing a speech that came not from any pen but straight from his heart.
"Pastor, before you conduct a wedding ceremony today, Leisha and I are

conducting a special ceremony this morning, just in honor of you and La' Dear." He handed Nathan the white gift bag, and Leisha presented Leah with the lavender. "I know we're tempting you, but don't open your bags yet. We've got more to say." He saw the puzzlement on their faces and smiled. "Ephesians 6:2 and 3 say, 'Honor your father and mother. This is the first of God's ten commandments that ends with a promise. And this is the promise: that if you honor your father and mother, yours will be a long life, full of blessing.' Also, Proverbs 23:25 says, 'May your father and mother be glad; may she who gave you birth rejoice!'

"In those bags, you'll find cards and a special gift from Leisha and me signifying our regard for you. Since we weren't with you this year for Mother's or Father's Day, we didn't honor you as Chance and Victor did. However, today before God and our family, we're making a declaration, and we're proclaiming the truth." Daniel glanced toward Leisha, and she then stepped forward, her hand on Leah's arm.

"La' Dear, Psalm 127:3 says, 'Children are a heritage of the Lord,' and Proverbs 14:26 declares, 'In the fear of the LORD is strong confidence, and his children shall have a place of refuge.'

"You've blessed Daniel and me with life, and you've opened your heart, home, and family to us for the last six months. You've showered us with love, you've encouraged us in faith, and you've motivated us in spirit. Today, we're blessing you and Pastor, first by retiring the names of La' Dear and Pastor. We love you both, and Daniel and I have mutually decided that name changes are in order." She nodded toward Leah. "With your permission, we'd like to call you 'mother' and Pastor 'daddy.'" She tilted her head. "Does that sound all right?"

"Like music to my ears." Tears rolled down Leah's cheeks. "I'll gladly be mother."

Daniel looked at Nathan. "What about you, sir?"

"I'm honored to be called your daddy. Are you both sure you want our relationship made public, though?"

"Leisha and I aren't ashamed to be your children, nor do we have a problem anymore with recognizing you publicly as our birth parents."

Nathan leaned forward, engulfing Daniel in his strong arms. "Thank you, son." He then turned and hugged Leisha. "Thank you, daughter.

Neither Leah nor I are ashamed of claiming you either." He stepped back in front of Daniel, positively beaming contentment.

"Mother, this rose, which symbolizes love at first sight, is for you." Leisha extended the lavender rose. "You began working your way into my heart from the first day we met. Since I've already given you my heart, today I offer you a daughter's love, honor, respect, trust, and devotion. Do you accept?"

"I do." Leah accepted the rose and hugged Leisha tightly. "I love and accept you, too, Daniel." She stepped over to hug and kiss him.

"Open your bag, Mother, and remove your gift." Daniel glanced back toward his parents, the Winwards, and saw that they too were supportive, smiling even, and his mother, Marissa, nodded affirmation, with tears in her eyes.

Leah shifted the lavender paper aside and pulled out a crystal heart with a silver engraved plaque on its back, matching the shape of the heart. Aloud she read the title, "Mother's Promises"; then, she recited the verses etched beneath. Afterward, Leah clutched the gift to her chest. "Thank you both. This is priceless, and I'll cherish it as long as I live."

"We're glad you like it." Next, Daniel put his right hand on Nathan's shoulder. "Open yours."

Nathan lowered his hand into the white bag and removed a crystal cross with a gold-plated plaque at its base. Aloud he read, "Daddy's Promises," then recited the corresponding verses. Afterward, he bestowed more hugs and kisses. "Thank you, son. Thank you, Little Heart."

"You're welcome. You two can be seated now." Daniel watched as Nathan escorted Leah back to her seat at the table. His gaze went from them to his newfound brothers, still sitting at the breakfast table. "Chance and Victor, please come forward."

Both exchanged curious glances before rising to their feet and advancing toward him and Leisha.

"First, I want to thank you both for all you've done, for all you've sacrificed. By recognizing Mother and Daddy, I'm also recognizing you as my brothers. As such, I'd like you to stand with me as I marry Taryn this afternoon."

Chance's jaw dropped. "You want us at your wedding party?"

"Yes."

"We don't have tuxedos."

Daniel smiled. "Yes, you do. I shared my plans with Mother last month, and she gave me your sizes. Presently, your tuxedos are outside in the Faith mobile. You can try them on after we leave here so we can take care of any alterations you might need before the ceremony. Also, at the church, Chance, you'll be escorting Salena, and Victor, you'll be escorting Leisha. Any more concerns?"

"I guess not. Thanks."

"This is beyond great, Daniel, and it's an honor for me to stand as your brother."

"Likewise, Victor." Daniel turned to Leisha. "Your turn, sis."

Leisha cleared her throat, looking from Chance to Victor. "Six months ago when Victor appeared in my office announcing that I was adopted and that I had a twin brother, my life changed irrevocably. Since then, I've had to adjust to a new normal and a new family. At first, I was running, withholding my heart and my love, denying you all a place in my life. Today, I'm not running anymore. I've finally accepted the truth— that Mother and Daddy are as much my parents as the Laurences were and that you, Chance, and you, Victor, are a part of my new life, too." She leaned forward, hugging Chance, then pulled back. "I love you."

He grinned, playfully tweaking her red nose. "I love you, too."

She confronted Victor, her arms extended—open—and he walked forward good-naturedly, wrapping his arms around her. "I love you, Victor."

"I love you, too, more than you know." He pulled back so he could see her face clearly. "I'll be here for you too, whenever you need me. Always. You can count on that." He thumbed tears from her eyes. "And it'll be an honor for me to escort the most beautiful lady after the bride up the aisle."

Leisha nodded wordlessly, then stepped back, and Victor did the same, retreating to Chance's side.

Daniel clapped his hands, reclaiming everyone's attention. "Now that we've bonded, given our gifts, and cleared the air, let's get out of here! We've got a busy day: a bride waiting for her groom and a wedding two years overdue." He said farewell to all his parents, telling them he'd see them at two o'clock at the church; then, he ushered Chance and Victor from the room so they could get their tuxedos from his truck.

As Daniel walked with his brothers, he felt like a new man beginning a new chapter—a new journey—and he wasn't afraid to confront the unknown—to travel the road ahead. After all, he had taken a chance with his heart six months ago, and he had come out richer—even more blessed, a victor.

Chapter Forty-One

For no matter how many promises God has made,
they are "Yes" in Christ. And so through him the
"Amen" is spoken by us to the glory of God.

2 Corinthians 1:20 (NIV)

Increasing Faith Worship Center
Saturday, December 24

That afternoon on Christmas Eve, Daniel was overcome with emotion standing beside Taryn and before his family and friends as Nathan proclaimed him and Taryn husband and wife.

Nathan beamed before them. "What God has joined together, let no man put asunder." He aimed bright, wet eyes at Daniel, who stood in his black and blue-accented tuxedo barely able to contain his love, his joy. "Daniel, you may kiss your bride."

Indeed, Daniel kissed her with much pleasure before finally pulling back and facing their audience. "Meet my wife, everybody." He grinned and grabbed Taryn's hand before whisking her down the aisle amid cheers, claps, whistles, and chants from his congregants of, "Pastor Win!" Later, he and Taryn returned, rounding up the wedding party and families for photographs. As Daniel then stood with Elec and Marissa, Nathan and Leah, Victor, Chance, Leisha, and Salena, he could hardly contain his elation or tears.

Back at the hotel, he and Taryn even included Nathan and Leah in the festivities at the reception, blessing each of them with a dance—Taryn in her elegant white gown gliding across the floor with Nathan and Daniel in his black tuxedo gracefully leading Leah. The two couples eventually returned to the Dearlings' table.

Nathan kissed Taryn's forehead. "Be blessed, daughter; put God first in your marriage, trust and respect your husband, keep the communication open, the love alive, and walk in faith, trusting God. If you follow those few steps, you'll have a strong marriage—one that will survive the storms and oncoming years."

Taryn kissed Nathan's cheek. "Thank you, Daddy Dearling. I welcome the advice."

He then offered Daniel the same pearls of wisdom, and Daniel, too, expressed his gratitude before settling with Taryn at the table so they could converse more before returning to their own table of honor.

After they had chatted some, Leah excused herself to visit the restroom, Victor requested a dance with Taryn, his new sister-in-law, and Bennett invited Salena for a swirl on the dance floor after Leisha and Chance respectively declined their offers.

Nathan took Bennett's and Salena's absence as an opportunity to speak privately with Leisha and Chance, and Daniel had no choice but to eavesdrop.

Nathan reached over, covering Leisha's hand with his. "You've become quiet, Little Heart. How are you?"

"Fine, Daddy."

"Truly?"

"Yes."

"That's good news, then, because today's a day for celebration and smiles, not for sadness and worry." He squeezed her hand, reassuringly. "Now that I've seen Daniel married, I pray that one day I can stand beside you on your wedding day, walking you toward the man God has chosen for you." He pressed their bound hands against his chest, even as tears welled in his eyes. "Now that I've found you, though, I'm only entrusting you to the right man—the one the Lord has destined for your heart."

Leisha raised her head, her eyes wet, too. "If he's a god-sent man of faith, courage, and family like you, then I'll gladly let you hand me over, putting me into his care, and I won't feel abandoned but loved—cherished."

"You're definitely loved and cherished, so never doubt that. And when you've found your prince, don't surrender him or renounce your love for anything or anybody. Fight for him and for all that God has promised you because love is always worth defending."

She smiled weakly. "Sometimes, it's hard to fight for love, especially when you're doing it alone. Sometimes, it seems easier to accept defeat and move on."

"That's when you rely on God's strength—the power of His might. Regardless of the circumstances, you never give up on love."

"He's right, sis. Love is precious when you find it, and you shouldn't let fear deprive you of it, or lose faith, letting it slip through your fingers."

Nathan raised her hand. "Promise me you won't settle for less than God has for you, Leisha."

"I won't, Daddy."

"Good." He smiled, released her hand, and kissed her forehead, then he turned to Chance. "Now that I've settled that with Leisha, do you have any news for me, son?"

Chance met his father's stare, then sighed. "Mom told you about the engagement ring, didn't she?"

"Of course, she did."

Daniel leaned in. "Whose engagement ring?"

"Salena's."

Leisha's jaw dropped, and she flashed stunned eyes on Chance. "You're proposing?"

"That's the plan."

Giddy, Leisha clapped her hands, then leaned over, hugging Chance. "I'm so happy for you! Salena doesn't have a clue, but she'll be thrilled."

Chance cut his eyes at her. "It's a secret, so don't you tell her."

"I won't. I promise." Her eyes sparkled. "When are you popping the question?"

"New Year's Eve."

"She'll love it."

Chance smiled. "I know she will. She's a firecracker and crazy about fireworks."

"Congratulations, Chance! I can't wait to attend *your* wedding."

"Thanks, Daniel." Chance faced his father again. "I'm sorry I didn't tell you sooner, Dad. I had planned on keeping this all a secret until I had actually proposed, but Mom found out by accident this morning when she dropped by the room and saw the ring on a table."

"Don't worry about me. I'm fine, and I understand your motives. I'm just glad you're finally settling down and that you've found a woman you love enough to make your wife."

"Salena's the one, Dad—the woman God knew I needed, the one I didn't even know to pray for. She loves me in spite of my past, and I love her enough to leave the past behind and move forward—Godward—with her."

"Well, for that, I'm grateful, and you have my blessing."

"That means the world to me." Chance stood, closing the gap between them, and hugged him. "Now, I'd better rescue my intended bride and dare to dance with her." He left Nathan's side, traipsing onto the dance floor to reclaim Salena.

At that moment, Leah returned and sat, snuggling beside her husband, and within minutes, Bennett settled beside Leisha, folding her hand in his, and Victor arrived, relinquishing Taryn to Daniel.

Offering their excuses, Daniel and Taryn rose from the table and left to mingle with the others in attendance, and later, they engaged in a couple of time-honored wedding traditions: cutting and eating the wedding cake and tossing the bridal bouquet.

Although all the single ladies, including Salena and Leisha, crowded on the dance floor, jockeying for the best positions, the lady to victoriously catch the prize seemed the most shocked and least enthused about it. Later, as they prepared to depart, Taryn and Daniel pulled the lucky lady aside.

Taryn winked. "Congratulations, Leisha. You're next!"

"I seriously doubt that." Leisha loosely held the blue and white rose bouquet at her side. "You and Mother have already claimed the best men—Daniel and Daddy."

Daniel leaned over, whispering in Leisha's ear. "Don't give up, sis! Fight for love. Fight for *him*."

She pulled back, clutching his arm. "Fight for whom?"

"Victor. Fight for *him* and his love." Daniel kissed her forehead, then returned to Taryn's side, his hand resting on her waist. "The best advice I can give you now is this: Love Victor and forgive him."

Tears wet Leisha's lashes. "How long have you known about Victor and me?"

"I suspected after your assault, during our first weekend in Crossland, but I knew with certainty this morning after breakfast when he stood before you baring his heart. I saw that deep bond between you—that ribbon of love. However, it was love frustrated—unsatisfied." Daniel raised her chin with his index finger. "He loves you, sis, and you evidently love him, so fight for him and never quit. You're meant for each other, and both of you deserve happiness, true love."

"He chose Alessia over me. He hurt me, carelessly broke my heart."

"He made a mistake, sis. He knows that now. Forgive him." Daniel turned, nodding toward Taryn. "My wife here knows what it means to defend love. She waited two years for me, fighting for our love, even when I challenged her. Now, we're married, about to embark on a new life together."

"Victor rejected me, Daniel. He betrayed our love. How do I forgive him? How do I forget?"

"With God, with mercy, and with grace, which is *unmerited* favor."

"Daniel's giving sound advice, Leisha, so heed his words. If you love Victor, stop wasting time, remove any mountain standing between you, and claim your man—your life mate. If you don't, someone else will, and you'll have nothing left to hold on to but memories and regrets." Taryn leaned forward, hugging Leisha. "Be strong, sister; don't be proud."

"I don't know if I can trust him anymore, especially with my heart."

"Trust God, then, and let Him soften your heart and guide your steps."

"It's not that easy, Taryn."

"Yes, it is. Let go and let God do the rest."

"I'll try. But it's hard."

"You won't be able to submit to any man, sis, if you don't first learn to submit to God. If you can't surrender your heart, soul, mind, and might to Him, what hope is there in surrendering any part of your heart to anyone else, including Victor?"

Leisha frowned. "This is about submission?"

"Yes, and your pride. A submissive heart humbles itself and honors God; a proud heart exalts itself and honors you." Daniel drew Taryn to his side. "Now, if you'll excuse us, it's time for us to leave. We'll see you tomorrow at church, then later at the house."

Leisha waved. "Enjoy your wedding night."

"We will, sis. And you be encouraged, be loved, and be blessed." He waved farewell; then he and Taryn raced toward the doors amid cheers and whistles, both of them excited about the coming night, their new lives, and their future together, as husband and wife.

Chapter Forty-Two

A man's wisdom gives him patience;
it is to his glory to overlook an offense.

Proverbs 19:11 (NIV)

The Harlington Hotel
Saturday, December 24

*L*ater, after the wedding reception and after they had bid farewell to the Winwards and Bennett Ford who had to catch a flight to Virginia to spend Christmas with his family, Victor, Leisha, Victor's parents, Salena, and Chance stepped into the elevator, ascending to their respective floors.

After he had punched the corresponding buttons, Dad grabbed Mom's hand, caressing it. "God just dropped some pearls in my spirit. As a family, we're overcomers. We've journeyed from grief to gladness, from Crossland to Sutton, from a church called Kingdom Family to one called Increasing Faith. God has favored us, individually and collectively, and He's blessed us, increasing our family, our hearts, and our faith."

Victor's mom leaned against his dad, her smile as bright as her eyes. "God is good, isn't He?"

"Yes, love. He is—all the time, every day." Dad kissed her hand, pressing it over his heart. "Indeed, like we always say, God is good, God is just, and God is love."

At the third floor, the elevator stopped, and Victor's parents bade the others a good evening, telling them that they loved them and reminding them that they would see them the following morning before they departed to the church for the Christmas service. Victor, Leisha, Chance, and Salena all wished them a good night, calling out, "We love you."

After his parents left, the doors closed, and the elevator resumed to the fifth floor, Victor stood back against the wall, his eyes resting on Leisha in her royal blue gown. She clutched the bridal bouquet and waited in front, near the control panel, her back to him. Chance and Salena stood between them, whispering to each other, but he wasn't interested in their hushed conversation. He was only cognizant of the woman he loved—the one he had let escape.

Finally, when the elevator reached the fifth floor, Chance, holding Salena's hand, spoke, garnering Victor's and Leisha's attention. "I'm escorting Salena to her room so she can change and we can tour the gift store together. Victor, you can escort Leisha to her room."

Leisha raised her head, looking squarely at Chance. "The hotel is secure. I don't need an escort."

"You may not need an escort, but you're getting one, just the same." He confronted Victor. "Do you mind?"

"Not at all. It would be my pleasure."

"Thanks, little brother."

As the doors opened, Salena leaned over, hugging Leisha. "We'll speak later."

"Definitely, friend." She pulled back, her eyes trailing Salena and Chance from the elevator. When the doors shut again, she became silent, her face thrust forward and the bouquet firmly gripped in her hand.

"You made a beautiful bridesmaid."

Leisha turned. "Thank you."

Before she could resume her pose, giving him her back again, he pointed toward the bouquet, his eyes never wavering from hers. "That was some catch you made."

"It just fell into my hands."

"Maybe that's a sign, then."

"That I'm destined to marry next?"

"That with God, *all* things are possible."

"You're the doubter. Maybe you're the one who should take that verse to heart."

He heard the accusation in her voice and knew he deserved it. "Was what you said true about you and Bennett—that you and he are just friends who enjoy each other's company?"

"Yes."

"Does he know that?"

"Of course, he does."

"He loves you, maybe even wants to marry you, too."

"I'm not in love with him, and he knows that because I've been upfront with him."

"What did you tell him?"

"That I couldn't commit to him because I loved someone else." She lowered her hand to her side.

"He wasn't discouraged?"

"He said he'd wait on me as long as necessary."

Unlike Victor with Alessia, Leisha had been honest with Bennett, and based on what Victor had observed of Bennett's interactions with Leisha all day, the man cared deeply about her. Bennett had always put her first, catering to her, supplying her every need, and treating her like royalty. "He seems like a gentleman—a good, decent man." If Victor was truly selfless, he would politely step aside, paving the way for the man. However, he had discovered in the past six months that he couldn't forsake his heart and renounce his love. He loved Leisha, he wanted her, and he needed her, so he couldn't let her go again. Not now, not ever.

"Bennett is a good, decent, *mature* man, and he'll make the right woman a great husband."

"He probably will, but that woman's not you, is it?" The bell dinged, then the elevator stopped and opened. Reaching over Leisha, Victor pressed a random button for another floor, then confronted Leisha again, his right hand caressing her face.

She pushed his hand away. "You don't have a right to touch me anymore, nor can you dictate my life, my relationships, or my future."

"Yet, I'm right, Leisha. You and Bennett may be compatible as a couple, but you're not meant to be, because you love me, and I still love you."

Leisha shrank from him, creating distance between them. "You lost faith, Victor. You gave up on me—on us—even before we began—and you fled to another woman—Alessia de la Cruz."

"I know, and I regret my faithlessness and cowardice, the pain that I inflicted on you. I'm sorry, and I realize you deserve better—a man like Bennett Ford—but I'm not prepared to lose you again." He reached out, grasping her left hand. "I love you, and I'm ready to fight now—for you, us, our love. Forgive me."

"What about your parents—your fear of disappointing or scandalizing them?"

He raised both hands to cup her head and draw her closer. "All resolved. After I ended the relationship with Alessia, I told my parents the truth—that I was in love with you and had been for months."

Leisha gasped. "They know about us?"

"Yes."

"For how long?"

"More than a week."

"They haven't said anything. How did they react?"

"First, with shock, then with disappointment because of my secrecy and deception, and finally with acceptance and goodwill." Victor thumbed the tears from her eyes. "If we love each other and want to pursue a relationship as a couple, we're free to do so with their blessing."

"And Chance?"

"He's on board, too." Victor smiled, lifting her head higher. "There are no roadblocks, Leisha—no other mountains—unless you don't love me anymore or you can't forgive me."

She closed her eyes, inhaling deeply before opening them again, her eyes seemingly delving into his soul. "What do you want from me?"

"Forgiveness. Love. Your trust. Your heart."

"If I give you those, what future do you envision for us?"

"A lifetime together—a marriage, a home, some children."

Her eyes widened, shimmering with fresh tears. "You want to marry me?"

"With all my heart."

"We haven't been on a date. We're not even a couple."

"I don't need a date to know you're the only woman I want, the one God created just for me."

"We only met six months ago, and we've hardly had any time alone."

"I already love you, Leisha, and if you accept me, we'll have a lifetime to learn all we need to know about each other. Any more concerns?"

"I don't know your favorite color."

"Green, and yours is purple."

"How did you know?"

"I'm attentive, especially to you. Everything about you fascinates me, including your favorite color." The elevator stopped and opened on another floor, and he again pushed a button, buying himself more time. "Now, is there anything else bothering you?"

"I'm a lawyer based in Corinth, and you're a teacher planted in Crossland. If we did commit to each other, how would it work? "

Victor brushed wayward dark-brown curls behind her left ear. "Wherever you are, my heart will be, Leisha, and if we both take Jesus with us, He'll be wherever we are." He rubbed his thumb softly across her cheek. "Crossland is only my present home; you're my future hearth."

"You love Crossland."

"I love you more."

"You'd leave your home and life there for me?"

"That's how much I love you, how much I want to build a life with you. Whatever the cost, I'm willing to pay because you are worth it." He pressed a soft kiss on her forehead, then pulled back. "Now, will you forgive me?"

Leisha nodded. "I forgive you."

"Thank you." He hugged her, tears stinging his own eyes. "I love you."

"I love you, too."

"Then, let's make this official. Leisha Denise Laurence, will you be mine to love and cherish till death and only God separates us?"

"Before I answer, tell me *your* middle name."

"Roberto. Now, what do you say?"

"Yes, Victor Roberto Dearling, I will." She covered his hand with hers. "Will you be mine?"

"Always." He captured her chin in his hand. "Now that we've bound ourselves by heart and word together before God, I'd like to respond with a Proverbs 24:26 token. Do you recall that verse?"

She smiled and nodded, anticipation reflected in her eyes. "Yes."

"Refresh my memory, then."

"An honest answer is like a kiss on the lips."

"So be it, my love." He lowered his head, then covered her soft lips with his—pouring his heart out and declaring boldly in that single kiss, "I love you, and from this day forward, you're mine, and I'm yours. Faithfully. Always."

Chapter Forty-Three

Love is patient, love is kind. It does not envy, it does not boast, it is not proud. It does not dishonor others, it is not self-seeking, it is not easily angered, it keeps no record of wrongs. Love does not delight in evil but rejoices with the truth. It always protects, always trusts, always hopes, always perseveres. Love never fails.

1 Corinthians 13:4–8 (NIV)

The Harlington Hotel
Sunday, December 25

On Christmas morning, Leisha rose early in her hotel room with a smile plastered on her face and a prayer of gratitude and praise on her lips.

After she and Victor had reconciled in the elevator, pledging their hearts before each other and God, they had gone to their separate rooms, changed into sweaters, coats, and jeans, then reunited in the hotel lobby before strolling outside into a clear, star-lit night, officially on their first date.

"Where would you like to go?" Victor had wrapped strong arms securely around her waist. Then he led her away from the revolving glass doors along the sidewalk so they could wait for their taxi to arrive.

"It doesn't matter as long as we're together. Where you lead, I'll follow."

He stared at her. "Really?"

She nodded. "Yes."

"Are you sure?"

"Yes." She was ready to surrender her heart completely, to release that tight grip on the steering wheel of her life enough to let the man she loved do what God had created him to do—lead, love, and protect her. "I love you, Victor. I trust you, and I trust God."

"I've made mistakes with you in the past. I don't want to disappoint you again."

She caressed his face. "I have faith in you, in us, and, more importantly, in God, and I believe that together you and I are stronger than we ever were alone." She pressed a hand over the silver cross necklace covering his heart. "Since you first confessed your love for me, Victor, I've had this recurring dream—a vision of our future together as husband and wife, friends and partners—as helpmates and co-laborers for the cause of Christ."

Leisha stared into his eyes and saw that vivid dream reflected there, shining brilliantly back at her. "I envision us happily married and surrounded by children, working side by side and fishing for the souls of lost and wounded kids—boys and girls who've been abandoned, abused, rejected, and cast aside. We're their advocates, waging war for their hearts, minds, and souls—for their future—and although my field of battle is the courtroom and yours is the classroom, by the authority of Jesus Christ and through the power of the Holy Spirit, we're both able to victoriously conquer every adversary, gain even more territory, and win even more young souls for the Kingdom of God."

Victor covered her hand with his. "That's your dream for us?"

Leisha smiled. "It's what God shared with me, even after you renounced your love for me and started dating Alessia and even after I agreed to entertain Bennett Ford. At first, I fought for that dream and that future with you, but then when you kept parading Alessia in front of me, my faith wavered, and I gave up—afraid that I was mistaken and the dream was nothing more than wishful thinking or an overactive imagination. *Now*, tonight, my faith is renewed, and I know that God never fails and with Him, all things *are* possible. He's brought us together and united us in love for reasons that we can't even imagine yet, but we're meant to love each other and work together for His purpose and glory."

Victor brushed his fingers through Leisha's curls. "I'm glad that God knows our hearts better than we do, that His promises are always true, and that He perseveres—never failing, and I'm beyond grateful that He's blessed me with a second chance with you—an opportunity to love, cherish, encourage and protect you as I've wanted to since that first encounter.

"I had to nearly lose you to another man before I finally realized how much I genuinely loved and needed you in my heart and my life." He leaned down, pressing his forehead against hers. "I was stupid and ungrateful, undeserving of a gift as precious and beautiful as you, but God is merciful and forgiving. He softened your heart toward me again and blessed me with your love, and for that, I am truly humbled." He kissed her forehead. "I'm not taking you for granted again, nor am I wasting any more time. Tonight, on Christmas Eve, that dream, that promise, and that family portrait will come to completion."

Leisha had lifted wet lashes, her eyes meeting his. "What are you saying?"

"I love you wholeheartedly, and I'm not denying it anymore." He thumbed her tears dry, then cupped her face in his hands. "Tonight, my heart's a symphony, and it's even singing, and I don't want this sweet melody to ever end." He raised her head, lowered his, then kissed her tenderly, lovingly, and thoroughly until she was breathless and her own heart applauded.

Finally, Victor pulled back, his hands resting on her shoulders. "At times I wish I had God's foresight or even Abraham's faith."

"Why?"

"I would have known with certainty that you were destined to catch that bridal bouquet, I would have realized that you still loved me and that you and I would reconcile tonight, and I would have come prepared with chocolate kisses, a bouquet of lavender roses, a truly heartfelt card, and a priceless engagement ring." He sighed, shaking his head. "I don't have any of those symbols of my love for you tonight, though. I only have one gift of value to offer you now—one that expresses my regard for you and one I pray you'll accept tonight and cherish for a lifetime."

"What is it?"

Victor lowered his hands from her shoulders, enfolded one of her hands in his, then kneeled on the sidewalk on one knee. "Me." He brandished a smile. "Tonight, I'm offering you everything—two of the most precious possessions in my life—my heart and my last name. So, Leisha Laurence, will you marry me?"

Leisha gasped, covering her mouth with her free hand. For the second time in her life, she was utterly speechless. She and Victor hadn't even begun their first date. A genuine marriage proposal was the last thing she had expected.

Despite her silence, Victor continued in love, in faith. "Leisha, will you take my last name as yours, live with me, and love me through old age as my wife, friend, partner, and lover?" He kissed her hand, his eyes never wavering as they searched hers. "Finally, will you create a family with me?"

Scalding tears spilled from Leisha's eyes as she saw God's dream for them drawing closer. *Victor loved her, and she loved him. She didn't need an official date or even more time to realize that love and happiness, even her chosen husband, were already standing right in front of her, awaiting her answer—her acceptance. All she had to do was be strong and courageous enough to step out on faith, reach out her hand, surrender her heart, and accept everything that Victor was offering—all that God was blessing her with.* "Yes, I will." She pulled Victor up until he stood before her, his full heart exposed and the love in his eyes shining bright. "I'll marry you!"

Exuberant, Victor lifted her from the ground, swinging her like a merry-go-round in his arms and smothering her face with kisses before returning her to the sidewalk and sealing their engagement with one thoroughly tempting, heart-stopping, toe-curling kiss that gave Leisha a glimpse of what married life would be like with a passionate, demonstrative husband.

She sighed, pulling back. Then, she pressed one hand over Victor's heart and curled the other around his silver cross. "We've got to be careful. We can't get carried away or give in to passion."

Victor wrapped his hand around hers. "I know, and I'm sorry if I got overly excited with that last kiss. I'll be more careful next time and confine our kisses to sweet, tame ones. After all, I love God and I love you, and I can't live without either of you."

"Really?"

"Really. I respect you, and I appreciate your trust—your confidence in me—and I don't want to lose it or make you feel awkward, like you can't be alone with me or trust me to protect your virtue until our wedding night. Like you, I've been saving myself for the right person."

Her jaw dropped. "You're a virgin?"

Victor smiled. "I'm celibate. When I was fifteen, I made that decision. I promised God that I would keep myself physically pure for my wife and only make love to her *after* marriage." He caressed her face. "Despite that final kiss we just shared, my resolve hasn't changed. I'm still completely committed to celibacy until marriage."

"Really?" she echoed.

"Yes, *mi amor*. If anything, I'm more selfless than selfish. I won't do anything that will damage our relationship or the one we both have with God, nor will I pressure you for a physical relationship, putting either of us in an uncomfortable or tempting position." He brushed a wayward curl from her face. "I love and respect you, so I'm not going to take advantage of you or coerce you into an intimacy neither of us is ready for. Instead, I'm going to do all in my power to uplift and encourage you, to strengthen your faith and lessen your burdens, and I'm going to treat you like the precious gift from God you are, doing so with great tenderness."

"Thank you."

"You're welcome." He stepped back, placing his hand on her arm. "Now that we've got that settled, let's celebrate our engagement by finishing this date."

Their taxi arrived, and Victor held the door open for Leisha.

She slid into the back seat, her eyes still on him. "Where are we going?"

"Outdoor ice skating."

"What if I don't know how to skate?" She recalled all those embarrassing times as a schoolgirl when her friends had gone skating and she had always found herself either sitting alone in a corner or, worse, out on the floor, forever stumbling, falling, and landing on her rear.

"Do you?"

"On the ice, I'm clumsy. I always fall."

Victor leaned in, kissing her forehead. "Don't be afraid. You can lean on me, and I'll be patient, teaching you as long as it takes, and even if you do stumble, I'll catch you before you fall."

Leisha nodded, her fears fading. "Okay. I'll trust you."

They had climbed into the backseat of the taxi, holding hands and snuggling together and merely enjoying each other's company until their driver arrived at the Holiday Square ice skating rink nestled among white winter-frosted trees twinkling with golden lights, and true to his word, Victor had been lovingly patient with Leisha after they donned their skates. He had offered his arm, his protection, his wisdom, encouragement, and strength, and he had taught her to skate, but, more importantly, he had taught her that when she was insecure and fearful and traveling into unknown territory, she could trust him now and depend on the strength of his love.

Now, on Christmas Day, Leisha was an engaged woman—promised to Victor Dearling—the man of her dreams. She was happy, truly blessed, and she couldn't wait to see Victor again. It was going to be hard for her, though, to act as though nothing extraordinary had occurred between her and Victor since Daniel and Taryn's wedding reception—since that elevator ride—especially when she was ready to declare their love from the rooftops. However, she and Victor had decided last night to postpone announcing their engagement until the family had returned from church and gathered at Daniel's and Taryn's for the family Christmas celebration.

Leisha knew she would be antsy, periodically checking her watch until it was time to reveal what both she and Victor had hidden for so long—their love—but she would get through it. After all, she wasn't unfamiliar with waiting—being patient.

Although Victor had assured her that all of the Dearlings were supportive of a relationship between them, Leisha was still somewhat nervous. Now that she and Victor had made a commitment to each other, she didn't want any more interference, even from well-meaning friends or family members.

She was contemplating how she would hide the truth from Salena when the phone rang beside the bed. Reaching over, she removed it from its cradle, lifting it to her ear. "Hello?"

"This is a day the LORD has made. Let us rejoice today and be glad! Let us give thanks to the LORD, for he is good; his love endures forever," her caller said, referencing Psalm 118.

Warmth spread through Leisha's chest, and she smiled. "Good morning, Victor."

"Good morning, sunshine. I love you."

Leisha laughed because she couldn't stop smiling. "I love you, too."

"Are you dressed for breakfast yet?"

"I haven't even risen from bed."

"Well, it's already seven, so you'd better crank into gear, love. We've got to meet everyone, including Daniel and Taryn, in the breakfast room, then leave later for the church. Daniel already warned us that traffic would be horrendous today, and he said Increasing Faith Worship Center is going to be filled to capacity for the Christmas program."

"Don't worry. I'll be ready in time. After we get married and start living together, you'll discover that I'm very low maintenance and always punctual."

"Does that mean you *won't* spend hours taking a bubble bath or applying makeup and fixing your hair when I'm in dire need of the bathroom, you *won't* keep me waiting impatiently in the car while you search the house for some forgotten personal item, you *won't* coerce me into sitting with the other husbands and holding your purse in a department store while you're in a fitting room, trying on new clothes, you *won't* make me sleep on the couch whenever I upset you, and you *won't* ever embarrass me by making me purchase feminine hygiene products?"

Leisha laughed, imagining his flushed face and bewildered eyes if she ever did send him to buy some feminine products. In her mind, that look was priceless, positively funny. "I'm a woman, Victor, so naturally you'll have to be patient as I adjust to living as your wife, just as I'll have to be patient as you adjust to living as my husband."

"Seriously, though, I look forward to being married to you. I want us to live and laugh together, to build a solid relationship, and create a loving home—one just like my parents'. Theirs is a good marriage—a strong one. It's been tested over the years, but it has always survived, and so have they—together—both of them leaning on each other and on God."

"I want our marriage to be like that, too. I want to be the kind of wife to you that Mother is to Daddy. She's strong and independent, but she's also Daddy's complement and helpmate, and together they make perfect sense."

"So do we, Leisha. We have all the ingredients we need for all that we've ever dreamed to come true: God, love, faith, trust, commitment, and prayer. If we hold on to all of those, even when times get tough, then we'll be able to survive anything life tosses our way."

"That's what you believe?"

"Yes."

"Then, I'll agree with you, and I'll pray that our marriage is one that endures."

"Well, the Bible does say 'where two or three gather in my name, there am I with them.'"

"I love when you do that."

"What?"

"Easily apply God's Word to our lives. Those scriptures—those verses—more than the candy and roses, were instrumental in me falling for you in the first place. Before you, no man had ever romanced me by quoting from the Bible. Those words nourished my spirit and edified me, drawing me closer to God, and, ultimately, to you.

"You were able to capture my heart not because you appealed to me—the woman—but because you appealed to me—the believer—both uplifting and encouraging me, advising me to put my trust foremost in God. You were different—committed, godly, passionate, and intense— and I couldn't help but be both fascinated by and frightened of you."

"Do I still frighten you?"

"No."

"You wouldn't rather be with Bennett Ford?"

"No, Victor. You're exactly the man I need—someone who motivates and challenges me, daring me to leave my comfort zone, and someone with whom I can grow spiritually."

"I feel the same about you."

God, I love him. I can't wait. Leisha pressed a hand over her pounding heart, tears stinging her eyes. "Victor."

"Yes?"

"I can't do this anymore; it hurts."

"What?"

"Keeping secrets. I love you so much that it feels like my heart is flooding, and I can't stop it, nor can I hide it anymore. I don't even want to try."

"Neither do I."

"I know we agreed to wait until after church to profess our love and announce our engagement, but I physically can't wait anymore. I feel like I'm carrying a bomb in my chest, and any minute it's going to explode."

"We can't keep any more secrets, not even for a few hours. It's Christmas, a time for rejoicing—for celebration—and I want our friends and family to know that we're in love and engaged. Today, I want to be able to hug you anytime I feel like it and kiss you beneath the mistletoe. I want to walk confidently among everyone with your arm protectively around me, and I want to enter that church this morning and sit beside you in the presence of God, Daddy, Mother, Chance, Salena, Daniel, and Taryn, with the truth known—that I'm your fiancée—the woman you love—the one you've chosen to marry. That's the only gift I'm requesting today—the truth."

"When do you want to tell them?"

"At breakfast—*before* we eat."

"We'll make the announcement then."

"Thank you."

"I love you, Leisha. I don't want you doubting that again."

"I feel the same, and I'll meet you downstairs in twenty minutes."

"Until then, be blessed."

"You, too." She returned the phone to its cradle, hastily, leaped from bed, then sped barefoot to the bathroom so she could shower, change into a white pleated blouse and red pantsuit, and mentally prepare for one of the most important announcements in her life.

Twenty minutes later, she and Victor stood outside the doors to the breakfast room, their hands bound.

Victor gently squeezed her hand. "Are you ready?"

Even though butterflies were having a field day in her stomach, Leisha nodded. "Yes."

"Then, let's enter." He twisted the knob, opening the door and leading her inside where everyone had already congregated around the breakfast table: Nathan and Leah, the newlyweds Daniel and Taryn, Elec and Marissa Winward, and Chance and Salena. At their entrance, all eyes turned toward them, and those who knew their true hearts were clearly curious about their arrival together, but Nathan was the only one who spoke. "Good morning and Merry Christmas. It's nice to see you both here."

"Merry Christmas, Dad." Victor kept his fingers twined with Leisha's as he led her from the door within a few feet of the table—in front of his parents.

"Merry Christmas." Leisha felt flushed beneath the intensity of everyone's stare, especially Salena's.

Nathan palmed his hands over his plate. "Once you grab your plates and have a seat, we'll give thanks for the food."

Victor glanced toward Leisha, and she nodded her consent. It was time. "Before we do that, Dad, Leisha and I have some good news to share with everyone."

Nathan traded glances with Leah, then faced them again. "Go ahead, son. We're all listening."

Victor reassuringly squeezed Leisha's hand. "Leisha and I are in love, and we're not running from each other, dating other people, or hiding our feelings anymore."

"Good!" Nathan clapped his hands and beamed benevolently at them. "If you're in love, you shouldn't hide it. After all, love is a gift from God, and it should be celebrated, not rejected, especially if it's shared with the right person—someone God has chosen for you."

He's not upset, surprised, or disappointed. He's actually encouraging us to love each other. Leisha stared at Nathan with tears welling in her eyes. "Do you approve?"

"Yes, Little Heart. You have my blessing."

"As well as mine." Leah smiled with her hand pressed over her heart. "You and Victor make a beautiful couple, and I'm glad you found each other and realized that your love—your relationship—was worth defending."

Leisha turned toward Chance. "Do you have a problem with Victor loving me?"

"No, I don't. I wish you well, nothing but a life of happiness and love."

"Thank you." Leisha confronted Salena. "Do you have anything to add?"

"Congratulations, friend! If you and Victor are in love and make each other happy, then I have no objections. I'm on board, cheering you both on."

Leisha smiled. "Thank you."

"Congratulations, Leisha, Victor."

"Thank you, Taryn."

"I'm happy for you, sis." Daniel draped his arm over Taryn's shoulder. "You, too, Victor. You both deserve the best, and I believe God's given it to you in each other."

Both Leisha and Victor thanked him for the compliment.

Nathan clapped his hands again, garnering everyone's attention. "Now that that's settled, Victor and Leisha can fix their plates, take their seats, then we can bless this food, and enjoy this wonderful Christmas breakfast. I, for one, am so hungry I could eat everything on that buffet table."

"Dad, Leisha and I weren't finished."

Nathan raised curious eyes toward them. "You love Leisha, and she loves you. Now, you're a couple. What else is there, son?"

"Last night I proposed and Leisha accepted. We're engaged."

Leah fanned her face dramatically. "What did you say?"

"We're getting married, Mother."

Leah leaped from her seat, shouting and dancing before rushing toward Victor and Leisha, hugging and kissing them both before returning to her seat, still bouncing with joy. "Hallelujah! Praise the Lord!"

"You and Leisha are really getting married?"

"Yes, Dad, we are."

Leah dabbed at her wet eyes. "It's about time. You both deserve some happiness."

"Congratulations!" Daniel whistled, Chance clapped, Salena squealed, and Nathan sat as though stunned in his seat, wiping tears from his eyes. Taryn, Elec, and Marissa each hugged the couple, wishing them well.

"Dad, are you okay?"

"Yes, son."

"You're crying."

"That, I am."

"Aren't you happy for us, Daddy?"

"I am. Truly." He rose from his seat, then walked around the table, approaching them and placing his hands on both their shoulders. "These are tears of joy I'm shedding today because God is good, God is just, and God is love. Since I learned that you two loved each other, I've been on my knees toiling and praying for your reconciliation, and today God answered that prayer in a mighty way.

"Last night as I lay in bed, the Lord even gave me a vision of you two together. At that time, I thought it was nothing more than a dream, wishful thinking on my part. Anyway, you were married and happy, each of you sitting beside the other on a swing, holding the cutest twin babies in your arms: a little olive-tan boy in the image of his curly-haired father and a little dark-haired girl blessed with her mother's pretty eyes. When I asked you who they were, you said the boy's name was Eliander and the girl's name was Eliana."

Leisha's heart leaped for joy in her chest. "You dreamed that Victor and I got married and had twins?"

Nathan nodded, smiling and stepping back from them. "Yes, Little Heart. I most certainly did. I do believe the Good Lord gave me a glimpse of your new family—my future grandbabies."

Leisha turned to Victor, fresh tears in her eyes. "Victor, what do you think about that—about us having twins?"

Victor looked at her with eyes full of love and certainty and faith. "I don't have to think about it, Leisha. I already know what it means:

with God, all things are possible." He turned then, cupping Leisha's face, and there, in front of family and friends, he branded her with a kiss—a heartfelt promise and a tender love note of all that was to come. As he pulled back whispering that he loved her, then led her to the buffet table, his hand still twined with hers, Leisha glanced back toward Salena who gave her a thumbs-up sign, and she laughed, happy and ready to celebrate life, love, God, and family because she was still harboring one final secret—a good one—that Salena would love to know—that of Chance's proposal.

Like He did for Ruth in the Bible, God was giving both of them a Boaz blessing, and soon, she and Salena would be more than just sisters in Christ; they would be sisters-in-law—both of them Dearlings.

Chapter Forty-Four

For he has rescued us from the dominion of darkness
and brought us into the kingdom of the Son he loves, in
whom we have redemption, the forgiveness of sins.

Colossians 1:13–14 (NIV)

Corinth, Texas
Saturday, December 31

Tonight, Chance was reaching out, daring to make his dreams come true. He was going to propose to Salena, asking her to be his life-long partner, his helpmate, his wife. He had prayed earnestly over the decision, and God had confirmed what he already knew: He loved Salena, and she was the right woman for him.

She was an extraordinary woman of faith, courage, and compassion, and she genuinely cared, not only for him but for others—those less fortunate. She had even been keeping abreast of Ray, selflessly becoming a mediator between him and Chance. At Christmas, she had shared with Chance the most recent news regarding Ray. Pastor Antonio Bienvenido, who had some influential connections in the medical community, had worked diligently on Ray's behalf, rallying support to get him reinstated as a full-time doctor. Following the media coverage of Ray's delivery of the battered woman's baby and Salena's subsequent human interest story chronicling Ray's life and his road to Redemption House, Pastor Bienvenido had been successful in garnering support from people throughout the city. So, Ray now had full-time employment as a doctor at Nazareth Memorial Hospital. Since his and Chance's last meal at the diner, Ray had even left Redemption House and was now living modestly in an apartment at Uptown Place.

Chance had received the news with a sense of relief. He had forgiven Ray, and even if he didn't envision a typical father-son relationship with him, he wished Ray well in this new season of his life. He had even added Ray to his prayer list, requesting that God bless him with pure, abiding love.

Salena returned from the restroom to their table near the balcony. "Did you miss me?"

"Profoundly." He consumed her with his eyes, appreciating her beauty—the shimmering gold dress that accentuated her curves and the flaming curls unbound and falling down her back.

She caught him staring intensely at her face, and she blushed. "What's wrong?"

"You're breathtaking—incomparable—and I'm just admiring you."

Salena flashed a Cheshire-cat smile. "Keep flattering me, and you'll definitely see fireworks when we kiss at midnight."

He absently patted the diamond engagement ring hidden inside the pocket of his jacket. "I look forward to midnight then."

After the waiter arrived with their dessert, he and Salena ate quietly, content to enjoy the soft music wafting overhead. Occasionally, they broke the silence, sharing their insights and discussing the latest family news.

"This is the first time in four years that Leisha and I aren't spending New Year's Eve together." Salena pushed her dessert plate aside. "Typically, we'd drink hot chocolate and gorge on junk food, with Orion at our heels, and we'd stay glued to the television, watching the New Year's Rockin' Eve celebration in Times Square. After the ball dropped, signaling the advent of another year, we'd celebrate with prayer and praise. This year, though, Leisha's celebrating in Crossland with her new love and her new family, and I'm here with you, the man I love."

"Any regrets?"

"This is right where I want to be—with you."

"I feel the same." Chance was mindful of how significantly their lives had changed. "In the past, my parents would always invite me to welcome in the new year with them at church, but I would always decline, dreading those hours spent in church before God, and I'd consign myself to hours of loneliness."

"How do you feel about being in church or in the presence of God now?"

"Willing. Hungry. Thirsty. I'm not the same man I was six months ago, yet I'm still not perfect either. I'm a work in progress—with a renewed mind and a clean heart."

Salena reached across the table, grasping his hand. "Eileen would be proud of you. You've fulfilled that childhood promise to her."

"Maybe I'll meet her in heaven one day and thank her for loving me enough to pray for me and teach me about Jesus. Although I ran from Him for years, He drew me back, using those seeds of faith she planted with her prayers and advice. Her final gifts to me were hope, love, and faith, and for those, I'm grateful."

"When you remember her, dwell on her love and those gifts, not on her abuse or her suffering. She's living in peace now, and so should you." Salena gently squeezed his hand before pulling away.

Later, at a quarter till twelve, Chance asked her to accompany him to the balcony, and she complied, rising from her chair and walking with him. Turning, Chance faced her, his heart a warm well of love and his mind decidedly made up. He brushed Salena's face with his hand. "Five months ago, you challenged me, daring me to dream, to love, to live, and to dance. Tonight, beneath heaven and before God, I'm daring to do all those things." He lowered his hand from her face, secured her left hand in his, then dropped to one knee.

Salena gasped, and tears swelled, then escaped her eyes. "Chance, are you—"

He removed the ring from his pocket and extended it. "I love you, Salena Kyleen Blake, and I want to spend what's left of my life with you. I want to be that daring man that you love through old age, and I want to father your children—a little red-haired girl named Channing and a blue-eyed boy named Chandler—and I want to make a safe, loving, and godly home for you and them." He lifted hopeful eyes to hers. "Will you marry me?"

Salena enthusiastically bobbed her head, laughing through her tears. "Yes, Chance Holden Dearling, I'll marry you!" She bounced as he slid the diamond ring on her finger.

He rose to his feet, still holding her hand. "I love you, and I thank you for just making my life complete."

Salena removed her hand from his, framing his face in both her hands. "I love you, too, and there's no greater honor and privilege for me than to live as your wife and be a mother to all of your children."

Inside the restaurant, the countdown commenced, accompanied by drum beats, and Chance smiled, wrapping loving and protective arms around his new fiancée. "Are you ready to bring in the new year together?"

The countdown sounded at ten seconds, and her eyes twinkled as bright as the overhead stars. "More than ready. I love you."

"I love you, too. Happy New Year." He lowered his head and possessively claimed her lips as the clock struck midnight and cheers, bells, and whistles filled the air, followed by a lively rendition of "Auld Lang Syne"—the Good Old Times.

Even as fireworks burst overhead, streaming through the black, star-blanketed sky with rainbow colors, he kissed her thoroughly— flooding her with his love, pouring his dreams into her, and sharing his passion and promises with her. Finally, he pulled back, resting his hands on her waist, and he saw beauty standing before him with shining eyes and flushed cheeks. Smiling, he removed his hands from her waist and extended his right hand—his own olive branch—to her. "Dare to dance with me?"

Salena placed her hand in his with confidence. "Always."

Then, together they danced under the stars, beneath heaven, and before God, in love and, quite simply, redeemed.

About the Author

Terra Blakemore is an educator and former college professor with more than twenty years of teaching experience in colleges, universities, private and public schools. She is an avid reader and creative writer, with a master's degree in English and a minor in Writing, who often blogs devotions and pearls of wisdom on her professional website (www.godswordprofessor.com) and tweets Bible verses and offers words of encouragement throughout social media as she endeavors to wield words for good and wield words for God, as GOD'S WORD PROFESSOR.

She lives with her family in East Texas and loves writing faith-affirming stories about families and relationships, using diverse characters, Southern settings, redemptive themes, and real-life solutions for real-world problems, and her greatest desire is to change the world one good word at a time, one great book at a time, and one unique person at a time.

CPSIA information can be obtained
at www.ICGtesting.com
Printed in the USA
BVHW051333160323
660599BV00013B/989